THE GIFT
OF *Second Chances*

The Styles of *Love* Book Three

USA TODAY BESTSELLING AUTHOR
N.D. JONES

THE GIFT
OF Second Chances

The Styles of *Love* Book Three

N.D. Jones

KUUMBA PUBLISHING
CREATIVE MINDS.
PASSIONATE HEARTS

Book Layout © 2014 BookDesignTemplates.com
Cover Design by Limabean Designs
Logo Art Design by Najja Akinwole
Editor: Kathryn Schieber
All art and logo copyright © 2018 by Kuumba Publishing

The Gift of Second Chances/ N.D. Jones. -- 1st ed.
ISBN-13: 978-1-7325567-7-5

THE GIFT OF SECOND CHANCES

Whatever happens beyond "I do" is up to us . . .

Facing the choppy waters of marriage, infidelity, and the vows that bind us, a sea of choices stretches out before a couple on the brink. For Dr. Angela Styles-Franklin and her husband Sean, the past twenty years come to a head when the truth about a brief affair threatens to dismantle their family. Angie must face the rough road before her. In these trying times, the rosy haze of memories past and the history of their relationship flash before them and force both Sean and Angie to come to terms with what it means to invest a lifetime in a person and what a life lived together truly means. In the process, faith, trust, forgiveness and the power of family weave together into a tapestry of trials and patience that engulfs their road to reconciliation. Is love enough to hold together the fabric of a family and a second chance at forever?

DEDICATION

Trayvon Martin

February 5, 1995-February 26, 2012

"The vision preached by my father a half-century ago was that his four little children would no longer live in a nation where they would be judged by the color of their skin but by the content of their character. However, sadly, the tears of Trayvon Martin's mother and father remind us that, far too frequently, the color of one's skin remains a license to profile, to arrest and to even murder with no regard for the content of one's character." ~ **Martin Luther King III**

REFLECTING ON INFIDELITY:
AN INTRODUCTION

The Gift of Second Chances is a novel about a seasoned married couple's efforts to find their way back to each other after a short-lived, but still very painful, affair. The story is not about the hero's affair but the couple's love for family and their growth as individuals and as a couple.

In the novel, Sean and Angie decide the best way to learn how to heal from Sean's affair and to strengthen their marriage, is to engage in marriage counseling. Their therapist poses several questions, during their initial session. I asked similar questions to Facebook friends and newsletter subscribers. They included the following:

- Cheated-on partner: Do/Did you blame yourself for your partner's affair? Briefly explain.
- Cheated-on partner: Are/Were you willing to change, in some areas, if it meant healing yourself and working to heal your marriage/relationship? Explain.

- Cheated-on Partner or Cheater: Do you believe cheaters can change? Why? Why not?
- Cheater: Do/Did you feel remorseful about your infidelity? Explain. Please note, remorse is not the same as guilt.
- Cheater: Why were you unfaithful?
- Cheater: Were you and your partner able to move past your infidelity? Why? Why not?

The information was gathered on a Google form, where respondents could answer the questions openly and honestly and with anonymity guaranteed. No demographic information was collected, and the results aren't meant to "prove" anything or intended to serve as scholarly research. However, infidelity is a serious and painful experience within many romantic relationships. Some relationships survive and thrive after an affair, while others crumble and die.

Read Angie and Sean's story of guilt, shame, and anger, but also love, strength, family, and growth. Once done, read Reflecting on Infidelity: Survey Results. If you'd like to share your story, you can fill out the form here.

CHAPTER ONE

"Faster, Daddy, faster. They're going to beat us."

Kayla's long legs wrapped more tightly around Sean's waist, and her arms were vices around his neck. The ten-year-old may be a beanpole, but she wasn't light. At his oldest daughter's loud, ebullient urging, Sean increased his speed, chasing his brother-in-law down Excelsior University's football field in an unwinnable race.

"Uncle Malcolm's going to win."

Malcolm always won. The thirty-six-year-old Malcolm was not only ten years younger, but he carried Sean's pixie of a four-year-old on his back, which amounted to nothing more than an oversized book bag for the younger man.

From the sideline, Angie cheered for her girls. Only one could win, but that didn't stop their mother from encouraging them both to victory.

"Old and slow, Dad. Not a good combo," SJ's singsong voice mocked, the teen sprinting past Sean with energy, breath, and youth to spare.

"I got your old and slow."

"You gotta catch me first, and that's not happening."

Dammit, it wasn't. But Sean wouldn't leave the field embarrassed. Well, he would, especially with his wife recording the family race and his pathetic performance. Whose idea had this Saturday outing to Excelsior University been? That's right, Sean's.

He dug his heels in and ran as fast as he could while towing a laughing and screaming Kayla on his back. Malcolm and SJ ran the length of the field before Sean and Kayla even reached the eighty-yard line.

"We won, we won." Malcolm lowered an excited and chubby-cheeked Zuri to the ground, and she ran straight to Angie. "Did you see me, Mommy? We won! Uncle Malcolm is so fast."

"I did see you, baby."

Zuri galloped around her mother's legs, imitating a jockey and shrieking, "Giddy-up, horsey, giddy-up."

Angie, cell phone in hand, recorded the last leg of Sean's humiliating defeat. A hundred yards and he was gasping like he'd trekked up the Himalayas.

Kayla jumped off his back before he'd come to a full stop, also running to Angie. What was it with his girls and their mother? Sean, they treated like a pack mule, but they rushed to Angie as if they hadn't seen her in a month instead of only a few hours.

"Don't feel bad." Malcolm slapped Sean on his shoulder. He felt the force of his brother-in-law's heavy hand through perspiration and layers of clothing.

"What makes you think I feel bad?"

"If you don't, you should. Next time, I'll let you win. You know, to save face in front of your children." Malcolm pointed to his sister, who smiled and nodded as the girls talked her head off about some Adoptable drawing they'd seen on Instagram that was "so adorable" and "will you buy it for us"? "Your wife already knows you're a loser, but I hate to remind my sister how poorly she's chosen the father of her children."

Sean swung at Malcolm, who dodged the weak attempt to punch him in his face. "Don't let your mouth get you into something your ass can't handle."

He darted after Malcolm, faster now that he wasn't encumbered by a child on his back but still not swift enough to catch his brother-in-law. December in Buffalo was cold, but all the running kept Sean warm.

SJ ran past Sean and caught up with Malcolm in a matter of youthful seconds, grabbing his uncle around the waist but not strong enough to bring the muscular man down.

Sean collided into them, knocking Malcolm, SJ, and himself to the grass. He'd played high school and college football, so he knew what it felt like to find himself on the gridiron, blue sky overhead. But Sean didn't remember the ground being this hard and unforgiving on his body.

He really was getting old, and he and Angie had years before their last child would be going off to college.

"That was a great tackle, Dad. You've got to show me that move."

"Your father slammed into us. That's not a move, SJ. It's what happens when you're six-three with big feet. You can't help but fall over them and into whoever is unfortunate enough to be next to you."

Sean punched Malcolm in the arm, and they all laughed.

From his spot on the ground, he watched Angie stroll across the field and to his side. Rare though it was, Angie loomed over Sean. He couldn't help it, he grinned up at his lovely wife.

"Are the three of you done rolling around on the ground? It's cold, and the girls and I are ready to go."

SJ jumped to his feet more quickly and smoothly than Malcolm and Sean got to theirs, then the boy was off again, dashing across the field toward his playing sisters.

"No wonder that boy is always hungry." Angie smiled after their son. "You didn't have to bring the children here. I would've been home in another hour."

"It's Saturday. You could've worked from home or, better yet, not at all."

Malcolm drifted away, familiar with the old argument between Sean and Angie.

"It's just a half day. "

"It's not just half a day. It's a good chunk of one of only two days we have to spend time with each other and with the kids. Between their school and our work, we only see each other at meals and bedtime."

"You're exaggerating."

"I'm not. I'd like for us to spend more time together. We talked about it, remember?"

"When you're dealing with one of your high-profile discrimination or harassment cases, you work long hours at the law firm. You don't hear me complaining when you do."

"Maybe you should. Or maybe you don't complain because you don't want to give me an excuse to call you on the same thing. You've made it through the first two years of your college presidential contract. You don't have to sacrifice your Saturdays to prove yourself to anyone. Anything that needs doing here can be accomplished Monday through Friday. Unless it's an emergency or a big event, you don't need to be here on weekends."

"It's easy for you to say, you're your own boss and only accountable to your clients. I'm accountable to twenty-five thousand graduate and undergraduate students, over four thousand full-time employees, and twenty-one hundred faculty members."

Excelsior University was a respected public research university with an operating revenue of over four hundred million dollars and an endowment of five hundred million. Dr. Angela Styles-Franklin, President of Excelsior University, had started out as an adjunct professor at EU. Twenty years later, she led the three-campus institution, serving as Provost and Executive Vice President for Academic Affairs before earning the top leadership position.

His wife had worked hard to achieve her goal. More, Sean knew how dedicated she was to the academic success of every student, but Angie was burning the candle at both ends, and something had to give.

In truth, something already had, but Sean didn't want to think about that.

While Sean, Malcolm, and the kids wore tennis shoes, jeans, and sweatshirts--typical weekend gear--his wife dressed as if she were going to one of her many meetings. Light make-up accentuated high cheekbones, full lips, and dark-brown eyes. Her hair, normally worn down past her shoulders, was pulled back and up in a tidy bun, the conservative style showing off her beautiful face and dangling gold earrings. In her full-length winter coat, Sean couldn't see her outfit, but he knew what she wore underneath: a form-fitting navy-blue suit, single-button blazer over a blue-and-white cami, and dress pants. Her pointed-toe pumps added two inches to her slim, five-three frame.

She was professional and poised as always, but Sean preferred the less put-together Angie who wore her hair in a messy ponytail and spent Saturday mornings holed up in the house in leggings and a long T-shirt, eating leftovers with Sean and the kids because neither of them felt like cooking after a long work week.

He missed those lazy days of family fun and togetherness.

Sean took hold of Angie's hand. "You're up by five-thirty and out the house an hour later, driving to your first meeting. After that, it's even more meetings with deans, students, professors, community members. By two, you're lucky if you've slowed down long enough to have lunch. If there's no major event for you to attend, you may make it home by seven. Even then, you're checking work emails." He lifted her hand to his mouth and kissed. "You work over sixty hours a week. In your busy schedule, there isn't much time left for the kids and me."

Now wasn't the time to have this discussion again, but the location was appropriate. EU had seen more of his wife, these past two years, than Sean and their children. In a way, the university was Angie's fourth child, born of immaculate conception.

"I don't want to get an emergency call about you being rushed to the hospital from a heart attack or stroke. Our children need a mother, and I'd like to grow old with you. You need to slow down." Sean held his wife's hand. "Look around you, Angie."

"We're outside, what do you want me to look at?"

"Everything. You're the fifteenth president of this great institution. Those who came before you were all white men. That fact alone makes your appointment unprecedented and ups the stakes and pressure for you. But look at this place, dating back to the 1800s. It's not going anywhere. These buildings"—he stomped the grass underneath his feet—"these grounds, will outlast us, our children, and our grandchildren. The school won't crumble to dust if its president works reasonable hours and doesn't drag herself in here on Saturdays."

"I understand your point, but I can't get everything done working forty hours a week. It's impossible."

"I know, but there are ways to cut back if you really want to."

"If I really want to?"

Angie reclaimed her hand and began walking in the direction Malcolm and the children had gone. If he didn't know his wife so well, her brisk pace and silence could've been misinterpreted as an emotion other than annoyance. He'd seen her walk that way, business-like and focused, a thousand times. But Sean wasn't fooled. He'd hit a nerve, which Angie didn't like, so she'd walked away from him and what could've been a full-blown argument at her place of work.

Sean hadn't gone there to get into a fight with Angie, so he didn't continue the conversation as they made their way across campus and toward Roosevelt Hall where Angie's car was parked.

"That's Dr. Murphy's parking space." Angie shook her head at her younger brother, who leaned against his truck, the girls in the backseat and SJ sitting shotgun. "You're lucky one of the campus police officers didn't give you a ticket." Frowning, Angie glanced from Malcolm to Sean. "Why didn't you drive?"

"Because I'm riding with you, and the kids are spending the day with their uncle."

"Since when?"

"Since two weeks ago when we planned to use today to finalize our Christmas shopping."

Angie's eyes closed, and she shook her head. "I forgot."

"Yeah, I know."

He would leave it at that. Angie rarely forgot anything work-related and never forgot something involving the children directly. But when it came to the two of them, her mind became a sieve, filtering Sean out but retaining everything else--everything she placed above him in importance. An unfair assessment, she would argue, but Sean wasn't the one who'd forgotten yet another event they'd planned to do together.

"I'm sorry."

Angie looked as if she would offer more than her typical apology, but she closed her mouth and went to Malcolm's truck. She waited for her brother to unlock the doors so she could say goodbye to the children. Angie began with Zuri, checking the strap around her car seat. The act was more for her peace of mind than as an indication of Angie's lack of faith in her brother to secure her child properly.

For each of the children, Malcolm had gone so far as to buy a car seat for his vehicle when they were little, which was unnecessary but did save Angie and Sean from having to switch one of their seats to Malcolm's truck every time he drove the children. The man would make an amazing father whenever he got around to finding the right woman and settling down.

Several hours later, Sean and Angie were in their bedroom, surrounded by bags.

"I think we went overboard." Angie plopped onto their bed, her hands going to her shoes and plucking them off. A relieved sigh followed their removal. "Where in the hell are we going to put all of this stuff?"

"The usual spot."

"All of these gifts will not fit in our closet." Angie pushed to her feet, shrugging out of her blazer and tossing it onto the desk chair to her right. "Zuri's going to love the bike you got her."

"Flowers, pink seat, streamers on the handlebars and basket, what's not to love?"

"Don't take the training wheels off."

"She doesn't need them."

"She does need them, the same way Kayla and SJ needed them on their first real bike. Leave the training wheels on until she's used to riding a bike and has built up her confidence."

"Training wheels are nothing but a crutch. One day is all I need to teach her how to ride a bike on her own."

"Two crying children and scraped knees would suggest otherwise."

"SJ and Kayla learned."

"Learned what? That their father thinks yelling, 'keep your eyes straight ahead, don't stop pedaling, and try not to run into a tree,' is a perfect way to teach a child how to ride a bike?"

"It's how I learned. I fell once, got back up, and didn't fall again."

Angie rolled the Princess Flower bike to their closet and opened the double doors. Clothes and bins of shoes occupied the space. She was right. No way would all the bags fit in there. They'd have to ban the kids from their room until after Christmas and keep their bedroom door closed.

"You broke your arm. You always leave that part of the story out. It was weeks before you were able to ride your bike again."

"True. But I wasn't afraid to get back on and try again. It's called grit and perseverance. That's what I want to build in our kids. Everything in life won't come easy for them. They need to know it's okay to fail. But it's not okay to wallow in their mistakes. They need to learn to dust themselves off and go for it again."

"Zuri's four. She doesn't need to learn that life lesson now. No more than SJ and Kayla did when they were her age. There's nothing wrong with needing and asking for support. That's the kind of mentality that gets too many EU students in trouble, especially the freshman. When they find themselves floundering, their pride prevents them from seeking assistance and using services that could help them cope and succeed. You're right about grit and perseverance, our children need both. But they don't have to learn everything the hard way."

Angie didn't add "like you did," but he knew she'd thought it. Sean did learn things the hard way. He learned by doing, by jumping in with both feet and riding out the wave. Unfortunately, the wave, sometimes, crashed against hard rocks.

Sean helped Angie store the bags in any available space—underneath the bed, in the closet, beside the nightstands, on chairs. For now, the bike was stored in the master bathroom in front of the linen closet--totally in the way. They would have to definitely keep the kids out of their room, which wouldn't be a big deal for anyone but Zuri, who loved to crawl into bed between Sean and Angie. The more hours Angie worked, the clingier Zuri became and the more often she left her bed at night and went in search of her mother.

He sat at the foot of the bed, shoes, socks, and sweatshirt off. Angie still wore her cami, but she'd removed her pants, which left her in only underwear. Sexy underwear, at that, a white pair of jacquard, floral pattern, mesh panties. They fit her curves to perfection--the same way the matching bra did, a sensual set Sean had bought his wife a month ago. He'd also purchased her the combo in red and dark-purple, colors that complimented her gorgeous dark skin. Sean couldn't wait to see her in the garter and strapless bra set he'd bought her—him—as a Christmas gift.

When Angie made to walk past Sean, he grabbed her wrist and pulled her so she stood between his parted legs. They needed to talk.

Sean held Angie around her waist, his face at breast level but his eyes upturned and focused on his wife's face. "I meant what I said earlier. You pull too many twelve-hour days. It's not healthy. You're going to burn yourself out."

"I exercise and eat right."

"Which is probably the only reason you haven't crashed and burned yet. Slow down. Take time for yourself. Go to the movies or catch up on your reading. You have a stack of novels on your nightstand you haven't gotten around to reading yet. You also have a husband and children who'd like to see you more."

"You make it sound as if I'm not home by design. My job is demanding and time-consuming."

"I know, but like I said earlier, EU will be there long after you're gone. I'm not minimizing your worth, but if something happened to you, EU would fill your seat and keep going, business as usual. For your family, on the other hand, you're irreplaceable."

He wasn't trying to scare his wife when he'd mentioned her having a heart attack or stroke. Both were real possibilities with the level of stress her job put her under. Being a civil rights lawyer carried its own share of stress. But, as Angie had said, he was his own boss and had far fewer people relying on him. Angie did have a huge responsibility as a college chief executive officer, but she shouldn't let her job dictate so much of her personal life.

"The kids miss you." Sean kissed the delicate space between her breasts, the cami soft and silky. "I miss you." With a gentle tug, Sean had his wife perched on his left thigh, the right side of her body pressed deliciously close. He kissed her--long, deep, and slow. "I want us to spend more time together."

Angie claimed his mouth as soon as the words fell from his lips. One arm wrapped around his shoulder, the other hand cradled his cheek. His wife deepened the kiss, her tongue in his mouth and licking, just the way he liked.

Shit, they didn't kiss like this often enough. But when they did, it reminded Sean, even more, how little time they made for each other and how easily his wife could bring him to his knees with a single kiss.

Sean reveled in the feel of Angie stoking their mutual flame of desire. She enjoyed sex as much as Sean and, despite her overloaded schedule, they made love at least four times a week, which wasn't bad for two working parents. Sean would like to have sex with his wife every day, but what husband wouldn't?

He shifted, so they were fully on the bed, Angie on top of Sean and their lips melded in carnal bliss.

The kids wouldn't be home for hours, which meant they could be as loud as they wanted. Knowing Malcolm, he'd keep the children for the night and bring them home tomorrow morning. His brother-in-law had ample room and supplies for his nieces and nephew. Even if the kids didn't stay the night with their uncle, Sean and Angie had time to do this more than once and without rushing.

Off came Angie's cami, Sean ridding his wife of the attractive but unwanted layer.

Sitting up and straddling his waist, Angie reached behind her and unclasped her bra. "Take it off me."

"Gladly." Sean slid his hands up Angie's thighs and over her waist, his fingers stopping to appreciate her soft, toned skin.

Angie's eyes fluttered closed at his exploring touch, her own hands falling to her sides and granting him unfettered access to her body.

Deft fingers slid the bra straps off her shoulders and down her arms. The cups slid south, disclosing what they were meant to conceal. No matter how many times Sean saw his wife's breasts, the sight of them never ceased to arouse him. After nearly twenty years of marriage, Sean found Angie as attractive and as irresistible as he did when they'd gone on their first date.

With years of practice, they undressed each other. They had plenty of time, so there was no rush, which didn't stop them from getting each other naked as swiftly as possible.

Sean lavished kisses up and down his wife's body. Hands palmed breasts and fingers squeezed nipples before his mouth descended on them, sucking, sucking, sucking.

"Mmm, that's good." She arched into his mouth. "So good."

Sean could do better than good. He returned to her mouth, kissing Angie hard and deep, the way she craved when aroused and panting for more pleasure, as she was now.

Opening her legs wide, she lifted her hips and rubbed her moist lips against his hard, throbbing dick. Shit, he loved when she did that. Up and down she went, gliding herself over him. Every slick slide had him caressing her unhooded clit. Over and again, Angie used him to pleasure them both, his shaft an erotic pole taking his wife closer to an orgasm.

Sean repositioned himself, moving down a few inches, which was all Angie needed. This time, when she lifted herself, her clit came into direct contact with the bulbous head of his penis.

She moaned, he grunted, and she moved against him repeatedly, the sensation ball-tightening good.

Angie came, a sensual cry of release Sean would never tire of hearing.

His cell phone dinged, alerting him to a text message and interrupting their privacy.

Sean entered his wife who was still wet and pulsing from her orgasm. It didn't get much better than this, having intercourse with Angie after she'd come. Sean normally brought her to this state with his mouth or fingers, but he enjoyed it more when she took control and used his body to see to her own needs.

Afterward, she was suppler, her desire greater, and her moans louder.

He smiled down at her, and his cell phone beeped again.

Eyes opened and looked up at him, Angie's orbs lust-filled yet unbothered by the intrusion. "Do you want to get that?"

"I don't care who's texting me. I'm not stopping."

Her eyes closed again, and her mouth lifted into a contented smile. "Good, I don't want you to stop."

Sean didn't. Uninhibited and thorough, he made love to his wife.

His cell beeped a fifth time, and it took everything in him not to swear. Sean had also gotten a string of text messages while they were shopping. His failure to read the messages and respond to the sender hadn't gone unnoticed by his wife.

By the time Angie came for a third time, followed by Sean, neither were thinking about the texts and the persistent person on the other end of them.

CHAPTER TWO

Angie stood in the doorway of their bedroom, a bottle of cold water in each hand. A naked Sean sat on the side of the bed, head down and cell phone in hand. She watched him read what she assumed were the text messages that had interrupted their lovemaking. He'd ignored them earlier, the same way he had when they were at the mall.

She'd also ignored her phone while they were out, knowing each ding was a work-related email. Like Sean, Angie had waited until they weren't together to check her messages, which she'd taken care of while downstairs.

Angie hadn't enjoyed the feeling of guilt that had swept over her when she'd deliberately checked her work emails when her husband wasn't around to complain. She'd felt sneaky. Angie wondered if Sean felt the same.

"Who are all the texts from?"

Sean's head snapped up. "I didn't hear you come back."

"Obviously." She threw him one of the bottles of water but didn't move to join him in their bedroom. "So, who are they from?"

Sean had good reflexes. He'd caught the bottle with the hand not hold-ing his phone. The feat was especially impressive considering the force she'd used to lob the bottle at his head.

"Darryl. I gave him the Cavanaugh racial profiling case, and he had a few questions he needed me to answer."

Darryl O'Neal was one of three lawyers at Franklin & Associates. He was the first attorney her husband had hired, a fifty-year-old Georgian native who ate too much peace cobbler and all but bathed in cologne. She liked Darryl. The man was compassionate and open-minded, and his At-lanta-Buffalo accent a cute mix of Southern and Eastern urban.

For as long as she'd known Darryl, she didn't recall him ever blowing up Sean's phone the way he'd done today. "Why didn't he call? It would've been quicker if he needed the information right away."

"He knows weekends are off limits. I know I can't put every case on the backburner during the weekends. As much as possible, though, that's my goal. When I said I wanted us to spend more time together, I meant I had to adjust my work schedule, too." He looked at her quizzically. "Why are you standing over there?"

She didn't know. No, that wasn't true. Angie needed to ask Sean a question, and the distance helped force the words out her mouth and into the marital air between them. "Is there something you want to tell me?"

"Like what?"

"I don't know. Something."

"Something like what? Am I supposed to know what you're talking about?"

Sean dropped his cell phone and bottle of water onto the bed. She thought he would get up and put on a robe, like she had, or slip into a pair of boxers. Instead, he stared at her, his luscious brown eyes pools of con-fusion.

"If you have something you'd like to tell me, I wish you would."

"I have no idea what you're talking about. You aren't making sense. Come over here."

"No. Just tell me. Be honest." Her grip on the water bottle tightened, and her heart pounded with anxiety. "Be. Honest." The two words escaped on a whispered, angry plea. "Was that really Darryl texting you?"

"Come here and find out for yourself."

Her legs were like marble columns planted at the threshold of her bedroom. For the last two months, she couldn't have asked for a more loving and attentive husband. Not that Sean wasn't before, but lately, he'd taken notice of Angie the way he hadn't in years. He brought her flowers and gifts more often. He'd taken to surprising her at work with lunch. Sean prepared her breakfast so she'd have a decent meal to begin her day. And yes, he'd reduced his workload, coming home earlier and taking the weekends off.

The changes were sweet, but Angie couldn't help but wonder at the unexpected behavior and attitude shift.

As naked as the day he was born, Sean got to his feet and grabbed his cell phone. His long legs brought him to stand in front of her in mere seconds.

"Here, look for yourself." She stared down at the offered cell phone. "Take it. I don't have anything to hide. Check whatever you want. My texts, emails, call logs, Facebook page, whatever."

Angie had never been one of those women who searched her man's wallet, pants pockets, cell phone, or social media accounts. She didn't pull up the search history on his laptop when he wasn't around, looking for porno addiction and god knows what else that would give a woman a reason for concern.

She wasn't that kind of female. Angie had assumed, if a woman felt a need to go through all of that, then she might as well let the man go. Whether he was loyal or not, her actions proved she didn't trust him enough.

Angie trusted her husband, but she found it difficult to ignore her instincts. She snatched the phone from Sean's hand but didn't waste her time scrolling through the device. Even if her suspicions were correct,

Sean wouldn't be so stupid as to leave evidence around for her to find. And he certainly wouldn't offer up his confession on an electronic platter.

"I don't like lies."

"Neither do I. Tell me what's wrong."

She didn't want to utter the words. Her boyfriend before Sean had a serious case of insecurity. Angie never found out if it was due to past relationships that had gone wrong or an emotional deficiency in Craig. What she did know was how awful it felt to have the person you loved accuse you of cheating. Nothing Angie had said could convince Craig of her fidelity, so he'd broken up with her, thinking her a lying cheater. After all these years, the memory of the unfair judgment still stung. The wound of Craig's mistrust had long since healed, but she'd never forgotten how he'd made her feel—a little dirty and a lot insulted.

Sean was an intelligent, handsome, and humorous man with the material trappings of success. Angie had caught many women checking him out. When he was happy, his lips had a way of turning up into a crooked, adorable smile.

He wasn't smiling now and neither was she.

Angie shoved the cell phone back into Sean's large hand. "Forget it. I'm tired and imagining things."

"You're angry."

"A little. But it's my own fault."

"Do you want to talk about it?"

"It's not worth discussing. What do you want to do? We have the house and the rest of the evening to ourselves."

The topic change wasn't subtle. But Angie didn't want to push the issue. She didn't want to confirm her suspicions. God help her, she didn't want to know because knowing would break her heart and crush her soul.

Angie trusted Sean, she repeated to herself. Nineteen years of marriage and three children, he wouldn't risk all of that for a fling.

Would he?

"Malcolm called when I was downstairs. As you thought, he's keeping the kids for the night."

"Pizza, popcorn, and a movie?"

"Yes, his normal." Angie ran a hand through her hair, pushing long bangs out of her face and working hard to force her mind away from distressing fears and angry thoughts. "My brother needs a wife."

"Needs?"

"Yes, needs. Malcolm needs a wife and his own kids to fill his very nice, but empty, house."

"I had the same thought earlier about Malcolm finding a wife and settling down. He's an unusual Styles. The rest of you were long married by the time you reach your brother's age."

"Malcolm's too picky."

"I don't know if a person can be too picky when it comes to choosing a life partner."

"Good point. Tell me what I'm missing, Sean. You've been doting on me for the last two months, and I want to know why." Okay, maybe she couldn't fully let it go.

"Only a woman named after Angela Davis would question why a man pays special attention to the woman he loves."

Sean grabbed Angie's hand and led her to their bed. Yanking back the rumpled covers and displacing his bottle of water, which rolled off and under the bed, he climbed inside.

She laid her bottle of water on the nightstand, removed her robe, and followed her husband onto the bed and under the covers. Angie reclined on her side, her back to him, and Sean spooned around her.

Angie's hair had long since come undone, their earlier activity too much for the bun to survive. Her hair fell past her shoulders and onto her pillow. Sean moved her hair out of his way. His mouth went to her nape and kissed, his hand to her hip and caressed.

"Each of our children was a planned pregnancy. How many people can say that? Most can't, including our parents. We planned the birth of our children around our professional goals and timelines. Even Zuri, who everyone thinks because you had her at forty-two, was a surprise pregnancy." Fingers slid across her hip, a tantalizing back and forth motion.

"Now I wonder, if you'd known the former EU president would retire sooner than expected and you'd be tapped for his job, if you would've agreed to try for a third child."

"That's unfair. I wanted to start a family right after we married, but you were the one who wanted to wait until your law firm took hold."

"I know, and I'm not judging. My only point is that we've made personal decisions based on our professional aspirations and responsibilities." Lips kissed shoulder and teeth nipped earlobe. "When we were younger, it made a lot of sense to think that way. Now, I'm unsure if it still does. I'm afraid."

"Afraid of what?"

"Of waking up one day next to a stranger. Of sitting across from you at the dining room table, the children moved out and us with nothing to talk about. Of us living together but slowly growing apart."

Angie twisted in Sean's embrace, bringing them face-to-face. "You think we're growing apart?"

"If we keep going the way we have been, I think we will."

"You mean me working long days?"

"Not just you, honey. Me too. If our positions were reversed, I'd be putting in the same number of crazy hours at EU. But I don't have to because I have three attorneys to divide the caseload at the firm."

Even before he began flexing his hours, Sean was the one who got the children up in the morning and off to school. He'd also arranged for Angie's retired mother to pick the children up after school and to drive them home. The arrangement worked for all parties involved. Kim and the kids had more time to spend with each other, and Sean and Angie had a person they trusted to take care of their children while they were at work.

Angie tried not to miss SJ's sporting events, Kayla's ballet recitals, and Zuri's playdates. She spent every Sunday cooking dinners for the week. Angie froze the meals so they could be reheated when she wasn't home to guarantee her family had balanced meals to eat.

None of that, however, addressed her husband's larger concern.

Sean wore the serious face Angie knew well. Being a lawyer and dealing with emotional causes, he had no choice but to pull out his serious face. But her husband preferred laughter, jokes, and smiles, especially when at home with Angie and their children. When he spoke, his tone matched the emotion etched across his face.

"I don't want us to become strangers to each other. My parents are great examples of what I mean. I think they've been together so long they have no idea how to live without each other. The kindest word I can come up with to describe their marriage is content. That's a low standard for what should be a loving, happy, and fulfilling relationship."

Sean was from New Jersey, and his parents, Brenda and Edward Franklin, still lived there. He loved his mother but tolerated his father. That was more than Angie could say for Sean's four sisters who weren't on speaking terms with their father. The first time Edward had met Kim, at Sean and Angie's engagement party, he'd flirted with Angie's mother. To make matters worse, Edward had done it in front of his wife, complimenting Kim on her looks, standing too close, and asking her to dance instead of Brenda. It had taken a strong word from Malcolm and an even firmer grip to his arm to keep Charles, Angie's father, from knocking Edward on his behind.

They rarely visited the Franklin's, but Angie had never felt comfortable with the distance Sean insisted on maintaining between his parents and their children. She'd surmised Sean hadn't had the best upbringing. She didn't think he'd been abused, but he'd left New Jersey when he graduated college and never moved back to the state. His older sisters had done the same. Adults didn't flee the state of their birth and their parents if their childhoods were sunshine and rainbows. After almost two decades of marriage, Sean still hadn't told Angie what had driven him away from home.

"We both can be laser focused. It's one of the traits that makes us good at what we do. But being that way also means we sometimes fail to notice other things around us. I want another nineteen years with you. More than that, if we're lucky. What do you want?"

Angie had everything she wanted: a husband and children she adored, and a career she treasured. He'd asked her the wrong question. It wasn't about what Angie wanted but what she was afraid of losing.

"I want you, us, our family."

"So do I. You asked what I wanted to do tonight." Sean leaned in closer, their faces almost touching, his breath minty fresh. "This is it. Being with you in our bed. Chillaxin."

"Chillaxin?" Angie snorted a laugh. "You're supposed to rub off on our son, not the other way around."

"It's a perfectly good word. It's in the urban dictionary."

"Oh, well, since it's in the urban dictionary, by all means, Counselor Franklin, chillax away."

His tongue snaked out and licked her lips. "We could watch a rom-com. I won't even gag at the predictable moments, not even the lame meet-cute."

"Rom-com? Meet-cute? Who are you, and what have you done with my husband?"

He pinched her bottom then gave her a hard, quick kiss. "You've made me watch enough romantic comedies for me to know the tropes. An unlikely circumstance that starts the relationship. A cast of wacky friends as supporting characters. A grand gesture or declaration of love."

"We haven't watched a rom-com in years. Hell, when was the last time we watched an adult movie?"

"We can take care of that right now. We can pull up one of those free, online porn sites." Sean sat up, a sparkle in his eyes and scanning the room for one of their laptops.

Angie yanked him back down. "Not that kind of adult movie. You know what I meant." She snuggled against his side, her head going to his wide, hard chest. "Every movie we own has a G in the rating. Does Hollywood even make Rated-R movies anymore? Or do they think adults don't have movie aspirations beyond PG-13?"

"It's all about the financial bottom line. PG-13 movies are a perfect in-between for Hollywood. Those movies have enough action, drama, and adult themes to draw in old heads like us, but they are benign enough to be acceptable for the thirteen and below crowd."

"No nudity, little to no blood, the same with cursing. Implied drug use and sex, maybe. Kissing, a little. Do you know how many PG-13 movies we've watched that would've been much better if they threw in a hot sex scene and dropped a few F-bombs?"

"I think you do want to see a porno. I'm sure we can find one of those where the porn stars act out some shitty script that's a rip on a popular movie or television show."

"Like *Night of the Giving Head*?" Angie suggested.

Sean laughed. "Exactly. Or *The Sperminator*."

"*Friday Night Beaver*."

"You're on a role. What about *Good Will Humping?*"

Lowering her mouth to Sean's chest, she pressed a soft, teasing kiss over a nipple. "Those are great punny titles, but I wouldn't watch any of those movies."

"There's one I bet you'd watch." Sean rolled Angie onto her back and wedged his hips between her legs. "*Ocean's 11 Inches*."

"Eleven, huh? Hmm, yes, I'd watch that one. Would that movie fall in the Big Dicks category?"

"At eleven inches, it could be its own category. Why do you know porno categories?"

"For the same reason you know rom-com tropes. But we haven't watched an X-rated movie in years, either."

He nudged her entrance, teasing her the way she'd done him. "We can make our own porno. Not eleven inches but I'll be your *Bone Ranger* if you'll be *My Bare Lady*."

She grinned, and warmth suffused every part of her body in contact with Sean's. "My *King Dong*."

Sean slipped inside, and they moaned at being joined again. They rarely had sex more than once a day, anymore. Today had been an exception. The second time was in the shower. Sean had pinned her to the tiled back wall, his strength and confidence soaking her sex and weakening her limbs.

"If you must work on the weekends, you can do it at my *School of Cock*."

Angie couldn't help it, she laughed. If not for Sean, this day would've gone very differently. Angie could've spent most of it working and the rest catching up on household chores, the way she did most Saturdays. Sean could've preyed on the guilt she did indeed feel at being away from home and missing most of the evenings with their children. He could've argued and complained and pushed every one of her defensive buttons. Sean could've also taken the children out himself, the house empty when Angie returned home from EU.

The bottom line was that her husband had options. The one he'd chosen had them spending hours Christmas shopping and talking about their children and the holiday season. They'd laughed and held hands, two people in a sea of strangers engaged in the same activity. When it came to her, Sean often took the path of least resistance.

"I love you." His voice held none of the humor from just a second ago and neither did his light-brown eyes. "No matter what the future holds for us, I need you to know I love you. The workaholic Angie, the sarcastic and shrewd Angie, the mother of my children Angie, and every other kind of Angie there is. I love all of you. Don't you ever forget that."

Sean's declaration of love didn't surprise her. Between the two of them, her husband said, "I love you" more often than she did. So, not a surprise, but his vehemence had her lifting her hand to his cheek and gazing deeply into his eyes for what hid behind his declaration.

Earnestness and an emotion she couldn't decipher lurked within.

"I love you, too. I love the care you take with our children and the care you take with me. I'll review my work schedule and see where I can cut out the fat. Just don't look at me like that."

"Like what?"

She pulled him down into a long kiss. Angie could now name the other emotion in his eyes.

Sadness.

CHAPTER THREE

"When will police learn brown and black kids in hoodies aren't, by default, gang bangers?" Darryl asked. But his question was more of an angry statement than a true query.

Sean sat in his office behind his desk. Darryl claimed one of the two black leather chairs in front of his desk. For the last hour, they'd reviewed the Cavanaugh case. Fifteen East Side Buffalo high school students, African American and Latino, were illegally arrested during a gang sweep. They were searched, questioned, and held for hours before parents were notified. No Miranda Rights were executed and one of the teenagers, Brandon Cavanaugh, had had an asthma attack while in police custody, his inhaler confiscated and not returned when he went into distress, leading to his tragically avoidable death.

The young man's family hired Franklin & Associates to handle the wrongful death case against the arresting police officers. The African American and Latino communities wanted justice and the Buffalo Public Schools aligned with the community leaders in their opposition to the criminalization of students of color. An attorney from the American Civil Liberties Union's Racial Justice Program was handling the class action suit. She'd contacted Sean a few days after local news reported his firm's involvement in the Cavanaugh case.

Sean had given a brief statement to reporters. Brandon's mourning parents had stood beside him, strong, despite their obvious anguish and anger. He couldn't imagine the depth of their grief. When Sean had returned home that night, he'd gone straight to SJ's room and hugged his son. He'd held the fourteen-year-old for a long time, breathing in his innocent scent and appreciating the presence of his safe form.

SJ hadn't questioned Sean's odd behavior or tried to extricate himself from his firm hold. The teen had said nothing, quietly submitting to his father's bout of fear and gratitude.

How many times would a young African American male have to lose his life before the country woke the hell up? This shit had to end. Brandon Cavanaugh was one more victim in a long, shameful list, with too few people held criminally and civilly responsible.

Sean had embraced SJ and counted his blessings. Like the Cavanaughs, Sean and Angie did all in their power to keep their children safe. But a parent's protective reach didn't extend beyond their home and into the harsh Buffalo streets.

After an emotional conversation with SJ about racial profiling, police brutality, and the all-around danger of being a young black male in America, Sean had called his wife. Angie was still at EU, but she'd left a budget meeting to speak with him. Sean had felt foolish interrupting his wife at work for a non-emergency, but her calm voice had helped settle his protective hackles. Later that night, she'd tugged him from SJ's doorway where Sean had stood watching their son sleep. When they'd settled into their room and bed, she'd comforted him in a different way.

Darryl tapped his chin with his thumb, a quirk the older man didn't realize he had. "Different face and name but the same old shit. We fight the good fight, but it's hard when it involves our children. North or south, east or west, it doesn't matter. This sickness is everywhere, an epidemic no one wants to truly address. Payouts to the families are nothing compared to their loss."

"I know."

Jury selection in the Cavanaugh civil case would begin the following day. A blue wall of silence had gone up around the accused police officers, adding to the growing tension between the BPD and members of the African American and Latino communities. Darryl, like Sean, wasn't immune to the deep feelings race-based crimes evoked, which explained Darryl's current mood.

Sean hadn't removed himself from the case. He'd simply shifted from first to second chair. The change enabled Sean to reduce his level of responsibility, freeing him to go home at a reasonable hour. He'd learned, from awful experience, the price of staying at the office late at night with no one else around except for—

A knock had both men turning their attention to the closed door.

Patricia, Sean's secretary, had gone home for the day. She would've locked up behind her. The only other person in the suite of offices was Lillian Withers, a self-proclaimed "bleeding heart liberal attorney with shark teeth."

"Come in, Lily," Sean called.

The door opened, and a familiar figure stood on the other side. But it was not the woman he'd expected.

Sean and Darryl rose. Darryl, broad-shouldered and lean at five-eleven, maneuvered around the chairs to reach the woman. His long arms wrapped her in a fatherly hug.

"It's about time you came for a visit." Darryl stepped back, eyed the woman from head to toe, and proclaimed with professional affection, "You look good." Darryl pulled the woman into Sean's office. "Doesn't Trinity look good?"

Darryl didn't wait for Sean's response before he launched into twenty questions about their former legal assistant's new job at Damseoux, Luster, and Bettis, PA. Sean knew Roger Damseoux from law school, so it had only taken a phone call, an email with Trinity Richardson's resume, and a recommendation from Sean to earn her an interview.

Two days after the interview, Roger had offered Trinity a job. Two weeks after Trinity accepted, she'd left Franklin & Associates, and left Sean in a state of relief to see her go.

She was supposed to be in his rearview not in his goddamn office carrying on a conversation with Darryl.

"They're treating you right over there?"

"They are. Mr. Damseoux is demanding, but I'm learning a lot."

"His firm is bigger than ours, their caseloads heavier. You can handle it, though. You learned from the best."

Trinity's gaze moved to Sean. She hadn't given him her full attention since entering his office, but she did now. The twenty-seven-year-old was pretty and bright--not too much of either, but more than enough to leverage both to her advantage. She spoke and carried herself with sensual confidence. Five-seven and built like a plus-sized model, Trinity left most men salivating in her wake. Most men, including him. Not anymore but, for a short while, he'd crossed the sacred line between employer and employee and between a married man and a single woman. He'd screwed her and fucked himself in the process, and now the devil had come calling.

"Being under Mr. Franklin taught me a lot. I'll never forget his lessons. They'll stay with me forever."

There was a hard, biting edge to her words, the double entendres meant for him. Trinity hadn't so much taken Sean in with her seductress wiles, as he had willingly followed her siren's call, dick out and eyes closed to the dangerous waters ahead.

"Sorry to run, but I promised the missus I'd be home for dinner, and I'm already late." Darryl grabbed the Cavanaugh file from Sean's desk. "Don't be a stranger," he said to Trinity. "Sean, see you tomorrow in court." Darryl slapped the folder he held in his hand. "A little bedtime reading."

"Yeah, see you tomorrow. Drive safely, and give Val my best."

"Will do. My wife is looking forward to having dinner with you and Angie next week."

Darryl gave Trinity a quick hug before leaving Sean's office, and he pounced the second they were alone, his voice rough and his heart pounding wildly. "How did you get in here?"

"Darryl's barely down the hall. And is that really the first question you want me to answer?" She closed the door. "I thought you would've started with the most important one."

"I assume Lily let you in on her way out, not that it matters. You shouldn't be here." Sean neither returned to his chair nor offered Trinity a seat. He didn't want her getting comfortable. She wouldn't be staying long. "You should've called instead of stopping by unannounced."

She flipped her waist-length braids, in that haughty way of hers, and claimed the seat Darryl had vacated.

Shit.

Sean sat, literally on the edge of his seat.

"You don't answer my phone calls or text messages. You left me no choice."

"There's nothing for us to talk about. We're done. Finished. I made that clear two months ago."

"You think too highly of yourself, Sean. I don't want a man back who I never had in the first place. It was fun while it lasted, though." She smirked at him then to his cluttered desk, her point clear about what kind of fun they'd had and where. "You can't brush off what I texted you last week. I didn't want to tell you like that but, as I said, you don't return my phone calls."

Hell no, Sean hadn't called Trinity back. He'd deleted her number from his phone and every text they'd exchanged, even work-related messages. Then he'd cleared his call log after he'd broken things off with her. The affair had been brief, barely two months, and he'd made no promises to leave Angie for her. That would never happen.

Sean had helped secure her another job then washed his hands of the ill-advised affair. He'd buried his lies and guilt and prayed, in time, he'd forgive himself for what he'd done. His single saving grace was Trinity's disinterest in causing trouble for him with his wife. For her, screwing the boss was an amusing past-time with no repercussions. She didn't have a husband and children waiting for her when she returned home late. She didn't have to take a quick shower before her spouse got too close, making sure to wash off evidence of her time with another man. She hadn't lived seven weeks of deception, turning into someone she despised.

Sean slumped against the back of his chair, still shaken from Trinity's last text message. He'd read it after Angie had gone downstairs. Her message had been squeezed between the ones from Darryl. After he'd read the short text and deleted it, Sean couldn't stop staring at the screen, even after the phone had entered sleep mode.

I'm pregnant. Call me.

One line of text brought back everything he'd worked so hard to forget and to hide. *I'm pregnant.* Trinity couldn't be. They weren't together but a handful of times, his stupid brain had supplied, desperate for a life preserver.

I'm pregnant.

Sean hadn't used a condom in years. He'd pulled out, not so far gone he would come inside a woman who wasn't his wife, but the act had been a sophomoric move his old ass knew better than to employ. He hadn't even been that reckless in college, but marriage and monogamy had spoiled him. Between pregnancies, Angie was on the pill, so Sean was used to skin-on-skin sex. But that was with his wife, not a woman he had no business touching.

"Are you sure?" he asked, grasping at straws. "Have you been seen by a gynecologist?"

"Yes, to both of your questions. I wouldn't have contacted you if I wasn't positive. Ask your other question."

"Is it mine?" he asked, relieved he kept the tremor from his voice and his hands from shaking, but not as thankful as he would be if her answer was no.

In the two years Trinity had worked for him, Sean had never known her to hesitate, not even when she should've. But his question had her eyes falling away from his and to the picture of Angie and the kids on his desk.

She picked it up.

Sean wanted to snatch the family photo from her. But he kept his cool. He couldn't allow his roiling emotions to escalate an awkward meeting into a hostile confrontation.

The picture Trinity examined was taken on Zuri's first birthday. The Styles had gathered in Sean and Angie's home for the celebration, and Malcolm had served as photographer. Angie had chosen one of the pictures from that day, framed it, and then gifted it to Sean. In the picture, Zuri sat on Angie's lap, asleep in her mother's arms. Sean sat on the sofa beside his wife, and Kayla and SJ flanked their parents, wearing big smiles for the camera.

Until two months ago, he'd kept the picture on the nightstand on his side of the bed. Its presence on his desk now was like screeching to a stop after running a red light. The illegal act had already been committed and couldn't be reversed.

"Your son and oldest daughter look like you. They even have your tall frame. But the little cutie is all her mother. She's beautiful."

"Zuri—"

"I meant your wife. Beautiful, classy, smart. She didn't stop by the office often, but when she did, Dr. Styles-Franklin made a point to speak to me, even if nothing more than polite small talk." Trinity returned the photograph to Sean's desk, her gaze back on him. "No, I'm not sure if the baby is yours."

Sean feared as much.

"But it could be, which is why I contacted you. You needed to know."

Needed to know? Yes. Wanted to know? Hell no.

"When will you know for sure?"

"Not until after the baby is born. A test can be done then."

"I read there's a prenatal paternity test available. It's non-invasive and can be done as early as the eighth week of pregnancy."

"I should've known you would've done your research." Trinity laid her hand on her stomach, her heavy coat making it impossible for Sean to see whether she was showing yet. Too soon, he thought. "I don't know how reliable prenatal tests are. I'd rather wait until the baby is born. The results will be accurate."

From what Sean had read, prenatal test results were also accurate. An accredited DNA Diagnostic Center was in Buffalo. If she wanted, Trinity could schedule an appointment. With Christmas next week, she may not be able to get in before the New Year. But Trinity could at least call and find out. Sean would pay for the test, of course, and anything else she required … if the child she carried was his. He would have to accompany her to supply a DNA sample, which meant he'd have to heap one more lie atop the ones he'd already told Angie. Lies of omission and commission, both weighed him down.

"Think about the prenatal paternity test. I'll email you the link to the Diagnostic Center. Read the FAQs and give them a call if you have questions or concerns. Just don't rule it out as a viable option. I don't want to wait months to find out if the baby is mine."

"You're going to have to tell her."

"We're not talking about my wife."

"She either learns about the baby and me now, giving her months to grapple with the knowledge of your affair and the baby created from our carelessness, or later when the baby is born, and news of its existence smacks her in the face."

Sean wouldn't discuss Angie with Trinity. His wife had never been a topic of conversation between them, and he wouldn't begin today.

"This is my fault. The responsibility falls on me. If you're carrying my child, then we'll have to figure something out."

"I only slept with one other person while we were together."

They hadn't been "together." He hated the way the word sounded in reference to the two of them. They hadn't been a couple. They'd screwed, fucked, and now she might be pregnant with his child.

"It's a good chance the baby is yours. I'm sorry. I really am. I didn't want this for either of us. If you're wondering about abortion, for Jehovah Witnesses, non-medical abortions are an act of high crime in the sight of God."

"I wasn't." Sean didn't know much about Trinity's faith, but he doubted Jehovah Witnesses condoned premarital sex and sleeping with a married man, yet Trinity had no compunction engaging in both of those activities. Sean felt like crap wishing Trinity had aborted the child and never told him she'd been pregnant. But, god help him, he did. "You can't call or text me on my cell anymore. If you need to get in touch with me, call me here during office hours. We can talk then. But I don't want you doing anything that might risk Angie finding out."

"You're going to have to tell your wife everything. If you confess now, she'll be hurt. If you wait until after the baby is born, she'll be devastated. Either way, you can't spare her pain, but you can try to minimize the impact."

Minimize the impact. Spare Angie pain. There was no way to spare his wife pain, or himself the horror of his bitter truth. Angie may forgive Sean his affair, but she would never forgive him if he had a child with another woman. Angie would likely castrate him before throwing his lying ass out of the house and filing for divorce.

The thought of castration was less terrifying than the prospect of coming clean and losing his wife. There was no falling down and getting back up from this. The tumble to the ground wasn't like the bike discussion they'd had a few days ago. Scraped knees and broken arms hurt but they also healed.

Did a bleeding heart?

Sean didn't see Trinity leave or hear her parting words. He didn't even recall driving home or letting himself into the house. He went through the normal evening routine, muscle memory doing all the work. By the time Angie arrived home, Kayla and Zuri were in bed and SJ in his room finishing homework.

She snuggled beside him on the living room sofa, the Christmas tree the only illumination in the room.

"Sorry, I'm late. My meeting ran over."

"You called to let me know, so it's fine. I wasn't worried."

"Not worried, but are you upset? You're distracted tonight. Did you have a bad day at work?"

"Something like that."

"Do you want to talk about it?"

Sean lowered his head to Angie and kissed her. She tasted of the red wine she'd had with dinner and of trust and love.

"You're going to have to tell her everything."

His hand slipped under her dress, removing her panties and then seeking her center.

"If you confess now, she'll be hurt. If you wait until after the baby is born, she'll be devastated."

At his urging, Angie reclined on the sofa with Sean between her legs, his hand fumbling with the button and zipper of his pants.

"Sean, SJ is still awake."

"I know but ... " He pushed his pants and boxers down enough to free himself. "I need you." He kissed her again, his lips trembling from fear and guilt. "Let me make love to you. Please."

"Either way, you can't spare her pain, but you can try to minimize the impact."

Angie took hold of Sean, stroked his length until he was long and hard in her hand and then guided him to her entrance. Desperation had Sean plunging deep. His movements were fast, thrusts hard and kisses needy. Angie buried her face in his shoulder and muffled her cries of pleasure.

"Either way, you can't spare her pain, but you can try to minimize the impact."

Sean gave her everything he had. He didn't hold anything back. Nothing ... except for the truth.

"Either way, you can't spare her pain, but you can try to minimize the impact."

CHAPTER FOUR

Sean stood at the bottom of the stairs in Gershwin Hall, his coat on and Angie's slung over his arm. She waited for him at the front of the building near the glass doors. At this point in the evening, Sean wasn't surprised to see who stood next to his wife. Like most of the men in attendance, the short man wore a black, notch lapel tuxedo with black tie and shoes and a pristine, white dress shirt.

Sean hated suits, although he wore one every day to work. If not for Angie and the fundraiser gala at EU's Reich Concert Hall, a five-hundred seat venue inside Gershwin Hall, Sean wouldn't be in a suit on a Friday night. Since he had to wear one this evening, he wanted to look good for Angie because his wife rocked her Styles name tonight.

Neither of them had settled for the classic, but predictable, black formal wear. Sean's tuxedo, while traditional in cut, was midnight blue and paired with a black, butterfly bow tie, silver and onyx cufflinks, a white shirt, and black, leather shoes. He'd shined the shoes himself, the way his father had taught him. It was one of a handful of lessons about manhood Sean deemed worth taking from Edward Franklin.

Angie was gorgeous in a cold-shoulder, draped, metallic gown in smoke. The cowl neckline displayed her smooth, rich skin, which he'd adorned with the teardrop necklace he'd bought her for Christmas. She'd permitted Sean to clasp the necklace around her neck after she'd put on the matching earrings. Unable to help himself, he'd kissed her neck, his hand at her nape and fingers gliding across the necklace's clasp. He'd also taken pleasure in helping Angie slip into her high-heeled, silver glitter shoes, not that she'd required assistance. But any opportunity to touch his wife's soft skin, Sean was there.

And so was Dr. Derrick Murphy, Provost and Executive Vice President for Academic Affairs. He hadn't seen the man touch Angie beyond a handshake and the dance he'd requested of her. He saw Angie five days a week. There couldn't be much more for them to talk about. But there was Dr. Murphy, inserting himself next to Angie whenever space and opportunity allowed.

Sean had been gone for no longer than three minutes, retrieving their coats so they could go home and relieve Kim and Charles. SJ had whined that he was "too old for babysitters," and that he could "take care of Zuri and Kayla while you and Mom are out." Yeah, that wasn't happening anytime soon.

Dr. Murphy at least had the good sense not to interrupt Angie's conversation with the biggest EU donors at the event and neither would Sean. His wife knew how to part rich people from their money. She had a great sales pitch, made easy by the fact that EU students, faculty, alumnus, and their premier programs were recognized nationally and internationally for excellence.

This was Angie's element, and she soared among the eagles. Fundraising was a huge part of a college president's responsibilities. Not all her fundraising efforts involved getting dressed to the nines and attending a concert. But everyone was still in a post-Christmas and New Year giving mood, making mid-January a surprisingly great time for a fundraiser.

"Are you sure you have to leave?" Murphy asked Angie.

She smiled at Sean over Murphy's shoulder when he approached. "I'm sure, Derrick. It may not be late for a bachelor, but it is for an old married couple like us."

"You're hardly old. Don't forget, I see you walk this campus every day, and I can barely keep up."

"You keep up just fine." Sean held Angie's coat open for her so she could slip it on. She smiled up at him gratefully, murmuring, "Thank you."

Because Sean didn't like the way Murphy's dark eyes sparkled when he spoke to Angie, he placed a kiss under his wife's ear, hands possessive on her shoulders and eyes on the forty-something-year-old man with a crush.

Dr. Murphy stared back at Sean then nodded. He had no idea what the gesture meant, but he had bigger concerns tonight. Sean didn't have the energy to worry about a baldheaded, goatee-wearing runt of the litter provost with a crush on a woman who was oblivious to his interest.

He kissed his wife again in the same spot, lingering until she raised her hand and caressed his cheek with affirming affection.

"That was nice. You're being extra charming tonight."

Half of her body had turned away from Dr. Murphy and toward Sean and, just like that, the sparkle in the provost's eyes dimmed. Angie didn't see him, at least not in the way Sean suspected Murphy wanted her to. Then again, Sean could be imagining it all. His affair and Trinity's pregnancy weighed on his conscience.

Sean had thought he could cope with the lies, but he'd been wrong. Trinity was right. He had to tell Angie the truth. He couldn't bring himself to do it during Christmas and ruin the holiday for everyone, so he'd waited. Then New Year's rolled around, and Sean pulled out and dusted off the same excuse for keeping his mouth shut. He didn't want to spoil the holiday.

Now, the children were back in school and the two of them back at work. Valentine's Day and Angie's birthday were next month, so the same excuse applied for February. That would put them in March and about five months before Trinity's due date. He could wait until then, but March was his and Angie's anniversary month. Mother's Day was in

May and Father's Day in June. That left July, the Fourth would be celebrated at his in-laws and his son's birthday was on the twelfth.

Angie patted Murphy's arm, her smile for the man warm and friendly. "Enjoy what's left of your weekend. I'll see you Monday."

"Right, Monday. It was good seeing you again, Mr. Franklin. Take care."

"Same to you."

Murphy turned and took two steps away from Angie and Sean before stopping and turning back to them. "By the way, Angela, you look amazing tonight. I couldn't let you leave without telling you."

Angela? No one called her that, not even her parents. Dr. Styles-Franklin or Angie worked. But her complete name, coming from Derrick Murphy, came off as, not only too formal but like the man was trying too hard to set himself apart from everyone else who called Angie by her preferred nickname. Did Murphy think using her given name, when no one else did, made him special to her? It was a small and insignificant point but, for some reason, it grated.

"Thank you." Angie smiled and waved goodbye to her provost.

Murphy reminded Sean of a shorter version of the rapper and actor Common. The next time Sean saw Murphy, he'd ask him to bust a rhyme.

Angie accepted Sean's arm and permitted him to escort her out of Gershwin Hall and into the cold, winter air. It smelled of rain but not of snow. They were overdue, which meant February might be a beast.

Sean wrapped his arm around Angie's shoulders and pulled her close, using his body to keep her warm.

"Thank you for being my escort. Did you have a good time?" Angie asked Sean.

"I always have a good time when we're together."

"You're sweet. Come here."

When they'd arrived home, Angie had hugged and thanked her parents for watching their children. While he locked the door and turned on the security alarm, Angie had retreated upstairs. Her actions tonight were no different from what she did every time she returned home after the children had turned in for the night. Beginning with SJ, who was normally awake but cloistered in his bedroom, she checked on the children.

Then, in the privacy of their bedroom, Angie used Sean's suit jacket to pull him to her, her smile naughty and full of carnal promise.

"I love the way you look in this tux. No other man at the gala could compare to how well you fill out your suit."

"I bet you do like the way I look in the tux. You picked it out and bought it for me."

"I have great taste, and you're the ideal model. Tall with an athletic build, but not so brawny that your muscles minimize the stylish effect of the suit."

"And handsome. You didn't say I was handsome."

Hands slid up his chest to his shoulders and pushed off his suit jacket. "I could never forget something like that. You're what, when I was younger, my friends and I would call a 'pretty boy.' " Her hand found his face and caressed. "Yes, definitely a pretty boy. No mustache or beard, but a strong jaw, wide nose and deep-set brown eyes. Now lean down so I can kiss those sexy lips of yours. I've waited the entire night, and your teasing kisses to my neck earlier weren't fair."

Never one to refuse his wife, he obeyed. Angie wasn't a shy woman, not even when they'd met. She spoke her mind, when the mood struck her, and went after what she wanted. Lucky for Sean, she'd deemed him an object of her interest worth pursuing. In truth, there wasn't much of a pursuit. They'd liked each other.

Angie kissed him, arms around his neck and her on tip-toe.

Sean sank into the kiss. The girls were asleep, SJ was playing video games in his bedroom, and their bedroom door was closed. Sean wanted everything Angie's kiss offered. The taste and feel of her were an invitation to the primal male that lived inside him. Sean could, as he'd done these past weeks, bury himself inside his wife and drown in her heat. Being with Angie pushed back the nightmares, but they always returned.

"Wait."

Angie kept kissing him. This wasn't right. He couldn't do it. Not again.

"Angie, honey, wait. Just wait a minute."

Arousal brightened the eyes that opened. "What's wrong?"

"Nothing. I mean ... we need to talk."

"Now?"

Months ago, but now would have to do because if Sean waited another day, he wouldn't be able to muster the courage again. Trinity hadn't arranged for them to have the prenatal paternity test performed the way he'd hoped.

Beyond Trinity's illogical decision not to have the test done, his guilt ate at him. She'd sent him a prenatal picture, even though he'd repeatedly asked her not to contact him on his cell. The picture had looked the same as the ones he had of SJ, Kayla, and Zuri. Sean adored those black and white images. In them, he saw the life he and Angie had created from their love.

Sean had deleted Trinity's "first pic of our baby." He didn't want to think of *her* baby as *their* child. But the image had brought the truth of her pregnancy home. The child was real. It would be born. And it could be his. He couldn't ignore those facts. Not anymore.

It was past time Sean faced his sins and his wife.

"Sit down, please."

"Why?"

"Please, this will be hard enough. Would you just sit on the bed?"

Angie wasn't the type of person who did something without knowing the reason. They shared the trait, so he understood his wife's apprehension and reluctance to comply with his request. She eyed him with a wary mix of confusion and concern. Sean putting a halt to Angie's kisses and his serious tone had shifted the expected trajectory of their night.

Angie sat on the side of the bed, back ramrod straight. She didn't know what Sean had to say, yet she had braced herself to hear the worst. Short of telling her he had an incurable disease, there wasn't much else he could reveal that would be as devastating as this confession.

"Aren't you going to sit, too?"

"No, I need to stand."

If Sean sat beside Angie, he would crumple at her feet, a spineless jellyfish underserving of her forgiveness and love.

"Does your strange behavior have to do with the kids?"

"No."

"My parents?"

"No."

"Malcolm?"

"Angie, no, nothing like that. No one is sick if that's what you're thinking. What I have to tell you has nothing to do with your family or our children."

"That leaves the two of us. What's going on? You're scaring me."

Sweat rolled down his back and formed in his armpits, his dress shirt suddenly sticking to him. "I'm sorry. I didn't mean to. I'm scared too. Terrified, actually."

"Terrified? Of what?"

Sean bent and picked up the tuxedo jacket that had fallen to the carpeted floor when Angie had pushed it off him. Giving himself a few precious seconds, he hung the jacket in the closet before turning back to his wife.

Angie's face had shuttered, which didn't bode well for Sean. His wife was one of the sweetest people he knew, except when someone pissed her the hell off. When that happened, self-preservation dictated the target of her ire should make a quick retreat.

"Before I begin, I need you to know I love you and our children. Whatever happens between us, it's important you know how I feel about you, our family, and the life we've built together."

"I already know you love us. What I don't know is your sudden need to declare it. What do you think is going to happen between us that I need to be reminded of your love?"

Sean glanced over his shoulder and to the closed bedroom door. Confessing to Angie would be bad enough, no way did he want one of the kids to overhear.

"Tell me."

Sean's head whipped back to Angie, her voice colder than he'd ever heard it.

More sweat formed, and his skin felt hot and itchy.

"Tell me," she repeated. Angie's chest heaved, and her fingers gripped the comforter. "Tell me what you've done."

Shame had his eyes lowering, but respect for his wife had them lifting again. The least he could do was look Angie in the face when he told her the truth.

"I had a brief affair."

The words weighed down his tongue even as they slithered from his mouth, a venomous statement that poisoned the space between them. He'd finally spoken the dreaded words, and they'd tasted as repulsive as he thought they would. The fate of his marriage shouldn't hinge on the power of five words, none more than two syllables.

Sean didn't know what he thought Angie's reaction would be. Most women would cry, yell, or curse, maybe throw something and break some shit. Not his wife. She sat on the bed, unmoving. Her face was blank, her eyes unreadable.

Angie's eerie calm was the stuff of horror movies, and Sean was very afraid.

"You slept with another woman."

She hadn't phrased it as a question. Sean wasn't sure if her words were meant for him or if they were a stunned clarification for herself. But he responded anyway, unsure what else to do.

"I did. I'm sorry. I'm so sorry."

"You're sorry."

"I am. I didn't mean for it to happen."

"You didn't mean for it to happen."

Angie sounded like a humanoid robot, but without the emotion program that would allow her to integrate, undetected, into human society.

"No, I didn't mean for it to happen. I didn't go out looking to cheat on you. I don't chase women, and it was only the one. Like I said, the affair didn't last long, and I was the one who broke it off."

"You broke it off, and you didn't mean for it to happen."

Angie's grip on the comforter tightened. All the emotions she didn't reveal in her face and voice were transferred to her knuckles.

"Do you walk around with your pants down and with an erection?"

"What?"

"You heard me. Maybe you were sitting under a tree on a bench at Delaware Park with your pants down. And, out of the blue, a naked woman fell from the tree and onto your erection. Because, short of that preposterous scenario, I don't see any way in hell you didn't mean to put your dick inside another woman."

Damn, Angie's voice wasn't emotionless now. The first fissures in her emotional armor were on full display.

"How long?"

"Two months."

"Who? And don't you dare lie to me."

With the sleeve of his shirt, Sean wiped the sweat from his brow and took a deep breath that didn't slow his hammering heart. "Trinity Richardson."

Angie laughed, a low, grim sound that broke his heart. "Of course, it was. Youthful, pretty, and built like a brick house. She's young enough to be your daughter, for god's sake. I suppose her age and big ass drew you in, a horny moth to her easy flame."

"It wasn't like that."

"I don't care how it was. You cheated, and you lied. You ended it, then you came back to me with your 'we need to spend more time together' bullshit."

"It wasn't bullshit. Nothing I've said or done has been bullshit. I don't want to lose what we have."

"What we have?" she scoffed. "We don't have a damn thing, Sean. You made love to another woman, for two goddamn months."

"I don't love, Trinity." Sweat and anxiety clung to Sean like dandruff on a dry scalp, uncomfortable and embarrassing. "I don't feel that way about any woman but you."

"What was it then?"

"Fucking," he blurted, before thinking better of his answer. But it was out, and Angie's jaw ticked, and her hands gripped the comforter that much harder.

"Not lovemaking but fucking. Thank you for the clarification. I feel much better now that I know my husband *fucked* his young employee but didn't make *love* to her. Because, lucky me, he only makes love to his stupid, trusting wife."

"Angie, don't. Please."

"Please, what?"

"Please listen."

"Oh, I heard everything you said. But I don't want to hear the details of how you ran around on me with a woman almost half your age. I don't want to think about the times you claimed you had to work late when you were probably with Little Miss Legal Assistant. Because that's when you fucked her, right, Sean? When you left our children here with my mother on nights you knew I would get home late from work. Those were prime fucking Tiffany nights, right?"

"Angie, don't. Come on."

"Don't. Don't. You keep saying that. Maybe you should've used that word on yourself instead of screwing another woman."

This was so bad, and he hadn't confessed the worst of it.

"Why tell me now? You got away with it."

"I didn't want to lie anymore. I felt like shit deceiving you. I wanted to unburden myself and begin the healing process."

"You're lying."

He shook his head. "I'm not. I didn't tell you because I didn't want to lose you. I still don't. I hope we can get past this. I know it'll take time, but we're stronger than my lies and affair."

"You're still lying, but you do it so well. I didn't realize, until tonight, how little effort it takes for you to lie to me."

Risking Angie's wrath, but needing to close the distance between them, Sean walked to his wife and knelt in front of her. Sarcasm and anger were her defenses against revealing the depth of her pain. Her true feelings bled through, though, around the edges of her eyes and the corners of her mouth.

He'd married a strong woman. Angie was fighting to keep it together. She wouldn't permit him to see her cry, and her effort to hide her heartache hurt like hell to witness. Because, the greater her effort, the deeper he'd wounded her.

Sean reached for Angie's hands, wanting to comfort her, but her hissed, "Don't you dare touch me," had his hands retreating.

"No more lies, Sean. Let the other shoe drop."

Not a shoe, but the deadly blade from a guillotine to his neck and their marriage.

Taking two deep breaths, Sean made his final confession. "Trinity is pregnant, and the baby is either mine or another man's."

The strike landed before he'd finished the sentence. Not a slap, but a short, hard punch to his cheek. Charles Styles hadn't raised a girly-girl who pulled hair or scratched faces when she fought. He'd taught his daughter how to protect herself, which meant using her fists. Sean had thought it cute when Angie would pull out her boxing gloves and wack away on her punching bag in the basement, a birthday gift from her father.

He didn't find being on the receiving end of her punches cute though. Neither were the tears streaming down her face.

"Get out."

"Angie, I—"

She pushed his shoulders. "Get out of my sight."

"Wait, I need you to lis—"

"Get out. Get out. Get. Out!" Her screams of hurt and fury slammed into Sean harder than her fist had. "You can't stay here."

"Umm, okay. If that's what you want. I'll sleep in the guest room, for the night."

A vehement shake of her head had her earrings swinging and his heart pounding even stronger.

"I don't want you in the house."

"W-what?"

Angie stood, knocking into him when she pushed past. She went to the closet and pulled out Sean's gym bag and tossed it to the floor. "Get your shit and get the hell out."

Dazed, he stumbled to his feet. "You can't be serious. Where am I supposed to go?"

"You can stay with your pregnant whore, for all I care." She kicked the duffle bag toward him. "I can't stand to look at you. It hurts too much. Get out, Sean. Just get the hell away from me. The thought of what you've done makes me sick to my stomach."

Angie bolted into the bathroom, slamming the door behind her. Seconds later, he heard her retching and crying.

Sean tried the doorknob, but she'd locked him out. He glanced down at the duffle bag. She wanted him to leave--not just their bedroom but their home. Sean could argue the point that the house was as much his as it was hers. But what would that accomplish? He'd literally made his wife vomit.

He picked up the bag and filled it with two days' worth of supplies. Sean would give her time to cool down, then he'd try speaking with her again.

Short of castration, this night couldn't have gone worse. Whoever said the truth would set you free didn't know what in the hell they were talking about. The truth was ugly and smelled of a rotting corpse.

His corpse.

He knocked on the bathroom door, a soft tap to get her attention. "Angie, honey, I'm going to go. I'll get a hotel room for the night. I'll text you the details, so you'll know where I am in case you need me or want to talk. Or I can stay here in the guest room. I don't have to go. I want to stay. Please, Angie, I want to stay here with you and the kids. Will you let me?"

More retching, then dead silence.

Eyes downcast, Sean slung the duffle bag over his shoulder, grabbed a coat from the closet and did as his wife had demanded.

He left.

CHAPTER FIVE

Angie dry heaved into the toilet, her body expelling nothing but her disgust and tears.

A soft knock came, followed by Sean's voice. She blocked out most of his words, but the last sentence seeped under the door on a ghost of a whisper. "Please, Angie, I want to stay here with you and the kids. Will you let me?"

He wanted to stay? She wanted to open the door and do bloody, violent harm to him. Neither of them would get what they wanted tonight.

"Trinity is pregnant, and the baby is either mine or another man's."

Her body clenched again, finding nothing but bile to expunge. Angie cried and gagged on saliva and the news of her husband's utter betrayal. She closed the lid and dropped her head to the plastic, her eyes a waterfall of blinding tears.

Sean had had an affair. A small part of her had suspected the truth, while a larger part hadn't wanted to know, so she hadn't pushed for answers to questions she hadn't wanted to pose.

Angie jumped to her feet, turned on the water in the sink and found her toothbrush and the toothpaste. She brushed her teeth. Her gums. Her tongue. Over and over, she reapplied toothpaste and brushed until her mouth overflowed with foam.

Again.

Again.

She had to cleanse her mouth of him, of *her*. Every part of Sean that had touched that bitch had also touched Angie. He almost certainly hadn't used a condom. Why else would he think the child Trinity carried could be his?

She snatched off the necklace Sean had gifted her for Christmas, breaking the clasp and throwing it and the matching earrings onto the vinyl tile floor. Angie stripped off her dress and underwear, ripping her panties in her haste. She had to get clean. His mouth, his tongue, his penis, they'd all come into contact with another woman. So dirty. How could he touch her with his tainted body?

Visions of Angie and Sean making love this morning assaulted her. She staggered into the shower. His tongue in her. Her mouth on him. God, he'd let her give him blowjobs after he'd had unprotected sex with Trinity.

Hot water beat against Angie's shivering body. Forgoing a washcloth, she scrubbed with the bar soap. Every inch of Angie needed to be cleaned.

Two months of at-risk behavior. Two months of endangering Angie and the kids. What in the hell had Sean been thinking? Why would he do it? Was he so anxious to be inside of Trinity he couldn't stop and sheath? Was their love life so unfulfilling he needed to find a woman capable of satisfying him? Or was he bored, after almost two decades of marriage, of sleeping with the same woman? Was Trinity the tip of Sean's mid-life crisis iceberg?

She fell to the tub bottom, legs too weak to hold the weight of her broken heart. How could Sean do this to her? She'd trusted him, given him her faith and loyalty, yet he had abused both.

Angie stayed in the tub until the water turned from scalding to ice cold. Grabbing her robe from the hook on the back of the bathroom door, she wrapped herself inside the thick, white cotton. Her eyes were swollen, and her head hurt. Despite Angie's best efforts, her tears wouldn't stop. So, she crawled into bed and under covers that smelled of Sean's cologne and wreaked of his infidelity. Angie had never before cried herself to sleep.

She did that night.

Two in the morning. Sean turned over in bed and away from the clock. He'd been at the hotel for three nights. When Sean had checked in late Friday, he'd paid for a single night. The next day he'd checked out and gone in to the office, thinking Angie would answer one of his text messages or phone calls and he'd be back at home in time for dinner.

Dinnertime had come and gone with no phone call or text message from his wife, so Sean had driven back to the hotel and booked a room for another night. Sunday had proven to be no different from Saturday, which left Sean with no choice but to extend his stay at the hotel.

Sean glanced over his shoulder to the clock. Another hour had passed, and he still couldn't sleep. He snatched his phone from the nightstand, then placed a second pillow under his head.

For two hours, after leaving his house Friday night, he'd sat in his truck, hoping Angie would change her mind and call him back. She hadn't.

Sean had returned home Saturday and Sunday nights, parking in front of the house instead of in the driveway next to Angie's four-door, red sedan. For three nights, he'd sat in his truck and watched his house. They lived in a nice neighborhood with safe streets and low crime, and Sean had, years ago, had an alarm system installed. Moreover, Angie kept the doors and windows locked and was sure to set the security alarm before turning in for the night and whenever everyone left the house.

This also wasn't the first time Sean hadn't slept under the same roof as his family. Business trips had taken him away from home before, although he tried to keep them to a minimum. If Angie needed it, Sean had a registered gun he kept in a lockbox in the bedroom closet. Angie knew the combination to the lockbox and how to shoot his gun. Neither the security system nor the gun settled his mind, however. He should be at home to protect his family in case a predator thought a woman alone with three children was easy prey.

Sean had to stop thinking like that. But he couldn't. Each day that passed, with Sean at the hotel and Angie at home, was one day closer to their separation turning permanent.

Pulling up his phone's gallery, for what felt like the hundredth time this weekend, he scrolled through the pics. The most recent images were shot the night of the fundraiser gala. Charles had used Sean's phone to take pictures of him and Angie before they left the house, playing the role of a proud father sending his daughter off to the prom.

Angie hadn't asked Sean to crouch or for them to sit on the couch so the height difference wouldn't be as evident. Angie was secure being five-three to Sean's six-three. His wife never felt a need to diminish him to elevate herself. But hadn't his affair diminished her, while elevating Trinity to a status in his life she didn't deserve?

For the pictures Sean had smiled, but he'd been hanging on to his lies by his fingertips. If Sean closed his eyes, he could see, behind him, the judicial executioner standing next to a guillotine, ready to carry out Sean's death sentence.

He looked at pictures of SJ at the final football game of the season. His son hadn't taken after him and tried out for quarterback. SJ was wiry, quick, and had good hands, making him an ideal wide receiver.

Interspersed between pictures of SJ's last game were close-ups of Zuri's smiling face. His little girl was forever messing with his and Angie's cell phones and taking the silliest selfies. Sean smiled at Zuri's sweet, laughing face.

What he wouldn't give to hear his little girl's laughter now. Sean could use the pick-me-up.

He kept scrolling until he found pictures of Kayla. Trinity was wrong. Kayla may have Sean's tall, lean frame, but her full lips, long bridge nose with a wide base, oval face, and prominent cheekbones were Styles' family trademarks.

Sean had never met a more outgoing or fearless child. School and their backyard weren't enough to satisfy her need to stay in constant motion. So Sean and Angie had enrolled Kayla in ballet and gymnastics classes when she was four. They'd had no idea if either physical activity would interest her. Fortunately, she loved both. More, she was good at both. In time, though, ballet claimed her heart. Now, Kayla devoted most of her free time to ballet, but she still attended gymnastics class once a week.

What would Sean do if Angie divorced him? With his infidelity and a possible child from his affair, any judge would grant Angie's divorce request. Who would get the house? Would Angie want to sell their home and purchase one closer to Excelsior University for her and the children? Would they share custody, or would the judge only grant Sean weekend and holiday visitations? The thought of a third party dictating when or if he could see his children had him struggling to breathe through his anger and panic.

Then there was Angie. He'd never messed up so badly. He couldn't retreat from his actions. He'd known he would have to own up to them. Sean had put off the inevitable for as long as possible, but he hadn't lied to his wife about the guilt eating away at his insides. Sean had needed to purge his sins, not only for her sake but for his own. Angie hadn't deserved a cheating, lying husband. She also didn't need a shamefaced, guilt-ridden one.

He either had to convince Trinity to go with him to have the prenatal testing done, or Angie to hold off on filing for divorce until after they knew the results of the paternity test. Sean may have a shot at saving his marriage if the baby wasn't his. He couldn't see his wife giving him a second chance if he'd fathered a child with Trinity.

He had to confess, at least to himself, that if it were the other way around and Angie had become pregnant from an affair, Sean sure as hell wouldn't take her back. Funny, how a man could cheat on his woman, yet hope, if not expect, with a bit of sweet talk, time, and gifts, that she'd take him back, while knowing he wouldn't extend her the same second chance. Men tended to hoard their distrust, striking back at women, in small but hurtful ways, even when they'd proclaimed their forgiveness and wish to continue the relationship.

He'd done the research and most men neither forgave nor forgot. Many women didn't either. Yet fractured relationships often persisted, with the couple choosing to stay together.

Would Sean and Angie prove to be ants carrying a piece of food one hundred times their body weight, an impressive feat of grit and survival? Or would their marriage be like a dinghy in a tsunami, small, defenseless, and overwhelmed by a stronger force?

Sean tossed his phone onto the bed in frustration and fear, yanking the comforter over his head, in an instinctive effort to shield himself and his vulnerability. He could not lose his family. If he shed a tear or two, there was, tragically, no one in the hotel room to notice, or to care.

CHAPTER SIX

"How come no one told me the party was in Mom's room?" SJ ran from the open door and jumped onto Angie's bed, bouncing and smiling as if he wasn't fourteen and five-eight.

"You're too big. There's not enough room for all four of us." Kayla shoved her brother, a playful push to his side that had SJ howling like a werewolf, and then pouncing on his sister, teeth bared. "No, no, get off me."

"I'm going to bite your neck and drink your blood."

Kayla giggled, fending off her brother with two stiff arms to his chest. "Big bully. Get off me."

Zuri jumped on SJ's back, her small arms going around his neck and holding him tight. Angie didn't know if she was trying to help Kayla or finagle a piggyback ride from SJ. A little of both, maybe.

"Help me, Zuri, help me."

"Giddy-up, SJ, giddy-up."

That solved it then. Zuri, the little opportunist, couldn't care less about her older sister's efforts not to be turned into a werewolf by their brother.

From her safe spot at the far side of the bed, Angie smiled at her children. No matter how awful the last week had been for her, the kids had managed to warm her heart with their rays of sunshine. When they weren't around, however, the cold returned like a deadly blizzard. During the day and busy at work, Angie could almost forget her troubles. The evenings were a different matter, though.

Fifteen minutes after Angie had gotten home from work on Monday, Kim had asked her, "What's going on? The kids said Sean is out of town on a business trip. But that can't be right. He's in the middle of the Cavanaugh case. Poor kid. At least the parents had the satisfaction of winning the first case against one of the interrogating officers. I'm sure he'll win the others, too."

Angie had walked her mother to the front door, Kim talking the entire time while also slipping into her coat and holding on to her car keys and shoulder bag.

"My point is that Sean can't be out of town on business. So where is he? He's the one who relieves me, not you. And why are you home so early? You're rarely here before six."

"We're too old for Twenty Questions, Mom."

"One then, and it's my original question. What's going on? With you and Sean?" Kim had qualified as if Angie would use the vague phrasing of the question to respond in an equally vague manner.

"I don't want to talk about it. At least not now."

If she did, she'd break down in tears. With the children around, Angie hadn't wanted to fall apart. Again.

"Come here." Kim had opened her arms, and Angie had filled them. She'd cried, despite her best efforts to hold her emotions inside. She'd coughed and hiccupped her sad story through a tear-choked voice "Oh, my sweet girl. I'm so sorry," her mother had said after her watery purge had concluded.

Kim hadn't asked further questions. She didn't push Angie to share details or to verbalize the depth of her pain. She didn't castigate Sean or ask Angie her plans. Kim had simply held Angie, soothing her with her presence and respectful silence.

SJ managed to extricate himself from Zuri's hold, tossing her onto the bed next to Kayla. The girls screamed, SJ roared and went in for the "kill."

Laughter ensued.

By the time they'd finished, Angie's bed was a mess. All the pillows and most of the covers were on the floor, as were her giggling children. Through it all, Angie had sat at the head of the bed, knees to her chest and a broad smile on her face.

Breathing hard, the children got to their feet, and then collapsed onto her bed.

"When will Daddy be home?"

Zuri asked the same question every day. Each morning, since Angie had thrown Sean out in a fit of rage, Zuri would look around the kitchen, as the family ate breakfast, and ask about her father. It began with, "Where's Daddy?" which SJ and Kayla wanted to know, too. After Angie had fumbled out a lie about Sean having to leave on an unexpected business trip, the question had shifted to, "When will Daddy be home?"

"Yeah, Mom, it's been a week." SJ sat up, his tone serious and gaze focused on her. "When will Dad be back? I have a game next week, and he always attends."

Three sets of dark-brown eyes peered at Angie, waiting for an answer she couldn't provide.

"I don't know," was her inadequate reply but the only answer she had to give them. Sean had left more than a dozen text and voicemail messages this past week, none of which Angie could bring herself to answer. She wasn't ready to speak to him, let alone prepared to decide about their marriage. "I'll attend your game."

SJ's face revealed what she knew. Having his mother attend his basketball games was nice but not the same as having his dad there cheering him on.

"Don't you have to work?"

"I'll adjust my schedule, so I can attend. Text me the details, and I'll make sure I'm there."

Sean had SJ's basketball schedule memorized, even though the winter sports season had only just begun. She'd been hesitant when SJ had come to them about joining a sports team. As a high school freshman, she didn't want athletics to distract from academics. Angie and Sean discussed it and came to a decision. If SJ maintained a three point five average, he could play a sport. First semester, he had a three point eight grade point average.

Zuri climbed onto Angie's lap, her head going to her shoulder. "Sleepy?"

"I want Daddy to read me a bedtime story."

Kayla jumped off the bed, ran from Angie's room, and returned with her iPad, a Christmas gift from her grandparents. "Let's FaceTime him. It's after seven and Saturday, so he shouldn't be working, and we won't be disturbing him."

She hadn't prevented the kids from reaching out to their father. Angie never would. They'd called him a couple of times this week. Sean had gone along with Angie's lie. She hated the deception. This couldn't go on much longer. She must either permit Sean to return home or file for legal separation. Neither option appealed, leaving their relationship in limbo and her children missing a father who stayed less than ten miles away in a hotel.

Angie situated Zuri between Kayla and SJ, against the headboard. The fatigue in the four-year-old's eyes was replaced with happiness at the prospect of seeing her father, even if via an iPad screen.

She got out of bed. SJ and Kayla knew what they were doing. They didn't need Angie's help, and she had no interest in seeing her husband's face or hearing his voice. When they were finished, one of them would retrieve her for their movie night. Zuri probably wouldn't make it through the opening credits and SJ, after his sisters were asleep, would try to sweet talk Angie into renting an R-rated movie from On-Demand.

No sweet-talking would be required. They both enjoyed bloody, action-packed movies.

Considering her children liked to talk as much as their father did, they would be a while, so she grabbed a book from her nightstand and settled on the living room sofa. She'd read no more than five pages before the buzz from the doorbell interrupted. Angie didn't bother answering. She was comfortable, and her visitor was uninvited but expected. He also had a key, which he used when she'd ignored the buzzer for the third time.

Malcolm appeared at the threshold of her living room, his concerned gaze a greeting she didn't need.

"You should've called me." More than concerned, Malcolm was angry. Angie didn't need that either. "Why didn't you call me?"

He removed his coat and hat. It never ceased to amaze Angie how her younger brother managed to keep his Rapunzel-like dreadlocked hair pulled up and under his hats. It had to be a miracle of science that prevented his long hair from falling around his shoulders and down his back. The way he cared for his hair put most women to shame, including her.

"I had to find out from Mom." Malcolm's big body dropped onto the cushion beside her. "She said you were upset and Sean hasn't been around all week. The asshole fucked another woman, didn't he? That's what Mom said. Did he also leave you and the kids? So, help me, Angie, I'm going to—"

She gripped the hand that had turned into a fist. "This is the reason why I didn't tell you or Dad. I don't need either of you fighting my battles."

"It won't be a fight. One punch. I'm going to kick his sorry, cheating ass with one punch."

"Don't. Please, don't do anything stupid."

"It won't be stupid. But I lied about the one punch. One won't be enough for what he did."

Angie's sigh whispered from her, a long exhalation she felt from the depths of her stomach to her beseeching eyes. "Come on. I don't need this from you. I have enough of my own emotions to deal with without you coming over here with your testosterone breathing all over me. I can handle it."

"Handle it, huh? What have you done to handle it?"

Not much of anything, other than altering her work schedule to cover the gaps left by Sean's absence. It wasn't easy, but she'd managed to make the necessary changes so she could cook the kids breakfast and get them off to school. Thankfully, Zuri, a preschooler, attended the same elementary school as Kayla. Next year, when Kayla became a middle schooler, there would be three schools to drive to instead of two. The children could catch the bus, but that option had never set well with Sean. He preferred to drive the children himself, to be sure they reached their destination safely. Just because he wasn't around to drive them to school didn't mean Angie would uproot their routine because of her job and their father's poor choices.

"I have an appointment with my doctor on Monday. I can't think about next steps until I find out the results of the STD and HIV screenings."

Malcolm swore, and Angie had never seen her brother angrier, not even when he was bullied as a kid and had decided to strike back.

"You mean to tell me he didn't have the good sense to use a goddamn condom. Wait. What am I talking about? He cheated on you. Clearly, the asshole doesn't have any sense. But I'll knock some into him."

"I didn't tell you to set you off. Malcolm, I'm serious, no fighting. It won't solve anything."

Neither had punching Sean when he'd told her about Trinity's baby. She'd heard about people "snapping" when they found their spouse in bed with someone else. A murder sometimes followed. Angie understood the fury and sense of betrayal, but not the raw, uncontrollable impulse to kill the cheating spouse. No one deserved to die for their lack of fidelity. But that night, her fist had moved, without conscious thought, and she'd attacked her husband. Would she have shot Sean if she'd caught him in bed with Trinity? Angie would like to think she wouldn't have. The truth, however, was that she didn't know.

For that reason alone, Sean returning home, right now, wasn't a good idea.

Malcolm made no promises, but he did pull her to him.

Angie breathed in his scent, an aromatic cocktail of coconut hair oil and bay rum, a common fragrance used in shaving soap. She melted into her brother, the same way she had their mother. Angie let it all out. The awful story flowed from her like Lake Erie into the Niagara River, Malcolm's love and support strong enough to hold her emotional weight.

She hadn't wanted to share her problems with her family. Not because they would view it as a burden to bear, but because their knowledge would make the situation more real for her.

Having her brother there, though, an immovable tree in her winter storm, gave her the strength to remove the all-is-fine mask she'd donned for her children and colleagues. Even for her mother, who'd looked at Angie with compassion tinged with worry.

With her brother, she didn't have to put on a brave front. That's not the kind of relationship they had. If anything, Angie and Malcolm were too honest with each other.

"I'll go with you."

"To my doctor's appointment?" She pushed from his chest, wiping her face with the back of her hand.

"Depending on the time of your appointment, I could either pick you up here or meet you there. The choice is yours."

"Then I choose to go by myself." They were close, but Angie drew the line at having her brother escort her to her gynecologist's office and wait while she submitted to venereal testing.

"That doesn't make any sense. I can go with you. If not me, then Mom. Someone, Angie, dammit. You shouldn't deal with something like that on your own."

Malcolm was only partially right. Family support would be nice. At the same time, Angie dreaded explaining to Dr. Grace Raymond the reason for the testing. She'd been her doctor since before SJ was born and had delivered all three Franklin babies. Furthermore, her grandson attended EU. While they weren't precisely friends, she and Angie had a relationship beyond that of doctor-patient.

"I'll ask Zahra to go with me." Zahra was Angie's best friend and, unlike Sean, really was out of town on business. She hated lying to Malcolm, but her brother could be like a dog with a bone. If he thought she intended to go by herself, he would bug the hell out of her until she relented. Angie would rather suffer her embarrassment without an audience. "I'll call Zahra tomorrow and see if she has time to go with me."

Appeased, Malcolm nodded, but neither of them smiled.

She cuddled against her brother's side, and he kissed her forehead. "Say the word and I'll murder Sean for you."

"You can't murder your best friend and the father of my children."

"He's no longer my best friend. But you're right about the squirts. Sean may be a shit husband, but he's a good father."

Sean was a great father and, until this business with Trinity and the baby, Malcolm would've never referred to him as a "shit husband."

"Do you still love the asshole?"

She swallowed, her throat tight and scratchy from the truth she didn't want to admit. "Yes. I'm pathetic."

"You're not pathetic. Feelings aren't like light switches. Just know, whatever you decide to do, the family will be there for you. If you want to kick Sean's ass to the curb, we'll help you pack his bags. But if you decide to give him a second chance, we'll support that choice, as well. Either way, we're here and not going anywhere." Tightening his arms around her waist, he pulled her even closer. "I love you."

"I know, M and M. I love you, too. Thank you for stopping by to check on me and for offering to ruin your life by killing my husband."

"What's a felony between siblings?"

Angie laughed, which was so much better than crying.

"Sorry about missing your game."

"It's fine. We lost, so you didn't miss anything good."

Sean pushed his dinner plate to the other side of the wooden desk. Hotel room service was fine, for a few days, but Sean missed his wife's home-cooked meals, as well as waking up in his own bed. He missed his children, most of all, and felt like crap for having to skip SJ's basketball game. With the lie Angie had told the children, for which Sean was grateful, he couldn't very well show up at SJ's game and then not return home with the family.

As it was, every time one of the children called, they'd asked when his case would be over so he could return home. Like Angie, he'd been forced to lie, repeatedly, to their children. None of it sat well with Sean, but them knowing he'd done something so terrible that their mother had thrown him out of the house was even worse.

"I did miss something good. I missed seeing you play a sport you love. You won't always win, but you must always give one hundred percent."

"Yeah, I know, Dad. You say the same thing before every game and test."

"It's not all about what I say, but what I do and what you hear."

He'd raised his children to be loyal and honest. Sean had modeled the behavior, in a way his own father hadn't. In the end, though, he had proven to be more like Edward than his marriage and conscience could take.

Sean leaned back in the chair in the sitting area of the hotel room. The room came with a king-sized bed, a sofa bed he didn't use at all, a full kitchen he made coffee in, but not much else, and a desk he used for eating and working.

If Angie decided to make the separation permanent, he'd have to find different lodgings because renting a hotel room was a waste of money. Maybe he could find an apartment or condo close to the house. He'd refrained from giving his future living arrangement too much thought, even when he'd gone home, while the kids were at school and Angie at work, to retrieve suits and supplies for the work week.

He'd texted Angie to let her know he'd be in the house. Her only reply was for him to set the alarm on his way out. After days of being apart, her response had been less than he wanted but more than he expected.

"I know. Listen, Dad. Mom's been acting differently."

"What do you mean?"

"Kind of quiet. A little sad, maybe angry. I'm not sure. She's been in the basement, a lot, hitting on her punching bag. I asked her if something was wrong."

"What did she say?"

"She told me not to worry." SJ was too smart not to realize his mother hadn't answered his question. "But I am worried. I've heard her crying at night, and I don't know why. The next morning she looks fine, but I know what I heard. She won't talk to me because I'm a kid. But she'll talk to you."

Until Sean's confession, SJ would've been right. Guilt churned in his stomach the more SJ talked about Angie. The teen's concerns weren't unfounded. But his faith in Sean to help Angie through her difficult time was misplaced.

"Uncle Malcolm's been by twice this week. He watched a movie with us last weekend and had dinner here yesterday and on Monday. He sent me funny gifs from Mom's phone."

"Your uncle was on your mother's phone?"

"Yeah, fooling around. You know how Uncle Malcolm is. I saw him with Mom's phone, then he sent me a bunch of funny but lame sports gifs."

Yeah, he knew how Malcolm was, and he hadn't been "fooling around" on Angie's phone. Sean knew it would only be a matter of time before Angie told her family, then her brother or father would come looking for him.

"Have you finished your homework?"

"No, but—"

"We can talk tomorrow. Finish your homework before your mother has to ask."

"Yes, sir. I guess that means you won't be home tomorrow either."

His big son sounded no older than Zuri, and Sean's guilt increased.

"I'll be home as soon as I can."

"Promise?"

Dammit, Sean didn't want to offer a promise he wasn't guaranteed he could keep, but the words that exited his mouth were the ones his son needed to hear. "I promise."

Thirty minutes after the phone call with SJ, the knock he'd expected came. Angie's defender had arrived.

Sean opened the hotel room door, and a fuming Malcolm Styles greeted him with a punch to his face. He fell back into the room, nose and mouth bloody from the attack he should've expected but hadn't. Damn, Malcolm hadn't pulled his punch any more than Angie had.

"You're one sorry piece of shit."

"Yeah, I know. Were you trying to break my damn nose?"

Blood splattered his dress shirt, and his hand barely contained the flow from his nose. Leaving a fuming Malcolm at the door, Sean went into the bathroom.

"You make me want to break your fuckin' neck. I told Angie I would murder you for her, but she asked me not to."

Because she still loved him or because she didn't want her brother going to jail for killing her husband? Probably the latter.

"It's bad enough you fucked another woman, but you did it without protecting yourself, meaning you didn't protect your wife either. Know where Angie went on Monday?" Malcolm hovered in the doorway to the bathroom, as Sean washed his face and tried to staunch the bleeding. "To have a goddamn STD test done. You didn't even think. She has no idea if you contracted something from your legal assistant and passed it along to her."

No wonder Malcolm had had dinner with Sean's family on Monday. He probably used the visit to check on his sister and to find out how her doctor's appointment had gone, although she may not have known the test results before leaving her gynecologist's office.

Sean held the white towel over his nose, pinching his nostrils and cursing himself. No matter what angle his affair was viewed from, close-up or far away, he looked like a selfish, uncaring bastard. For all he'd said that dreadful night, it hadn't occurred to him to tell Angie he'd had a comprehensive STD test performed and that the ten-test panel results had come back negative. That would've meant having a lengthy conversation about his sexual activities with Trinity and revealing yet another lie of omission.

Malcolm was right. He hadn't protected himself or his wife. Sean dropped the blood-stained towel into the sink and turned to Malcolm. "You want to take another swing at me?" His arms rose and spread outward, giving Malcolm a defenseless target. "I deserve it. Take your best shot. I won't stop you."

His brother-in-law's headshake and disappointed gaze hurt more than the younger man's punch had.

"You're not the man I thought you were. Do you have any idea what you've done? Angie is holding it together, for the kids. But she's a mess. Do you know what's really sad? Only you can make it better."

Malcolm's softly spoken words were grenades to his heart.

"I'm going to set it right."

"You can't, especially if that woman's baby turns out to be yours."

True, but Sean had no control over that. He did over his actions.

"I have no good reason for what I did, so I won't bother offering an excuse. I did it, and it's done. I don't want to lose my wife, even though I deserve to. If Angie still loves me, I have a chance to fix what I've broken."

"Her heart."

Sean's eyes slid closed at the brutal reminder. "Yeah, I know I broke Angie's heart." He looked at Malcolm, who appeared as shaken by that reality as Sean. "I'll do my best to help her heal, if she'll allow me."

Angie was right. Every time Sean told the story about falling off his bike and getting back up, he'd leave out the part about him breaking his arm. He also omitted how, after the doctor had removed his cast, he'd been afraid when his father put him back on the bike. Sean had been terrified of falling and hurting himself for a second time. He had also been afraid to trust his father not to let him get hurt again.

With so many thoughts whirling in his head, he hadn't noticed when his father's guiding hands had released the bike. Sean had ridden a full block before he realized he'd conquered his fear. He'd stopped and turned around. His father had waved at him, his smiling face filled with pride. Edward hadn't let Sean down the way he'd thought he would. It would be several years before Sean would learn how thoroughly Edward had let the entire family down.

He felt the same fear and anxiety now as he had all those years ago. However, Sean was no longer that scared six-year-old. The training wheels of life had long since been removed. Sean had fallen. Now it was time for him to get up, dust himself off, and get his ass back on the bike.

If Sean didn't do something, he would lose his wife. Angie's anger, hurt, and his absence would be enough to drive her to a divorce lawyer. Sean had given her space, almost two weeks' worth.

It was time to go home.

CHAPTER SEVEN

"Take your time. Don't run down the steps."

Angie's words went ignored as her children bolted past her room and toward the stairs the minute they heard the front door open and close. Sighing, Angie set aside her papers and rose from her desk. She'd read the same section of the most recent draft of EU's strategic plan four times. Lately, her mind was less on work and more on the sorry state of her marriage and heart.

The girls squealed, and she made her way out of her bedroom and in the direction the children had gone. Angie stood at the top of the stairs, unable to see her children or the person who'd let himself into her house.

His house.

She'd had two days to prepare for this moment, but forty-eight hours hadn't been enough time. Her heart raced, a freight train shaking the foundation of her resolve. Sean had called and, for the first time in two weeks, she'd answered. He'd kept the conversation short, which hadn't made it any less emotionally perilous.

"I haven't seen the kids in two weeks. I was hoping I could come by this Sunday. Would that be all right with you?"

Sean hadn't mentioned his affair or their separation. But his question had carried a weight far greater than his desire to spend time with their children. Once the kids knew their father was in Buffalo, they would expect him to stay home. For their lives, in their minds, to return to normal.

By the time she ambled downstairs, Sean and the children were in the kitchen. Angie stood, on the opposite side of the room. She leaned against the white-washed cabinets, a cool monochromatic look when matched with the light kitchen flooring. Angie and Sean had selected every item together when they'd renovated two years ago. While their dress styles were different, Sean casual to Angie's dressy, their tastes in home décor were surprisingly similar -- classy yet comfortable.

"Here, Dad, put this on your nose." Kayla handed Sean the ice pack they'd bought when she'd twisted an ankle at ballet practice. "Were you in a fight?"

SJ punched the open palm of his left hand with his right. "Tell me what you did to the other guy." He bounced on the balls of his feet around the wide island in the kitchen. Kayla stood beside Sean, who sat with Zuri on his lap. "Uppercut. Jab. Right hook." SJ demonstrated each attack, punching at the air with eye-rolling enthusiasm for a kid who'd never punched anyone, let alone taken one. "Roundhouse kick."

"Roundhouse kick?" Sean held the soft, blue pack against his face. "I'm not Bruce Lee. No, Kayla, I didn't get into a fight." He lowered the pack, and Angie saw the damage. "I don't have a cool story to share. What happened is kind of boring. But I could make up something exciting for you to tell your friends."

The injuries weren't fresh, and she doubted this was the first time Sean had applied ice to the bruised regions. But he hadn't done a good job, or his nose wouldn't look as if he'd volunteered as a punching bag.

"I fell on a treadmill."

"You fell?" SJ sounded disappointed. "I've never heard of anyone falling on a treadmill."

"It happens more often than you'd think, especially if you lose your focus, the way I did."

"I can't tell my friends you took a nosedive on a treadmill."

"Well, it's the truth."

It wasn't the truth, and she'd have to have a word with her brother. Unlike the lies Sean had told Angie, to cover his affair, his treadmill story needed work. He'd had forty-eight hours to come up with a credible explanation for his injuries. She understood, though. Lying to their children wasn't in their nature.

"Daddy, will you read me a bedtime story?"

Sean squeezed Zuri to him, his face lowering to the top of her head and kissing before lifting and finding Angie watching him. He smiled, as handsome as ever in a dark-blue, hooded T-shirt and blue jeans. As always, his face bore no signs of stubble, and his hair was cut and trimmed to perfection. At forty-six, Sean had neither a receding hairline nor more than a few specks of gray hair. Angie, on the other hand, fought a valiant but futile battle, ammonia-free dye her monthly act of defiance and vanity.

Sean kissed Zuri again, the girl already dressed for bed in her pink-and-white, fairy princess nightgown. She'd had her evening bath, her school clothes were ironed, and her lunch was packed and in the fridge. The only Zuri-related task left on Angie's list was her nightly bedtime story.

"I'll read you two. How does that sound?"

Zuri rose onto her knees and hugged Sean around his neck. "I missed you, Daddy. Don't go away again."

The four-year-old clung to Sean, and he to his little girl. All the kids hovered around their father, Zuri having voiced the thoughts of her siblings. The scene should've been beautiful, a devoted and loving father surrounded by his children. In a way, it was. But Angie couldn't help envisioning Sean holding a baby. His and Trinity's newborn, a product of their unprotected and illicit "fucking."

"I'm going to the basement."

She made the announcement loud enough for Sean to hear, but not so loud she would interrupt Kayla, who'd claimed the barstool next to him and had started to tell her father what was sure to be the first of a dozen school-related stories he'd missed. Then it would be SJ's turn. Zuri wouldn't take a turn, not because she talked any less than her sister and brother, but because she never felt a need to compete for Sean's attention when he held her. For Zuri, her favorite place was snuggled against Sean's chest with his arms wrapped around her.

"I'll be down in a while."

Angie nodded to acknowledge Sean's response, then she slipped away from the kitchen and back upstairs. She grabbed the same novel she'd started when Malcolm had interrupted her reading last week. Angie hadn't made much progress since then, and she wouldn't tonight. But muddling through a trope-filled novel, while she waited to have a discussion she'd avoided for two weeks, was better than sitting in her room dreading the conversation to come.

It didn't take Angie long to find a bit of Zen in the anarchy of her mind. The gray sectional sofa was baby soft and the basement quiet. She'd closed the basement door, affording Sean and the kids their privacy and her some solitude. The book rested on her lap, closed, just as her eyes were.

Angie dozed, on and off, before hearing the door to the basement open and close and heavy feet on the steps. She sat up from where she'd slouched when she'd fallen asleep.

"You look good." Sean lowered himself to the opposite side of the sofa from Angie. "Really good."

Angie hadn't made an ounce of effort to prepare for her husband's arrival. She wore no cosmetics, not even lip gloss. Her feet were bare, as were her legs. After her evening shower, she'd thrown on a pair of black drawstring shorts and a white tank top over a black sports bra. If anything looked "really good," it was the hair she'd styled yesterday, loose curls that framed her face.

"I was hoping we could talk."

"I was hoping this had all been a horrible dream, but it isn't. Do you know the paternity of that...?" Words like bitch, whore, slut, and home-wrecker came to mind. Angie had used them all when she'd told Malcolm about Sean's affair. She didn't want to go there again. If she used any of those unkind but apt descriptors, she'd launch into a string of hurtful vitriol neither of them was prepared to handle. "Do you know the paternity of Trinity's baby?"

Sean's guilty eyes evoked frustration but not sympathy. Angie did, however, hate seeing him hurt. Malcolm had an understated protective streak and a vicious right punch. Either her brother had stopped after the first blow landed, or Sean had countered. No way, if Sean and Malcolm had gone all out, her husband would've escaped with only a puffy nose and split lip. Both men were too strong and skilled to leave the battlefield with minor injuries.

"No, she refuses to have the prenatal paternity test."

"So, we have to wait until the baby is born. Perfect. Just perfect." She threw her book across the room. It hit the top of an open storage unit filled with wicker baskets that held the kids' toys, books, video games, and whatever else they'd dragged from their rooms and to the basement. "This entire situation is unbelievable."

"I know. I'm sorry."

"I don't want to hear how sorry you are. Your sorrys don't change a damn thing. I can't ..."

Angie wanted something else to throw. Better yet, to hit. She glanced at her punching bag on its stand and in the corner of the room. Her hands still hurt from the abuse she'd done to them. Most days she'd worn her gloves, while others she'd gone without, smashing her fists into the heavy-duty vinyl. On those days, when anger and hurt got the better of Angie, she'd envisioned Sean's and Trinity's faces.

She wasn't ready for this conversation. Her rage ran too deep, and Sean's tail between the legs approach was infuriating.

Angie inhaled deeply and released it slowly. She could do this. "I moved your stuff to the guest room." She'd done it late last night after the children had gone to bed. Angie may not have wanted to see or to speak with Sean, but her children's needs trumped hers. "Until I know what in the hell I'm going to do about us, I don't want to disrupt our children's lives. They missed you, just as Zuri said."

"You're taking me back?"

Skeptical. He should be.

"No, I'm allowing you to move back into our house. The kids need a father, and I don't want to be the one to take you from them."

"I don't get it."

"Nothing has changed between the two of us. Until I know whether the baby is yours, I can't consider taking you back in any real capacity."

"So, we'll live under the same roof, but me in the guest room and you in our bedroom? Like platonic roommates?" He frowned as if he'd sucked a lemon and found the bitter taste not to his liking. "I think we should talk this out."

"There's no talking this out. I have no idea what you expect from me. It's only been two weeks since I learned of your affair, and that your Trinity may be carrying your child. What in the hell is there to talk about?"

"She's not my anything." Sean moved closer to Angie, but still left several cushion-lengths between them. "And there's plenty to talk about."

"Like what? Do you want to tell me why you fucked around? Do you want to tell me the when, where, and how of your affair? Do you want to get a plate of muffins and spill some tea on how you kept me from learning your dirty little secret? Or maybe, just maybe, you want to tell me when I stopped being enough for you."

"Angie, shit. You are enough for me."

Tears escaped, and she despised showing her weakness in front of him. She shook her head, denying Sean's lie and rebelling against her liquid traitors. "I wasn't enough. How could I have been, if you slept with another woman? Not once, Sean, although that would've hurt too, but many times. Two months' worth of times. No, I wasn't enough for you.

If you're going to continue to lie to me, then we might as well keep our communication to a minimum."

"I'm not lying."

Angie scooted from the sofa and retrieved her book. Her angry throw had left the paperback unscathed. She wished she could say the same for her heart. "We will talk and make a decision about our marriage after the baby is born and the results of the paternity test known. Or we could go upstairs and have a heart-to-heart with the kids. Zuri won't understand, but Kayla and SJ have friends whose parents are divorced. I won't tell them the reason why we're ending our marriage, but we'll have to come up with an explanation better than your treadmill lie."

"No!" Sean shouted, getting to his feet and stalking toward her. "We aren't having a goddamn heart-to-heart with the kids because we aren't getting a fucking divorce. I don't want a divorce."

"You should've thought of that before."

"I know. Dammit, I know. I'm sorry. Angie, I'm sorry. I don't want to lose my family."

"You won't lose the kids. We can work out an arrangement. We'll share custody. I wouldn't fight you on joint custody."

"Stop. Just stop." He spun away from her, agitation in every rugged line of his body. Just as quickly, he turned back to her, eyes wild and desperate. "You and the kids are my family. Don't take that from me."

"I'm not. You gave it away when you cheated. I'm only reacting to the series of events you set in motion."

Angie dropped her paperback onto the sectional. Tension radiated through her, and her head pounded. She slipped into her lightweight, red boxing gloves she'd left on the floor beside the punching bag. Setting her feet and holding her shoulders, elbows, and fists the way her father had taught her, she hit the bag.

Smack. Smack. Smack.

"No divorce."

Smack. Smack. Smack.

"Do you hear me? We're not getting a divorce. We'll get through this. It may not seem like it now, but we will."

Smack. Smack.

"I'm good with staying in the guest room."

Smack. Smack.

"I'm sorry for everything. An inadequate apology, but I mean it with every breath I take. I'm sorry I was unfaithful."

Smack.

"I'm sorry I lied."

Smack.

"I'm sorry I wasn't a better man when I was tested."

Smack. Smack. Smack.

Sean stood in front of his bedroom closest, or what used to be his closet. All his shoes and clothing were gone. When Angie had said she'd transferred his belongings to the guest room, Sean had assumed she'd moved a few items. But no, literally everything he'd kept in the master bedroom was gone, including the toiletries he couldn't take with him when she'd thrown him out of their home.

He looked around the bedroom, an ache of regret his reward for his affair but not for the truth he'd finally spilled. Sean wasn't built for deception, no matter the stereotypical perception of lawyers. His lies were acidic bubbles in the pit of his stomach, painful, corrosive, and with no chance of receding until he'd purged his soul.

Now, the sour taste of his truth, a grimy layer of film on his tongue, left him craving his wife's sweetness. But Angie felt nothing but bitterness toward him, a justified response to his affair. She wouldn't even have their conversation in their bedroom, where most of their private discussions occurred. Instead, she'd chosen the basement, neutral territory with no connection to the last place they'd spoken.

The place where he'd revealed his lies and broke the special bond between husband and wife.

She hadn't taken him back. If Trinity's baby also turned out to be his, Angie would file for divorce. His wife hadn't been that direct, but the implication was there. Angie was willing to have him back in the house and wait until the paternity test before she decided the fate of their marriage. Which meant what for Sean?

One, Angie wasn't ready, despite her anger and pain, to end their marriage now. Two, she'd left room for the possibility of a second chance and reconciliation, no matter how slim. Three, she didn't believe she could stay married to him if he'd fathered Trinity's child.

Sean walked from the master bedroom and down the hall to the guest room. The door was open and, as he'd known they would be, his possessions were inside. Two rolling suitcases were at the foot of the bed. Three garment bags hung in the closet next to Sean's suits. A neat row of dress shoes, winter boots, and athletic shoes was at the bottom. He spotted his shaving bag on the dust-free dresser and the small collection of magazines he kept on the nightstand on his side of the bed. He didn't doubt, if he opened the nightstand drawer, he'd discover everything that used to be in his nightstand in the master bedroom in this one.

Every item was as they had been when he'd last seen them, except they were in a different room of the house. Angie hadn't reenacted the popular scene from *Waiting to Exhale* when Angela Bassett's character, Bernadine "Bernie" Harris, had thrown her lying, cheating husband's belongings in his car and set them ablaze. Sean hadn't gone to see the movie with his own Angela, but he'd seen the famous clip of Bassett, a wife scorned. Her fury, but more so her sense of gut-wrenching betrayal, had been palpable.

When he'd watched the scene, the hurt in Bassett's eyes, her voice, hell, her entire trembling body, had brought back painful memories. Even as a man, his sympathy wasn't with the husband who'd lost a closet-full of expensive possessions, but with the wife he'd taken for granted, cheated on, and then left for a white woman.

Sean didn't view himself on par with John Harris, Bernie's husband, but had he hurt his wife any less than John had hurt his? Had Angie had her own meltdown moment, after he'd left? Had she considered taking out her fury on his clothing, in lieu of hunting him down at the hotel and meting out female justice? What had it cost her to invite him back into their home, his presence salt in Angie's open wound?

Sean plopped onto the bed, heart heavy and legs weak. He had five to six months to make amends with Angie before the baby was born. If she filed for divorce, however, he would have no choice but to let her go. It would kill him to sign the papers, but he wouldn't cause Angie more grief by keeping her in a marriage she no longer wanted.

But they weren't there yet. As grudging as it had been, Angie had permitted Sean to move back in. She'd done it for their children, not for him, or even for herself. But Sean didn't care. He'd take any leverage he could get if it meant saving his marriage.

Giving himself that much-needed pep-talk, he stood. Sean had a bed-time story to read and a wife's forgiveness to earn.

CHAPTER EIGHT

"I haven't changed my mind."

"Are you sure? It sounds like you have."

"How can I sound as if I've changed my mind when I just told you I haven't?" Angie opened her closet and selected her dark navy trench coat with leather trim. "I'm putting my coat on now. In five minutes, I'll be in the car and on my way to meet you."

"Do you have the address?"

Angie rolled her eyes. She'd known Zahra Whitfield since high school. Even as a moody, irreverent teen, she'd assumed everyone shared her highly selective memory. "You texted me the address this morning, two days ago, and last Monday. I may be turning a year older next week, but that doesn't mean my memory is already slipping. Relax, I'll be there."

"Three times, huh?" She chuckled. "That's anal, even for me. I guess I thought, with everything going on with you and Sean, you might not be in a partying mood."

Angie's wedding and engagement rings taunted her from the glass jewelry tray on her dresser. She hadn't worn the twin symbols of her marriage and commitment to Sean since the morning after her husband's confession. She'd told herself it was due to her swollen fingers from beating on her punching bag more often and harder than usual. A partial truth.

Angie had removed them the morning she'd awakened without Sean by her side, exhausted from a restless night and too much crying. She had shed the twenty-year-old rings the same way dieters lose the last ten pounds, with difficulty. If anyone had noticed her bare fingers, they hadn't said. Angie didn't know if she was preparing herself for an inevitable divorce or whether she'd felt too disconnected from Sean and the meaning the rings once held for her to wear them. Perhaps a little of both.

Angie belted her coat and checked her appearance in the mirror before flipping off the ceiling light and leaving the bedroom.

Zahra was right, Angie wasn't in a partying mood, but she needed to get out of the house. Specifically, she needed a few hours of breathing space from Sean. Angie didn't know which version of Sean was worse, the guilty Sean who brought her flowers and cards or the overconfident Sean who smiled and flirted and acted as if all was well between them.

Both versions grated because one reminded Angie how low her husband had fallen, while the other ignored the huge dent his cheating hammer had put in their marriage.

"As I said, I'll be there. Look, I need to say goodbye to the children, then I'll be on my way. See you soon."

Angie ended the call then slid her cell phone into a coat pocket. Everyone was still on the first level, which meant one thing: movie night with dad. She poked her head into the living room. "I'm about to leave."

Four sets of eyes shifted from the flat screen television and a slapstick comedy rental. Mouths full of popcorn, the children waved but didn't budge from their spots on the couch. That was Angie's cue to leave.

High heels clicked as she made her way down the hall and toward the front door. Her purse and a flat, pink-and-white gift box were on the front hall table. She claimed both. Angie reached for the knob of the front door, her mind already mapping the route she'd take to the event.

Angie didn't hear Sean approach, but she should've known he wouldn't let her leave without commenting on her Saturday evening plans.

"Where are you going?"

"I told you. Zahra's sisters are throwing her a bachelorette party." She turned away from the door to face him. From the look of him, Sean was spoiling for a fight. She didn't have time for an irritable husband tonight. "I have my cell. If something happens with one of the kids, call."

"I'm here. The kids will be fine." He stepped closer, bare feet on solid hardwood flooring and dressed in gray sweats and a bum-around-the-house T-shirt way past its prime. "I want to know the exact location of the party. You didn't tell me. Is there a reason why?"

Angie's comings and goings weren't Sean's business. She didn't owe him anything. Except, dammit, she did. Whether she liked it or not, they lived under the same roof, and he was still her husband. Considering his affair, those two facts didn't carry much currency with her. Yet, if something, God forbid, happened, Sean needed to know her whereabouts, so she told him.

His face hardened, and storm clouds formed in his eyes. "That's a strip club."

"It's a bar and lounge with adult entertainment, and Saturday is Ladies' Night."

"Same damn difference." Rigid arms crossed over broad chest, pulling the old T-shirt taut. "That's what you're into now?"

"Don't start. I didn't choose the location of the party."

"But you're going, so you must not have a problem with it."

"Zahra's my best friend. Of course, I'm going."

"This is her third marriage. I don't know why in the hell she needs another bachelorette party when none of her marriages stick. Zahra can't seem to keep a man."

She glared up at him and hardened her voice. "Not every man is worth keeping."

Sean took another step toward her, lightning in his eyes and his mood thunderous. Yeah, Sean wanted to fight, and Angie, when it came to her husband lately, stayed on a knife's edge of a bad temper. But she wouldn't permit Tropical Cyclone Sean to ruin her night before it even got started.

"Is that your way of saying I'm not worth keeping?"

"That's your interpretation."

"You implied it." Arms dropped, and so did his eyes to her hands. "Where are your rings?"

What? Angie thought he'd seen her ring-less fingers but had chosen not to comment and risk starting an argument. It had never occurred to her, after almost two weeks of being home, that Sean hadn't noticed. Then again, Angie spent as little time around Sean as possible, which may account for why he stared at her as if she'd committed the crime of the century.

"I took them off."

He waved his hand in front of her face. "I'm still wearing mine. Why in the hell aren't you wearing yours?" He hadn't yelled those sentences at Angie, as much as he'd snarled them. "You're still *my wife*, no matter what I've done."

"Our rings are meaningless."

"They aren't."

Now, those two words, he did yell.

"Lower your voice, or the kids will hear you."

"They aren't meaningless."

"What meaning did your wedding ring have for you, hmm? Did it prevent you from sleeping with another woman? Did it remind you of me, when you were buried in Trinity? Or was it nothing more than an inconvenient piece of jewelry, symbolic but ultimately meaningless?"

Angie stood her ground, undaunted by Sean's anger but afraid of her own, as well as her sudden desire to lash out at him.

"You're still my wife," he repeated, ignoring all she'd said and his voice still too loud. "Our wedding rings aren't meaningless, and your hands don't look the same without the rings I gave you. Put them back on." His voice finally lowered, and his heated tone softened. "Please, put them back on."

Sean was right. Their wedding rings weren't meaningless. The problem wasn't their lack of meaning but the unwelcome change his affair had on how she now viewed them.

"I need to leave, or I'll be late."

His face said this conversation wasn't over but that he was choosing to let it go. Good, but future discussions wouldn't yield a better result. Sean hadn't gotten their new but not improved relationship through his stubborn, arrogant skull. Yes, Angie was still his wife, but that role no longer fit her the way it used to. Sean had once washed her favorite wool skirt instead of taking it to be dry cleaned. The skirt was never the same afterward, despite Angie's ability to squeeze into the damaged garment.

Back then, Sean hadn't read the clothing care label and had ruined her favorite skirt. Now, he may have condemned their marriage to the same fate, unheeding the care label of her heart.

"You're all buttoned up. What are you wearing underneath that coat?"

She didn't like his accusatory tone, so she jumped into the petty end of the pool with him. "Nothing but the bra and garter set you bought. Did you also buy a set for Trinity? A buy one, get one half off deal? Or maybe you caught a great sale and paid full price for the first and nothing for the second. I bet the saleswoman wondered about the different sizes, though." She may not be in the mood to argue, but Sean had a way of bringing out her mean side. "I also have two hundred dollars in small bills in my purse. Do you think that's enough? I don't know the going rate for a lap dance."

"So much mouth for a small woman. You're trying to piss me off."

"You were pissed off when you came after me. Although, I have no idea why you're upset. I'm going to drink a little, dance and laugh a lot, and then return home."

"You forgot to add watch men shake their junk in your face."

"Not in my face, Sean. I don't get down like that." Angie reached behind her, found the doorknob, and turned. "But I'll watch and enjoy all the mouth-watering sights. Music, muscles, and men, how can I resist a combo like that?"

"Don't do something you'll regret. You won't be able to take it back." They stared at each other, but with each measured breath he took, his storm clouds dispersed, leaving Guilty Sean in their wake. "You won't be able to take any of it back."

If Sean was going to cheat, why couldn't he have fucked and forgotten about it, like most men? Why did he have to burst Angie's bubble of naïveté and doom her to this love-hate-distrust quagmire?

"I'll take a page out of the Book of Sean Franklin and do whatever the hell I want and with whomever I want. Don't wait up."

Angie left the house before her bravado exploded all over her. She hadn't meant a word she'd uttered to Sean. But a perverse part of Angie had wanted to hurt her husband and give him a small taste of what it felt like to question your attractiveness and appeal, even your self-worth.

In no time at all, Angie was walking into the bar. Loud music blared, and bodies gyrated. Angie hadn't cared when five people bumped into her. In a place like this, it was to be expected. But when a hand snaked around her shoulders from behind, she'd had enough.

Angie jerked away from the presumptuous ass who thought it okay to touch a woman without her permission—thank you very much Donald Trump and Bill Cosby—and spun around to give him an ear full.

A familiar body flung herself at Angie, hugging and squeezing her tight. "You came."

"I told you I would." She released a shuddering breath. "You scared me. I thought you were one of those handsy guys we used to see at the club when we were in college."

Zahra planted a sweet, loud smack of a kiss on Angie's cheek before releasing her. Forty-five-year-old Zahra, pretty and five-six, wore a black skater dress with a plunging neckline and mesh details. Her best friend loved Malcolm's long locs but didn't have the patience to grow her own.

Braid extensions were the next best thing, according to Zahra. To Angie, faux locs would've made more sense.

"You thought I was one of those jerks? I'm insulted." She squealed and reached for the present in Angie's hand. "Ohhh, is that gift for me?"

"Yes, but you'll have to wait to open it. Where's everyone?"

Zahra's pout of disappointment lasted a second. Then she grabbed Angie's hand and tugged her through the crowd and deeper into the bar. Angie followed Zahra up a flight of stairs and to a semi-private room with a bar, tables and chairs, and plush-looking red couches that lined the wall. In front of the elevated stage was a dance area. Women and men filled the space. Most of the women she knew, mainly because they were Zahra's relatives.

"Who are the men?"

"I have no idea. Ella rented the room for my party."

"Did your sister rent the men, too?"

"Funny. They're men from downstairs who saw a bunch of pretty women piling in here and decided to join us. They seem nice enough. If that changes, Ella will have security throw their asses out of here."

Ella, five years younger than Zahra and a Buffalo homicide detective, wouldn't require security to take care of the men if they got out of hand.

"Come on. Put that gift down and let's sit. The show's about to begin."

Angie added her gift box to the table with gold cloth and emerald decorations, Zahra's wedding colors.

As the guest of honor, Zahra sat at the table nearest the stage. Ella was already seated, as was Zahra's youngest sister, Amara. She hugged them both, happy to see the women.

"I'm glad you're finally here." Ella sipped from her glass of white wine. "Zahra can relax and stop driving us crazy worrying about you."

Angie didn't fear Ella referred to Zahra worrying about her situation with Sean but her friend's tendency to fret in general. Amara and Ella may be Zahra's sisters, but she'd always kept Angie's confidences. She didn't want everyone knowing her business, not even all her friends. Angie could do without their sympathy and pity, no matter how well-intentioned.

She removed her coat and settled into the seat next to Zahra. Within minutes, a Blue Hawaiian was in front of her—crème de coconut, pineapple juice, white rum, and blue curaçao—what Sean would call a "girly drink."

Lights lowered, and *Uptown Funk* by Mark Runson featuring Bruno Mars drifted from the speakers and filled the room. Women got to their feet, dancing along, then clapping and hollering when five men strutted onto the stage. Baggy jeans, hiking boots, open plaid shirts, and cowboy hats, the men reveled in the applause, their huge chests and six-pack abs glistening before they'd had a chance to work up a sweat.

Wonderful. Cowboys in Buffalo. Yee haw.

She picked up her drink, sipped from the straw, and gave herself permission to tuck her troubles away and enjoy the sight of a man's body other than her husband's. Not a single man, but men. Hard-bodied and tatted-up, the inked designs added to the men's sex appeal and drew the eye to the most scrumptious places.

Amara's, "Yum," followed the dropping of men's shirts, and Angie concurred.

Cowboy hats were tossed into the audience, tantamount to a wedding bouquet all the women in attendance wanted.

When the song ended and the women quieted, Buffalo cowboys were replaced by two men in leather biker gear and black bandanas on their heads. The duo, six-feet, all muscle and with a striking resemblance to each other, jumped off the stage and onto the dancefloor. Nelly's, *The Fix*, played in the background, explicit lyrics and all about sex, of course. Fucking, not love or even romance. That kind of raunchy, raw song was the last thing she wanted to hear.

Angie slid from the table, empty glass in hand, and walked to the bar on the opposite side of the room.

"You wanna order another drink, pretty lady?"

The bartender, Jason, according to his nametag, could've been one of the strippers. The width of his shoulders, handsome face and cocky smile earned him good tips, no doubt.

Angie handed him her glass. "After Shock."

He whistled. "You like to play with fire, huh? That drink will have you smashed faster than the twins get out of those tight ass leather pants. After Shock weighs more than you do. How about another Blue Hawaiian or a Red Sangria?"

Angie appreciated the bartender's concern, but not his opinion of her capacity to hold her liquor. She would have only one, and it would help take the edge off.

"An After Shock, please."

He shook his head but didn't argue further.

"Was your drink on fire, when you were at the bar?" Zahra asked when Angie returned to the table.

"Only for a few seconds. Is that dancer supposed to be an Egyptian pharaoh?"

"Yeah. Isn't his costume great?"

Angie doubted if anyone in the room gave two cents about the dancer's ancient Egypt-inspired wrap-around skirt, leather sandals, and a striped headcloth with lappets that fell down both sides of his face. Not when his bare, ripped chest and tree trunk thighs were more enticing treats to feast her eyes upon.

The pharaoh moved his hips and shook his ass in a way a male shouldn't be able to. When he'd danced over to the guest of honor, straddling Zahra's legs and yeah, shaking his junk in her face, her best friend reached around and smacked the stripper's ass.

Zahra's friends went wild, and more male dancers came into the audience, finding women to dance with. Or, more aptly, to grind against.

Angie hadn't given herself permission for this, although she didn't object when a man, built like an Olympic weightlifter, picked her up … well, Angie and the chair she sat in … and proceeded to carry her around the room. When the giant of a man, dressed in nothing but a G-string, stopped and put her down, Angie's head spun. From the strong drink, the hot room, or the dancer's semi-hard erection jutting toward her, she didn't know.

She reached out, forgetting for a minute a stranger's penis was in front of her and not the empty glass she'd left at the table. Angie yanked back her hand and went in search of Jason the Bartender.

Sean snatched the phone and answered it. "Hello."

"I can't believe you answered on the first ring."

"Is that you, Zahra?"

"Yeah."

"What's wrong? Why are you calling from Angie's phone? Where's my wife?"

"Slow down. One question at a time."

"It's two in the morning, where in the hell is my wife?"

After the kids had gone to bed, Sean returned to the living room. He'd tried not to worry when eleven o'clock had turned into twelve and then midnight slid into one. By one-thirty, he'd given up the pretense of watching a movie and not waiting up for his wife. Ten minutes ago, he'd thrown on socks and placed a pair of tennis shoes by the front door.

He'd wondered how mad Angie would be if he asked her brother to watch the children while he went wife hunting. When Zahra called, Sean was about to use the landline to contact Malcolm.

"Angie's fine. Drunk, but fine."

Sean jumped to his feet. "I'll be there in twenty minutes."

"Slow down. You have three sleeping kiddos at home. You can't leave. I rode with Ella and Amara to the bar. I'll drive Angie home, in her car, and Ella will follow. No way am I sending my girl home, like this, in a taxi or Uber. Not happening."

"How drunk is she?"

"Not falling down or cursing people out drunk. She doesn't get like that, but Angie takes classy drunk to another level."

Yeah, rare though the occasions were, drunk Angie was also flirty Angie.

"She said she wouldn't drink a lot."

"It doesn't take much when they are After Shocks. Two, maybe three."

"Two or three." Sean bit back a curse. What in the hell had Angie been thinking? At one hundred eighty-five pounds, Sean could barely handle one of those drinks. Yet his one hundred twenty-pound wife had downed two or three. No wonder she was drunk.

"Look, my sisters and I have her. She's strapped in her car, and I'm pulling out of the parking lot. We'll be there before you have a chance to burst a vein worrying about her. Better yet, use the time to calm down. I can hear the anger in your voice. Let her sleep it off tonight. She'll wake up with one hell of a hangover and remember why she hasn't gotten drunk in years."

Every now and then, Angie would have a glass of wine with dinner. Neither of them indulged much. When they did drink, though, they didn't do it to excess. Yet tonight Angie had, and Sean knew why. So did Zahra, but the woman had too much tact to blame him.

"Thanks. Call when you're in the driveway, and I'll come out and get Angie and her car keys."

While he waited, Sean ran to their—Angie's—bedroom, pulled down the sheets, set out underwear and nightgown, and ran a hot bath. He grabbed one of SJ's sports drinks from the fridge and placed it on Angie's nightstand beside a bottle of water. The electrolytes should help restore her salt and potassium loss while the water would aid the flushing of the alcohol from her system.

It didn't take Zahra long to get there. At two thirty in the morning, few drivers were on the road.

Sean waved at Ella and Amara, who waited in a blue sedan in front of the house. He didn't know them as well as he knew Zahra, but they were friendly, and Angie liked the sisters, which was all that mattered to him.

Wrapped in a warm-looking puffer coat, Zahra climbed from Angie's car and handed him the keys. "She fell asleep halfway here."

"I'll get her."

Sean took a step toward his wife's car, his heart slowing at the sight of her. She was safe. Drunk, but safe. Until now, he hadn't realized how worried he'd been the longer she stayed out. He knew she wouldn't call him, and he hadn't wanted to call and intrude on her evening. So, he'd watched television and waited for his wife to return home, the way she said she would.

He'd watched and waited and prayed Angie was a better wife than he'd been a husband. As angry as Sean had been to see her without the engagement and wedding rings she'd worn every day of their marriage, he was more upset with himself. It had taken every rational cell in his body not to blow his top. He had zero moral standing to judge Angie for taking off her rings.

To Sean's shame, he had also removed his wedding ring, but for a totally different reason from Angie's. Every time he had sex with Trinity, he would slip his wedding ring off his finger and into his pants pocket, as if that cheating man's trope prevented him from tainting what the ring represented. It hadn't, and the thought of Angie not bothering with that shallow pretense and going to a club with men looking for one-night stands had seized his heart and fueled his jealousy.

"Wait." Zahra tugged at the sleeve of his coat. "I know it's not my place to say—"

"Then don't."

"She's my friend."

"And I'm her husband. I know what I did to her. I don't need you to tell me."

"Do you really know? I don't see how you could. Have you looked at your wife? Listened to her?"

"Of course, I—"

"You have no idea how easy it would've been for Angie to do to you, tonight, what you did to her for two months. I've been through two marriages and two divorces, Sean. I don't want my friend to go through the pain of dissolving her marriage. But you didn't see her tonight, pretending to have a good time for my benefit. Men flirted with her, including the bartender. Angie could've taken any of those men up on their offers, but she didn't." Zahra shrugged, not at all nonchalant. "Perhaps she will later. No one's a saint, and you've given her no reason to continue to be faithful. You may not see or listen to her. But trust me, there's always someone who will."

"Are you finished?"

"Not quite." Zahra's leather glove covered hand took hold of his and squeezed. "I may be pro-Angie, but that doesn't also make me anti-Sean. I hate seeing my best friend sad and in pain, but I see the same in your eyes. I attended your wedding, twenty years ago this March, and I hope to help you celebrate your thirtieth anniversary." She released his hand and nodded toward a sleeping Angie. "I'm rooting for you both. Take care of my friend."

Stunned by Zahra's words, Sean could only nod and watch her get into the car with her sisters. They waved, and Ella pulled away from the curb.

Sean gathered his wife into his arms and carried her inside. Once behind the closed door of her bedroom, Sean settled Angie onto her bed and removed her shoes. When he reached for her coat, her hand stopped him, and her eyes opened.

"I can undress myself. Thank you for bringing me inside."

They were in the same position they'd been in when he'd told her the news of Trinity's pregnancy--Sean on his knees in front of Angie and his wife seated on the side of the bed.

She removed her trench coat, revealing a black, off-the-shoulder dress with bell sleeves and a side slit. Only his wife would wear a chic cocktail dress to a strip club. The sexy, form-fitting dress looked great on Angie and was perfect for holding her close and for slow dancing under a full moon's glow.

"I ran you a bath. After you're finished, drink as much of the water and sports drink as you can get down."

Sean wanted to touch her. He desired nothing more than to set his hands and lips on the expanse of exposed skin above the low-cut top of her dress. He also wanted to inquire about this evening's events and the men who'd offered to replace him, even if only for a few sensual hours.

Drawn to her, the way he always was, he couldn't deny the pull. Unconsciously, he leaned forward, her lips a temptation he couldn't resist.

Angie turned her face, denying his kiss "No." A solid hand pushed against his chest. "No." The hand on his chest fisted, but she didn't strike out the way she'd done before. "No."

Did that two-letter word answer questions Sean was too afraid to ask?

Do you still love me?

Will you ever let me touch you again?

Do you trust me?

Will you stay faithful?

Will you forgive me?

He pushed to his feet and helped Angie to hers. "Go take your bath." The water would no longer be hot, but it should be warm enough for a quick soak. "Don't fall asleep."

"I won't."

She moved around him and toward the master bathroom, peeling off her dress and underwear as she went.

Damn, Angie hadn't been screwing with his mind. She did have on his gifted bra and garter set. With a dress, thankfully, but still. The woman knew how to stab a man in the heart. She'd worn the silk items only once since Christmas, and that had been on New Year's Eve. They'd rung in the New Year making love and drinking champagne in bed. Two weeks later, he'd told her about Trinity.

Now, only a few days away from Valentine's Day and her birthday, his wife had decided to wear the gift again. Not for Sean and his pleasure, but for herself and a secret "go to hell" to him.

He would stay until she finished her bath. Angie was highly functional, but she was still drunk. And drunk people did mindless stuff like falling asleep in a bathtub and drowning.

"I'm fine," she yelled from the tub.

She wasn't, and neither was he. Sean stayed until his wife returned from the bathroom and kicked him out of her room.

CHAPTER NINE

"Where do you want me to put this one?"

Angie looked up from her computer screen to Jeanette Gregory, her executive assistant. Not that she could see the fifty-one-year-old brunette behind the bouquet arrangement.

"Mr. Franklin has gone all out this year. Every delivery is bigger than the one before. This arrangement has three dozen red roses. It's beautiful but heavy."

Heavy, that single word had Angie getting to her feet instead of staring, mouth agape, at the large floral arrangement, balloons, and box of chocolates Jeanette held in her capable but overwhelmed hands. Rushing from behind her desk, she took the balloons and candy from Jeanette.

"You can put the vase on the conference table."

"Are you sure? There're already three there, and you have a meeting in here in two hours."

When Jeanette had brought in the first bouquet, red roses mixed with three shades of pink roses and accented with assorted greenery, the ten-chair oak conference table seemed an ideal location for the flowers. The pretty arrangement brightened Angie's office. With today being both Valentine's Day and Angie's birthday, she didn't bother asking Sean to forego his normal extravagance and risk starting a pointless argument. Nothing she could've said would've prevented him from doing exactly what he'd done today–go overboard.

"Then put the vase on the credenza."

Jeanette, poised and professional in a pair of red, slim ankle pants and a black, crepe blazer, nodded to Angie. "Okay, there you are, you little pretties," she said to the flowers, almost cooing the words.

Jeanette placed the vase next to the three-foot white bear whose red paws held a red heart with the words: Be Mine. Fingering the letters on the heart, Jeannette glanced over her shoulder, chocolate eyes twinkling at Angie. "You've either been very good, or Mr. Franklin's been very bad." The second the words were out of Jeanette's mouth, her gaze dropped to Angie's hands that still held the balloons' strings and the box of chocolates. "I didn't mean …"

Angie didn't step into the breach, when her executive assistant went quiet. Jeanette was great at her job, observant yet discreet. Today, Angie wore her wedding and engagement rings. The same as yesterday and the day before. Jeanette and anyone else who'd noticed her rings' temporary disappearance could speculate as they would, but she'd be damned if she confirmed their suspicions. Much of Angie's job involved her image. Being the mother of three well-adjusted children and the wife of a respected civil rights lawyer was part of her image and fit EU's brand of family, future, and success.

The Board of Trustees wouldn't look favorably on a president whose marriage became fodder for gossip, especially not the kind of sensational gossip that would follow news of the birth of her husband's "love child." Angie and Jeanette may have a wonderful work relationship, but she never confused the role of executive assistant with that of a friend. Jeanette Gregory worked for the Office of the President, not for Angela Styles-Franklin. The distinction kept Angie vigilant, so she stared at Jeanette and waited for the woman to either complete her sentence or to leave.

"I … umm, I'm going to go finish preparing for the meeting."

"Good idea."

Jeanette hustled from Angie's office, pulling the door partly closed behind her.

Angie's office reflected the date on the calendar. Flowers, candy, balloons, and stuffed animals were everywhere. Angie dumped the red star balloon weight and box of candy on the right corner of her desk. There was nothing professional about her once pristine office. Two kissing stuffed bears were in a chair in front of her desk, and a Valentine ladybug with a red bowtie in the chair next to it. On the floor and under her desk, where she'd tossed it out of sight, was a stuffed brown deer in a pink-and-white shirt that read: Dat Ass Doe. Her husband wasn't as funny as he thought himself to be, and she'd have to sneak the gift out so no one would see. Unfortunately, there was nothing Angie could do about the people who'd seen the delivery person bring the Valentine's Day deer into her office. Jeanette, for her part, had tried to repress a laugh when she'd given Angie the gift.

She retook her seat behind her desk. Angie had two reports to read before she met with her executive leadership team.

A knock sounded, and Angie sighed. At this rate, if Sean's deliveries kept interrupting her, she'd get no work done.

"Dr. Styles-Franklin." Not another delivery but her provost. Dr. Derrick Murphy peeked his head around the door, a wide smile his greeting. "Are you busy, Angela?"

She could count on one hand the number of people who called her Angela and still have four fingers left. For some reason, Derrick preferred the more formal name, and Angie didn't mind his preference. It was still her name, after all. He said it with respect, if not a little something extra she'd chosen to ignore.

"Never too busy for you, Derrick, come in." Untrue, but she knew why the man was there. It was the same reason more than a dozen EU administrators, faculty, and staff had stopped by her office today. Her mailbox was also full of emails wishing her a happy birthday. All her life, people had loved the idea of her birthday sharing the same day as Valentine's Day far more than she did. Sean and her family were no exception.

Derrick strolled into her office, his gait confident and his smile even larger when he approached her desk, a vase of Casablanca lilies in his hand.

"Not to be redundant"—his eyes took in Sean's extravagance—"but happy birthday. I hope you like lilies." He handed her the vase of white flowers, the sweet fragrance lovely, the big blooms beautiful, and the gift considerate, if not a tad inappropriate. "Beauty, class, and style, that's what the florist told me lilies symbolize. I thought they fit you perfectly."

"Thank you. The lilies smell wonderful, but you didn't need to get me anything for my birthday."

She'd have preferred if he hadn't. Angie had a strict personal policy about gift-giving. When she treated EU's employees, it was done on a group, not an individual level. As a woman and as president, propriety couldn't be neglected, or its importance minimized. A closed-door meeting, drinks after work, even a birthday or holiday card, all innocent until someone twisted the facts into something unrecognizable from the truth.

Derrick should've known better than to buy Angie a gift. He hadn't in the two years she'd known him. The only saving grace was his presentation of the flowers as a birthday gift and not as a Valentine's Day present. Although his beauty, class, and style comment delivered a different message.

"It's your birthday, and you're a great boss. They're pretty flowers, and this is your special day."

The entire time Derrick spoke, his smile didn't falter. His entire focus was on her, and she saw how easily this moment could turn into so much more if she allowed it to. A warm smile, a lingering touch, a dinner suggestion, off campus, of course, and it could grow from there, a seed planted.

How had it started for Sean and Trinity? Long work nights and conversations? Flirty smiles and silly jokes? A hug of gratitude and a friendly kiss to the cheek?

"Thank you," Angie repeated, her tone professional and polite. The man was handsome, no doubt about that. He was also intelligent, confident, and kind--traits she valued in a man. Traits he shared with Sean.

Angie hadn't been interested in a man, other than Sean, in a long time. She wasn't now. Even if Angie wanted to begin her own affair, she wouldn't choose Derrick Murphy. Not because he wasn't attractive and fit and would likely make a good lover. But Angie loved her job and career too much to risk either on an office romance born of a sick desire for revenge.

She found space on top of a file cabinet for Derrick's flowers. They were beautiful, as she'd told him, but lilies weren't her favorite flower. Roses were, which Sean knew. No matter how many other kinds of flowers he brought her, he made sure the florist added at least two red roses-- love and beauty.

Derrick finally left with an, "Enjoy the rest of your birthday."

She didn't know if she would. Sean was back to acting as if nothing was wrong between them, except their house was filled, like her office, with flowers forged from guilt. On her birthday/ Valentine's Day, he'd upped his gifts and charm.

She'd awakened to steaming, fragrant coffee and a tray of her favorite breakfast foods. Sean hadn't treated Angie to breakfast in bed in years, yet he had this morning. A new silk robe hung on the back of the bathroom door and the shower had been stocked with coconut frosting shampoo, shower gel, and bubble bath. Angie had used the shower gel. It left her skin feeling soft and smooth, the scent lingering for hours.

Sean had also left a box of Valentine's treats in her car: chocolate-covered strawberries, black bottom cupcakes, heart-shaped red velvet cookies, and a raspberry-chocolate parfait she'd eaten an hour into her workday. On her way out the door, he'd pressed her stainless-steel water bottle into her hand. Except, when she made to drink the contents, the bottle contained mint-lime iced tea, another of her favorites.

Angie comprehended her husband's point. The bludgeon of gifts wasn't necessary. The night of Zahra's bachelorette party, he'd told Angie she was his wife. The corollary, of course, being, he was still her husband. As Angie's husband, Sean was intent on proving to her how well he knew his wife and the extent he would go to earn her forgiveness.

They both knew, however, despite the seeming romanticism of Sean's gifts, his extravagant tactics would increase his credit card bill but not raise his value in her eyes.

"Here, Mommy." Zuri handed Angie two folded pieces of construction paper, pink inside red. "I made it all by myself."

That wasn't exactly true. Sean played a little role in helping Zuri with her gift for her mother. She knew more words than she could spell and didn't like the idea of sounding them out and possibly spelling them wrong. Of course, at four, she would spell many of the words incorrectly, which was part of the learning process. But Zuri wanted her card to be "perfect for Mommy."

As the youngest, Zuri had an adorable but fierce way of claiming Angie, when she thought her older siblings could upstage her. The children didn't often compete for their parents' attention and praise, but there were times, like today, they reminded Sean his children were as much Franklins as they were Styles. The Styles clan loved three things: their family, the Buffalo Bills, and winning. Malcolm and Angie weren't as competitive as their father and cousins, but they hated to lose … at anything. Zuri was no different from her mother and uncle, when it came to her attitude about winning and being the best. She'd wanted her gift to Angie to outdo Kayla's and SJ's gift.

Angie sat on the living room sofa with Zuri wedged between her legs. Zuri's face was so close to Angie's she barely had enough room to read the card.

This year's birthday and Valentine's Day festivities were smaller than in years' past. The Styles enjoyed nothing more than going all out for holidays and birthdays, especially when they overlapped, as in the case of Angie's birthday. This year, however, with the tension between Sean and Angie, he'd only invited Angie's immediate family to her birthday celebration. He didn't know how many in the Styles clan knew of his affair, and the last thing he wanted, on Angie's birthday, was a similar incident to what had happened with Malcolm.

Malcolm was his best friend, so he'd taken his punch without retaliating. The younger man had a right to defend his older sister, but Malcolm's single punch was the exception, not the damn rule. Sean wouldn't tolerate any other Styles thinking to put their hands on him. Sean would have to eventually face the Styles clan, but he wasn't prepared to deal with more disapproving glares tonight. As it was, Malcolm wasn't speaking to him and Angie barely spoke. His in-laws, incomprehensibly, treated him as if he hadn't broken their daughter's heart.

"Let me see what you have here, baby." Angie pressed a kiss to Zuri's forehead then read her card. "Happy birthday, Mommy. You are the best Mommy in the whole wide world. You hug me and kiss me and read me bedtime stories. You let me sleep in your bed when I'm sick and when I have a bad dream. You watch movies with me and sing songs with me…"

Angie turned the page and kept reading, and everyone smiled. The little girl had a lot to say. Zuri had only needed help with her spelling. Everything else, including the decorations, glitter hearts and all, were done by her. She'd made a complete mess on the kitchen table after school today, but her sister had helped her clean it up before Angie arrived home from work.

"Wow, you did an amazing job. Thank you. I'll put your card on my desk at work."

Zuri beamed, and Sean had to coax her away from her mother so SJ and Kayla could give Angie their gifts. The children already flanked her on the sofa, while Sean sat in a chair across from his family. Charles and

Kim reclined on the loveseat to Angie's left, and Malcolm leaned his shoulder against a wall, a gift bag in his right hand, his focus on his sister.

When Sean had married Angie, he'd not only got a prize of a wife but a cohesive, loving family in the Styles. He hadn't realized, until he met Angie's family, how much he'd craved the closeness Malcolm and Angie took for granted. Styles family celebrations were the norm. They crammed into one house, on special and not so special occasions, food and laughter always on the menu.

That wasn't his normal, growing up. As a man who would turn forty-seven in March, Sean had a closer relationship with his wife's family than his own. As he watched his children give handmade gifts to their mother, a pang of sadness and regret hit him. That had been Sean, a long time ago, happy and carefree. Where had that vibrant little boy gone? When did he become disillusioned by his family, the joy of youth and innocence sucked from him?

Sean knew the answers to both of those questions. Family memories, long buried, found their way to the present, his mind and heart unable to continue to keep them separate. He'd pushed them deep down for years, now he couldn't force them back inside. Tentacles of insecurity gripped him, the hold tight, the pull great, and the monster's whispers cruel. *"You're just like him. I knew you'd succumb. It was only a matter of time. Welcome home, Sean, welcome home."*

More gift-giving followed SJ's and Kayla's presents. As always, Angie's parents and brother gave her both birthday and Valentine's Day gifts. She also had two cakes in the kitchen, again one for her birthday, a heart-shaped cake Kim made, and an ice cream holiday cake Malcolm purchased. Knowing Malcolm's love for sweets, he'd probably bought himself one too.

Angie hugged everyone, happier than he'd seen her in a month. He hadn't given Angie his gift, but he knew better than to expect a warm embrace from his wife. Sean had already gone overboard today, with the deliveries to her office and the flowers in the house and her bedroom. What would one more gift matter?

Sean stood from the chair and went to his wife. She still sat on the sofa, the kids around her, and the eyes looking up at him so very brown and beautiful.

"You have one more present to open."

"You didn't have to. Look at this place, you've given me more gifts than I know what to do with."

"You deserve them." He held out the velvet box to her. "And this."

She took the box from him, for which Sean was grateful. He had a great eye for what appealed to his wife and what would look stunning on her. He purchased Angie lingerie more often than he should. But his wife had a wonderful figure, toned and curvy, and he enjoyed seeing her decked out in sexy, silk underwear he could run his hands over before stripping them off of her.

"That's so pretty," Kayla crowed, leaning over Angie's shoulder and looking at the open gift box in her mother's hand. "Get it, Dad. Grandma, come look at Mommy's necklace."

Dutifully, Kim pushed from the loveseat to examine her daughter's birthday gift. "Kayla's right, Sean, you've outdone yourself this year. Angie, lift your hair and let me put it on for you."

Complying, Angie stood and turned her back to her mother. At sixty-nine, Kimberly Styles was still a beautiful woman. The women resembled each other in facial structure and build, although not in temperament. Angie was more subdued and serious than her mother, but when Angie got going, she could be as boisterous and outgoing as any other Styles.

When Angie turned back around, Sean's gift settling into the V-neckline of her purple blouse, he couldn't help grinning. He'd been right. The pendant, rose gold curved to meet a line of round diamonds, was set in 10-carat white gold. It didn't disappoint. The necklace looked as gorgeous on his wife as he'd hoped it would.

"So pretty."

"You aren't looking at the necklace, Sean," Kim teased.

"Guilty as charged. But nothing is as lovely as my wife." He moved into Angie's space, wishing she'd say something about his gift. "Do you like it? It has two hearts."

"I noticed."

"Who wants cake and ice cream?" Charles patted Sean on the back. "We'll be in the kitchen helping ourselves to dessert."

His father-in-law didn't have to repeat the question. As soon as the words cake and ice cream were out of his mouth, the children stormed from the living room. Malcolm and Kim slipped away, too, perceptive of the privacy Charles wanted to give Angie and Sean.

"Happy birthday." Normally, he would lean down and kiss the hell out of his wife, and she would return the kiss with matching ardor. Now, awkward silence was all they managed to share. "Happy Valentine's Day. I know I went a bit overboard, but—"

"Way overboard. It's too much."

"It isn't."

"Yes, it is, and you know it."

"So, you don't like anything I gave you today?"

"You know me, including my likes and dislikes. The flowers, balloons, and candy were all wonderful but too much. Breakfast in bed was delicious and sweet, and you could've left it at that." Angie touched the pendant. "This necklace is precisely what I'd buy for myself, but it had to cost you a grand."

With taxes, it had. But Angie was missing the point or perhaps Sean was missing hers. "I wanted to make today special for you."

"I know, and I appreciate it. But it's too much and doesn't change anything between us. Did you really think grandiose gestures would fix what's broken?"

Sean hadn't, but he'd hoped. Without hope, what else did he have?

"I want things to be different between us. Normal. I'm slipping under the water, Angie, and I can't find a single life preserver. I'm trying to hold on to something, anything, but our marriage is like water, and I can't get a grip."

Her face registered nothing he hadn't seen this past month—polite tolerance with an edge of sadness and anger.

"I can't be your life preserver, Sean, not when you're the one who sailed our marriage into an immovable iceberg. I'm doing my best to keep my head above the water, too."

"What does that mean for the two of us?"

"I don't know. I wish I did. This is my birthday, and I spent most of it feeling like crap, comparing this day to last year's. I thought I was happy then. I thought *we* were happy. Now I must reevaluate what I assumed to be true. Six months after my birthday, you started your affair with Trinity. What am I supposed to do with that knowledge? How do you expect me to feel, realizing that, even as you were treating me to flowers, candy, and jewelry on my birthday, you were likely already attracted to another woman, maybe even flirting with her and building up your courage to take the mutual attraction to the physical level? I'm wearing your rings again, and you're living in our home. Beyond those two concessions, I don't have anything else to offer you."

Nothing hurt worse than the brutal truth. Angie didn't sugarcoat, not even for herself.

Sean said nothing when she walked away from him and out of the living room, the scent of roses a bitter perfume of rejection. He collapsed onto the sofa, his head in his hands. Sean had kept most of the details about his affair with Trinity to himself, but Angie had an unerring way of figuring them out.

She'd been right about Sean using her late nights at EU to be with Trinity, just as she was correct about his mindset of a year ago. It had taken Sean months to get on board with the signals Trinity had thrown his way. Subtle, at first, but more blatant when he didn't shut her down, and his eyes began to wander over parts of her he'd once ignored.

Courage to cheat on his wife and to keep cheating, yeah, he'd worked himself up to the point of no return. A caress, a nibble, a squeeze, and finally a kiss, the floodgates to the forbidden garden had opened to Sean, and he'd strolled inside.

A hand touched the top of his head. Sean wanted it to be his wife's, offering him comfort, but it wasn't.

"You want to talk?" Kim sat beside him, silver hair pretty in a classic bob cut. Her bangs covered her right eye, which she pushed behind her ear to take in Sean in that scrutinizing way of hers.

He supposed it was only a matter of time before one of Angie's parents brought up his affair. Between a sometimes-gruff Charles and his mother-in-law, he preferred Kim.

She took his hand in hers and leaned against the sofa cushion. "I think we should talk."

"Do I have a choice?"

"Life is nothing but choices."

Sean shifted to his side, taking in the petite, older woman dressed in a long-sleeved, burgundy dress with a belt. "You're going to chide me on my poor choices with my former legal assistant?"

"No, from the look of you, you're doing a fine enough job. I wanted to talk to you about my choices."

He turned even more to face his mother-in-law. "You're choices? What do you mean?"

She glanced to the opening of the living room and then back to him. She still held his hand, sweet but also strange. "Charles and I decided not to tell Angie and Malcolm what I'm about to tell you. By the time they were old enough to understand, it didn't matter anymore." Shoving even more of her hair behind her ear, she shook her head. "Well, that's not true. It never ceases to matter. It just stops mattering so much."

"You do realize I have no idea what you're talking about, right?"

Kim's soft laugh sounded conspiratorial. "Of course not, dear. I haven't spoken about it in so long, I must dust off the cobwebs. I want you to know I understand what you're going through with Angie."

It took him a minute to process her words, but he still wasn't sure he'd interpreted them correctly. "Are you saying Charles cheated on you?"

"I don't know who cheats more. Perhaps men do, so your assumption is probably a fair one. But you didn't listen to what I said."

"You said you understood what I was going through with Angie."

"Yes, I didn't say I understood what Angie was going through with you."

Sean dropped Kim's hand and twisted fully to face her. "Wait. Are you saying you cheated on Charles?"

"You sound so surprised."

"That's because I am. I thought you two were ... were ... I don't know."

"A perfect couple?"

"Yes. No. Well, kind of."

She laughed again and reclaimed his hand. "Fifty years of marriage, my dear boy. A lot happens between a husband and wife over five decades. We haven't gotten this far without more than a few bumps in the road. My affair was the biggest bump, and it nearly ended my marriage."

The woman had blown his mind. Every Styles, age thirty or older, was married, except for Malcolm. As far as Sean knew, they were all happily married and adding to the Styles' clan. Kimberly and Charles were also happy. He'd known them over twenty years. The kind of love he'd witnessed between them couldn't be faked. But there Kim sat, having confessed to infidelity.

"The point in revealing my secret isn't to get into old details you don't want to hear, and I have no interest in sharing, but to, hopefully, soothe your restless heart and worried mind." Kim used both hands to gesture to the bouquets of roses in the living room. "You went the flowers and expensive jewelry route. I used the way to a man's heart is through his stomach tactic. Do you know what both of our strategies have in common?"

"They didn't work?"

"Smart dumb man. Yup, I knew it, but I kept the fridge stocked with Charles's favorite foods. You know it, but you'll keep this house looking like an overgrown flowerbed. But this is what you may not know, Sean. Once you cross a Styles, it's hell to regain their trust. Worse, if you lose their love, you won't get it back. When I told Charles what I'd done, he took Angie, who was three at the time, and moved out. In one day, I lost my daughter and my husband."

"Charles took Angie from you. Why would he do that?"

"For the same reason Angie threw you out of the house, to hurt you because you hurt her."

"Did he come back? I mean, obviously, Charles came back. But how long were you separated?"

"A lot longer than two weeks. But yes, Charles returned home with Angie but things between us were awful for a long time. He was angry, quiet, and distant."

"The way Angie is towards me."

"Right. Charles slept in the basement because he couldn't stand to share the same bed with me. Even after he moved back into our bedroom, there was still a wall I couldn't break down. It took a very long time for my husband to forgive me. It took Charles even longer to trust me again. Love and our child brought him back to me physically, but his presence in our home was all of himself he was willing to give me. His sisters and brothers each have a carload of children, but we only have two. You don't know pain until your husband tells you he doesn't want to have more children with a woman who could give her body to him and another man." Tears fell from pain-filled eyes. "Charles wasn't trying to be malicious. It was simply how he felt. Ten years later, Malcolm was born. Anytime in those ten years, either of us could've walked away. In the years that followed, we still could've."

"You're point is that Angie won't forgive me anytime soon, if at all."

"Yes, but you need to understand how deep the pain is for her. I was so caught up in my need to make amends and be forgiven, I failed to grasp, for too long, the magnitude of my betrayal of my husband. I became impatient with him. Months passed, and I thought he should've gotten over it already. I thought he should be able to see how repentant I was and forgive me. That he should acknowledge my newfound commitment to him and our marriage and cut me some slack. Everything I did was more about me and not enough about him. Charles could see it when

I could not. Angie is unlike her father in most ways. But, in this, she is Charles's daughter. If that woman's baby is also yours, she won't share you with another family."

He slumped against the cushions, the air knocked from his lungs. Kim had voiced every one of his fears, leaving him breathless.

"Angie loves you." He shook his head, but Kim continued, "Trust me. I know my daughter. She still loves you, although she'd rather cut her tongue out than admit it."

"What do you recommend I do?"

"For one, stop beating yourself up about it. What's done is done." She narrowed her gaze, voice suddenly hard. "It is done, isn't it?"

"Months ago. I was a fool once. I have no intention of being one again."

"Good, then my best advice would be to become best friends with patience and your hand, because you're in for the long haul, and Angie won't be having sex with you for a while."

Had his mother-in-law suggested he give himself handjobs? Good lord, she had.

"Oh, don't look at me like that. It's the truth. If Angie hasn't already, she'll buy a vibrator or dildo. I guess, nowadays, you can buy a vibrating dildo." Kim smirked, a pretty devil. "Technology is a wonderful thing. Maybe not for you. But if Angie's able to get herself off, every now and then, she won't be as grumpy, which will be good for you. If you really want to give her a happy birthday, Sean, you should run out and get her one of those sex toys. Angie won't thank you, but she'll use it."

Sean dropped his head in his hands again. Instead of the despair he'd felt fifteen minutes ago, he found himself repressing loud laughter. This was his wife's mother at almost seventy.

He could envision her fifty years ago as a young, beautiful bride of a military man. Charles Styles had done what any smart guy who'd caught the eye and favor of an attractive woman would do, he'd snatched her up and put a ring on her finger and a baby in her belly. They were both probably too young for marriage and the responsibilities of that kind of commitment. Not an excuse for Kim to cheat, but it didn't take much to imagine how it happened.

Loneliness, temptation, and an absent spouse were the breeding grounds for poor choices and reckless behaviors.

"When I was in the kitchen, with your greedy children, I sent a link to a song to your phone. Take a listen, then join us. Unless you want me to distract your family while you run out for that vibrating dildo." Kim winked at Sean, then got to her feet.

A bit stunned by the entire conversation, he watched Kim leave the living room. He knew his mother-in-law to be blunt, but she'd never spoken to him with such personal candor. He'd loved her, like a mother, for a long time. He loved her even more after he listened to the song she'd sent him.

Sean hit play again, closed his eyes and listened to Pastor Donnie McClurkin sing *We Fall Down*. The gospel crooner sang about falling down but getting back up. For months, Sean had felt like a sinner and defined himself by his sinful acts of adultery. Without a doubt, he was. But McClurkin reminded him that saints were also sinners who'd fallen but got back up. The spirit of the song wasn't about falling into sin but the strength to rise from it. To get up when it would be easier to stay down.

"Hey, Dad," SJ yelled from the kitchen, "you're missing all the cake and ice cream. If you don't get in here quick, Uncle Malcolm's going to eat your share."

Malcolm would too. The greedy junk food junkie.

The last line of the song ended, and Sean got back up.

CHAPTER TEN

Twenty-One Years Earlier

"What do you think?" Angie examined herself in the mirror, unable to decide between the red dress and the black one. Both looked good on her, although the red dress--tight with a low neckline and high split--was more daring than the black. She turned to Zahra, who reclined on Angie's bed. "Well, what do you think?"

Zahra rolled her eyes. "I don't know why you bothered buying two new dresses."

"It's Valentine's Day, and Sean is coming over for dinner, why wouldn't I buy a new dress?"

"It's also your birthday, and Sean is stupid in love with you and couldn't care less what you wear. It doesn't matter anyway because that dress will be on the floor five minutes after I've left the apartment."

"Shut up. No, it won't." Angie ran her hands down her dress, unsure why she was nervous about tonight's date with Sean. "Red or black? His favorite color is—"

"Whatever you're wearing is Sean's favorite color. Whatever you cook is his favorite food. By the way, I may or may not have cut a slice of your pot roast."

"You ate the dinner I made for my boyfriend?"

"Heck no. What kind of friend do you think I am?"

"A greedy one who hates to cook."

"True. But it smelled so good, and I didn't have lunch." Zahra patted her stomach and gave Angie her trademark puppy dog eyes. "I only cut a few slices for a sandwich."

"Oh, now it's a few slices. At first, it was a single slice."

"Don't blame me. You're the selfish one who cooked Valentine's Day dinner for her boyfriend while leaving her best friend to starve. What was I supposed to do? Give me some credit, at least. I didn't cut into that cute heart-shaped cake you made."

"You want credit for not raiding everything in the kitchen, none of which you purchased or cooked?"

"Pretty much, yeah."

Angie laughed, her hands going to her hips. "You're a food mooch. If I didn't have the greediest brother ever, there's no way we could live together."

"Malcolm's a sweetheart." Zahra, dressed in black, fitted jeans and a red, long-sleeved turtleneck sweater, stood. "He's also cute as sin. Why won't you let me date him again?" Zahra gestured for Angie to turn around so she could zip up her dress.

"He's sixteen, and you're twenty-four."

"I'm only eight years older than Malcolm, and he's so loveable."

"Mom would kill you for seducing her son."

"Well, a killer mother. Our love story is doomed before it's even begun. There you go, birthday girl. The red dress is the one."

"Why, because I'm wearing it and you're tired of the dress conversation?"

"Pretty much. Seriously, though, your mother is going to have to watch Malcolm, now that he's no longer her chubby little boy but a hormonal, weightlifting teen. Females are going to be all over him, and I don't just mean teenage girls."

Angie opened her jewelry case and took her time finding the right accessories. "Trust me, I know. He's too handsome for his own good. I tell him that all the time. But Malcolm's also smart. I can't see him letting some girl turn his head around."

Malcolm and Angie's ten-year age difference wasn't insignificant. By the time she was ready to go off to college, Malcolm was only eight. Still, they were close, and Angie would protect and defend her brother, especially from an older woman who thought to take advantage of his youth and kind nature.

"I know you've had a tiring work week," Angie said to Zahra. "It's fine, if you want to stay home."

"No, I'm good. My sisters and I have plans of our own. Me being gone for the entire night is my birthday present to you and my Valentine's Day gift for Sean. You both can be as loud as you want. Although, considering the sounds I've heard coming from your room, if you get much louder the neighbors will call the police."

She snorted. "We aren't that loud."

"Liar, liar, red bondage dress on fire."

Angie recalled the last time Sean visited. Halfway through their lovemaking, loud music blared from the room next door. They should've quieted it down, but the music gave them the excuse to be even louder.

"I'm a terrible roommate. Sorry."

"You are. Remember this conversation the next time I eat your food. Yes, those earrings but not the necklace. Try the other silver one."

Angie did, swapping out one necklace for another, not seeing a big difference but content to take Zahra's advice.

"Much better. You look beautiful, and I'm going to have to find a new roommate."

They'd had this conversation before.

"You won't."

"Keep telling yourself that. Your man has different plans."

"Sean is too busy to think about getting married."

"Like I said, keep telling yourself that. Before you know it, you'll be married, and I'll be minus a roommate. It's been three years. One of you needs to pop the damn question already and be done with it."

As liberal as Angie was, she couldn't see herself proposing to Sean. She could, however, envision herself accepting a proposal from him. But Sean was only two years out of law school and dreamed of forming his own law firm, not of becoming a husband of a doctoral student and part-time adjunct faculty member at Excelsior University. Yet, Angie couldn't deny how much the thought of being Sean's wife appealed.

The doorbell chimed, and Angie smiled. Her heart picked up its beat, and she wondered, not for the first time tonight, why she was so nervous. They'd had dinner at her apartment dozens of times. Angie had also cooked for Sean before, as he'd done for her at his apartment. But she'd never dressed up for him just to eat in, Valentine's Day notwithstanding.

Last year, they'd spent her birthday weekend in New York City. A fun but expensive gift from Sean--but he'd insisted, and Angie hadn't wanted to say no. This year, however, he'd requested dinner and a night in. He hadn't expected her to cook. In fact, he'd offered to order food from their favorite restaurant on North Johnson Park. It was Angie who'd decided to cook them dinner instead of accepting another expensive birth-day present from Sean. If he didn't save his pennies, he'd never be able to open his law practice.

"You finish up I'll grab my bag and let Sean in."

Zahra exited the bedroom, humming Whitney Houston's *I Believe in You and Me*. The song was about a woman with ultimate faith in her re-lationship with the man she loved, even when times were bad. The song ran through her mind, Houston belting out the romantic lyrics in that powerful spinto-soprano voice of hers.

Angie's heart pounded harder as the song continued to play in her mind. How could anyone believe so much in themselves, let alone another person? Sure, her parents, aunts, and uncles had enviable marriages. They were all wonderful role models, but Angie couldn't help viewing their happy marriages as exceptions, not the rule.

"She's still in the bedroom," Angie heard Zahra say. "Dressed to impress, I see. I thought you hated suits."

"I do, but my lady likes me in them. So, here I am. Are you going to have dinner with us?"

"Are you suddenly into threesomes?"

"No. That was me being polite. I was hoping you were about to scram."

"Ahh, you're such the sweet talker. You'll win every case with that silver tongue."

Angie closed her eyes and breathed deeply, ignoring Zahra and Sean's good-natured banter. She didn't know what was going on with her, but she didn't like it. The stone that had formed in her stomach wasn't painful, but it felt like an omen. Whether good or bad, who knew? The best anyone could hope for was to experience more good tidings than bad.

"I have my overnight bag," Zahra yelled. "I'm off, Angie. Happy birthday and try not to have the cops called on you for all the loud sex you'll have with Mr. Handsome."

As Angie emerged from her bedroom, she heard the door close. She saw Sean standing in front of the closed door, a hand over his face and laughing.

"She's a mess." Angie walked toward Sean, who'd stopped laughing at the sound of her voice. Now, he watched her approach, his sexy, crooked smile a beautiful sight. "Zahra was right. You do look handsome in that blue suit. Is it new? I don't think I've seen it before."

"It's as new as what you're wearing. Wow, you're smokin' hot." For flattering seconds, Sean's eyes traveled her body, his gaze appreciative. "You're so damn fine. I can't believe you're mine."

"Did you mean for that to rhyme?" she asked, the stone in her stomach growing heavier.

Sean claimed her hand and pulled her to him. "I'm no poet. Happy Valentine's Day." He bent his head and kissed her lips. "Happy birthday." He kissed her again--a sweet, slow, wet kiss she happily returned.

They wrapped their arms around each other. One of Sean's hands touched her hair, his fingers threading through the strands and holding her face close for his tongue and mouth. The flowers he hadn't yet given her fell from his other hand, freeing him to explore her waist, hip, and ass.

She groaned into his mouth, the stone in her stomach dissolving, slowly, with each slide of their tongues and bodies. Angie wanted him, right there in front of the door Zahra had gone through less than five minutes before.

Angie stepped away from Sean.

"W-what's wrong? Why did you stop?" Sean sounded as dazed and as aroused as she felt.

"Zahra said we'd have sex within five minutes of her leaving us alone."

"I always said you had smart friends. Zahra's my favorite."

"Because she knows how horny you are and doesn't complain, too much, when you knock my bed into the adjoining wall?"

"Exactly. But you're as horny as I am, so don't try to put all that bed banging on me." He glanced over her head and toward her bedroom. "Speaking of bed banging."

"We should eat first. I made dinner."

"I can eat your dinner later. But I want to eat you now." Sean reached for Angie, but she sprang away from him. "Oh, you're playing hard-to-get. Fine, it's your birthday, and I don't mind hunting my food."

Angie kicked off her dress shoes and darted away from Sean and around the couch. There wasn't much space in the living/dining room. This would be a short evasion. Sean was tall and fast. Angie's movements were encumbered by a tight dress and, let's be honest, she wanted to be caught.

He dropped his suit jacket on the floor beside the roses. If Angie weren't so keen on this form of foreplay, she'd pick up the jacket and hang it in the front closet. Just because Sean disliked the confines of a well-made suit, that was no reason to treat his new clothes like stinky socks.

They ran around the room, Angie careful to keep a piece of furniture between them.

"I'm going to catch you."

Angie planted her hands on the dining room table, where they should be sitting and enjoying a home-cooked meal. "This may be Buffalo, but you're not a lion, and I'm not your prey."

"I don't hunt buffalo." Sean ran around the table and toward her, forcing Angie to seek refuge in front of the couch with him behind it. "I prefer cute little pussy cats to big, ugly buffalos."

Angie snorted a laugh. "That was your less than subtle way of saying you like pussy."

"Yeah, it was. But only yours. Only ever yours." He leaped over the couch, catching Angie off-guard and bringing her down onto the soft cushions. "Got you, my wily Valentine's Day cat."

Sean did have Angie and not because he pinned her to the couch. She wiggled under him. He was heavy but in a way that brought an ache of need. "What's that in your pocket?" She shifted, curious.

Sean moaned and dropped his forehead to her neck. "Stop doing that. You know what it is."

"It's hard." She moved again.

"It's supposed to be hard. And your wiggling is making it harder."

She gave him a quick peck to his lips. "Not that, you sex fiend. It's hard and small. It feels like a—"

Sean hopped off Angie and the couch. "I knew I shouldn't have kissed you. You and your tasty lips and sexy body, you make a man forget what he's supposed to do."

Angie sat up, aroused and confused. "What are you talking about?"

"I had everything planned." Sean scooped his suit jacket off the floor, shaking it out before putting it on and then picking up the dropped red roses.

"I still have no idea what you're—"

"Love and beauty." Sean handed first one rose to Angie and then the second, his hand trembling. "Love and beauty," he repeated. Smiling, Sean lowered himself to Angie's height--not on one knee, but two.

The stone in her stomach returned, as did the pounding of her heart.

"When I think of you, those two words come to mind. When we first met, your sweet smile and sexy body drew me in and made me want to learn more. What I learned about Angela Rosa Styles, an around-the-way girl with Ivy League brains, was more than I could've imagined. You accept me, for the man I am and for the man I aspire to become. You push and praise, knowing when I need one but not the other. You listen with your heart, as much as you do with your ears and your mind."

Angie questioned whether she breathed or even blinked. She couldn't tear her eyes away from Sean. His light-brown orbs held her captive, twin beacons of vulnerability and hope.

"I ran this over in my head dozens of times. I memorized the lyrics to your favorite song and poem. I bought a new suit, for the occasion, and here I am on the floor. But I don't care. I also don't care I can't remember a damn thing I planned to say to you. I wanted romantic and smooth, but I ruined that when I chased you around the apartment and called you a pussycat."

Angie laughed, her eyes filling with tears. Her charming and confident Sean was nervous. That knowledge made him even more endearing and this moment more touching because it was unrehearsed and real.

Sean removed the roses from her grip and placed them beside her on the couch. His large hands raised one of hers to his cheek and the other to his heart. "You're a beauty. More importantly, you're my love. Yours is the face I want to see every morning and each night. The voice I want to hear calling my name and laughing at my jokes. The arms I want to be wrapped around me when you're happy but also when you're sad. The lips I want kissing mine, even when we're too old to do anything beyond kissing and holding each other close." Lowering her hand from his cheek to his lips, he kissed Angie's palm. "Love and beauty. We can have both, if you'll do me the honor of becoming my wife."

The stone in her stomach exploded.

Sean released her hands and dug into his pocket, pulling out the object she'd felt earlier. He held a wooden, monogramed ring box with the centerpiece 'A' encircled in rose petals.

"I made the ring box myself. I hope you like it."

She did. Very much. "It's pretty."

"Pretty?"

"Yes. Unique. Special." She touched his cheek again. This time, without his guiding hand. "Unique and special, like you. And the *yes* was for your proposal."

"Yes?"

Angie nodded vigorously. "Yes, I'll be your wife."

"And the mother of my children?"

"Yes"

He tackled Angie again, smothering her under his fierce embrace. "You've made me so happy."

"You've made me happy. May I see my engagement ring, please?"

"Oh, oh, hell, I forgot. You weren't supposed to accept before I showed you the ring."

"I could always take back my *yes*. It would make for the shortest engagement in history."

"Unless you want to see my heart explode from my chest, you better not." Sean slipped out of his suit jacket and sat close beside Angie, his roses on the other side of her. He opened the wooden box. It was lined with red velvet and on the soft material was her engagement ring.

"Will you put it on?"

"Yeah, of course."

Angie tried not to cry at Sean's shaking hands. To witness such a large man, so full of emotion and tenderness, touched her deeply.

He slid the ring onto the fourth finger of her left hand. It was a stunning white gold ring with alternating amethyst, her birthstone, and round, brilliant-cut diamonds set in a channel that framed the diamond in the center.

Despite her best efforts, the tears came. "It's perfect. I love it." Angie kissed Sean, hard and with everything she felt for him. "And I love you."

"I'll take care of you and our kids."

"I know you will."

"I'll make you happy," he earnestly promised her. "So very happy."

"We'll make each other happy. I believe in us," she said, thinking back to Whitney Houston's song.

His hand found her thigh through the slit of her dress. "A Valentine's Day wedding. We can have it next year."

She groaned, and not from the tantalizing hand massaging her thigh. "Not a Valentine-themed wedding. There wasn't one birthday I had that my parents didn't also link to Valentine's Day."

"But it's romantic and perfect. How could you have a problem with that?"

"You've already added another layer to this day with your proposal. I don't want to lump our wedding anniversary on top of it." She didn't stop the hand reaching around to unzip her dress. From his angle, Sean wouldn't make much progress, so she shifted to help him. "I have a better idea."

For all that Sean was a man, he undid her zipper and bra clasp with skillful fingers. Plump, wet lips settled at her neck and kissed, her hair held to the side and out of Sean's way.

"What's your better idea?"

"Your birthday."

"There's nothing special about March twenty-ninth."

"It's the day you were born, which makes it plenty special to me. You added an engagement to my birth date. It's only fair I add a wedding to yours."

Hands pushed dress and bra straps from shoulders and down arms. Sean's warm mouth kissed its way from her nape, across a shoulder and down her back, leaving a trail of heated passion.

"I had my heart set on a Valentine's Day wedding, but I can be persuaded to change my mind." The cups of her bra fell away. "The persuasion can begin here."

Fingers caressed nipples, and Angie leaned against Sean, her back to his chest and her head to his shoulder. She closed her eyes. From his initiation, she wouldn't have to do any persuading. But ...

Angie craned her head around and captured Sean's mouth. Marriage was about shared responsibility. She would begin practicing her part tonight.

"March twenty-ninth." Twisting, Angie pushed Sean onto the couch cushions and made him her willing mattress. A nip to the underside of his jaw, mouth shy of his shirt collar. "March twenty-ninth of next year, I'll take you as my husband."

"And I'll take you as my wife. It'll be the best birthday present ever. For the rest of our lives, we'll have two months to celebrate our love and commitment to each other." Sean flipped them over. "Now, my little pussycat, about my meal."

Angie's dress went up, and Sean's head went down.

CHAPTER ELEVEN

"Hey, SJ," Sean yelled from inside his bedroom. He hated to think of the guest room that way, but that's what it now was, and everyone in the house knew it.

SJ kept walking toward his bedroom. Sean jumped from the bed and to the open doorway. "I called you, son."

SJ stopped, but he didn't turn around. Okay, this was the third time since Angie's birthday that SJ had acted this way toward him. Sean didn't tolerate disrespect, in any manner, from his children, and his son giving him his back, instead of turning to face him, was damn sure disrespectful.

"When I call you, I expect you to come see what I want. Turn around. I'm not going to have a conversation with your back."

Sean disliked SJ sighing his obedience almost as much as SJ strolling past his room as if he hadn't heard his father call his name. Sean had wanted to ask his son if he would like to watch the baseball game with him. Now he had a different question.

"What's going on with you?"

"Nothing."

Sean also didn't do petulant teen, despite having been one. "Try again. What's up with you?"

Arms crossed over his chest, SJ's stubborn chin sticking out in defiance, he accused, "You're still in the guest room."

Sean and Angie hadn't talked about how to explain Sean's new sleeping arrangement to the children. They should have. The inevitable, like SJ's statement, was bound to happen.

"I know where I'm sleeping."

"But why in the guest room? I don't get it. You're not sick, and neither is Mom. So why are you in the guest room?"

It had taken his son two months to pose his question. All the children had noticed, but none had mentioned the change until tonight. As the oldest, it made sense SJ would be the one to mention what Sean and Angie pretended wasn't obvious.

"Your Mom and I needed a little space, so I moved out for a while."

A horrible, incomplete answer, but Sean couldn't tell his son the truth.

"It's been weeks. Did you have a fight?"

"Something like that. But we are fine. Everything is fine."

"If everything is fine, when are you moving back into your bedroom?"

Sean had no idea. He'd like to say *soon* or even *tonight*, but that would be too big of a lie. As it was, telling SJ things between Angie and him were "fine" was tantamount to a high crime.

Sean closed the distance between SJ and himself. Reaching out, he lowered SJ's arms. "Me staying in the guest room is temporary. I don't want you or your sisters worrying about it. You know I love you, right?"

"Yeah, I know but—"

"Then that's all that matters. Your mother and I love you and the girls. We're in our house together, and we're a family. Not a perfect family, but a family. Do you want to watch the ballgame with your old man?"

"No, I don't want to intrude on the space you must need. Besides, I have stuff to do in my room. May I be excused?"

Whoever said moody girls were worse than pubescent boys hadn't met his son. SJ had never turned down an opportunity to watch a baseball or football game with Sean. It was Saturday, so SJ didn't have homework he needed to finish tonight. He'd gone from ignoring Sean, to asking permission to end their conversation, then retreating to his room to get away from him.

Sean wanted to say more, but nothing came to mind. He had no way of reassuring his son because he had no reassurance for himself. Since returning home, his relationship with Angie was as broken as it had been since the night she threw him out. Their anniversary was a few days away, and she hadn't mentioned it, any more than she'd spoken of his birthday.

Kim had advised him to become friends with patience and his hand. The hand part of the equation was easy and met with success. But befriending patience was a challenge. In his mind, it was tantamount to doing nothing. Sean despised having no control. Practicing patience came perilously close to accepting his lack of control over this situation.

"Maybe we could do something together tomorrow."

"Yeah, maybe." SJ waited for a beat, then he turned and walked away.

Sean let his son go, relieved he hadn't pushed for more answers but also disheartened. He hadn't wanted his affair to touch his children, yet it had. Sean and Angie could conceal the truth of his affair from them but not the fracture in their marriage.

He returned to his bedroom and closed the door. Sean needed to do something to move things along, and he could think of only one action to take.

Picking up his cell phone, he called the only other person responsible for his sorry predicament. She answered on the third ring.

"Hi, Sean. Did you get the pics I sent?"

He'd given up on asking Trinity to stop sending him pictures of her growing belly and calling him for frivolous matters. No matter how many times he told her, she did whatever the hell she wanted, regardless of his feelings or opinions.

"I got them, but that's not why I'm calling." Hooking a foot around the leg of a chair and pulling it from under the desk, he sat.

"Great, you changed your mind about going to my next doctor's appointment. It's on—"

"I'm not going to your doctor's appointment. We've had this conversation before."

"The baby could be yours, you know."

"Yes, I know. That's why I'm calling. I want you to have the prenatal paternity test."

"As you've said, we've had this conversation before. My answer hasn't changed."

Damn Trinity. Sean paused before he said something he would regret. The last thing he wanted to do was antagonize her. If he wasn't invested in maintaining his marriage and reconciling with his wife, he would blast the legal assistant to hell. But Sean was invested, which gave Trinity a power over him he abhorred. Anytime she wanted, she could call or write his wife, spilling every ugly detail of their affair, thereby destroying Sean's last shred of hope for keeping his wife and family.

Sean hadn't spent his time with Trinity bashing Angie and their marriage. He hadn't lain in her arms after sex and whined about his home life and how being with her was so much better than being with his wife. She had no anti-Angie stories to share. Although, if inclined, she could make them up and dispense the lies like poisoned Halloween candy.

She didn't have his balls in a vice but damn near. Without medical proof, Trinity couldn't compel Sean to treat her as the mother of his child and her unborn baby as his. But she could set his entire life ablaze, not with lies but with the truth.

Right now, only his wife, a few members of her family, and Zahra knew of his affair. The Styles and Angie's best friend were a tight-lipped group, and none of them would do anything to harm Angie, so he didn't worry about his affair leaking from them. His colleagues were unaware of his relationship with their former legal assistant, and he hoped to keep them ignorant. His clients were also in the dark. If Trinity had told anyone, she'd kept that to herself.

There were no pictures or videos. Sean had neither sent Trinity romantic texts nor had he purchased her gifts. He never stayed at a hotel with her, treated her to an expensive restaurant, or made up work trips to be with her. Unless Trinity recorded their conversations and sex acts, she had no proof of their affair. No proof, except for the child she carried, if it proved to be his.

In his business, however, irrefutable proof wasn't necessary to ruin a man's reputation, career, and marriage. He saw the pain caused by his recklessness in Angie's eyes, and in the tight lips that held back her words of condemnation. She grasped all he'd risked for sex with another woman. Angie kept it inside, a powder keg with a slow-burning fuse. Angie hadn't exploded yet, but she would if Trinity contacted her and threw her affair with him in her face. Such an ill-advised act wouldn't bode well for Trinity or Sean. His wife reminded him of an Australian cassowary bird, rare in its colorful beauty but, when motivated, aggressive and strong. With Angie's connections from being president of a tier one university, she could hurt Trinity in ways more painful than fists capable of doing bloody harm.

"I can schedule for us to have the test done. If we do, we'll know. Me or the other guy. If it's me, I'll step up."

"But you don't want to step up, do you?"

"If the baby is mine, I'll step up. Listen, Trinity, I won't spend the next five months going with you to your doctor's appointments." He wouldn't subject Angie to that level of humiliation. Sean had no intention of doing anything to remind Angie of his infidelity and all the reasons she should divorce him. "If you want me to act the role of dad, then give me proof I'm the baby's father."

When she didn't immediately reply, Sean hoped his words had finally penetrated her stubborn skull. But no, her next statement proved Sean wrong and Trinity delusional and so very young.

"You knew the risks when you fucked me. I don't deserve to be treated like a thot and then discarded once you've had your fun."

"I never treated you like a whore, and you know it. Was I wrong for crossing the line with you? Hell yes. Did I tell you I would abandon my wife and children to be with you? Hell no. Did I say I wouldn't take care of the baby if it's mine? Again, hell no. I'm sorry about everything. I should've kept our relationship professional. I didn't, so I must deal with the consequences."

"The baby being one of the consequences?"

"If your baby is mine, then yes. It'll be the most significant consequence of our time together. But understand, I won't treat your child as mine without knowing for sure that it is. I love all my children and will love this one if the test proves I'm the father."

Even for his wife and marriage, he wouldn't abandon a baby he'd help create. Nor would Angie ask him to make that kind of no-win decision. Kim was right. Angie wouldn't share him with Trinity and a baby born of his affair, even if he were no longer in a sexual relationship with the younger woman. The sad part was that he wouldn't blame Angie for divorcing him. He'd created a terrible situation for them all, including the woman on the other end of the phone.

"Have the test. You're needlessly dragging this out. You want the father of your child by your side while you go through your pregnancy. I get it. I really do. If you had the test, you'd know who'd fathered your child."

"Hey, Mom," he heard SJ say in the hallway. "May I plug my game system to the big television in the living room, or are you still reading down there?"

"What's wrong with the television in the basement?"

"Nothing, but the TV in the living room is ginormous, and the fight scenes look epic on the huge screen."

"I only came up here to retrieve my laptop, but I plan on returning to the living room."

"Is that a no?"

"Yes, it's a no. I told you before, I don't like you and Kayla plugging your game systems into the living room television. It messes up the settings and wires."

The games didn't mess up the settings. Angie just didn't know how to get the television back to the Cable setting, if one of the children forgot to do it after they played their games on the television. SJ, kinder to his mother than to Sean, didn't mention the real issue.

"In your room or the basement. Those are your options."

No sighing or backtalk from SJ, just a, "Yes, ma'am. I guess I'll be in the basement if anyone needs me."

Angie laughed. "If anyone needs you? Who are you expecting? Do you have a harem of high school girls coming by you haven't told me about?"

"Maybe I do."

"Really?" Angie joked. "A harem of teenage girls? Hmm. Should I order pizza or hire a referee? Will there be blood when they fight over you, or will you pick one and send the others home crying and heartbroken?"

"That's the last time I ask you to watch an action harem anime with me."

Angie laughed again, and Sean could envision a pouting SJ. The teen took anime and manga far too seriously. But, like the rest of the family, SJ had a good sense of humor.

"Is my big boy salty? Don't act like that. Come here and give Mommy a hug."

Sean was lost in the conversation on the other side of the closed door, Trinity and the baby temporarily forgotten. He laughed to himself. SJ hadn't called Angie "Mommy" since he turned thirteen and deemed the word "for babies, not teens."

"I'm too big for hugs." SJ didn't sound as opposed to the idea as he would probably like his mother to believe. "And you're teasing me."

"Of course I'm teasing you. It's one of my favorite pastimes. But I would like a hug from my only son. You'll never be too big or too old for that."

Sean couldn't hear what happened next. He didn't need to. Despite his weak protestation, SJ, like his sisters, loved Angie's open affection. She withheld none of her love from them. Until recently, Sean hadn't realized all the small ways his wife expressed her love for him. The months building up to his affair and during his affair, he'd obsessed over Angie's long work hours and how little time they spent together as a couple. Sean wasn't wrong on either issue, but he'd drawn an unfair conclusion based on the two points.

"You don't have anything to say? Have you heard a word I said?"

Sean looked at the phone in his hand then back to the bedroom door. He missed the loving, playful Angie.

"I didn't hear you. What did you say?"

"It doesn't matter. I won't have the test done before the baby is born. That's all you need to know."

Sean had assumed as much before he'd called, but he'd hoped, for once, Trinity would be reasonable. She was deliberately dragging this out. What she hoped to achieve from the delay, Sean couldn't figure. Trinity hadn't demanded money for her silence or tried to guilt or seduce him back to her bed. Sean loved Angie, and he'd told Trinity the same. Her delay tactic wouldn't alter how he felt about his wife and the commitment he'd made when she'd accepted his engagement ring.

"Then don't text or call me again until your child is born and you're ready to have the paternity test done."

Sean ended the call before Trinity could say anything else. If she decided to confront Angie, there was nothing he could do to stop her. He may suffer the consequences, but so would she. What he could do, however, was put an end to her manipulation and concentrate on his wife. Angie wouldn't make a move toward Sean, so he had to do the chasing.

A smile formed, and Sean recalled chasing Angie around her little apartment the night he'd proposed. They used to have so much fun back then.

He unplugged his computer, wrapped the power cord and placed it on top of his laptop. He also grabbed his wireless mouse and the manila folder from his desk with documents from the Mercado sexual harassment case.

When Sean exited his bedroom, he wasn't surprised to see a vacant hallway. The girls' bedroom doors were open, but no sounds could be heard coming from them. He went downstairs and joined Angie in the living room. He wasn't surprised by that sight either.

Angie, laptop on thighs and head low, clicked away, oblivious to his presence.

"Are the girls in the basement with SJ?"

Sean stepped further into the living room. He didn't hear them on the main level. Deductive reasoning wasn't difficult, but he posed the question to his wife anyway.

For the last eight weeks, Angie only treated him as her husband when the children were around. Otherwise, she ignored his presence in their home. His wife wasn't hostile. She didn't lob verbal grenades his way, unless provoked. Some days, he wished she would. Arguing with Angie would be an improvement. At least when she quarreled with him he knew she cared about something other than their kids and her job. When Angie shut down, the Arctic was warmer than being in her presence.

Tonight, Sean was prepared to battle Mrs. Frost.

"I said—"

"I heard your question." Angie's head didn't lift from her laptop nor did her fingers stop typing. "They were in the kitchen eating a snack. But you know how they are. When they saw SJ with his video games, they followed him into the basement."

Sean deposited his laptop, folder, and power cord on the opposite end of the couch and turned on the lamp beside it.

Angie's head popped up. "What are you doing?"

"Work, like you."

"I see that. But why are you doing it down here?"

"Because the guest room isn't a prison cell."

"What in the hell is that supposed to mean?"

"It means I have full run of my house. Just because you're in a room doesn't make it off limits to me."

"I never said that."

"But you act like it." Instead of claiming the cushion where he'd put his belongings, Sean sat in the spot next to his glowering wife. If Angie wanted space from him, then let her be the one to find it by hiding in her bedroom. "Since our son doesn't want to watch the ballgame with me, I thought I'd come down here and work. Do you mind?"

"There's an entire room, why are you sitting next to me?"

"Because you smell good and look pretty." He batted his eyelashes at her and smiled the way she liked. "Why else?"

"I'm not going to fight with you."

If he pushed enough, she would. Was that what he wanted? Sean hadn't thought so when he'd decided to invade her space. He'd intended to share the living room with her, a reminder of how they used to keep each other company while engaged in independent work. Yet, when he'd entered the room and saw her, beautiful and remote, the attention-seeker inside him wanted to disrupt her peace and push her buttons.

Stupid and pointless.

"Fine, then we can talk."

"I'm busy."

"You're always busy. Tell me what you're working on. What's going on at EU these days?"

"I'm not doing this with you, Sean. I'm not going to have a conversation and act like we're good."

"Trust me, I know we aren't good. But I thought we could have a simple convo. Is that too much to ask?"

"I don't have anything to say to you."

"That's a lie. Your head is full of shit you want to say to me. You just don't want to lose your cool. What's the worst that could happen if you did? Are you afraid you'd actually feel something for your husband?"

Her laptop slammed closed. "One of these days, I'll slip into your bedroom while you're asleep. If you're lucky, you'll awaken before the pillow lowers to your face and suffocates you. If you're not, tell Grandma I said hello when you see her on the other side."

How could such a sweet-looking woman deliver such a cold-hearted threat? Nothing in her tone of voice or hard eyes suggested the threat was hollow.

"Would you actually kill me?"

Sean hadn't meant it as a serious question. He didn't fear for his physical safety around Angie. But the slow breaths she took and the brown eyes that turned onyx had Sean questioning the sanity of prodding an angry lioness.

"You may want to start locking your bedroom door at night."

Cold, hard steel. Yes, Trinity would do well to stay as far away from Angie as possible.

"I love you, Angela Styles-Franklin. You're my wife, and I'm not giving up on us."

Nothing in her countenance softened, and Sean chanted a single word in his mind: *Patience, patience, patience.*

Angie reopened her laptop and turned away from him. When the doorbell rang, she didn't acknowledge that either.

Sean answered the door and let Malcolm in. Angie greeted him with a warm smile, as if she hadn't been threatening murder just minutes before.

After ten minutes of listening to Malcolm go on about a female colleague who'd sparked his interest but who didn't return his attraction, Angie replied to her brother's request with a single word.

"No."

Malcolm should've known better than to ask Angie to leverage her position to get him into a leadership retreat with the female colleague who'd turned down his date invitations. A letter of recommendation, while easy for Angie to write, would compromise her integrity.

"Come on. Why not?"

"Did you really just whine those four words at me?"

"Yeah, he did. He's either devolved into a loser of epic proportions or the woman he wants is smokin' hot."

Malcolm sat in the chair across from Sean and Angie. For her brother, she'd put aside her laptop and schoolwork and had given him her full attention. The loving Angie appeared for everyone except Sean. He tried not to let it hurt him, but it did.

"Okay, two things," Malcolm raised his middle finger to Sean, "one, no one says 'smokin' hot' anymore, and the only loser in the family is you. Two," Malcolm's gaze moved meaningfully from Sean to Angie, his index finger lifting, "you owe me a favor."

Sean wondered if the favor Angie owed Malcolm had to do with him. Malcolm hadn't gotten in Sean's face since that night in his hotel room. He hadn't told Angie who'd caused his injuries, but she'd known. It wasn't a stretch to conclude the older sister had had a stern word with the younger brother. It was a stretch to think she'd done it because she cared about his physical well-being. More likely, she had wanted to prevent another incident that could alert the children to problems in the family.

"For the record, Dr. Styles, that's three things." Taking advantage of the opportunity Malcolm's presence afforded him, Sean lifted Angie's hand from where she'd laid it on the cushion between them and brought it to his lips. She hadn't permitted a single touch in weeks, and he shouldn't overstep now. Sean kissed her palm, his smile broad and all for his wife.

Instead of smacking him in front of their guest, Angie reclaimed her hand.

"A degree in African American History doesn't mean I'm poor at math."

Angie had never needed to do anything to capture Sean's attention. He was vulnerable to her allure and needed to taste her again.

"I know, man. I didn't mean anything by it. I was just ... well, you know, playing with you. Like old times."

"Listen, I came here to talk to my sister."

Growing up with four sisters, Sean had wished for a brother. He never got one until he married Angie. He loved Malcolm and missed their friendship. He no longer visited as much, and Sean understood why.

"Right, right. We don't talk anymore. I get it." He looked at his wife. "I know I messed up--with Angie, with the kids, and with you. I'm trying to fix things."

He might as well give Angie one more reason to see him dead. Sean leaned across the divide that separated them, metaphorically and physically, and kissed her on the cheek, stealing another taste.

Malcolm could be mad at Sean all he wanted. That was the man's choice, just as Angie had made her choice when she'd let him move back into their home. Best friend or not, Sean wouldn't allow anyone's attitude about his affair to get in the way of his efforts to mend the rift between Angie and himself.

Sean nodded to Malcolm when he got to his feet. He would understand what in the hell it meant. He left the siblings alone. It wasn't as if Malcolm had come there to speak with him about his new love interest. The woman must be something, though, because he'd never known Malcolm to obsess over, let alone chase, a female.

He turned on the television in the kitchen and found the baseball game. The Mets were playing the Phillies. The girls had left sticky jelly on the island. If Angie saw the mess, she'd call them from the basement and make them clean it up. Sean didn't feel like being bothered, so he wet a sponge and cleaned the entire island. Grabbing salsa and shredded cheese from the fridge, whole grain chips from the pantry, and a plate from the cupboard, Sean made his own snack.

The basement door was open, and he could hear the kids. SJ may have skills on the football field but Kayla was a better virtual game player. Eighty percent of the time, she kicked her brother's butt in the versus fighter games. SJ fared better against his sister with the sports games, but only because he knew the rules and the plays to call. Sean had no doubt, if Kayla cared enough about those games to learn the rules, she'd beat her brother in those too.

Kayla and Zuri cheered, and SJ was suspiciously quiet.

Poor boy. Sean knew the feeling of losing to a sister in an area you assumed you should excel in but didn't.

Halfway through his second plate of nachos, the house phone rang. Reading the name on the caller ID screen, Sean swallowed his food and answered.

"Hey, Mom. How are you doing?"

Turning off the television, he sat on a barstool. He loved his mother, but they didn't talk often or have the kind of relationship they should.

"I'm fine."

"You don't sound it. More like exhausted. What's wrong?"

"It's, uh, well, it's your father. He had a stroke."

"A stroke? When? Are you at the hospital?"

"Not anymore. Calm down, Sean. Your father is home. The stroke was mild, but I thought you should know."

Which meant Edward hadn't wanted Sean and his sisters to know, and Brenda had called them without his knowledge.

"How long was he in the hospital?"

"A few days."

A few days and she was only now contacting him. Typical.

"I'll be there tomorrow."

"No, no. That's not why I called. You're a busy man. You have a family. You can't just up and leave. I told you, the stroke was mild. Edward will be fine."

"I'm worried about you. You don't sound good. I'll work something out at work and with Angie. But I'm coming home to check on the two of you."

"Are you sure? I don't want to inconvenience you."

"It's not an inconvenience." The fact that his mother thought he'd view a visit to his sick father as a bother told the tale of their screwed-up family. "I'll make arrangements."

"Thank you, sweetheart. I'll prepare a room for you. Umm, I know the children aren't on a break, but will you bring them with you? I haven't seen them or Angie in a long time."

"I know, Mom. But the children are in school, and I don't want to pull them out and drag them to Jersey with me."

"I guess that also means Angie won't be coming with you either. She'll have to stay at home with the kids. I sure would like to see them, though. Another time, I guess."

First Trinity, then Angie, and now Brenda. This night was full of women evoking one emotion after another from him.

"Yeah, another time, Mom. Angie's busy."

"You both are. But you'll come, right?"

"I'll be there."

"That's great. Maybe you'll stay long enough for us to celebrate your birthday."

Why not? Angie didn't give a damn. She probably wouldn't even notice he was gone.

CHAPTER TWELVE

"Here, hold this for me."

Angie took the cell phone Malcolm all but shoved into her hand and watched her brother examine every overpriced flower arrangement in her living room. "What are you doing?"

"Looking for the perfect one."

"The perfect what?"

Malcolm didn't answer, and Angie didn't know whether she should worry about her brother or laugh at his strange behavior. Ever since he'd come to her home with a desperate plan unbecoming of a Styles, he hadn't been himself. Dr. Sky Ellis, whoever the woman was, had turned Malcolm's world upside down. If this was one of those versus video games SJ and Kayla liked to play, Malcolm would have a big L on his forehead because, from the anxious way he moved from one floral arrangement to the next, he'd lost this round.

"Why do you have Dr. Ellis's cell number again?" Angie yelled from her comfortable spot on the couch and into the hallway where Malcolm had moved. He'd texted Dr. Ellis in the middle of their conversation after she had turned down his request to write him a letter of recommendation for a college leadership retreat. As chair of Eastern Bluebird College's

African American Studies Department, Malcolm would make a great candidate for the professional development and networking opportunity. Apparently, Dr. Ellis intended to attend. Malcolm feared, if he didn't use the retreat to spend uninterrupted time with Dr. Ellis away from EBC, so they could get to know each other better, she wouldn't consider dating him.

Malcolm appeared in the threshold of the living room, a red rose in his right hand. "Found what I was looking for."

Angie pointed to two vases with red roses, one on the fireplace mantle, the other on a table in front of a window. "They're everywhere. Sean won't stop buying them."

"Guilt gifts. It's what stupid men do when they want to suck up to the woman they hurt, and their imagination is smaller than their ego."

Okay, well, that was more than her simple sentence warranted. The siblings often agreed, although they were rarely upset about the same issue to the same degree. This wasn't one of those times, however. But Angie wouldn't gang up with her brother against her husband. No matter what, they were all family. Sean wasn't the enemy, and they wouldn't treat him as one, despite Malcolm having flipped him the bird earlier and Angie having said nothing. In the end, no matter her stance on Sean, his affair, and their marriage, her husband and brother were friends who'd have to work out the issues between them. Angie would like to think their friendship didn't hinge on her decision about her marriage but knew it did. If she couldn't forgive Sean, Malcolm wouldn't either. The thought pained her and added a level of responsibility she didn't appreciate.

"Anyway," Malcolm walked into the living room and rejoined her on the couch, "I had a lot to choose from, and this flower is the best of the pricey bunch." He held the long-stemmed rose out to her. "What do you think?"

"I think it looks like all the others."

He scoffed. Malcolm's version of her snort. "This one is fully open but not so much it looks like the petals will fall off any second. It's vibrant and virile."

"Virile?"

"Yeah, and silky soft."

"Open, virile, and silky soft?" Angie's snort had Malcolm frowning. "God, M and M, you haven't gone on one date with Dr. Ellis, and you're already talking about sex."

"I wasn't... " Malcolm's handsome smile preceded his deep laugh. "Okay, I was. I can't help it, she's adorable."

"Adorable?"

"Not adorable like Zuri. But the kind of adorable a woman is when she doesn't realize how amazing she comes across to others."

"Adorable and amazing?" Angie grabbed the tip of Malcolm's nose and pulled. "Yup, it's wide open."

Laughing, he swatted at her hand, and she let his nose go. "Get out of here with that. I need you to take a few pics of me." Malcolm placed the stem of the rose between his lips, undid the top two buttons of his shirt, and struck a pose that had Angie gagging and jumping to her feet.

"Hell no. I'm not taking nasty sex pics for you."

Malcolm yanked the rose from his mouth. "Nasty sex pics? First, yuck, you're my sister. Second, I'm fully clothed."

"I don't care what you say, you're going for sex and sexy, and I won't help you." Angie tossed Malcolm his cell phone. "Take your own damn pictures. I'm out of here."

"Come on. Selfies won't look as good."

"You'll just have to make do because I'm not getting involved. You can stay as long as you like." Angie snatched her laptop and papers from the sofa and ignored Malcolm's pleas as she made her way out of the living room and toward the kitchen.

Too late, she remembered Sean had retreated to the kitchen after Malcolm had made it clear he'd come to visit her and not him. She watched him walk from the island to the counter, where he placed the wireless in the cradle. When Sean turned, their eyes met, his were filled with worry.

Angie strolled into the kitchen and unburdened her hands, placing the laptop and papers on the island across from a half-eaten plate of nachos.

"What's wrong?" For a second, she didn't think her husband had heard her. Sean stared at her, or rather, through her, so she moved around the island and closer to him. "What's—"

"Dad had a stroke."

Angie glanced from Sean to the phone, then back to him. He was upset, but he wasn't in mourning, which answered her most pressing question.

"What can we do to help?" He blinked but didn't respond. Angie reached out and set her hand on Sean's arm. "I assume you were on the phone with Brenda." She doubted Edward had been the one to call Sean. Edward and Charles were of the generation of African American men who kept quiet about their poor health, even if it killed them, which it too often did.

He nodded, slowly, but he seemed more focused than he'd been seconds ago. "Yeah, Mom called. Dad had a stroke, a week or so ago. He's out of the hospital."

"Okay, okay. That's good. What can we do for your parents?"

"I'm going home to check on them." For the first time since entering the kitchen, she felt as if Sean really saw her. "I'm sorry. I know I'm supposed to be here working on us, but I need to go to Jersey for a few days."

Angie's hand dropped from his arm. Were they in such a bad place, and did he think so little of her and the value she placed on his family? Angie may not have been as close to his parents and sisters as Sean was to the Styles, but she loved them and cared about their well-being.

"I'll take a couple of days off and go with you."

His shocked stare hurt more than it should've. "I've seen your work calendar. It's full, and not with minor obligations you can pawn off on other administrators."

She was about to ask him how he'd seen her work calendar but decided it didn't matter. Sean was right. She'd had a too-brief spring break. Like always, she planned to take off a few days during the kids' spring recess. But that wasn't until halfway through April.

"Tomorrow is Sunday. There's no need to pack up the kids and drag them to Jersey, just for you to turn around and drive them home for school on Monday." Worried eyes softened. Gratitude. His expectation bar for Angie couldn't get much lower. "Thank you. Your offer means a lot. Even if the last-minute trip wasn't inconvenient for your work and the kids' school schedule, I still wouldn't accept."

"Why not? If it was my dad who had a stroke, you'd be right by his side. I wouldn't even have to ask."

"You know I'd be there. That's a given. But it's not the same. If you came with me, that would put you in the position to lie and pretend the entire time we're with Mom and Dad. Mom will want all of us to stay in the house. She wouldn't understand our preference to stay in a hotel because we've never done that before. Nor would she understand us sleeping in separate rooms. I don't want to put you through that. And Dad will take one look at our interaction and know what I've done. I really don't want him to know. I don't want either of my parents to know what I've done."

She wasn't planning on telling Brenda and Edward. Angie also hadn't thought her offer through. She'd responded on instinct and with her heart. The practicality of their current predicament, while in Newark, hadn't registered. Sean was right. They always stayed with the Franklins when they visited. The house wasn't large, but the three upstairs bedrooms and the sleeper sofa in the basement accommodated their family just fine.

Angie didn't blame Sean for not wanting his parents to know of his cheating and a baby the potential blowback. If it was Angie, she would confess her sins to her parents, but only because they saw each other too often for her to keep such a big secret from them. She wouldn't relish seeing their disappointment, no matter how much they would try to hide or deny it. Angie imagined the same fear plagued Sean. With a sick father, he had enough to worry about. Though, she sensed a deeper reason behind his vehemence to keep knowledge of his affair from his parents. She doubted Sean would tell her, and she refused to ask.

Their last heart-to-heart had left her and their marriage in shambles They weren't strong enough to handle more honesty between them. Still, Brenda and Edward didn't see their grandchildren often enough. That needed to change. A couple of days out of school wouldn't put the children behind. If they wanted to travel with their father, Angie didn't see the harm in letting them.

"I think it would be good for Brenda and Edward to visit with the kids. You can ask them, and I'll help you prepare for the trip. If you want to stay longer than a couple of days, which you probably will, I'll drive down and pick up the kids and bring them home. I don't want you cutting your visit short to get the kids back here for school. But they need to see their grandparents more. Edward's stroke is a harsh reminder we shouldn't ignore."

The hug surprised Angie. Tight and heavy, Sean held her close and slumped his big body over hers. She didn't hug him back, but she also didn't push him away. For all his suave and success, Sean was a man with basic needs. For a time, Angie had failed to meet one or more of his needs, so he'd sought it elsewhere. She despised blaming herself for any part of Sean's infidelity. Wasn't that what too many women did, blame themselves instead of the unfaithful man?

Angie extricated herself from Sean's arms and stepped back.

"Sorry. I forgot. No touching."

He didn't sound apologetic but triumphant. This was the Sean Franklin, entitled and bold, who lied and cheated for two months. The man who saw an opening and took advantage. The man who interpreted Angie's kindness correctly, as a sign of her care and love. Sean's arrogance prevented him from analyzing their interaction clearly. Many couples, when they divorced, still had tender feelings for each other. Angie could still love him but also dissolve their marriage. For her, love and divorce weren't mutually exclusive. She didn't have to hate her husband to divorce him. Angie only needed to distrust and not forgive Sean, her love for him be damned.

Something in the way she looked at him must've registered her thoughts because his arrogance wilted back to gratitude.

"Thank you. I would love to take the children with me. Mom asked about them so this will be a nice surprise. Are you sure you don't mind making the trek south only to turn right back around and drive home?"

Angie collected her laptop and papers from the island. "I don't mind. But I don't think it's a good idea to have the kids out of school for more than a couple of days. So, I'll pick them up Tuesday evening and have them back in time for school on Wednesday. Will that work for you?"

"It will. Thanks."

"You don't have to keep thanking me. Married or divorced, we share three children, and I care about my in-laws."

"I know you do. I shouldn't have been surprised. But we don't have real conversations anymore. You don't want to talk to me or even be in the same room with me. That kind of change in our relationship is a lot to get used to. I hate it."

"It doesn't feel good to me either."

That was all she would say on the subject, no matter how long he waited for her to elaborate. When things were going sideways for Sean, he should've come to her instead of letting whatever it was that drove him to Trinity to fester until it popped and bled over into an affair. Why did men have to be so ass backward, sometimes? When they should open their mouths and speak up, they don't. But when everything has gone to hell, they develop diarrhea of the mouth, as Nana Styles used to say.

"Our anniversary and my birthday are next Friday. I'll make sure I'm home by then."

She should've left her thoughts go unspoken, but they tumbled out of her, a surging flow of mud down a steep slope. "You should spend your birthday with your parents. Beyond what the kids will want to do for you, I haven't planned anything for your birthday and definitely nothing for our anniversary. What in the hell would we celebrate, anyway? Trinity's pregnancy?"

His face fell, and her mouth slammed shut.

Shit. This was the reason Angie kept conversations with Sean to a minimum. Every time he acted as if they were normal, it grated, and awful--but truthful--sentiments bubbled to the surface. Most days she prevented them from escaping. Sean hadn't been so lucky tonight.

"Right. Thanks for the reminder that our marriage doesn't mean shit to you anymore."

Those were fighting words, and she almost swallowed the bait. Angie turned away from Sean and walked toward the kitchen's exit.

He stalked after her, stopping her in the hallway with a hand to her shoulder. "You were pretty quick to get rid of the kids and have the house to yourself. What are you planning on doing while I'm away?"

"You're being an ass."

"Yeah, I am, and you didn't answer my question."

Angie heard Malcolm's laughter ripple from the living room to where she and Sean were seconds from ripping into each other. The children were in the basement, they had a visitor, and Sean was upset about his father. She couldn't allow their conflict to escalate beyond low, heated words.

"I asked you a question. And you never did tell me what happened the night of Zahra's bachelorette party."

"There's nothing to tell."

"You got hammered. There's plenty to tell."

"You carried me into the house. Did I smell like another man?"

Sean stepped into her space the way he did a month ago when she was on her way to the club for Zahra's special night. "You smelled like booze, sweat, perfume, yours and someone else's, probably Zahra's, and cologne."

"I didn't smell like colog ... "

He smirked. "Remember something, *wife*? Who did you permit to get so close that he left his scent on you? Or were you too drunk to remember his name and what you did with him?"

Angie could smack Sean.

True, she didn't recall everything from that night, but she knew she hadn't kissed or had sex with anyone. Even if she was inclined, Zahra and her sisters wouldn't have allowed her drunk behind to go anywhere with a stranger. But she did remember dancing with Jason the Bartender. He'd asked and then whisked her onto the dance floor, instead of pouring her another drink.

They'd danced and laughed, and she'd forgotten until now.

"Have you seen him since that night? Are you planning on seeing him while I'm out of town with our children?"

"It would serve you right if I did. Would me stepping out on you make you feel better about cheating on me? It would certainly make us even." For a few painful seconds, Angie thought about the two months' worth of sex Sean had had with Trinity. "Wait, it wouldn't," she ground out. "A one-night stand wouldn't be nearly enough to even things between us."

He gritted out, "You're not funny."

"I'm not trying to be. But you're being ridiculous and paranoid about nothing all because I have no interest in celebrating our anniversary. Tell me, Sean, what is there for us to celebrate? I won't smile and pretend and act as if our twentieth anniversary is special when it's not. God, twenty damn years and you decide to screw things up now."

"No time is a good time to have an affair. But it's not true there's nothing to celebrate. We have our health and our children. And, despite everything, we still have each other. Celebration may be too big of a word, right now, but twenty years means something, Angie. You talk about not pretending, but you're pretending when you act as if two decades of marriage means nothing." Sean's voice lowered and softened, although too late for Malcolm not to have heard most of their conversation. "Twenty years is china, and the twenty-fifth is silver. I want us to make it to the twenty-fifth. Fortieth is ruby and fiftieth is gold. I want us to have those too. We'll be old, and our children will be grown with children of their own, by then. I'll still love and want you on our fiftieth wedding anniversary. This is a speed bump, Angie, not an impassable crater."

Sean went from damn near challenging her to cheat on him to professing his love and eternal commitment. Whiplash would've been less jarring.

She backed away from him again. "Go speak with the kids, and I'll run upstairs and pull out suitcases." SJ could manage his own packing, but Zuri and Kayla would need help.

Sean didn't budge, his eyes still on her for long, uncomfortable seconds.

"Fine, whatever you say, as long as you don't forget what I said."

Angie refrained from uttering a comeback. Why in the hell was she always the one practicing restraint? She knew why, and so did he. For all Sean's talk of wanting Angie to open up, he was ill-equipped to handle an unchecked Angie. Not when he was the source of her anger. So much anger it took every ounce of her self-control not to lash out at him in every vile way, including fucking another man.

Working together but separately, it didn't take them long to pack bags and corral the children into Sean's truck. Their goodbye was quick and awkward and done for the children's benefit.

"I should be off too. I didn't mean to be here so late." Malcolm kissed Angie on the cheek. The two of them stood in her foyer. "I hope Mr. Franklin will be fine."

"So do I. If it was serious, I'm sure Brenda would've told Sean."

"Probably right. It makes you think, though."

"About our parents and their mortality? Yes, it does. But I try not to think about it and neither should you. Besides, you have better things to worry about. Like that colleague you're stalking."

"I'm not stalking Sky. You have it all wrong." Malcolm buttoned his leather coat and slipped on his hat. "She likes me. I know she does. If she didn't, she wouldn't have played with me tonight."

"Text messages don't mean anything. Dr. Ellis was probably bored and took pity on you."

"Thanks a lot. There's nothing like family to kick you in the teeth."

Angie laughed then hugged her brother. "Don't push her, Malcolm. If she's apprehensive about an office romance then there's probably a very good reason."

He wouldn't listen. Malcolm was as bullheaded as Sean.

"Let's do something tomorrow, since you're flying solo for two days. You can treat me to ice cream and candy."

Angie opened her front door and pushed her brother outside. "Three children are gone but one remains. I'm not buying you ice cream and candy."

Malcolm's tongue came out the same way it did when he was five and she was fifteen and wouldn't let him eat more than two chocolate chip cookies when they were home alone.

"You're the worst older sister ever."

"Good, now go home."

He stuck out his tongue at her again. "I'm going. See you tomorrow. I'll bring the ice cream, you buy the chocolate candy, or I'm telling Mom."

Angie watched her brother drive down the street before closing and locking the door. Finally, peace and quiet.

Her cell phone rang, and she ran upstairs and into her bedroom to answer the call. A name she hadn't thought about until tonight blazed across her screen--Jason. How in the hell had he gotten her cell phone number? A better question was how had be managed to program his name and number into her phone without her noticing.

Scratch that. Angie knew how. She had been drunk, as Sean had reminded her.

She let the phone ring without answering. To her surprise, Jason left a message.

Angie considered not listening and deleting the message and his number. But curiosity took hold and wouldn't let go, so she went to her visual voicemail and played the message.

I have an After Shock w/ur name on it. Hit me up, if you're thirsty. The heated drink feels real GOOD going down. Smooth and filling.

TTYS.

J

Angie deleted the message, and didn't answer when, an hour later, Jason called back and left another message. She erased that one too. But when he called a third time, a quarter past midnight, she stifled a yawn and answered.

"Finally. How have you been, Angie ...?"

CHAPTER THIRTEEN

"This is where you grew up, Daddy?"

Brenda bent to Zuri, who held Sean's hand, both curious and shy and not yet ready to leave his side or trust the woman in front of her. Luckily, SJ and Kayla hadn't treated their grandmother as a stranger. When they'd arrived, his older children had gifted Brenda with smiles and hugs.

The kids had slept for most of the six and a half hours they were on the road. SJ woke first, groggy eyes opening when Sean had taken the exit onto Interstate 280 East toward the New Jersey Turnpike. From there, SJ peppered Sean with what felt like a hundred questions about Newark and Central Ward, where Sean grew up and where his parents still lived. At their heart, SJ's questions were no different from Zuri's and revealed the same sad truth--his children knew next to nothing about his side of the family.

"Yes, your daddy did grow up here. Look at you, such a big girl. The last time I saw you, you were an itsy-bitsy thing." Brenda brought her hand to a few inches below Zuri's shoulder. "No taller than this, and you gave me a big hug when you left."

Intelligent, brown eyes lifted to Sean. Zuri knew what her grandmother wanted, no matter how indirectly Brenda had asked.

Still holding his hand, Zuri stepped forward and permitted her grand-mother to embrace her. His daughter even went as far as kissing Brenda's cheek. A quick peck, but more than the obligatory hugs from her older siblings.

Sean smiled at her. The little monster was building goodwill credit, which she'd cash in, probably around dessert time when she'd, oh so sweetly, ask her grandmother for seconds. Brenda, never one to refuse a sweet-talker, would cave, the way she had done his entire childhood.

"Oh, aren't you the cutest thing ever. Go into the living room with your brother and sister. I turned on a cable station with cartoons."

Zuri glanced up at Sean, who nodded his approval, then she took off running down the short hall.

He shook his head. "She has no idea where she's going."

"Living room, dining room, and kitchen. Those are her choices. She won't get lost. Although, if you brought the children here more, she would know where everything is and wouldn't look at me as if I'm going to kidnap her."

There was nothing to say to that, so Sean pulled his mother into a belated hug. He'd missed her. "Angie said she'll bring them for a visit during their spring recess, which is next month."

"Wonderful. I haven't seen my only daughter-in-law in too long. She calls, though."

"When?"

"Once a month. Sometimes twice."

He tried not to sound surprised, but he was. "You're kidding me. Since when?"

"Since forever. I always know when Angie is busy at work because a month or two will slip by and she'll forget to call. When she does call, she apologizes for forgetting about me, which isn't necessary. But it's nice to know she cares about my feelings."

The unspoken was that Sean and his sisters didn't care about her feelings because they rarely visited. He ignored the passive-aggressive dig. "When was the last time you spoke with her?"

"Well, I called Angie on her birthday, so that was our February talk. Then she called me the first week of March. I remember because it was before Edward had his stroke."

He'd had no idea. Angie's actions proved what he'd forgotten. His wife valued family above everything else. On the surface, it may not appear that way, especially when Angie was swamped at work. Once that layer was stripped away, however, the truth seeped into the light. She juggled and prioritized and sometimes Sean didn't end up on the top of her priority list. For him, Angie and the children stayed in the number one spot. His wife would likely disagree, but she would be wrong.

"Is that coffee I smell?"

"With the overnight drive, I figured you'd be tired but not too tired for a cup of decaf coffee and breakfast."

It had to be almost six in the morning. Despite the early time, Sean's mother was dressed as if she'd been up for hours. Sean and his sisters had had little choice but to grow to a height that dwarfed most people. While Sean was six-three, the tallest of the Franklin children, his father still had two inches on him, while Brenda, long-legged and beautiful, stood at five-eleven. At seventy-five, Brenda's dark-brown hair had slowly given way to an elegant shade of silver she kept cut in loose curls she could style with her fingers. Sean inherited his love of comfortable clothing from his parents, although his mother, come Sunday morning, dressed up for church.

"Jeans and a long duster? It's Sunday, Mom. Aren't you going to the eight o'clock service?"

"Don't be ridiculous. I haven't seen my son and grandchildren in two years. I'm not going to miss a minute of your visit. The Lord knows my heart. The church is just a building. I don't need to go there to worship."

That was different. Every Sunday, when Sean was little, Brenda would drag the Franklin children to church. His father rarely went, which bothered his mother to the point of her spending even more time there, teaching Sunday school and serving on the Usher Board.

"Come on, let's get a hot cup of coffee in you and then I'll cook everyone breakfast. After you called last night and let me know about the kids coming with you, I got the two guest rooms ready and put bed linen on the sofa bed in the basement for SJ. Unless you want him upstairs with the girls."

"No, the basement will be fine. It was good enough for me, when I was SJ's age, and look how well I turned out." Sean hugged his mother to him again and kissed her on the cheek. "I promise to visit more often. Is Dad asleep?"

"He'll drag himself downstairs when he smells bacon and eggs."

Sean followed his mother down the hall, stopping at the living room where the children watched television but not the cartoon channel Brenda had mentioned. Zuri sat between SJ and Kayla on the couch, her head on Kayla's arm and her eyes closed, while her siblings' gazes were glued to an action movie.

"Did you call your mother?"

SJ craned his head toward Sean. "Yeah. I told her we got here safely."

"Did Angie say anything?"

"Like what?"

Sean had no idea. It would've been nice if she'd asked after him. He'd figured Angie would rather get a progress report from her son than her husband. If one of them hadn't called Angie, by the time she'd driven to work, she would've called him, worried and upset.

"Nothing. Grandma's about to cook breakfast. While she is, you and Kayla need to get the luggage and bring it all into the house. Your stuff in the basement, everyone else's upstairs. Be quiet, while you're up there, so you won't disturb Granddad."

"What about her?" Kayla pointed to a sleeping Zuri.

They may have slept in the truck, but nothing was like getting a good rest in a bed. After they ate breakfast, they would all follow Zuri's lead and crash. Sean would check on his father first. Afterward, Sean had a hot date with a shower and bed.

"I got her." Sean scooped up his little girl, who opened her eyes just enough to confirm it was her father who held her, then closed them again. He tossed his keys to SJ. "Don't make a mistake and lock them in the truck. And don't turn it on."

"I wouldn't do that."

"Sure you would. You're fourteen, and I just gave you the keys to a sweet ride. Lesser things have tempted bigger men than you." Sean would know. "Just remember, anything you do you'll have to confess to your mother when she picks you guys up on Tuesday."

Odd, how such a small woman carried off the might of a person his size, but Angie did. Many people, like their children, weren't so much afraid of Angie, but they hated to disappoint her. And he'd met enough of his wife's colleagues to know she also intimidated people with her confidence and intelligence, two traits that made her attractive to him.

"I get it. No messing around with your truck. I should've stayed home with Mom."

Sean had been surprised when SJ agreed to the last-minute trip. With his crabbiness toward him, he thought SJ would grumble about spending time with him. But his son had been excited about the road trip to Newark and hadn't given Sean a single attitude. He guessed, miles away from home, SJ now regretted his decision.

"Mom's by herself. I should've stayed with her so she wouldn't be in the house alone."

Just like that, Sean could see everything Angie and he had gotten right with their eldest child. Not sulking about the vibe he'd picked up from Angie and Sean's marital issues or annoyance at being asked to pack and miss school with no notice, but concern for the well-being of his mother.

Sean squeezed Zuri between them when he hugged his son.

"Ah, come on, Dad. You're as sappy as Uncle Malcolm sometimes."

"You're squishing me, Daddy," Zuri complained.

"Sorry, sweetie. Go back to sleep."

He looked over at Kayla, who'd not only ignored the scene between father and son but had changed the station while SJ was preoccupied.

Leave it to his ballerina daughter to find a documentary about Alvin Ailey dancers. Sean had completed the request form for the AileyDance Kids summer program. Kayla had attended the New York location the last five years. But there was a site in Newark. He would have to first speak with Angie about a location change. If she agreed, maybe Kayla could spend the summer with her paternal grandparents. Brenda would love it, and he doubted his father would mind having a ten-year-old around he could get to run errands for him.

"Okay, you two. Get the bags out of the truck and then see if there's anything Grandma needs help with in the kitchen."

Two minutes later, he was upstairs. It didn't take Sean long to undress Zuri and place her into bed. This room, the smallest of the three bedrooms, had once belonged to his two youngest sisters, Danielle and Vanessa. A double bed had long since replaced the well-used bunk beds. The flower print wallpaper, stylish at the time, was also gone. Mellow yellow paint added a refreshing, sunny, and serene feel to the room his girls would enjoy.

Tip-toeing from the bedroom, Sean didn't close the door. The last thing he needed was for him not to hear Zuri awake and the girl burst into tears and yell for her mother because she was behind a closed door and in a room she didn't recognize.

"She's as cute as a button." Edward peered into the room and at Zuri. "Don't look a thing like you, though. You sure she's yours?"

The first sentences his father had spoken to him in six months and they reminded him of all the reasons he'd left home and taken years to return. In less than a minute, Edward had complimented Sean's daughter and disparaged his wife. Maybe he wouldn't permit Kayla to spend the summer there after all.

"Really, Dad?"

"Lighten up, Sean, and learn to take a joke." Edward slapped Sean on the shoulder. "Did your mother tell you I was dying or something? If she did, you drove all the way here for nothing. I couldn't feel better."

Edward's attitude and smart-ass mouth hadn't changed, but so much about him had. Thinner and grayer, his father didn't wear his age well. Until Sean had left Newark, everyone who'd known him and Edward swore he was the spitting image of his father. He despised the comparison, not because Edward wasn't a handsome and fit man and the physical comparison apt, but because there was so much more to his father than a female-stealing smile and good looks. Edward didn't have the appearance of a man who drank too much or used drugs, years of hard living etched across his face and body. Nothing so extreme as that. But there were other lifestyle choices that took their toll on a man.

"I know Mom cooks, so why have you lost so much weight?"

Edward patted his flat stomach, his button-down, long-sleeved, blue shirt tucked into black jeans held up by a belt with too much extra leather at the end. "Haven't you heard? Skinny, old man is in. We're the flavor of the month."

"Flavor of the month," Sean repeated, his tone mocking and tinged with irritation. "For once, can we have a normal conversation?" Sean glanced back at a sleeping Zuri. "But not here. We'll wake my baby girl."

Edward also looked into the room, his drawn face shifting into a genuine smile. "It's nice to have kids in the house again. That one will be a heart-breaker when she grows up. The sprout really does look like her mother, which isn't a bad thing at all. I always told you and your sisters not to marry an ugly or stupid person because you'd have ugly and stupid children. It's nice to know you listened to me instead of acting like everything that comes from my mouth isn't worth a damn because I don't have a college degree. In my day, a high school diploma and some college courses were good enough to get a decent job and raise a family."

"Not that again." Sean walked away from his father and into the room next door. Again, no bunk beds or visible signs of his older sisters' childhoods lived out between the four walls. No stuffed animals, fuzzy carpet or scratched furniture. No flower print wallpaper, like in Danielle and Vanessa's room. His older sisters, Tanya and Ebony, had been into metallic geometric shapes, begging their father to buy them that design of wallpaper. After two months of their whining, the father of five had given in, swearing the entire time he put up the wallpaper. In the end, Tanya and Ebony were happy and Edward proud.

Sean was tempted to slip out of his sneakers and sweatshirt and into bed. If he did that, though, he'd miss his mother's breakfast. What he refused to do, while at home, was to entertain his father's nonsense. He didn't understand how a man could encourage his children to pursue higher ed but scorn them when they achieved his and their goals. Instead of being happy for Sean, the way any normal father would be, Edward viewed his children's accomplishments as criticism of his potential. Being a bus driver was good, honest work that had put clothes on their backs and food on the table.

"How are you feeling, Dad?"

"I told you, I'm fine."

"You had a stroke. That doesn't sound like you're fine. You've also lost a lot of weight."

"I don't need you nagging me. I get enough of that from Brenda. I eat when I'm hungry. I just don't have an appetite the way I used to."

"For food or women?"

"Right for the jugular, and you haven't been home an hour. For the record, counselor, I don't do that shit anymore. I told you that years ago, but you never believed a thing I had to say. I suppose you won't believe me now either."

"You're seventy-seven. I'm sure your dick doesn't work the way it used to. There is help for erectile dysfunction, by the way."

"What in the hell makes you think I have ED?"

"The fact that you called it ED, for one. You being nearly eighty, for two."

"What in the hell is wrong with you? If you were only going to bust my balls about old shit that's none of your damn business, you could've stayed the hell in Buffalo. Are you trying to give me another stroke?"

"You said you were fine. And you being a serial cheater was all of our business."

"I told you. I don't do that anymore. Why can't you and your sisters forgive me? How long do I have to pay for my sins?"

Sean dropped to the edge of the bed, his mind more fatigued than his body. "Sorry, Dad. I shouldn't have said any of that. I didn't mean to dredge up old wounds. That's not why I'm here."

"But it's why you don't call enough or come home often. You at least try. Your sisters won't even do that much. I bet Brenda called all you kids." Edward spread his arms wide. "Do you see anyone else here? I could die tomorrow, and my girls wouldn't give a damn."

"That's not true."

"For a lawyer, you need to work on your lying skills. Tell me what's going on with you and Angie."

"What do you mean?"

"As I said, you need to work on your lying skills. Fine, don't tell me. I'm hungry, and you look like you're going to pass the hell out if you don't get some food in you soon. Get your butt up and let's eat."

With two hands on the bed, Sean pushed to his feet. This visit, if he didn't alter its direction, would be long and painful, especially if his father kept asking him about his wife.

"By the way, Angie called last night to check on me."

"Does she call you once a month, too?" He sounded churlish and didn't care.

"Once a month? Hell no. But Brenda gives me the phone after she's gabbed the poor girl's ear off for an hour. I get five minutes, fifteen tops, which is all we need to catch up."

"She makes time for everyone else but me," Sean mumbled, his gait slow as he followed his father down the steps.

"What did you say?"

"Nothing, Dad, nothing."

CHAPTER FOURTEEN

"Are you out of your damn mind?" Angie winced at Zahra's loud, judgmental voice, and pulled her cell phone a few inches from her ear. "You need to get your little ass out of there before he arrives."

"It's only drinks."

"This time it may only be drinks. Damn, Angie, you're smarter than this."

"A woman can have a male friend."

"Oh, please. Stop the bullshit." At that, Angie pressed the phone back to her ear. "Wounded pride and a broken heart, that's what this is all about. You're acting stupid because Sean was even stupider. But you don't want to do this."

Angie scanned the bar from her spot in the last booth on the right side. From this angle, she couldn't see the front door but had no concern Jason would find her. She'd arrived fifteen minutes ago, which was ten minutes early.

"Trust me, I'm not going to do something stupid."

"Because you don't intend on screwing around to get back at Sean, or because you won't view a one-night stand as stupid if it fulfills a twisted, but fleeting emotion?"

Her wedding and engagement rings felt like cement blocks pulling her under the water and into an ugly, black depth she wouldn't be able to escape. Angie shouldn't have spoken to Jason on the phone, even if it was only for ten minutes. She certainly shouldn't have agreed to meet him.

"Despite how this may seem, I'm not going to do anything."

"Then why are you meeting him?"

She'd asked herself the same question. More than once she'd been on the verge of canceling and forgetting her temporary bout of insanity. Yet, an entire Sunday had lapsed, and she hadn't snapped out of whatever drive had overridden her common sense. An affair or even a quick hook-up wasn't Angie's goal, not even to spite her husband. She had no interest in hurting Sean the way he'd gutted her.

"He's so apologetic. I believe Sean's sorry for his affair," Angie mused.

"That's good. He should be sorry."

"The problem is that I can't actually feel that emotion from him. It's all cognitive, on my end. When I look at him, I wonder what in the hell went on in his mind when he decided to stray. Not cheat, Zahra, but stray. To my way of thinking, they aren't the same. His mind strayed before his body cheated. The cheating was a psychological culmination of all the reasons he gave himself to take a lover. Before he slept with Trinity, he had to have given it a lot of thought, weighing the pros and cons. That's how he is, methodical. I can't see him driven by passion and reckless impulse. Not even the first time. He decided, then he acted. And he kept acting until he decided to stop."

"Being smart is a double-edged sword. What you said makes sense, but I don't know if you're right. What I do know is that you're overthinking everything and driving yourself crazy. You want to know what motivated Sean to cheat but won't ask him because you're afraid of the answer. You want to know how Sean could lie and betray you, seemingly with ease, so you agree to a rendezvous with a virtual stranger with the asinine hope of gaining insight into your husband's psyche of months ago. You're also hurt and angry, and the attention of a younger man makes you question, even more, why your husband cheated. You used the word cognitive. But what you want to know is Sean's metacognition. What was the thinking behind his thought process? Let me tell you something, you won't find your answers in a dark bar sitting across from a handsome, young man who'd fuck you a hundred different ways if you let him. In the end, you'd still be no closer to mending your heart."

Angie closed her eyes, taking in her friend's wisdom. Zahra, with her first husband, had traveled this rocky road. When it was all said and done, emotional scars were all Zahra had to show for a five-year marriage.

"Don't talk yourself into doing something you don't want to do."

"What makes you think I don't want to have sex with a young man who has muscles on top of muscles?"

Zahra laughed. "Yeah, well, there is that. But you know what I mean. You wouldn't have called me if you were committed to this meeting and taking Jason up on his offer. You're being reckless because you've never done a truly irresponsible thing in your life, and you want to see what it's like. You follow the rules. You always have. Now, though, you feel played by Sean and wonder what good comes from adhering to the rules when he didn't. A cheating spouse makes you question things like your self-worth and morality. It sucks, and it's unfair."

"It does, and it is. I feel stupid and angry at myself, which makes me angrier at Sean."

"It's only been two months. Give yourself a break. You need time to heal. It would be great if it happened overnight, but that's unrealistic. Healing takes time. And I mean for you and Sean. Is he there yet?"

Angie opened her mouth to respond in the negative when she spotted Jason coming toward her. He'd already removed his coat, the leather biker jacket hanging from a hand.

"He just arrived. Thanks for the talk, but I need to go. "

"Be smart, not vengeful. Call me later."

"Promise. Bye."

"Sorry, I'm late." Jason stopped on her side of the booth. Big brown eyes swept over her, a slow, sensual perusal. "Wow, you're a real snack."

"I have no idea what that means." Uncomfortable with his towering form and her sudden spark of apprehension, Angie stood and extended her right hand.

Jason's smiling eyes laughed at Angie's formal greeting, but he took hold of her hand and brought it to his lips and kissed.

"Your hair, make-up, and outfit. You're all put together like you were the night of your friend's bachelorette party. You're one of those women who takes pride in the presentation, but for her own sake, not for someone else's."

"You don't know me."

"Right, I don't. But I know your type." Her eyebrow arched and Jason stepped back. "I definitely know your type, and I just shot myself in the foot. A snack means you look really good, which you do." Tossing his leather coat onto the empty bench of the booth, Jason slid in after it. "You could've figured out the meaning of that slang, but you wanted to remind me, and yourself, of our age difference."

"I'm forty-seven." She retook her seat.

"And I'm thirty. We swapped ages last night. I told you, I don't care."

"I'm also married."

"That I should care about, and if your husband was behind me, I would pretend to."

"He's out of town."

"Lucky for me."

Angie observed Jason. He was indeed an attractive man. He wore jeans and a navy blue, tight fitting, knit pullover shirt that showed off the muscles on top of muscles she'd mentioned to Zahra. Smart and outgoing, she doubted Jason ever wanted for female attention. But he was also young and she was unavailable.

"I'm not sleeping with you. This is my fault. I shouldn't have agreed to the meet. You may not care I'm married, but I do."

Leaning forward, elbows on the table, his too-knowing gaze challenged her. "You aren't happily married. I can tell when a wife isn't."

Angie snorted. "Is that part of my 'type'?" Out of politeness sake, she'd decided to wait for Jason before placing a drink order. Now, she wished she'd swallowed a glass of liquid courage. "I apologize for giving you the wrong impression about my intentions."

"Working at the club, I see all kinds of women. Some, like you, pretend to be happy when they're not. They smile and laugh on the outside while secretly crying on the inside. When I meet a married woman as beautiful and as smart as you are, but who is unhappy, it's normally for one reason."

"What's that?"

He leaned back, smirking at her, revealing, despite his youth, the wealth of experience he'd had with women. "You know, or you wouldn't be here. Your husband's a loser if he picked another woman over you."

"People cheat and, based on what you've said, you sleep with married women, so you have no room for moral judgment."

Jason winked, his face alight with good humor. "I don't sleep with married women. I put it down, and they pass out afterward." He was toying with her. Not about having sex with married women, but in his approach to their conversation.

"You really are cute … and young."

"Sexy and tempting would be better words, but I'll take cute if that's all you're giving away."

Good lord. Fresh out of his twenties and Jason knew far too much about women and how to wiggle himself between their thighs.

"It is all I'm giving away."

"A shame, but I'm not surprised. Disappointed but not surprised. You want to order drinks and food? They make decent wings and fries here, and I'm hungry."

"What am I missing? You know I'm not going to have sex with you, but you still want to spend the evening with me? I'm not going to change my mind."

"Maybe you will, maybe you won't." Jason rose from his side of the booth and joined Angie on hers. "I like my sex partners willing and guilt-free." A long, muscular arm settled across the top of the booth and inches from around her shoulder. "This is probably the closest you've been to a man, who wasn't your husband or family member, since you married. And the only reason you haven't told me off for invading your space is because you're forcing yourself to stay calm and deal with me and this situation because you let tonight happen against your better judgment."

Eucalyptus and spearmint. The strong scents tickled her nose, and she couldn't recall if Jason had worn the same cologne two months ago and if it had been this combination of scents Sean had smelled on her.

Angie didn't back away from his challenge. Most women her age would've reveled in having the interest of a man almost twenty years their junior, clothes and inhibitions gone with one sensual glance.

"I'm not a MILF or a cougar."

"You know those words but not snack." Jason edged closer, his big body emitting waves of heat. "Your knowledge of slang is spotty. I can help you with that."

"I don't need your help, and you're too damn close."

"I know I am, and you know I'm teasing. If I tried to kiss you, what would you do? Would I leave with a bloody nose and a lesson on distance and respect? Or would I find out if your lips are as soft and as sweet as they look? I'm betting on soft and sweet. You also look like you're considering taking a swing at me. So, Angie, a kiss to test the depths of your fidelity, after your husband's cheating, or a punch to my nose because of my audacity?"

Jason wasn't audacious. Her actions, coming there, had been, though.

A single kiss? Angie hadn't kissed another man since she'd begun dating Sean. After meeting him, she hadn't wanted anyone else. Even now, as she watched Jason watch her, waiting for her response, she still didn't want another man. Having and wanting weren't synonymous. For Sean, though, he'd wanted and had Trinity.

Repeatedly.

Why then couldn't Angie travel the same path as Sean? Why couldn't she give herself to someone else the way he had shared his body with another woman? Like Sean, Angie could confess her sins afterward. She could claim it as a mistake--just fucking, not lovemaking--and promise to never do it again. Because, well, she loved Sean but not Jason, just as he had claimed to love her but not Trinity. Sean would understand, right? After all, he'd opened the adultery door. Why should he then be surprised if Angie followed him through it?

She didn't desire Jason, although she found him very attractive. His full bottom lip was perfect for kissing and sucking on, and she didn't doubt he'd mastered the art of kissing before he was old enough to legally drink. Angie could also envision his lips on other parts of her body. It didn't take much to imagine every wicked and wild thing Jason could do with his mouth. He wanted her to think about his lips on her, which was why he'd asked for a kiss and sat temptingly close.

How had Sean done it? Being there with Jason, his youthful manliness surrounding her with an offer of a kiss and so much more, Angie's guilt alarm blared. But Sean had slept with Trinity for two months and, presumably, hadn't felt a goddamn bit of remorse while doing it. Was his heart made of stone or was hers made of gossamer, unable to withstand the breeze of a solitary kiss?

Angie felt defeated as if Sean had taken something else from her. Would this be her fate, if they divorced? Would Angie, for god knows how long, find it difficult to accept the sexual attention of a man other than Sean, unable to return the desire with intent and action? Would she pine for a lost marriage and love while Sean moved on to greener pastures with Trinity or other women like her?

"If you don't want me to kiss you, I'll back off. If you do," Jason's hand swept the hair from Angie's shoulder, and his lips blew warm air across her exposed neck, "I'll make it so good for you, you'll forget your husband ever looked twice at another woman. Do you want to forget, Angie?"

With every beat of her bleeding heart, she did.

CHAPTER FIFTEEN

"Are you sure you've had enough rest?"

Brenda eyed Angie with a concerned gaze Sean remembered well. She'd bestowed the same on him every time he'd borrowed her or Edward's car when he was a high school senior, his license brand-spankin' new and his enthusiasm greater than his driving skills.

Angie, eyes a little red after her Brenda-imposed nap, smiled up at her mother-in-law. "The rest did me good. I wouldn't drive myself, let alone my children, if I wasn't certain I could get us home safely."

Arms crossed over his chest, as if a sentry on duty, he hovered in front of the open door, his focus split between his children outside and his adult family inside.

"If she says she's fine, Brenda, then trust the girl to know her limits." Edward stepped forward and beside Brenda, his hand lifting to her shoulder and squeezing before dropping back to his side. "The grandbabies are already in the car, and Angie slept for two hours. She also has a travel mug full of steaming coffee to keep her awake if she needs it. Stop worrying and let her get on the road before it gets even later."

For the second time since Angie arrived, Edward hugged her and kissed her cheek. "Drive safely and call us when you and the kids arrive."

"I will. I'm glad you're feeling better."

"You don't think I'm too skinny? That husband of yours told me I reminded him of a skeleton in old man clothes."

"That's not what I said."

"Close enough." Edward looked from Sean to Angie. "I'll kick him out in another day or two, so he'll be home for your anniversary. Twenty years, right?"

"Good memory."

"My only son's birthday and the fact that I was at your wedding, it would be hard for me to forget the day. Two decades of marriage, that's nothing to sneeze at. Many marriages don't make it that long nowadays, especially with this new crop of kids. They have one good argument and throw in the towel."

Tense, but trying not to show it, Sean spoke kindly but firmly. "Dad, Angie has to leave. Like you said, the kids are in the car and waiting. Everyone has said their goodbyes, and you're holding her up."

"I'm not holding her up. You can wait with the children outside, if you're so worried about them sitting in a locked car in front of my house for all of three minutes. You worry too much."

Sean did worry, but not about SJ, Kayla, and Zuri. Angie hadn't spent more than a few minutes speaking with his parents before Brenda hustled her upstairs and into the bed Sean had slept in last night. In that small span of time, Edward couldn't have noticed the tension between Sean and Angie. Yet, his father seemed to be on a fishing expedition, and Sean didn't like it.

"Sean and I have had our share of arguments, like any other couple. Twenty years is a long time to know someone without a fight or two."

"Or a dozen," Edward said, with a soft smile and a meaningful glance to Brenda.

"Yes, or a dozen. No worries, Edward, Sean and I won't argue if he chooses to stay here to celebrate his birthday with you and Brenda and miss our anniversary. He only turns forty-seven once."

"And you only have your twentieth anniversary once."

"True. I guess that's the drawback to having our wedding on Sean's birthday."

Brenda sighed, the way she did when she watched a holiday romance on the Hallmark Channel. "I always thought the choice of date romantic and sweet."

Sean agreed with her but refrained from adding his two cents and played it cool. If he continued to push the issue of Angie leaving, Edward's perceptive antennae would go up even more. Sean leaned against the doorjamb and waved at Zuri, her smiling face and little hands pressed to the rear driver's side window, no doubt leaving smudges.

"It's a nice thought, Brenda, but Valentine's Day would've been better."

Sean couldn't help it, he smiled. No matter how "romantic and sweet" people found their decision to marry on his birthday, if they knew Angie's birthday was on the most romantic holiday celebrated the world over, they thought that an even better choice. Sean didn't disagree with his father, although he did love sharing the date with his anniversary. After twenty years, the two fit perfectly together in his mind. The same way Angie and he fit perfectly together ... or used to.

"On that all too familiar note, I should leave now if I want to reach Buffalo by one, so I can get a few hours of sleep before getting ready for work and driving the children to school."

Sean left his wife with his parents, trusting her to make the second round of goodbyes quick, and went to the car. He'd already hugged his children goodbye, which didn't prevent him from taking his fill of them again. Spending uninterrupted time with the children the last two days had been nice. He'd missed Angie, but he'd given her the space she needed, meaning no phone calls, emails, or text messages.

She hadn't contacted him either. Not that he'd thought she would. Two days home alone. Sean wondered how she'd spent her time, other than working.

Angie strode toward him, her pace quick and self-assured. Straight black hair fell past her shoulders and onto a khaki, double-breasted,

THE GIFT OF SECOND CHANCES · 169

skirted raincoat that hit just below her cute behind and showed off toned legs in black, fitted slacks. Heels added several inches, and Sean imagined those spikes digging into the back of his thighs as he claimed his wife with needy thrusts.

"Thank you for driving down here. Did you go in to work today?"

"I took a half day."

"You should've asked Malcolm to come with you."

"He offered, and I would've accepted if I didn't know how desperately he wanted to have dinner with Dr. Ellis tonight."

"Dr. Ellis?"

"The woman from EBC he likes."

That was Malcolm's colleague's name. He'd had no idea.

"Are you okay?"

"I won't fall asleep. I told your parents—"

"Not that. You . . . I don't know ... seem different. Are you angry with me? I mean, beyond the fact you've been pissed at me for two months. I promise I haven't—"

"I don't care," Angie snapped. "Do what you want."

"Do what I want?" What bus had he missed? "Do what I want? Since when do you not care about what I do?"

"My caring didn't factor into your decision the first time you messed around. Why should it now?" Angie opened the driver's side door, grabbed an envelope from the center console, and then slammed the door shut. "Here." She shoved a blue envelope at him. "I'm giving it to you now in case I don't see you on Friday."

Her less than cordial attitude didn't make him want to take anything from her, but he did.

"What is it?"

"A birthday card," she answered, as if annoyed by her own thoughtfulness, meager though it was. "After school on Friday, I'll take the children shopping so they can select a gift for you. I'll also pick up a birthday cake. Brenda will probably bake you one, though. If you don't want two cakes, I could purchase you something else. Pie and ice cream, maybe."

"Why am I in a bigger hole than I was before I left?" Sean kept his voice low and leaned closer to Angie. "Did Trinity call you? Did she and the other man have the paternity test done? Did he turn out not to be the father?"

Every question left Sean feeling as if he rammed a blade into his wife's chest, yanking it out only to shove it back in, the blood unseen but the pain in her eyes all too visible and ghastly.

"I haven't spoken to your whor ..." Angie's scrutiny shifted to her car behind Sean before sliding back to him. "The kids are watching us, and your parents are in the doorway waiting for me to drive off."

"None of that matters, right now. Tell me what's going on with you." The way Angie looked at and spoke to Sean reminded him too much of the night of his confession. If Angie hadn't heard from Trinity, why did Sean feel as if his wife had slipped further away from him? If Edward hadn't mentioned their upcoming anniversary, she would've come and gone and not said a word to him about their special day. Even her birthday card was more obligatory than sincere.

"I'll call when we arrive home. It'll be late, and I'll probably wake you."

"You know I don't care about that. I want to talk, Angie. Really talk. Let's do that when I return home."

"Have a good birthday."

Angie hopped into her car, beeped her horn at his waving parents, and then drove off.

He watched Angie's car until he could no longer see the red vehicle. Red, her favorite color. Red, like her anger. Eyes dropped to the envelope in his hand. Blue, like Sean's mood. He ripped open the envelope and snatched the card out and read. Angie had signed it, but that was all she'd written on the inside.

Not, *I love you.* Or, *With all my love.* Not even, *I hope you have a wonderful birthday.* Nothing but her name.

He stalked into the house, his birthday card crumbled in his hand.

"Where are you going?"

Ignoring his father, he bounded up the stairs, rattling the house with the force he used to close his bedroom door.

Sean collapsed onto the bed, angry with his stubborn wife and furious with himself. He couldn't reach her. Sean didn't know what to do to make things right between them. He'd suggested talking it through but had no idea how to go about that without causing more damage to their tenuous relationship. What if she asked him questions about his affair he wasn't prepared to answer? Worse, what if Sean disclosed every shameful deed and Angie couldn't stomach the truth.

Would airing his dirty laundry ruin whatever chance they had for reconciliation, slim as it may be? Or would Angie decide he'd tainted their marriage too much for her to get past his affair and Trinity's baby?

Sean heard floorboards creak outside the bedroom and sat up just as his father opened the door.

"You could've knocked."

"It's my house. I own every room, I don't have to knock."

"You used to say the same thing when I was a teen. Any excuse to barge into my room. What did you think you would catch me doing alone in the basement? Jerking off?"

"Why in the hell would I have wanted to catch you doing that?" Edward bent, slow but steady. When he stood again, he held Sean's birthday card in his right hand, crumpled but readable. "It's from Angie. Why would you treat her card this way?"

"It doesn't concern you." Sean kicked off his sneakers and scooted against the headboard. "I may not be in Buffalo, but it doesn't mean I don't have work to do. You can throw that card away on your way out."

While visiting his parents, he'd worked on the pleading on the LeRoy case. Ideally, he'd like to have the document filed in court next Monday. While he took every case seriously, the ones involving children were the closest to his heart. Too many public schools were under-resourced, the teachers overworked, neither of which excused the lack of services provided to Antoinette LeRoy, a third-grader with autism.

Leaning to his right and toward the floor, he unplugged his laptop and placed it on the bed beside him. When he straightened, it was to find Edward still there, Angie's card in his father's hand and a frown aimed at him.

"You have a smart mouth and the wrong attitude. Brenda and I didn't raise you to be disrespectful, especially to us."

Something inside Sean snapped. The train of frayed emotions he'd tried to keep on the track veered off course and careened into Edward.

"No, you raised me to be a cheat who hurts his wife." He vaulted from the bed, so angry and with no one to take it out on other than the unfaithful bastard in front of him. "I knew this shit would happen one day. I fucking knew it. You and your goddamn affairs."

A long, thin finger came up and pointed at Sean. "You're blaming *me* for what *you* did?"

"Hell, yes. What kind of role model were you, Dad? You couldn't keep your dick out of women who weren't your wife. Your supervisor at NJ Transit. Ms. Brown across the street. You even fucked the preacher's wife. I remember when Mom stopped taking us to Belmont Baptist Ministries, and I had no idea why. That was her church home. Most of her friends and some of her family attended too. I also remember that was when you stopped going to church with us. Older sisters are good for a lot of things. One is talking in front of a brother they think is too young to understand. Even if I didn't know, at eight, what was happening between you and Mom, you gave me plenty of opportunities to learn, as I got older."

The crumpled card hit Sean in the chest. "Don't blame me for your weakness and stupid choices. It was your dick inside a woman other than Angie. Not mine. You were the one who cheated on your wife. Not me. Grow the hell up, Sean. Even with my stroke, I remember every speck of dirt Brenda can lay at my feet. I earned the pile of filth I slog through every goddamn day. I did my shit and enjoyed it while I was doing it. As men, we always enjoy being inside a woman, including the little thrill that comes from doing something we know we aren't supposed to be doing."

Sean shook his head, a quick denial. "It wasn't like that for me."

"Bullshit. You fucked someone other than Angie. If the sex wasn't good, what was the point of risking so much on a shitty lay?"

"That's my point. No sex is good enough for what I risked. I'm not like you. At least, that's what I always told myself. For years, I watched your affairs tear Mom down. One by one, and you didn't care. I promised never to do to my wife what you did to yours." Sean picked up the birthday card Edward had thrown at him, trying to smooth out the damage he'd done to it, and failing. "For nineteen years, I kept my promise. I looked, sometimes, because I'm a man and not dead. But that's all I ever did. I love my wife."

"And I love mine."

"How in the hell can you say that with a straight face?"

"The same way you did. What? You want me to believe you cheated on Angie but still love her. Yet you can't believe the same about me?" Edward jerked the wooden chair from under the desk and sat, his back to the single window. "I'm not heartless or a monster."

"You were both. You knew how much your affairs hurt Mom, yet you kept seeing other women. She was so unhappy. Angie tries to hide her pain from everyone, especially the kids. You beat Mom down with your infidelity so much she couldn't even manage Angie's stiff upper lip. How does that not describe someone who's heartless? Unjustified cruelty is the mark of a monster. Make no mistake, Dad, how you mistreated Mom back then was damn sure cruel. She should've left your ass. I never understood why in the hell she stayed."

"Or why she still stays?"

"Yeah, that too. You don't deserve her." Arms crossed over his chest, he leaned his bottom against the decade-old wooden dresser. "You've never been good enough for Mom. She gave, and you took." Until Sean had moved away for college, Edward had been the most selfish person he'd known.

"Spitting venom at me doesn't absolve you of your sins. It may make you feel better, raking me over the coals, but it doesn't make your shit stink any less. If you want to talk about what an awful husband I was to Brenda, fine. We've never really done that. I get it, though. You and your sisters think I'm the most awful kind of man. So horrible you don't want to have anything to do with me. I know, the way I know my name is Edward Louis Franklin, if Brenda and I had split, she would have a better relationship with you kids, and I would have none. I would be nowhere in the picture. Don't bother denying it."

Sean wasn't going to deny it, but he also wasn't planning on agreeing, no matter the truth of his father's words.

"I have no valid justification for all my years of cheating. I have excuses, which were enough to get me by at the time. Everyone who cheats has excuses. We lie. Not only to our wife and children but also to ourselves. We wrap ourselves in them and happily swallow our own bullshit. We think we're better men than we are. The truth is that we're only better in our heads."

"I am better than cheating. I have to be. If I'm not, what in the hell am I going to do? If I'm only going to turn out like you, I might as well let Angie go."

"You're so damn dramatic. You messed up. Once, I bet."

"I had an affair for two months."

Edward nodded. "I meant with one woman, but your short affair tells me something too. It was more than a single screw but not a drawn-out affair. You need to think long and hard about that. It may not have lasted long, but you returned to the buffet for seconds and thirds. That's what's going to stick in Angie's craw for a while. Look, I know you don't want advice from me."

"You're right, I don't. But you're not going to budge from this room until I listen, so have at it."

Edward's gaze fell to his feet, and his hands fisted then relaxed in quick succession. When he raised his light-brown eyes again, they glistened with tears.

"The first time is the hardest, believe it or not. The second is also difficult but not as much as the first. The third woman is easier. And all the others that follow don't even register. Not really. By that point, you're kind of numb to it all. You do it because you don't think you're capable of being better than you are. Because it's easier to sink into a female you don't give a damn about than it is to look into the eyes of the woman you love. In your wife's eyes, you see her high expectations of you quiver, shrink, and eventually die. Right now, you may feel like shit for breaking your vows and betraying Angie. As bad as that may seem, there's a world of difference between feeling like shit and thinking you are shit for your cowardice and weakness."

Edward stood with tears streaming down his face, and Sean should feel sorry for him. His father had confessed to thinking of himself as worthless. With the way he'd strutted around the house, as if Brenda was overreacting each time she found out about another one of his lovers, Sean would've never guessed the man felt anything other than callousness overladen by hubris.

Shaky hands cleared away tears. "You're right, I didn't set the best example for you and your sisters. I embarrassed myself and Brenda, and I embarrassed you kids. You never told Angie about my cheating, did you?"

"Why would I have done something like that? Angie would've taken it in stride because that's how she is. But the truth is that, no matter how much she would tell herself, and me, that the apple fell far from the Franklin tree, a part of her would've wondered if I would do to her what you did to Mom. If I told her now, she'd think I didn't share before because I'm more like my serial cheating father than I'd wanted her to know."

Edward nodded again. "When I first cheated, Brenda suggested therapy. No one I knew did stuff like that. We also didn't have money to waste on a crackpot counselor."

"You never sought professional help then?"

"No. I wish we had. I lay awake thinking about all the mistakes I've made in my life. I can't take any of them back. It's a terrible feeling to know how much you've wounded the person you love most in the world. It's even worse to continue to take from them, knowing how awful you've been, and that the person would've been much happier without you."

As Sean listened to his father, thinking about his mistake with Trinity and the possibility of having fathered a child with her, a horrible realization struck.

Sean's arms dropped, and he stood from the dresser, body tense as he allowed the new thought to formulate and take hold. His father had cheated for years and with many different women. In all that time, however, he'd never impregnated one of his lovers. Sure, Sean knew some cheating husbands had babies with their lovers and hid the children from their family. But Sean's oldest sister, Danielle, needing to know if they had half-siblings out there, had tracked down every one of Edward's former girlfriends. She hadn't uncovered any other children by Edward Franklin. The five of them were it.

Five, but there should've been six. Between Sean's two youngest sisters, there was another pregnancy, a second Franklin son. One afternoon, his father had driven Brenda to the hospital when her water broke. When they'd returned home, they didn't have a new baby with them. Who knew a child could be "born" dead?

"You selfish, manipulative ass. You kept Mom pregnant and with children to take care of so it would be harder for her to leave you. Out of all the women you screwed, you only managed to get your wife pregnant. How in the hell was that possible?"

Edward pushed to his feet, frame slim but not weak. "Yeah, I'm an ass. I would've done anything to keep my wife."

"Except stop fucking other women. That's all in the hell you had to do. Why didn't you just stop."

"I don't know," he yelled. "I. Don't. Know."

Edward may not know why he'd kept cheating, but Sean knew why he'd ended his affair with Trinity. One reason stood in front of him, weeping like the pathetic man his choices had turned him into. The second reason had just driven away, having made no promise to break down the barrier separating them, so they could talk and begin to build bridges.

"I'm not you. I never want to become you. You can't truly love a woman and treat her the way you treated Mom."

"Remember those words when SJ comes to you, twenty years from now, and throws them in your face for the pain you caused his mother. What will you say to him? Will you tell your only son to go fuck himself because he doesn't know what in the hell he's talking about? Or will you admit that, in marriage, love drives pain and pain drives love? That as much as you love Angie, when you were with that other woman, you traded Angie's pain for your pleasure. Love be damned."

Sean sank onto the bed, and Edward joined him. To his surprise, he found himself asking his father a question.

"How did you get Mom to forgive you?"

Edward's reply surprised Sean even more than his question had.

"She hasn't. I don't think she ever will."

"She hasn't?" Sean knew he was frowning but couldn't help it. "But Mom's still here when she could be any place else." Like living on her own or with one of her grown children.

"She's found peace within herself that has nothing to do with me. I don't question it because I don't want to rock the boat and risk Brenda changing her mind. You're right, I don't deserve her. I never have. Brenda's a good woman."

She was, but that wasn't the primary word Sean would use to describe his mother. He shoved the unkind thought away.

"If you're asking for my advice, then I'd say give Angie time and space."

"That's what her mother told me."

"You should listen."

Sean could give Angie all the space she wanted, but time wasn't on his side. His father got one thing right. None of his affairs had resulted in a pregnancy.

"Yesterday, you asked about Angie and me. How did you know something was wrong between us?"

"I didn't. Not really. The last three times I spoke to Angie she didn't mention you. She normally gives me a quick rundown on you and the kids. The updates on the kids stayed the same, but she omitted you."

"Did that begin in January?"

"I think so. Oh, I get it. That's when Angie found out."

"Yeah, I told her."

Edward blew out a long breath. "You're either brave or stupid. Probably both. A woman like Angie will leave you, you know."

"I know. What I don't know is how to earn her forgiveness and set things right."

"And you didn't touch her, that's how I knew for sure."

"What?"

"When Angie arrived, you didn't touch her. Not a hug or a kiss. Nothing. When a woman is upset with a man, the first things she denies him are her body and affections. I could see how badly you wanted to touch your wife, but also how hard you were trying not to. Angie's eyes also told the story. It's always the eyes, Sean."

"What did you see in hers?"

"Anger. A lot of it. But also sadness. Both are normal, so don't go slamming more bedroom doors. She'll get past the anger. No one holds on to that much anger and breathes. One of these days, she'll exhale and let it all out. Until then, you have to be patient."

Kim had told him that too.

Edward got to his feet. "We haven't talked this long in years. It was nice."

"We talked about cheating on our wives. What's nice about that?"

"Nothing. But I still enjoyed our talk. It gives me hope you may one day forgive me."

Did that mean Edward had given up hope of being forgiven by Brenda? Probably.

No, Sean did not want to end up like his father--broken by his mistakes.

CHAPTER SIXTEEN

Two months ago, Zahra had accused Angie of being stupid when she'd decided to meet Jason. Her best friend hadn't been wrong. She owned her decision, no matter how ill-advised. Angie would also own today's choice, despite the stupidity of this meeting, too. When did Angie's intellect begin to fail her? When had she begun to allow her emotions to overrule her common sense? She knew when--the first time she'd suspected Sean's infidelity but had chosen denial over confrontation.

Roger Damseoux, a partner in Damseoux, Luster, and Bettis law firm, kissed Angie's cheek, lips soft and blue eyes warm yet shrewd. Except for the color, Roger's gaze reminded Angie of Sean's. The law school friends were similar in many ways, their analytical ability one of them. She doubted the lawyer believed her story, despite her having brought along a gift box, wrapped in blue paper with multicolored balloons, as supporting evidence to her lie. If she'd learned nothing else being married to a lawyer, it was the importance of making a lie look like the truth and sticking to that falsehood with steely resolve, steady hands, and unwavering confidence.

Roger may suspect there was more to Angie's story than met the eye, but nothing in her voice or pleasant smile gave away the oddity of her appearance in the man's law firm, on a Friday, an hour before close of business. Angie should still be at EU. Instead, she'd canceled a meeting, driven to the nearest shopping center and picked up a gift box, transparent tape, and wrapping paper. She'd wrapped the box while in her parked car, her mind racing a mile a minute with a plan she'd conjured a month before. In truth, the impetus to do this had invaded Angie's thoughts further back than that. Not to visit Roger Damseoux with a ruse, but the idea of confronting the face of so much of her pain and anger.

Angie would spare herself anyone's pity and disapproval by remaining silent about this meeting. She could upbraid herself, she didn't need her friends and family telling her how foolish she'd been. A more critical person would use the word pathetic. They wouldn't be wrong. Angie felt pathetic, holding an empty, gift-wrapped box and lying to a man she only knew through her husband. As she followed Roger into a brightly-lit conference room, with law books on shelves lining the walls and a wooden table surrounded by four mesh office chairs, she wondered if he knew Sean had used him to wiggle his way out of an uncomfortable work situation.

Angie didn't question whether Sean had cued Roger in. Her husband had divulged his secret to few people, none of whom were outside of their family. He'd surprised her when he'd returned home after his trip to Newark, informing her he'd spoken with his parents about his affair. Sean hadn't gone into details, only noting Edward had suspected a rift in their marriage. Suspecting a rift and Sean revealing his affair failed to align with how she knew his mind worked. While she didn't relish more people knowing, even her in-laws, at least she no longer had to lie and pretend when they spoke on the phone.

"She's in the file room. I'll let her know she has a visitor and send her your way." Pencil-thin in black, pinstriped dress pants and white shirt, Roger straightened to his full five feet, eight inches and smiled at Angie over his shoulder, a Cheshire cat grin contorting his handsome face into pure scheming devilment. "I won't tell her who's come calling. I'll let it be a surprise."

Oh, yes, Roger Damseoux, a proud member of the New York State Bar Association, hadn't missed anything. He knew without being told. His employee's physical condition, Sean's referral, and now Angie's visit, when combined, amounted to circumstantial evidence that wouldn't hold up in court. But in the court of common sense, Roger didn't require more.

"Thank you."

"Of course. I'm sure she'll love your gift."

Angie grinned. Roger had a wicked streak.

She settled herself into a chair opposite the conference room door, crossing her legs and folding her hands on her knees. Angie told herself to stay calm and to keep her hands where they were. Roger Damseoux may have more than his fair share of the devil inside him, but that didn't equate to him turning a blind eye to assault against one of his employees.

The door opened, and Angie breathed in through her nose and out through her mouth. In through her nose and out through her mouth. In through her nose and out through her … The woman entered the room and stopped. She stared at Angie, blinked, and appeared as if she would turn on her heel and run. Perhaps a graceful retreat would be for the best.

For them both.

"Come in and sit down."

"Do you have a gun you're hiding under the table?"

Angie's low, angry laugh came from a place deep within her. A place where she stowed her resentment and plots of revenge lest she did something idiotic, like going and speaking with a woman she hated. Hate was such a harsh word, and she'd never used it before. However, the longer she took in the woman--her youth, her attractiveness, her protruding belly--the more the four-letter word felt right.

"If I wanted you dead, Trinity, I wouldn't have waited four months to do the deed." Unable to stop herself from taking another look, her eyes traveled from Trinity's face to her pregnant stomach. Her own stomach clenched at the sight and the thought that the baby the younger woman carried could be Sean's. Hands rose and settled on the conference table, palms down. "See, no gun. Now come inside and close the door. If you were bold enough to sleep with my husband, then be brave enough to face me."

Trinity shut the door. She appeared no more comfortable with the prospect of being in a closed room with the wife of the man she'd slept with, but she'd risen to Angie's challenge and displayed a backbone critical for her line of work.

Good. Angie wanted to see the real Trinity Richardson. Not the one who'd smiled in her face and spoke with a kind but forked tongue when she'd visited Sean's office. Not the woman who'd indulged an older man's fantasies and who possessed no sense of sisterhood. No, Angie didn't desire to speak with any of those versions of Trinity Richardson.

Angie wanted to confront the woman who thought herself cunning, Sean easy prey, and Angie's family a mechanism to achieving her goal.

"Have a seat. I don't bite, kick, slap, or even pull hair. You do have lovely fake hair, though. All those wonderfully long braids. I assure you, those extensions won't end up on Roger's shiny conference room floor by anything I'll do to you."

"Funny, I recall Sean liked my hair, pulling on it when he had me sprawled over his desk, fucking me from behind."

Angie smiled, showing Trinity her white teeth. "The legal assistant has claws. They aren't big enough to claw your way into Sean's life the way you want, but they might be sharp enough to trap a lesser man than my husband."

"I'm not trying to trap Sean. He didn't wear a condom when we had sex." Trinity patted her second-trimester belly, maybe third, depending on the date of conception. "This is what happens, and there's nothing any of us can do about it. I'm going to have Sean's baby."

"Listen, I didn't come here to argue with you. I didn't even come here to curse you out or to push you down a flight of stairs."

She laughed at the look of horror on Trinity's face and her own ridiculous words. The woman thought Angie serious, as if Sean's affair would drive her to injure a child. Harming a guilty lover was one kind of temptation, but hurting a child went against everything Angie held dear.

Trinity didn't know that about her, so her statement landed the way she'd intended. The same way Trinity's statement about having sex with Sean had hit her target. The reminder hurt, but so did this whole conversation and the sight of Trinity's pregnant body.

"Why are you here then? You shouldn't be. I don't want my boss knowing about Sean."

"You can't be that dense. From what Sean told me, you aren't married or engaged, yet you're pregnant. You may have a boyfriend, although I doubt it. Roger is a smart man. As soon as you stopped being able to hide that belly of yours, Roger knew the truth, even if he's been too polite to say."

"That I'm pregnant with Sean's baby. Maybe he does know."

Trinity did enjoy her less than subtle digs, but Angie only smiled and didn't allow the pain from Trinity's claws to show on her face. She wouldn't give her the satisfaction.

"Get it all out."

"Get what all out?"

"The rest of it. Surely you have more grenades to drop at my feet. I know you slept with my husband. Sean told me. I know the affair lasted two months. I also know Sean broke it off with you." Angie pointed to Trinity's stomach. "He also told me about your baby. *Your* being the operative word. No matter how many times you tell yourself the baby is Sean's, you don't know for sure."

"So that's it. You want me to have the prenatal paternity test. Like I told Sean—"

"You're not having one done. Yes, he told me that too."

Trinity's flared nostrils and rolled eyes telegraphed her mean thoughts before she spat them. "You think you know every damn thing. You didn't know your husband was screwing me and loving every minute of it, did you?"

Angie tilted her head at Trinity, staring at her as if she was an alien who'd gotten lost and landed on Earth yet decided to stay. It wasn't hard to see what had drawn Sean to his former legal assistant. Trinity Richardson was plus-size model pretty, with ample curves and hips to hold on to for a man with big hands like Sean. But there was also much to the younger woman that wouldn't appeal to Sean, let alone encourage him to alter his life to be with her.

"That really is all you got. You don't have anything else to throw in my face, do you? Your ammunition ends with sex with my husband and a baby with indeterminate paternal parentage."

"I know who the father of my baby is," Trinity declared, spittle flying and anger flaring.

"Careful there, dear, your cracks are showing. You have no clue which man's swimmer fertilized that little egg of yours. You only want it to be Sean's, but you also know he's too smart to take your word at face value. He would want proof. You could give him that proof, but you don't want to." Angie tapped the wooden table with her nails, a small release of banked anger. "He's confused by your refusal. Well, only a little. He thinks you're stalling with the hope of him changing his mind about being with you. Sean's only partially right. You do hope he'll change his mind, but you don't think he will as long as I'm in the picture." More tapping, harder and faster. "Your stalling isn't about wearing Sean down but waiting me out. What you really hope will happen, because of your delay and the stress you think your pregnancy has put on Sean's marriage, is that I'll get fed up with him, you and the entire mess, and end my marriage."

Angie's hand slammed against the table, and Trinity jumped.

"He won't change his mind and choose you, even if I file for divorce. If the baby is Sean's, he'll be the father your child deserves. You know that already, and I'm positive he told you the same. You've seen Sean with our children. You know the kind of man he is, which is why you didn't stop him when he didn't use a condom. No woman gets so caught up in the moment that she doesn't remember the minute the man enters her. We're wired that way, to protect our bodies and futures, because lustful men won't think to do either. I'll give you the benefit of the doubt and not assume you planned all of this. Even if you did, Sean made his choices, including not only having sex with you but also doing it without protection. It was a dumb move, but you were smart and took advantage of the opening he gave you. Now, you hope to use your baby to get a husband."

"That's not what I'm doing."

"It is. I'm not Sean. I'm not so full of guilt and shame that I can't see the selfish, desperate, maybe even scared, woman underneath. He can't discern the truth of you because his mind is clouded by his own lies. Trust me, Trinity, Sean's emotional blinders won't be there forever, no matter the state of his relationship with me. Whatever window of opportunity you thought you had has long since passed."

For the first time since entering the conference room, Trinity didn't appear nervous, shocked, or arrogant. She reminded Angie of too many freshmen who entered EU with a footlocker full of hopes and dreams, only to drag that same footlocker to their parent's car a year later when they've failed to meet their own high expectations. But Trinity wasn't a green, eighteen-year-old just beginning her life. Sean hadn't manipulated her into having an affair with him. They'd entered their liaison willingly, understanding the potential repercussions but choosing to ignore them. Both were to blame, although not to the same degree. In the end, Trinity had no responsibility to Angie and her children. That rested with Sean.

In mere seconds, Trinity's lost look morphed into something ugly and mean, and Angie didn't bother bracing herself for whatever the woman would hurl at her. Trinity had no power over Angie, other than whatever she was stupid enough to give her, and she gave her nothing. Everything with Trinity was rinse and repeat. Sean had had sex with her, and he was the father of her child. Beyond those two points, one a truth, the other wishful thinking, Trinity had nothing else she could use to wound Angie.

"If I really wanted Sean, I could've taken him from you." She snapped fingers in the air. "Like that. Easy. It would've been so easy to take Sean away from you ... and your kids."

See, the woman should've ended the sentence with *you*.

Angie marched around the conference table and right up to Trinity, leaving no space between them.

"This is what you'll learn when you become a mother. You'll do anything to protect your children, even from yourself. Most importantly, you'll do all within your power to shield them from pain. You can't, because life doesn't work that way. Let me say this one time, no amount of education, self-control, or morality will keep me from you if you do anything to hurt my children. This is neither a threat nor a warning, but the strongest of maternal facts."

Angie backed away from Trinity and toward the closed door. Being so close to her husband's former lover, regardless of her pregnancy, tested the hell out of her. The primal woman inside Angie wanted to beat the shit out of Trinity. Her fists ached to connect with soft skin, leaving her feeling barbaric and unfulfilled. She shouldn't want to hurt anyone, least of all a pregnant woman. But, god help her, she desired nothing more than to have her revenge, Trinity's black eyes, broken nose and bloody lips a betrayed wife's pound of flesh.

"I know there are people who think the way you do. They believe they have the power to 'take' a person from a spouse, boyfriend, or girlfriend. That's never the case. You may go after the person, be a satellite they can't avoid. But take is the wrong word. It gives you too much power and the other person not enough responsibility for their own decisions. Which is what everything boils down to, you stupid, stupid heifer. Sean is still my husband, not because you chose not to *take* him from me, but because he decided he wanted *me* and *not you*. You can't take a person. They either give themselves to you, or they don't. You know what part of Sean he gave you and so do I. If he'd wanted to give you more, he would have. That's how it works. Too many husbands are quick to share their dicks with other women, but few of them share their hearts, too."

"That's what you came here to tell me? That Sean fucked me but loves you?"

"Not exactly. I brought you something."

Trinity looked to the wrapped box on the table then back to Angie.

"What's inside is everything I see when I look at you and all you'll ever be in life if you continue the way you have been."

Trinity grabbed the box and shook it. "It's light. It doesn't feel like anything is in here."

"Why in the hell would I buy you a gift? There's nothing inside. It's empty. "

"I'm *not* nothing," Trinity screamed at her.

"You're right." Angie snatched the box from Trinity, crushed it with hands that wanted to do the same to the fuming woman, and squeezed it into the small wastebasket. "You're less than nothing."

There went her telegraph again--flared nostrils and rolled eyes. "And you're an old, jealous bitch."

Angie cracked her knuckles before granting Trinity her most luminescent smile. "Oh, sweetie, you have no idea how much of an old, jealous bitch I can be. But you can find out. If you *really* want to know, I'll be glad to show you what we old, jealous bitches are capable of. You won't like the lesson, believe me, but I'll enjoy teaching it to you."

She opened the door. Deep breaths sounded behind Angie, and she exited the conference room before Trinity calmed enough to think of a comeback. Angie needed to leave before she spiraled any more out of control and did something wrong but that she wouldn't regret.

Damn, Sean, and damn herself for permitting this situation to turn her into a cheated-on wife trope.

CHAPTER SEVENTEEN

"Maybe I should leave."

"No, don't do that. I'm sure Angie will be home soon. Something must've come up at work that kept her. She's normally good about not forgetting her appointments."

For the last thirty minutes, Sean had entertained Dr. Sky Ellis, Malcolm's colleague at Eastern Bluebird College and recent girlfriend. Entertained may not be the correct word, although he'd done his best to make her laugh while she waited for Angie. He'd used the time to get to know her better. Angie had invited Sky over for Saturday lunch a couple of times, but they hadn't spoken beyond pleasantries.

Like all of Malcolm's girlfriends, Sky was attractive and intelligent. Unlike the others, Sky was more observant than talkative and more reserved than outgoing. She also didn't have a desperate aura that often clung to single, thirty-something women ready for wife-and-motherhood and all too willing to leg shackle themselves to a man who could give them both, whether they were a good match or not.

Light-brown complexion with brown-green eyes and an Olympic runner's tall, fit frame, Sky Ellis was a beautiful woman. No wonder

Malcolm had come to Angie for help. What single man wouldn't want to date and get to know Sky better.

Sean and Sky sat across from each other at the kitchen island. At his urging, she'd followed him into the kitchen. Angie was late for her dinner date with Sky, the least he could do was provide her with light fare while she waited. For Sky, light fare meant cold water, no ice, and a bowl of green, seedless grapes she ate with a fork. He'd considered cooking fries to see if she'd eat them with a fork too.

Probably.

What in the world would junk food junkie Malcolm Styles do with a woman who didn't expect an engagement ring from him and who ate perfectly good finger foods with a fork?

Sean laughed. He knew precisely what his brother-in-law would do. Malcolm would marry the lovely Dr. Sky Ellis of Annapolis, Maryland.

"Hey, Dr. Sky."

SJ stood behind Sky at the edge of the kitchen. His smile couldn't get any brighter or his crush any harder.

Sky swiveled on the barstool to face the teen. "Hi, SJ. It's good to see you again. What have you been up to?"

Beaming, SJ strutted into the kitchen--a peacock in heat without the colorful feathers. "Nothing much. Do you like basketball?"

"A little. Maryland doesn't have a basketball team."

"That sucks. Knicks, Liberty, Nets -- New York has three basketball teams and that's not counting minor league. Dad recorded my championship basketball game and uploaded it to Google Drive. Want to watch? My laptop is already in the living room."

"SJ, I'm sure Sky doesn't want to—"

"No, it's fine." Sky picked up Sean's cell phone from the island and handed it to him. "I'll watch SJ's game, and you can answer the person who keeps calling you. I don't want you missing a call on my account. If Angie doesn't come home soon or return one of our calls, I'll go home and get in touch with her later." Sky patted his forearm and stood. "No worries, Sean, you've been a wonderful host. Spending time alone with you wasn't as horrific as I thought it would be."

What had she said? Was the woman serious or yanking his chain? Sean couldn't tell. Her blank expression revealed nothing. Then she smiled--a wide, toothy grin and twinkling eyes. Oh, man, Malcolm would be swimming in the deep end of the pool with Sky. Sean self-corrected, Sky was unlike any of Malcolm's other girlfriends. She had the power to break his heart or to elevate his world.

"Great." SJ's loud clap had Sean wincing. The boy had a lot to learn about girls and playing it cool. "Come on, Dr. Sky. I can't wait for you to see all the points I earned. I wasn't the highest scorer, but I left everything on the court the way Dad always tells me to." SJ's hand found Sky's and he led her out of the kitchen.

Maybe his son knew a thing or two about females after all because Sky only smiled and allowed the smitten teen to lead the way to the living room.

Sean's phone vibrated again. How many damn times would she call him? He'd told Trinity, unless it was an emergency, not to contact him.

The vibration stopped. Sean didn't look away from his phone. Sure enough, less than a minute passed before the vibration started again. He'd never forgive himself if the baby was in distress, and Trinity needed his help, and he'd blown her off. A true emergency should have Trinity calling 9-1-1, though, not him.

Punching the phone with his knuckle, Sean answered.

"It's about damn time you picked up. I bet you were sitting right next to your phone every time I called, looking at it and ignoring me."

No goddamn emergency, as he thought. The woman was unbelievable, and he was a fool.

"What do you want?"

"For you to keep your crazy ass wife the hell away from me."

"I have no idea what you're talking about."

Sean shoved from the island and went to the backdoor that led from the kitchen to the backyard. Kayla pushed Zuri on the swing, the girls laughing and enjoying the warm May evening and the end of the school week.

He watched them for a minute, before strolling from the kitchen and up to his room. With the toe of a shoe, he closed the door. Sean didn't know what was going on, but he would be damned if Sky or one of his children overheard him speaking to Trinity.

"Tell her to stay away from me, or I'll call the cops the next time I see her."

"I still have no clue what you're going on about. Calm down."

"Don't tell me to calm down. You aren't the one your crazy wife threatened."

"You saw my wife?"

"That's what I said. You aren't listening to me."

"I'm listening, but nothing you've said makes sense."

From the room's south window, Sean could keep an eye on his girls in the fenced-in yard. Sometimes Zuri got it into her mind to jump from the swing at the highest point. Her jumps were perfect. Her landings not so much.

"She came to the law firm and spoke with Roger. I have no idea what she said, but he found me in the file room and told me I had a visitor."

"The visitor was Angie?"

"Yes, it was your wife, and Roger didn't tell me. If I'd known, I wouldn't have walked in there like a blind fool. I wouldn't have gone into the conference room at all."

It had to be true. Trinity wouldn't make up this kind of lie. Still, Sean found it difficult to wrap his head around the news. Then again, he had no idea what went through his wife's mind nowadays. They shared the same house but little else. Sean and Angie had developed a peaceful co-existence, these past months, as long as he didn't mention his affair or their reconciliation. She refused to talk about their future until they knew the baby's paternity. With Trinity's obstinance, Sean and Angie's relationship remained in limbo, frustrating the hell out of him.

"What did she say?"

"That she should push me down a flight of stairs. I can't believe you're married to a crazy bitch like that."

"Watch how you speak about my wife."

"Oh, you don't like that I called her a bitch, which she is, but you don't have anything to say about her threatening me?"

"I won't tolerate anyone calling my wife names. You don't get a pass because we had sex. Angie wouldn't hurt your baby, no matter what she may have said to you."

"Don't think I missed how you narrowed Angie's threat down to my baby. What about me?"

Sean turned away from his playing girls and sank to the foot of his bed. Angie was the most logical and balanced of the Styles. During an emergency, she was the epitome of cool, calm, and collected. Little unsettled her, mainly because she kept an iron grip on her strong, "undesirable," as she viewed them, emotions. Sean's affair, however, had shaken Angie to her core. He'd never seen her so driven by her harsher emotions than she'd been since his confession.

Those same emotions, apparently, had compelled Angie to confront Trinity and to offer a hollow threat she had to have known the younger woman would take to heart.

His wife wasn't a crazy bitch. Angie was a woman in pain. A woman Sean couldn't reach. A woman who, with each passing week, he was losing.

"Angie doesn't care anything about you beyond whether your baby is mine. We hurt her. More me than you. If you've never experienced that kind of betrayal, then you have no idea what our affair did to her. I don't expect you to know or to even care. That's for me to do."

"You're right, I don't care. The only thing I care about is you keeping her away from me."

"If you would stop cancelling every appointment I schedule to have the test done, she wouldn't have felt a need to visit you at work. All we want to know is whether the baby is mine."

Trinity had no immediate response so Sean returned to the window. Zuri ran around the yard, kicking and chasing an inflatable, rainbow-colored beach ball while avoiding a flipping Kayla.

"That's not why she came to the office."

"It isn't? Tell me what she said then."

"If you want to know, ask her."

He could. Angie would either ignore Sean or they'd argue. Dear god, something just occurred to him. "What did you say to Angie?" Fingers clutched the phone, and beads of sweat broke out on his forehead. "What did you tell my wife."

Trinity's self-satisfied laughter streamed through the line and punched him in the gut. "I guess you do care about Angie visiting me after all, even if you don't give a damn about my welfare."

"This isn't a joke or a game. It's my marriage."

"Right, your marriage, not mine. You're awfully concerned about your wife and marriage now. Where was all that concern when you had your dick in my mouth?"

Sean closed his eyes and slid to the floor. "Is that what you told Angie? That you gave me blowjobs?"

"I told her you fucked me on your desk. You know, the same desk that has the picture of your smiling kids and blind, naive wife."

Head dropped to raised knees, and he felt like the passengers aboard the sinking Titanic, more fearful of the freezing water and unknown than staying on a doomed ship. "You shouldn't have told her that."

"Why not? It's the truth. You confessed, right? I guess not everything, though. She took the blow like a champ. But the way she smiled at me ... She's scary. I don't know how you sleep under the same roof as her. She'd sooner slit your cheating throat than forgive you. FYI, Angie won't ever forgive you. The woman I saw today is incapable of forgiveness. The sooner you realize you're spinning your wheels waiting for her to get past our affair, the quicker you can move on with your life."

He lifted his head, feeling the ship under him heeling to one side. "With you, you mean?"

"Maybe. If you want to."

"I don't want to, and Angie will forgive me, not that it's any of your business."

Trinity's scoff grated. "She won't. You're delusional. What will you do when you finally realize how wrong you've been and that you've wasted months on a heartless woman?"

Not heartless. Too much heart.

"Don't call me again until you've had the baby. If I must go through the court to force the issue of a paternity test, I will. I won't be your emotional prisoner, and I won't allow your delay to ruin what's let of my marriage."

"Don't treat me as if your messed-up marriage is my fault."

"It's not your fault, but you're deliberately dragging out our connection. I told you, I'm never going to leave my wife for you. Just to be clear, I'm not going to leave my wife for anyone. I love Angie, and I hope she still loves me after what I've put her through."

Sean heard a bouncing basketball in the upstairs hallway. How many times did Sean and Angie have to tell SJ not to play ball in the house? If his son was upstairs, did that mean Sky had gone home?

He got to his feet. Nothing about Sky left him with the impression of her being the kind of person who would leave a house without saying goodbye. Which meant one thing. Angie was home.

"I have to go."

"That's it, then?"

"Yeah, that's it. You don't want me. I'm too old and too married for you. I was before our affair and I should've left it at that. I still am, but I have no intention of revisiting my error in judgment."

"Error in judgment? That's all I am to you?"

"You know what I mean."

"Yeah, I do." *Click.*

Sean tossed the phone onto the bed. Trinity would punish him, and it wasn't a leap to figure out how. She would make him wait until after the baby's birth to have the paternity test performed. So be it. He'd made no headway convincing her to have it done sooner, anyway. Early August felt like years away. It couldn't come soon enough for Sean.

He rushed from the room and down the stairs, coming to a halt when he saw Angie at the front door with Sky.

"I'm really sorry I'm late and for not returning Sean's and your calls. I must've left my phone in my office because I can't find it in my car or pocketbook."

"You don't have to keep apologizing. It's fine. Sean was great and SJ gave me a tutorial on all things basketball."

"Don't tell me, he talked you into watching his championship basket-ball game with him."

"He offered, and I agreed. I didn't mind. It made SJ happy to share his success."

"You're very nice, Sky, and I feel bad about keeping you waiting. If you're still up for dinner, we can leave for the restaurant as soon as I hunt down my girls for a quick hug and kiss."

"They're in the backyard." Hands in pockets, Sean walked toward the women, his gaze on his wife. "I was watching them from my bedroom window. They're fine. Kayla may be dizzy from all the jumps, spins, and flips I saw her doing. Some days, I don't know if all those ballet and gym-nastics lessons will yield us a contemporary ballerina or a circus performer."

"I'll be right back, Sky."

Angie hustled down the hall and toward the kitchen, not a word to Sean. She hadn't even met his eyes when he'd approached.

"I ... um ... Let Angie know I'm in my car and will follow her to the restaurant. No rush, if you two need to talk before she leaves."

"Angie will be right back. You don't have to wait in the car."

"It's fine. Malcolm sent me two silly texts I've ignored but should an-swer. I'll do that in my car, which will give Angie a few extra minutes. It was nice seeing you again, Sean. Take care."

With a polite smile, Sky exited through the door Sean opened for her. If Malcolm hadn't told her about Angie and his marital problems, she sure knew now.

Sean waited for Angie by the front door. True to her word, she didn't take long. The click of her heels preceded the sight of her rounding the corner.

"We're talking when you get back, whether you want to or not."

"You're standing in front of the door, please move."

"We're talking when you get back, whether you want to or not."

"I heard you the first time, now move. I've kept Sky waiting long enough."

Sean moved but repeated his sentence.

Angie ignored him and left.

Sean stewed the three hours she was gone. He played one-on-one in the backyard with SJ, his son beating him three games to one. "Your mind isn't on the game, Dad, and I'm killin' it."

His mind hadn't been on the game but the conversation to come. If he left it up to his wife to seek him out when she returned home, she wouldn't, so he took the choice from her.

"We need to talk," Sean said the moment Angie entered her bedroom and saw him sitting on a bed they no longer shared.

She slammed the door. "Why?" Kicking off shoes, Angie picked them up and stored the heels in the closet, along with the black blazer she shrugged off. "I don't have anything to say to you, and I'm tired. I want to shower, spend time with the kids, then go to sleep."

"Which leaves no room for us. The way you like it."

"It's not the way I like it. It's the way you've made it and the best way I can deal with you."

"By not dealing with me, you mean?"

"Yes," she snapped, "by not dealing with you. You act as if I'm supposed to fall into line, accepting and getting past your affair because you're sorry and you want me to. You walk around here with those god-damn guilty eyes of yours and I hate them. I hate the hole in my heart that refuses to heal. I hate being angry all the time almost as much as I hate being sad. I hate coming home because I know you'll be here and nothing about seeing you will bring me joy the way it used to. And I hate that you've stolen that once taken-for-granted pleasure from me. I hate that you always want to talk, and I don't. Not because it's not the healthy action to take, but because I can't bring myself to delve any deeper into the wound that is our hemorrhaging marriage. You want to talk? You want to know what I'm thinking and feeling? Fine, by all means, let's talk."

A petite ball of fire and vulnerability, Angie stood in the middle of the room, arms crossed over chest. Trinity was right, this Angie was frightening, not because she was a danger to anyone but for all the anguish she'd buried inside. Hurt he'd asked her to excavate each time he pushed for a real conversation. They did need to talk to each other, to irrigate the wound so it could begin to heal. But they couldn't do it on their own.

"I think we should see a marriage counselor." She opened her mouth but Sean cut off whatever she'd been about to say. "Just hear me out before you reject the idea because I suggested it. I told you I don't want a divorce, and that's still true. I want us to work. I think, deep down, so do you. If you didn't, you would've hired a divorce lawyer and thrown me out of the house again. I also know our chances of working things out depends a lot on whether I'm the baby's father."

Sean wouldn't mention the phone call he'd received from Trinity. Angie had to have suspected she would've contacted him after her surprise visit to the law firm

Edward and Brenda hadn't sought counseling, and while they remained together, their "marriage of convenience" wasn't the kind of marriage he wanted to have with Angie.

Sean stood, but didn't force the issue by going to his wife and invading her space with his need for closeness. "Don't answer now, but please think about it. You can choose anyone you like, or we can select a counselor together. Either option will work for me as long as we do this together."

Trinity had told Angie they'd had sex in his office and on his desk. No wonder she'd forgotten about her dinner date with Sky and hadn't come home right after meeting with Trinity. What had she done afterward? Had she sat in her car and cried, cursing him for cheating on her? Had she second-guessed her decision to permit him to move back into their home? Perhaps she'd decided to hire a lawyer, letting him find out when he was served divorce papers. Or maybe Angie was exhausted, as she'd said, and needed sleep and time alone to digest another awful detail of his affair, refortify her heart, and shore up her defenses.

All of those scenarios were possible but none of them pleased Sean, although, some were worse than others.

"Will you think about it?"

She stared at him. The North Pole would've been warmer. Shaking her head, she walked away from him and back toward her closet. "I'm going to take a shower. Leave and close the door behind you."

"I'll leave after you promise to think about marriage counseling." Sean held no leverage, which didn't dissuade him from acting as if he did. "Marriage counseling, Angie, we need to go. I'll stop nagging you about having heart-to-hearts, if you agree to seriously consider going to counseling with me."

She swung around to face him, pants fisted in a hand. "Why in the hell should I go to counseling? You're the one who cheated. That's something you need to deal with."

"I know it is. But it makes the most sense for us to go together. Like I said, don't answer now. Let my idea marinate. Look up a few local marriage counselors, and see what they do and how it works. I don't mind going for my issues, but we'll get the most out of counseling if we go together. It's unhealthy to keep so much bottled inside. You'll give yourself a heart attack or stroke."

Angie turned away from Sean again and continued to undress, heedless of her nudity, his presence, and the fact that they hadn't made love in three months. Three long months ... his wife's naked body looked as good as he remembered.

She wasn't trying to tease or tempt him, although he wished she would. Angie held no ulterior motive for undressing in front of him. She simply didn't give a damn because she had no intention of lowering the drawbridge to any part of herself.

Body or heart.

"Mother's Day is Sunday," he said for lack of anything else to say that wouldn't be redundant. Forcing his eyes to obey, he dragged his gaze from Angie's breasts to her cold eyes. Too late, he caught his mistake.

Mother's Day was Sunday. He'd cheated, and his former lover was pregnant. Of course Angie had gone to see Trinity.

Shit.

"Angie, I—"

"Get out. I don't want to talk to or see you."

Wetness glistened in her eyes, and the hurt shining through them twisted his gut in painful spasms of guilt.

"Right, yeah, okay. I'll leave."

Angie wouldn't consider therapy. If their marriage remained intact through the summer, it would be a miracle.

CHAPTER EIGHTEEN

Sean stored Angie's small, rolling suitcase in her trunk and closed the hood. "Make sure you call me when you get to Newark."

"I always do." Leaning against the driver's side door of her freshly washed sedan, she looked up at him. "Thank you for helping Malcolm and Sky. They can't keep their office romance a secret forever."

"Four months is a pretty good run, but you're right. While EBC doesn't have a policy forbidding romantic relationships between colleagues, a letter of mutual consent, signed by them, is good security. Malcolm didn't need a lawyer to draw up the letter, but he's smart and understands the added credibility an attorney affords to that kind of document. I was just glad he asked."

At first, the conversation had been awkward, with Malcolm and Sean having spoken little to each other since Malcolm had become aware of Sean's affair. He didn't blame his brother-in-law for withdrawing from him, no matter how painful the loss of his friendship.

So when Malcolm had come to Sean requesting a personal favor couched as a professional service, he'd jumped at the opportunity. For the first time in too long, they'd had a real conversation. As far as progress went, it was a small step, but reconciliations were paved with steps of all sizes.

"Malcolm's still your friend. He'll eventually come around."

"He's your loyal brother first."

Malcolm wouldn't change his mind about Sean and their friendship if Angie divorced him. Brother and sister were a package deal. Like everyone who enjoyed deals, Sean wanted both. He would soon know whether he would continue to have a wife to come home to or a lonely apartment after she got rid of him.

Sean took hold of Angie's hand, small and warm. January to July had been the worse months of their marriage. As SJ's birthday month ended, Sean feared his marriage could follow.

"I don't want to keep anything from you," Sean told Angie.

"I know."

"If I could think of a private place other than my office or her apartment, we would meet there. But the baby's only a few days old."

"I know," she repeated, voice soft and eyes cast downward instead of up and on him.

"I'm only going there to have the test done. I want to ensure Trinity goes through with it. It's the reason why I bought the DNA home paternity test instead of relying on her to make testing arrangements."

"I said I know."

Sean released Angie's hand, when she tugged. He prayed it was the only part of her he'd have to let go.

"I'm sorry. I didn't want to lay this on you before you left to spend the weekend with Kayla and my parents. But I didn't want to do this behind your back, especially since I must go to her apartment. Nothing is going to happen between us, and nothing has happened since I broke it off last year. You can trust me."

Brown eyes snapped to his, and he thought she would object to his assertion that she could trust him. Angie didn't. Instead, she pushed from her car and got inside.

Sean caught the door before she closed it in his face. Barely. "Kayla's last day with the AileyCamp is August tenth. I'll drive down and bring her home."

All summer, they'd alternated spending weekends with Kayla in Newark. At ten, Kayla was old enough to spend six weeks away from Buffalo, but she missed home, and Angie missed her eldest daughter. The weekend visits made Angie and Kayla happy, so Sean didn't complain.

"I'm going to take care of everything. One way or another, we'll know the truth in three to five days."

"Three to five days?"

"It's the time frame given for the test results after the paternity test kit is received in the company's lab. I guess it'll be longer than that, if you take into consideration mail time and it being the weekend. Since I'm the one who ordered the kit, the testing company will call me with the results, followed by an email and a certified letter, if I request one."

"What if the baby is yours? What will you do?"

He wanted to ask her similar questions but feared her answers. Angie's questions had nothing to do with their marriage and everything to do with legalities.

"If the results say I'm the father, I'll upgrade the privacy test to a legal test, which includes a professional sample collection." He could go into more details about the process but chose not to when his wife looked as if she would hurl. Sean crouched to her level and reclaimed her hand. "Don't give up on us yet. You've stuck with me for six months, give me another week before you decide the fate of our marriage. Please, Angie."

"Sean, I—"

He hugged her, hard and desperately. Hair tickled his nose as he inhaled Angie's amber-vanilla scent. Sean nuzzled her pulsating neck and squeezed twice before standing. Unfazed by her lack of reciprocity, Sean smiled down at her. Angie hadn't castrated him for daring to touch her. In Sean's book that was a minor miracle. "Drive safely. I love you."

He moved away from her car, so she could close the driver's side door and reverse down the driveway. Sean waved, and so did Angie.

An hour later, Sean stood in a nursery with dark-blue walls and cloud decals. Two mobile airplanes hung from the ceiling--one black, the other white--over the crib of the sleeping baby. Big bold letters were affixed to the wall behind the crib and between the cloud decals. A single name. Not Sean, thank god, but Trayvon. He didn't know whether Trinity had named her son after Trayvon Martin, a seventeen-year-old African American male unjustifiably shot and killed by George Zimmerman, whether it was a family name or one she just liked, or whether it was the name of the other potential father. One thing was certain, Trinity had known the gender and name of her child before his birth.

Sean hadn't because he hadn't wanted to know.

"You didn't waste any time bringing me this." Trinity hovered behind Sean as he watched the sleeping baby. "What am I supposed to do with this?"

"There are two buccal swabs inside. One for me and one for Trayvon. They're non-invasive, so they won't harm him." He faced Trinity, as tired-looking as any mother of a newborn. Dressed in blue leggings and an oversized black shirt, no bra, he could tell, she frowned from the box and to him. "A swab to the inside of the cheek. Ten seconds, that's all the time it'll take to get a sample. I'll secure the swabs, the way it's explained in the instruction booklet, then I'll mail everything off to the lab. We'll know the result next week."

"You got it all figured out. Two swabs and then you're done with me, huh?"

If Sean was lucky, he would be finished, once and for all, with Trinity Richardson. If not ...

"I just want to know the truth. We all deserve to know, especially the baby."

"He's asleep. You'll have to wait until he wakes up for his next feeding."

"When will that be?"

"A couple of hours."

"Fine. I'll be back in two hours."

"Wait. You're going to leave?"

"There's no reason for me to stay."

Sean glanced over his shoulder at Trayvon. Dressed in a white onesie and covered with a blue receiving blanket with baseballs, the little guy had a headful of wavy, dark-black hair and was a cutie. Trayvon's honey-brown complexion matched his, and he was as long as SJ had been as a newborn. But Sean could see none of himself in the baby. Perhaps that would change, if he was awake or older. Babies appearances changed weekly. It was no telling who Trayvon would favor in three or six months.

Trinity had given birth a little earlier than Sean had expected, which could mean everything or nothing at all.

He left the nursery, swallowing his anger at yet another delay. When Sean reached the front door he stopped then swung around to confront Trinity who'd followed his retreat.

"This is bullshit. Even now you're playing games. Did you put my name on his birth certificate?"

"I told you I didn't. I didn't put a father's name."

"Is the other guy going to take the test, or did you have it done for him and know the results?"

"You're out of your mind." She still held the paternity test kit in her hand. "He's a sweet baby. The delivery was painful but not as bad as I heard it could be."

"I'm glad you're both fine, and Trayvon does seem like a sweet baby. But I need to know if he's *my* sweet baby or some other man's."

"Why are you acting like this? We had a good time together. If we were a family, we'd have an even better time."

"I have a family."

He'd visited Trinity's apartment once before. It was the last time he'd had sex with her. When Sean had entered her apartment and laid in her bed, he'd feared he'd crossed into potentially irredeemable territory. Sex in Trinity's bed was a level of intimacy he'd avoided. It had been dangerously close to entering the realm of a real relationship, a relationship beyond the boundaries of illicit sex in his office.

Sean couldn't have that, so he'd ended their affair and hadn't looked back. He'd regretted much the last year but never that decision.

"I know you do, but we could also be a family. Why don't you want that?"

"I don't want it because I don't love you. And you don't love me, so don't act as if you do. We crossed a line we shouldn't have. But nothing we did was remotely close to love. That baby in the other room could be the result of what should've never happened between us. That's not his fault. It's ours. Or it's yours and another man's. Either way, there's no future for us. We've been through all of this before, and I sound like an old, broken record."

"You're just old, Sean. An old man who has been a pain in my ass with all your whining over a self-absorbed woman you cheated on. You and Angie deserve each other."

"We do deserve each other." Sean wouldn't bother correcting Trinity's assessment of Angie. Her opinion of them didn't matter. All he cared about was her acceptance that Sean wouldn't leave his family for her, regardless of Trayvon's parentage.

A shrill sound he hadn't heard since Zuri was a baby lifted his spirits and brought a smile to his lips.

"Not two hours after all. Your son is up. Let's go check on him and get my DNA sample."

"You're a real bastard."

Yeah, a bastard who would either become a father for the fourth time, or a man released from prison on a technicality.

Trinity cursed Sean the entire way to the nursery and his smile didn't dim one watt.

Angie glanced over her shoulder and to her right before changing lanes. She disliked driving behind big vehicles, like the white moving van she'd just switched lanes to avoid. She'd be at her exit soon, so she might as well get over early.

As much as Angie loved her in-laws and was pleased with Sean's idea to have Kayla attend summer dance camp in Newark, she couldn't wait to bring her baby home. Yes, Kayla was no longer a baby and Angie worked to remember not to treat her as one. But all her children were her babies, no matter their age, and not seeing Kayla's exuberant face every day had brought out the side of her that spoiled her children and dared anyone to question her maternal instincts.

No matter how much she may wish to stop time, her children would continue to grow and develop, no longer needing her as much as they did now. SJ turned fifteen this summer and Zuri five. Her youngest would begin kindergarten in the fall, another milestone for the Franklins. Kayla would turn eleven in October, her birthday month the same as Malcolm's and Kim's. Her children were getting older and she would have to learn to let go so they could spread their wings and discover the depths of themselves. Sean referred to it as a "gradual release," a term Angie knew well as an educator.

Angie and Sean hadn't spoken, beyond a compulsory phone call to him when she'd arrived at the Franklins'. Before she'd hung up, he'd said two things: "I mailed off the paternity test kit" and "No matter the result, know I love you and our children."

She hadn't been able to think of much else the entire weekend. This time next week, she'd know whether Sean had fathered a child with another woman. The awful thought had kept Angie from enjoying Mother's Day. The knowledge of Trinity's impending birth had put a damper on most family functions, Angie obsessed with not knowing the truth. She couldn't see past Trinity's pregnancy to get to a place where she could begin to truly deal with Sean's lies and affair.

It had left Angie paralyzed and Sean in a perpetual apologetic state, buying her one unnecessary gift after another. He had no clue how to deal with her because she herself had no idea how to grapple with her emotions and move forward without sacrificing the last twenty years of her life.

Slowing, Angie took the next exit. She'd left Newark at almost nine in the evening. She'd made good time and should arrive home around four. Her first meeting on Monday wasn't until ten, leaving her time for a few hours of sleep before heading out to EU. Sean liked for her to call him, when she was close to home. No matter the time, he would drag himself out of bed and downstairs, greeting her at the front door with a chilled pineapple and kale smoothie. In those moments, Angie forgot he'd broken her heart and made her cry.

The light turned yellow and Angie eased off the accelerator, while two cars to her left sped up and powered through the light just as it turned red.

She wouldn't call Sean this time and disturb his rest. She'd be home soon enough.

Beep. Beep.

Her wayward thoughts had her missing when the light changed to green.

Beep. Beep.

"Okay, okay, I'm going." She moved into the intersection.

Beeeep. "It's not that serious, lady. The light just chang—"

Screeeech. Bang.

Sean bolted up in bed, heart pounding and head aching. Breaths came hard and fast and still he felt as if he couldn't breathe. Shoving the comforter away, he tumbled out of bed, almost falling into the nightstand. He steadied himself, one hand going to the wall beside the bed, the other to his heaving chest.

Was he having a heart attack? If not, what in the hell was wrong with him? A panic attack, maybe. He'd never heard of a person having a panic attack while sleeping, though. A nightmare? Sean couldn't recall dreaming, although a nightmare would explain the sense of fear radiating through his body.

"What time is it?" The room was dark, and the blinds closed, but he could see the glowing numbers from the clock on the nightstand. "Four thirty." He rubbed his face, working to shake off the remnants of a bad dream he couldn't recall.

Cold water to the face would help. Sean started for the door, hoping he'd make it to the bathroom without falling flat on his face. He stopped. "Four thirty. Angie should've been back by now. Why didn't she call me, so I could meet her at the door?"

Heart beating wildly and body slick with perspiration, he marched from his room to his wife's. The door was as wide open as it had been when Sean had passed it on his way to bed. When Angie turned in for the night, she pulled the door almost closed. That hadn't changed since Sean stopped sharing the room with her. If not for the children, particularly Zuri, Angie would close the door all the way.

Sean entered the room and turned on the light. No rolling suitcase. No Angie.

"You should've called, if you were going to be late," Sean muttered, continuing his one-sided conversation. "Come on, Angie, you know how this works." Grabbing the phone from Angie's nightstand, Sean called his wife and waited. "Come on, come on, pick up." Voicemail. He called back. She didn't answer. Sean called over and again, each time thrown into voicemail after a string of unanswered rings.

She wouldn't not answer her cell. Angie knew Sean worried when she made the trek between Newark and Buffalo by herself. They'd long since gotten past the point of Angie avoiding his phone calls.

Sean called for a tenth time. "Dammit." He slammed the phone onto the cradle only to pick it back up and dial again.

The phone rang four times and, thank god, someone answered. "Hello."

Sleepy and annoyed but Sean couldn't be happier to hear the voice. "Dad. It's me."

"Why in the hell are you calling this time of morning?"

"I'm sorry, but would you put Angie on the phone? She's not answering her cell, and I'd like to speak with her."

Edward's muffled yawn and pause had Sean biting back an impatient command for his father to get the hell out of bed and go check on Angie.

"You sound breathless. Don't tell me you've become one of those health fanatics who gets up at the crack of dawn to jog or some other stupid exercise like that."

His fist clenched, and he contemplated putting it through a wall. "Dad, just put Angie on the line then you can go back to sleep."

"Maybe the air in New York is different than in Jersey because your brain isn't working right. Angie left here hours ago. I asked her to give us a call when she got home. I didn't really expect her to call us at four, but later in the morning once she got settled at work. You know, Angie and Kayla—"

"She's not here. I called her phone so many times, but she hasn't picked up."

"Okay, Sean. Calm down."

"Calm? My wife's not with you, and she's not here with me. She should be here, Dad."

"Look, it's only a little before five. Traffic, even this time of morning, can be terrible. Don't go off the deep end. I'm sure Angie's fine."

From the moment he'd awakened, everything had felt terribly, horribly wrong. The deep end would be a relief compared to the fear assaulting him.

"She's probably in traffic and her phone died. Don't get yourself worked up over nothing. Angie will be pulling into the driveway any minute now, you'll see. Do you hear me, Sean?"

He heard Edward, but every fiber in his body screamed his life had taken an awful turn.

"Listen, why don't you ... What's that?"

"Someone is calling on the other line. Hold on, Dad." Sean switched to the new caller, body taut and mouth dry. "Franklin residence."

"This is Officer Fitch of the Buffalo Police Department. Are you related to Angela Styles-Franklin?"

Two sentences had never been so hard to force from his throat. "She's my wife. What's happened?"

Somewhere between the words "car crash" and "air ambulance" Sean's world shifted and fell apart.

CHAPTER NINETEEN

"What in the hell is taking so long?" Sean forced himself to stay seated and not to rush the nurse's station again and demand an update. A fist slammed down on the arm of his chair. "I hate all this waiting. It's driving me crazy."

"Come on, bro, let's go for a walk."

Sean shook his head. "I can't leave. What if something happens while we're gone?"

Malcolm swore under his breath. Unwilling to leave Zuri and SJ alone in the house until his in-laws arrived, Sean had arrived at the hospital after Malcolm. Sure, SJ was old enough to stay home alone with Zuri, but Sean would've had to wake him and explain what had happened to Angie. He couldn't have that conversation yet, not until Angie was out of surgery and he'd spoken with the surgeon.

"You're right. But you have to keep it together."

"Keep it together? Some asshole ran a red light and plowed into my wife's car, and now she's in an operating room fighting for her life. How am I supposed to keep it together?"

Sean, hunched over in his chair, straightened and looked at his brother-in-law. Like Sean, Malcolm's face wore the ravages of worry and fear. His long dreadlocks were free from their normal confines, and he was dressed in baggy jeans, a wrinkled T-shirt and untied sneakers. "She's your sister. How are you doing?"

"I feel like I'm breathing with a knife in my chest. It hurts like hell. I'm trying not to think about what happened to Angie or what's going on in the operating room."

"Because those thoughts lead to other thoughts, I know." Like, what would they do if Angie didn't survive. "I'm blocking them out the best I can, but it's damn near impossible the longer she's in there."

Eleven other people sat in the surgery waiting area. From how they were clustered, they appeared to be from four different families. Two mounted, flat screen televisions were on. The one to Sean's right was turned to a cable news station. The other, on the far wall in front of him, displayed a patient status board. The color-coded board indicated each patient's progress from admission to surgery to recovery. According to the status board, Angie was still in surgery. Sean and Malcolm would have to wait until she reached the green recovery phase before visitors would be allowed to see her.

"We'll get through this together. We're family. It's what we do." Malcolm got to his feet and reached out his hand to Sean, who took it. The shorter man pulled him to his feet and into a tight hug. "My sister is the strongest person I know, and the stubbornest. Angie won't leave us, and she sure as hell won't leave her children. Have faith."

Sean held on to Malcolm and his words of support. What else did he have but his brother-in-law's reassurance and supporting arms? He wasn't in this alone. After Sean had hung up with the police officer, he'd stood in Angie's bedroom with no idea what to do next. His arms and legs wouldn't move, and his brain had skidded to a helpless stop. His senses had narrowed to the bed where his wife should be and where two of their children had been conceived.

In those minutes, Sean had replayed the laughter and love Angie and he had shared in that room. His mind had then conjured an image of a weeping Angie, himself kneeling, his confession of Trinity's pregnancy dripping from his lips. The wretched memory had jolted him out of his malaise and into action.

"Thank you." Sean slapped Malcolm's back before releasing him. "You're right. If I give in to worst-case scenario thinking, I'll be no good to the kids or to myself."

Over Malcolm's shoulder, Sean saw a set of familiar faces coming toward them. Malcolm turned, wrapping Kim in the same bear hug he'd gifted to Sean. She wept, and Sean wanted to turn away from her pain. Charles spread his big arms around his son and wife, holding them close. Sean went to step back, but Charles grabbed his shirt and yanked him forward, bringing him firmly into the family hug.

"We came as soon as Debbie and Gary got to your house." Aunt Debbie was one of Charles's many siblings, Gary, her husband of forty years. "Don't worry about the kids. We got them covered while you're here. The aunts, uncles, and cousins will take shifts. Whatever you need, they'll take care of, son. Don't worry."

The Styles never ceased to amaze and humble Sean with their closeness and love. He hadn't met a Styles who didn't possess a big heart. They were big believers in acts of kindness. They were unique individuals as well as a cohesive clan. He valued each of them and wouldn't know what he'd do without Angie and them in his life. He'd risked so much with his affair with Trinity. Sean hoped he'd have the chance to fix what he'd broken.

"What's Angie's patient ID number?" Kim asked him, glancing over her shoulder to the surgery patient tracking board."

"It's four, seven, five, three, two."

Kim nodded, and Sean felt a small weight lifting from his shoulders. His mother-in-law would keep track of Angie's progress.

By silent agreement, the quartet moved to sit in the chairs to wait, with Kim and Charles flanking him, each holding one of his hands. At some point, Malcolm called Sky and Sean thought the man would break down when he heard her voice. Malcolm's reaction spoke volumes about the depth of his feelings for Sky.

"Is she coming to the hospital?" Kim asked. "Charles and I haven't met her yet."

"No. She's at a summer leadership retreat in Hamilton, New York. Sky offered to fly home early, but I told her not to."

"It's sweet she would offer. Why didn't you accept?"

Malcolm shrugged. "Look at me, Mom, I'm an emotional wreck. I don't need her seeing me like this. Besides, Sky's new to her job and EBC's president wanted her to attend the retreat. After Dean Alston confronted me about our relationship this past Friday, it wouldn't look good for Sky to ditch the retreat because of me."

Charles grunted. "It's no one's damn business who you're dating. You're grown-ups. But you need to bring your lady around to meet your mother and me. Everyone's met her except us."

"Not everyone. Only Sean, Angie, and the kids."

"That's everyone in your immediate family except us. Is there something wrong with the girl you don't want Kim and me to know about?"

"No, Sky's great, Dad."

"Marriage material great or temporary girlfriend great?"

"Leave him alone, Charles."

"What? You want to know too, Kim. Stop acting as if you don't. So, back to you. Girlfriend or wife? If she's just another one of your girlfriends, then we don't need to meet her. It'll be a waste of our time."

"That's so wrong. I thought you liked my previous girlfriends."

"I liked them well enough. But I'm old and already know a lot of people. I don't want to spend what time I have left getting to know women who won't become a member of our family."

"Sky's marriage material." Three sets of eyes shifted to Sean. "Well, she is, if Malcolm doesn't screw it up."

"Thanks a lot."

The men shared a short moment of friendship.

Kim squeaked, followed by a deep exhalation. "Angie's status just turned pale-green. That means she's out of surgery and in recovery, right?"

Yeah, it did. "Green is a good sign. When I asked, one of the nurses told me we can see her when there is a Y next to her pink identification number."

Charles grunted again. "I wonder how long that'll take. You'd think someone would come out here and give us a personal update on our Angie. All this waiting around is making my ass itch, which makes me want to break something." Dark, angry eyes found Sean. "Did the cops arrest the dipshit who smashed Angie's car to bits? You spoke to one of the police officers on the scene, right?"

"I did. He told me everything he could. The driver of the other car was arrested."

"Was the piece-of-shit driving drunk, talking on his cell phone, or in such a hurry he didn't care the light was red and he didn't have the goddamn right-of-way?"

People having quiet conversations in the waiting area or simply sitting in silence turned to Charles whose angry voice grew louder the longer he spoke.

"Calm down." Kim moved to sit beside her husband, her hand going to his hard jaw and stroking. "Our daughter is out of surgery. Take that as the good sign it is."

"We don't know if it's a good sign, only that she didn't die on the operating room table."

"Then we should be grateful, which we all are. You taught Angie how to fight. You must trust her to have the strength to fight her way back to us."

"I know. I just ... she's our baby girl. You saw her car. God, Kim, we saw what that asshole did to her car. It's totaled. How could anyone survive that crash and not be seriously hurt?"

Social media was a bitch. Before the local news broadcast the "near-fatal" accident, a mere ten miles from Sean and Angie's home, pictures of the crash scene were already online. Because of Angie's public status as President of Excelsior University, her accident was big local news.

Two local television stations had already contacted Sean. He had no idea how they'd gotten his cell number.

There were other calls from unknown numbers he'd refused to answer. Sean had been tempted to turn off his phone, but Malcolm reminded him he needed to stay accessible to family, friends, and colleagues.

They waited another hour before they were called into a private family room. A short, stout Iranian man with thin-rimmed glasses and green scrubs met them. He offered the family a seat, but no one sat.

"I'm Dr. Bandari. I'm the surgeon who tended to Mrs. Styles-Franklin." He looked to Sean. "Are you Mr. Franklin?"

"I am. These are Angie's parents and her brother. What can you tell us about my wife's condition?"

"Unfortunately, I see far too many of these cases. When a driver has on a seatbelt, as in the case of your wife, the injuries are not as severe as they could be when a seatbelt isn't used, but they can still be great. Head, neck, chest, and legs were my main areas of concern in the operating room. There were also many cuts and lacerations from the broken glass and torn metal. Nothing too deep but enough to require sutures. For now, my biggest concerns are her head injury and back contusions. We'll work on reducing the spinal pressure. She's hooked to an intracranial pressure monitor. That machine will help us monitor tissue swelling. Mrs. Styles-Franklin was given a CT scan when she arrived in the emergency room. We saw no evidence of fractures or bleeding in the brain. But there was evidence of bruised brain tissue and brain tissue swelling."

By the time Dr Bandari had finished his description of the damage and surgery, everyone in the room, except for the doctor, had taken a seat, mouths open in horror and disbelief. Like Kim, Sean had seen images of his wife's car on the six-a.m. news. He shouldn't have watched the footage on his phone. The sight had sent him running to the bathroom, throwing up the little food he had in his stomach.

For all their impatience to see Angie, after meeting with the surgeon, Sean and the Styles stood outside her room, afraid to go inside and witness the sight Dr. Bandari had described.

Kim held on to Charles as they entered the room. She buried her face in his chest the second she laid eyes on her daughter, sobbing softly. Charles's low whine could've matched that of any wounded animal.

Malcolm stared at his sister, fists clenched and eyes molten red and ocean wet.

The trio stayed where they were, frozen in place by the sight before them. White gauze was wrapped around Angie's head and the left side of her face, covering an eye. Both legs were elevated on pillows and immobilized in casts from her feet to the tops of her thighs. A black shoulder stabilizer peeked out from beneath her hospital gown and a cervical collar stabilized her neck and kept her spine in position, as Dr. Bandari had explained.

Nothing the surgeon could've said would've prepared them for this heartrending sight.

Sean understood Angie's family's stunned immobility. He, on the other hand, couldn't stay away. Sean rushed to her side, tears blurring his vision.

Bedside monitors surrounded Angie, checking her heart rate, blood pressure, respiratory rate and only god knew what else. It wasn't the monitors that had Sean grasping his wife's hand, burying his face in her pillow and crying like a baby, but her swollen and bruised figure that made her nearly unrecognizable.

The at-fault driver had T-boned Angie's car on the right side, slamming her body into the driver's side door and window. Upon impact, her car had flipped onto its side, skidding to a halt several feet from the impact. Thankfully, there were few cars on the road that time of morning, and no one else ran into her car.

According to Officer Fitch, the woman driving directly behind Angie was the first motorist to call 9-1-1. Apparently, she'd seen the fast-moving car and had tried to warn Angie by beeping at her. She'd also stayed with Angie until first responders arrived, talking to her, even though she'd been unconscious.

Sean held Angie's hand, soft and warm, the same as when she'd departed for Newark.

He cried harder. "I'm so sorry. For everything. Please, honey, please. Don't go away. You can't leave the kids and me. Please. Please."

Sean had no idea what he muttered to his wife, uncontrollable feelings he couldn't keep inside, let alone recall later. But they had to be set free, so Sean permitted their emancipation. He had to tell her how he felt. How much he loved her and how he didn't want to imagine his life without her in it. He didn't care who else was in the room or what they heard him say to her. He may be ashamed of his affair but not his bone-deep regret and heart-heavy sorrow.

He stayed with Angie all day, sitting beside her bed and holding her hand, afraid to touch any other part of her. Malcolm stayed, too, pulling up a chair on the other side of Angie's hospital bed. Every so often, Malcolm would kiss her forehead and whisper his love and encouragement in her ear.

Charles and Kim had left around three to check on the kids and to relieve Kim's sister, Aunt Linda.

"I'm sorry, fellas, but I can't allow you to stay any longer. Visiting hours ended twenty minutes ago."

Angie's night nurse, Mia, a fifty-something Puerto Rican woman with kind eyes but an unyielding bearing, stared at Sean and Malcolm.

They left, both of them tenderly kissing Angie goodbye.

Sean drove around before going home. He found himself at EU, although he didn't recall driving there or why he had. Sean left the school before a campus police officer saw him parked in his wife's reserved parking spot. He wasn't concerned the officer would question his presence there, but rather, that he might inquire about Angie. At this point, all of EU's employees would've received an email from Dr. Murphy, providing broad strokes about Angie's car crash and current health status. He assumed the man would, along with all members of Angie's executive leadership team, step in and step up until she returned to work.

If she's able to return. Sean couldn't shake off the negative thought, as he drove away from EU and toward home.

For thirty minutes, he sat in his truck in the driveway of his home, staring at the empty space where Angie's car should be. Hands gripped the steering wheel and squeezed. Fists pounded the dash, over and again. The horn blared, and Sean sat, oblivious to everything other than images of an unconscious and broken Angie.

"Sean?" A knock to his driver's side window and a familiar voice reached him. "Come on, Sean, get yourself out the truck and into the house." Charles pulled the truck's handle. "Unlock the door and get out."

Trembling hands turned off the vehicle and opened the door.

"That's it. Now get yourself out of there and into the house. One leg after the other, that's all you need to do."

Listening to the strong timbre of Charles's voice, Sean pushed from the truck then followed his father-in-law inside the quiet house.

Kim met them at the door, her arms going around his waist. "Did Angie awaken?"

Sean wished he could set Kim's mind at ease, but all he had was the frustrating truth. Dr. Bandari had used the word coma, but Sean hadn't believed him until he'd seen Angie, her eyes closed and not responding to light, sound, or touch.

"Not yet, but Dr. Bandari believes Angie's unconsciousness is temporary."

When Dr. Bandari had examined Angie, an hour after her parents had left, his diagnosis of her brain injury was one of reserved optimism. The doctor hadn't offered false hope, but he did say Angie's blood tests "looked good" and her latest CT scan was "promising."

What it all meant, Sean had no clue, but he didn't want to send his in-laws home thinking they'd lost their daughter to a traumatic head injury. Tomorrow and the days afterward would prove Sean's massaging of the truth an unintended cruelty or an empathetic gesture the Styles needed to get through the night.

Kim nodded, disappointed but with an air of hope.

Charles handed his wife a black, leather tote she slung over her shoulder.

"Where are the children?"

"Asleep." Kim pulled Sean's shirt, and he leaned down to accept a kiss to his cheek. "It's almost midnight."

Midnight? Malcolm and Sean had left the hospital at seven-thirty. Had he driven for all that time?

"What did you guys tell them?"

"Nothing more than what you told SJ earlier. All of us made sure to keep details of Angie's crash sketchy. Zuri only knows her mother is sick, but SJ's the one you'll have to deal with. He had a million questions and was angry when his grandfather and I didn't answer them to his satisfaction. You'll have to speak with your parents to find out if they told Kayla. If you didn't receive a call from her, they probably haven't."

"Listen, Sean," Charles began, tone gentle but voice deep, "we can drive to Newark and pick up Kayla, if you want. I know you have a lot on your mind, so sleep on it and let us know. Kayla should be home."

"I ... I ... I can't let any of the children see their mother the way she is now, not even SJ and certainly not Zuri."

"You don't have to make any of those decisions tonight, but you will soon." Charles hugged Sean, the scent of his aftershave weak with the lateness of the day. "Kim made you and the kids soup. It's in the fridge. She went all mother mode and made a pot for Malcolm, too, and had me drop it off at his house. Curtis will be here in the morning. He'll stay with the kids, so you can go the hospital. Rodney will relieve my brother and Damon will relieve him."

Rodney and Damon were two of Angie's cousins and the funniest men in the family.

"My sisters will work out a schedule for next week," Kim added. "Although you'll see them at the hospital tomorrow after church service, they wanted me to tell you they're keeping Angie in their prayers."

Sean's heart swelled as exhaustion weighed him down. "Thank you both. I know this isn't any easier on you than it is on me. I appreciate and love you."

"Family," Charles said, as if that explained everything. For the Styles, Sean supposed it did. "We need to get home. See you at the hospital tomorrow."

Sean watched his in-laws leave, locking the front door behind them and setting the security alarm before going up to bed. He checked in on Zuri and SJ then headed to his room. Stopping at his bedroom door, Sean shook his head and then walked back up the hall and into his wife's room.

Dragging off his clothes, he crawled into Angie's bed. Being there felt wrong without his wife sharing the bed with him. But there was no place he'd rather be than among Angie's things and surrounded by her sweet scent.

He was tired--emotionally more than physically. He wanted someone to talk to. Sean reached for the phone on Angie's nightstand but pulled his hand back. He doubted Malcolm was asleep, so he didn't worry a call would disturb him. They'd gotten along better today than they had in a long time. But bonding over mutual pain wasn't the same as resolving an issue. And the thought of calling Darryl or another friend, who would ask Sean well-meaning but ultimately painful questions about Angie's health status, left Sean feeling cold.

Despite his fatigue, he couldn't fall asleep. Sean picked up the first book from a stack of four on the floor beside the bed. He'd purchased three of them for her and Angie, as far as he knew, hadn't gotten around to reading even one. He wished she would take more time for herself. She didn't relax or treat herself enough. Once Sean got her home, he would work hard to convince her to slow down.

Cracking the fantasy romance novel, Sean began to read, unfazed by the opening argument between the husband and wife. It seemed all too fitting and so very depressing.

CHAPTER TWENTY

"What's going on with Mom?"

Light beamed on Sean's face. He shifted in bed, yanking the comforter over his head.

A shove to his shoulder. "Dad, I asked what's going on with Mom."

Sean groaned. Why wouldn't the annoying voice in his head shut up so he could get some sleep? And how was the voice capable of touching him, pushing him, and ... dammit, pulling off his toasty covers?

"Daddy. Daddy."

A small, soft hand squeezed his nose and he gasped awake, his head pounding. "What? What? I'm up. I'm up."

"Good. What's going on with Mom?"

"Daddy, where's Mommy?" A little body plopped on the bed beside a groggy Sean and found his nose again. "Where's Mommy? Is she sick?"

"Zuri, sweetie, you can't grab my nose like that."

"What's going on with Mom? You said she was in a car accident, but you didn't tell me everything."

Through grainy eyes, Sean met the hard, worried gaze of his son. He knew.

"You've been online, haven't you?"

"Yeah, but that's not how I found out. I have good friends. A few of them called to see how I was doing. Mom's the president of a prestigious university."

SJ's, "Of course I found out," implied but left unsaid.

"Come here, sweetie." Sean picked Zuri up and got out of bed. "Let me get her breakfast and then we can talk. Are you hungry?"

"No. I want to go see Mom. I can eat at the hospital."

"I want to go see Mommy, too. I can eat later."

"No one is eating later or at the hospital." He kissed Zuri's chubby cheek and lied to her face. "You're too young to go to the hospital. They don't allow kids your age in there. You'll have to wait to see Mommy when she comes home."

"Dad, don't."

"I said she's too young, SJ. Leave it at that."

"I'm not a baby, Daddy. I turned five in April, and I'm old enough to go to kindergarten now."

"I know you're not a baby. But rules are rules. Even if we don't like them, we have to follow them." He placed Zuri on her feet, making sure her nightgown was pulled down. "How about this? When Mommy is feeling better, you can talk to her on the phone. How's that?"

Zuri began to cry and Sean wished, for the first time, his children weren't so damn perceptive. In his bumbling, sleep-deprived way, he'd not only told his five-year-old Angie was too sick to speak to her, but too sick for her to visit her mother in the hospital.

"Way to go, Dad."

"Give me a break." He picked Zuri up again, returning to the bed and sitting. "Okay, okay. It's all right. There's nothing to cry about."

"I want to see Mommy."

"I know you do, but you can't right now."

"Why not?"

Shit. He couldn't tell her the truth, but he also didn't want to lie to her again.

"She's sick but the doctor and nurses are taking very good care of her. As soon as Mommy's feeling better, I'll take you to see her. Okay?"

"No." Zuri's tears wet his chest, where she had her face buried. "Mommy should be home with us, not at the hospital. Go get her, Daddy, and bring her home."

He held his daughter, rocking her and stroking her braids. "I need you to be a big girl for me, Zuri. I know it hurts not seeing Mommy here and knowing she's sick. But we all get sick sometimes. Remember when you had that bad cold and had to stay home from school?"

She nodded, clinging to Sean in a way she hadn't since her last nightmare. After today, the poor girl would likely have more bad dreams.

"I'm better now. No more coughing or fever."

"I know you are, sweetie, and Mommy will be better too. She just needs a little time, then I can bring her home. I need you to be patient. The doctor will make Mommy better just as the cough syrup made you feel better."

"It was nasty. Grapes are good, but the cough syrup was yucky. I hope the doctor gives Mommy yummy medicine, so she'll want to take it. If she takes it, she'll feel better and come home."

If only life was as simple as it was in the mind of a five-year-old.

Sean and Zuri stayed seated, with his arms wrapped around his daughter and her tears flowing until she grew tired of crying and fell silent. All the while, SJ hadn't moved an inch. He was dressed the same as Sean, in boxers and nothing else.

"Go put on a T-shirt and shorts. I'll take Zuri downstairs, fix her a bowl of oatmeal with fruit and be back up to speak with you. Or you could eat with your sister and we can talk afterward."

SJ's eyebrow arched in a way that reminded Sean too much of Angie. "Did you really think that would work?"

"No, but I'm tired, and you and your sister woke me before I could get all my rest in."

"Sorry."

"Don't worry about it. I would've had to get up soon anyway."

Because of the unplanned conversation he would have with his son, he wouldn't reach the hospital when visiting hours began. The Styles would be there, so Angie would have family with her. But Sean wanted to also be there, especially if she'd awakened last night. Before speaking with SJ, he would call the hospital for a status update. But first, he needed to get dressed and feed his little girl.

"Come on, sprout, let's get you breakfast."

Zuri wrapped her legs and arms around Sean and rested her head on his shoulder, acting like the baby she claimed not to be. Sean didn't mind, though. Zuri needed reassurance that, with her mother sick and in the hospital, her father wouldn't go away too.

Sean held her tight to him and kissed the top of her head. Zuri wasn't the only one who needed reassurance.

Fifteen minutes and one disappointing phone call to the hospital later had him back upstairs and in Angie's room. SJ sat on the unmade bed and Sean joined him.

"Dad, I—"

Sean hugged his son, as tightly as he had Zuri.

"Mom's that hurt, huh?" SJ returned the embrace, his forehead going to Sean's shoulder. "My friends said they saw pics online, but I didn't want to see them. I was afraid to see them. I heard you come in last night, and I really wanted to know about Mom. But I also didn't. You were gone all day. I figured she couldn't be good if everyone was going out of their way not to tell me and Zuri what was going on with her."

"You kids are too smart for your own good." Uncaring SJ was fifteen and not prone to physical displays of affection with his old man, Sean kissed the teen's cheek before letting him go. "Sometimes, SJ, you need to allow the adults in your life to protect you, even if that means lying or telling half-truths. We don't like it either but knowing can be worse than not knowing sometimes."

"Is this one of those times?"

"I think so. Knowing hurts."

"So does being kept in the dark, especially when everyone else isn't."

"Yeah, I know. "

"Is Mom going to die?" Tears burst from SJ and, right before Sean's eyes, his son crashed and burned, crumpling into his arms the same way Zuri had. But SJ's cries were silent, making his heartache even more devastating to witness.

"I got you, my big man. It's okay to let it out. I did the same yesterday. Twice. Maybe three times."

SJ cried and cried, and Sean recalled his son's words. He didn't say he hadn't seen the pictures of his mother's car online but that he was afraid to see them. Obviously, he'd pushed past his fear and looked.

Would seeing Angie in the hospital but in a coma be better than not seeing her and conjuring images of her untimely death? Sean didn't know. Anything had to be better than holding SJ's tear-wracked body and listening to him fight for control of his emotions.

"As soon as someone comes to babysit, we'll go to the hospital to see Angie." Sean couldn't recall which family member had first shift.

"Y-you're going to take me to see Mom?" He lifted his head, face wet and eyes red.

"Yeah, you can come. But I need you to understand what you'll see. If you don't think you can take it then you need to tell me and stay here. Your sisters are too young to see Angie hurt. You're at that weird age where I don't always know what direction to take with you--child or young man. If you go with me, I need you to be a young man. Mom needs all of our strength, so we need to be strong for her."

"I can do that." Steady hands wiped away tears. "Yeah, I can do that. I just needed to get that out. I'm good now."

"There's no shame in crying, son. Every man does, even if it's in private. Any man who says he's never cried is either a liar or a sociopath. I cry, and so do your uncle and grandfathers."

"Thanks, Dad. I'll go shower and get dressed."

"And eat. Your mother doesn't like it when you leave the house without having breakfast."

"I know. I'll make sure to get something." SJ used the heel of his hand to remove the remaining tears from his cheek. "Mom called me last night before she left Newark. I was playing a video game and rushed her off the phone, so I could get back to it. I figured I'd see her when she returned home, and we could talk then. It didn't occur to me that ... that ... I rushed her off the phone, Dad. She took the time to call me and I couldn't even give her five minutes. What if ... what if ...?"

SJ broke down again and Sean consoled his son the best he knew how, by holding him close and letting him embrace then push through his pain. By the time SJ climbed into Sean's truck, the teen had his emotions on lockdown.

When they'd arrived at the hospital, SJ's weak smile and slow, tentative steps down the hall and toward Angie's room had Sean worried he wouldn't be able to handle seeing his mother's hurt and unmoving body.

SJ pushed the door open, took one look at Angie's prone form and backed up into Sean, who steadied his shoulders with a strong grip.

"You don't have to go all the way in if you don't want to."

"I want to go in."

"This isn't one of your games. It's not a competition to beat your best score."

"If I was in that bed, Mom wouldn't run away, would she?"

"You know the answer to that."

SJ's shoulders stiffened, and he walked away from Sean and toward Angie. Zahra and Kim, who'd kept vigil beside Angie's bed, nodded at Sean and left the room.

"Hey, Mom. It's me." SJ glanced at him over his shoulder. "Can she hear me? Should I talk as if she can?"

"Do what feels right. What is your heart telling you?"

Shuffling closer, SJ took hold of his mother's hand then leaned down to kiss the cheek not covered by white gauze. "I played the new game you got me. The graphics are on fleek and the characters OP. Oh, sorry, that means overpowered. But them being OP is what makes the game so good. My favorite character is Bloodpaws. He's a Hellhound."

Sean slipped from the room, giving his son privacy. The hallway outside Angie's recovery room was filled with relatives on both sides of Angie's family.

"How's SJ doing?" Charles asked. "He looked a little blue around the gills before he went inside."

"As well as can be expected. He's talking to Angie. If she's capable of hearing anyone, it's one of the kids. By the way, my parents are going to bring Kayla home."

"That's good. When?"

"The end of this week. I decided I didn't want Kayla missing the last week of camp only to come home and not be able to see her mother. I'm hoping, by the time she arrives, Angie will be awake. Have you seen the doctor today?"

"Not yet, but the on-duty nurse said he'd be in to check on Angie by noon. They're also going to take her for another CT scan. They want to have that done before the doctor examines her."

Kim came up on her husband's left side, arm going around his waist and her other hand to Sean's arm. "You look tired. How many hours of sleep did you get?"

"Not enough, but I'll be fine. I read a book I bought for Angie."

"You read an entire book after we left?"

"I couldn't sleep, and the story helped settle my mind. I meant to bring it in from the truck. I want to read it to her."

"That sounds like a good idea. What's the name of the book?"

"*Bound Souls*. It's a fantasy romance set in the future and written by an African American female author. The author is one of the reasons I bought the novel for Angie."

The older couple nodded, and they floated from one distracting conversation topic to another as the day crept by with no sound or movement from Angie.

Sean stayed with his wife all day. Family members came and went, and Malcolm was kind enough to drive SJ home. After his initial shock, SJ had gathered himself and surged forward with grit. His son always made him proud, and today was no different. SJ had spent two hours holding Angie's hand and talking to her, from sports to video games to movies they both liked. He'd teared up a little when it was time to leave, disappointed she hadn't awakened during his time with her.

"Love you, Mom. I'll help Dad take care of Zuri and Kayla while you're in here. "He kissed her cheek again, scratched but healing. "Get better soon so Dad can bring you home."

SJ had hugged Sean before leaving with Malcolm. "Thanks, Dad. I get it now. Sorry about earlier."

"Don't ever apologize for loving and needing your mother. As old as I am, I love and still need mine. It's how a son should feel about the woman who gave birth to him. Angie loves you kids."

"I know."

"So do I."

"I know that too, Dad."

Sean plopped into the chair beside Angie's bed. Everyone had gone home except him. The same night nurse from yesterday reminded him of when visitation hours ended. He had less than an hour left.

He cracked open *Bound Souls* and picked up where he'd left off reading to her. With so many visitors, Sean hadn't managed to read beyond the second chapter. But Angie's room was quiet, and Sean was grateful for the time alone with his wife.

"Though exhausted, Zion didn't sleep. He watched his wife, the rise and fall of her chest, the anguished expressions that marred her features, telling him she wasn't sleeping peacefully. The poor woman was unable to let go of her anxiety over his impending death, even in her dream state.

Zion dug his fingers into her heavily coiled hair, finding sensitive scalp and massaging. He'd discovered, when they were courting, that Asiyans held their tension in their head, unlike humans whose stress often found its way to their neck and shoulders.

After several minutes, Lela's tense body melted under his expert ministrations, taking on a more natural posture. Her breathing grew deep and heavy.

Zion smiled at his wife and wrapped himself around her, using his left arm to pull Lela close to him, claiming her as his. She was still his, he reminded himself. For the next three years and one beyond that, she would be only his in mind, heart, and body. After that... well, life went on, even for the most loving and dedicated of spouses. Zion was sure Iman had forgiven him for finding love and happiness with someone else. And he could...would do the same for Lela. But not now, not tonight, not yet. He still had time. They still had time. She was his. Yes, his and his alone."

When Sean had read this part last night, a terrible sense of dread had washed over him. What if he got Angie back only for her to still leave him? Angie may be his now, but she wouldn't be if Trayvon proved to be his son. Tomorrow was Tuesday, and he'd mailed off the kit on Friday. Three to five days after its arrival he'd have the results. Zion and Lela's time was up. They may have been souls bound for eternity, but they'd also lost each other for a very long time.

He sighed and read the second section of chapter two.

"He reached for Lela, and she came, body still naked from when they'd made love last night. *The last time.* Or so Zion had told himself. Yet the way his equally nude body responded to Lela's nearness, he welcomed being wrong.

With a vigor that came from a reserve Zion hadn't known existed, he went about making love to his wife one last time. Knowing when they finished, when they exploded in rapturous, sensual glory, it would truly, inescapably, be the last time for Zion Grace and Lela of the House of Asheema.

When Zion reached his peak, when his heart raced, toes curled, and muscles clenched, there was only one thing he could say, 'I love you, Lela. My heart is forever yours.'"

Sean closed the book. If he didn't leave soon, Nurse Mia would kick him out. He stretched as he pushed to his feet, glad to be out of the uncomfortable chair but loath to leave Angie's side.

CHAPTER TWENTY-ONE

"Do you feel this?" Sean asked of Angie.

"No."

"What about this?"

"No." Angie looked down the line of her body, Sean at the end of her hospital bed, his hand on her foot. "I still can't feel anything south of my waist."

She closed her eyes, taking a visual break. The last thing she remembered, before waking in this hospital bed, were the lights of an oncoming car and the blaring of a car horn behind her. Her body had been whole and unharmed. Now…

"It's only been a few days since you awoke, and you still have swelling around your spine. The doctor said the contusions hinder the nerve impulses, so the normal messages that should travel from your brain to your body through your spinal cord are disrupted because of the inflammation."

Angie knew what Dr. Mucci had said, a redheaded Italian woman with an ego that seemed too big to fit inside the five-foot orthopedic physician. The doctor also hadn't said whether Angie would regain feeling and movement in her pelvis and legs. Dr. Bandari had also visited the first day Angie awoke from her coma, explaining her injuries and the operation.

"Do you need anything?"

Her eyelids opened. Sean had moved to sit in the chair next to her bed. His usual spot.

"You should go home and rest. You're here every day, all day."

After her discussion with the surgeon, she had waited for the doctor to leave before she broke down. Angie had almost died. The thought had frightened her. Not so much because she wasn't ready for her life to end, but because of the pain her death would've caused her family, especially her parents and children.

She could see the toll her car crash and two-day coma had taken on everyone, even though their relief softened the tension at the edges of their eyes and mouths.

"I'll leave when visiting hours are over. That's in another ninety minutes. Stop trying to get rid of me. You should know by now I'm not going anywhere."

"But you're so tired, Sean. You've developed dark circles under your eyes, and you don't eat enough while you're here."

"Listen to you. I'm not the patient here. Don't worry, our mothers make sure the kids and I are fed. I'm eating." His smile warmed her, for all the strength and security she found there. Sean's hand offered the same, when he twined their fingers. "You didn't answer my question. Do you need anything?"

"Other than mobility in my legs and waist, no."

Angie tried not to think of the possibility of living the rest of her life confined to a wheelchair. Many people were wheelchair users and lived happy, fulfilled lives. But the physical limitations and lifestyle changes were undeniable and terrifying.

"Spinal cord injuries take time to heal, honey. You'll get feeling back in your legs."

"What if I don't? I hate to think like that but—"

"Then don't. Positive thinking only. You survived the car crash. You survived the surgery, and you came out of the coma. You did that."

"Not by myself."

"God, Dr. Bandari, the medical staff in the operating room, the first-responders. But also you. I sat right here, for two days, watching you and praying you'd wake. When I went home that first night, I was so afraid of leaving you here. Afraid because I didn't know whether you'd slip away while I was gone. I didn't have enough faith in you."

Sean had it wrong. Angie was never as strong as he believed her to be. Her husband had a bad habit of treating and viewing her as if she were a super woman, capable of inhuman feats. Sean's perception couldn't be further from the truth. She was never as independent as he thought her to be. Focused, yes. Driven, yes. Stubborn, hell yes. But never a woman without need for help and support.

"I'm just a small woman who hurts and can be broken."

"I know, and I'm sorry."

"I didn't mean … I wasn't talking about …"

"I know you weren't talking about me and what I did. But it stays on my mind. I keep thinking about forgiveness. After your car crash, I can't stop thinking about it."

Sean wouldn't say the words they were thinking. What if she'd died having not forgiven him? She wouldn't have wanted that fate for him, regardless of the state of their unresolved marital issues, any more than she would've wanted to die.

"I don't want to talk about that now."

"Neither do I. Is there enough room for me in your bed?"

She didn't have to look at him to know he wasn't joking. Too tired to argue and too weak to stop him, she said nothing when he joined her in bed. Sean had to be uncomfortable, reclined on his side and with half of him off the bed.

"Nurse Mia would have my ass if she saw me like this. Rest your head against my shoulder and close your eyes."

"I want to see the kids."

"I know, and they want to see you."

She'd seen SJ but not her Kayla and Zuri. Angie missed her girls. Phone calls were fine, but nothing compared to seeing their beautiful faces.

"Maybe not in person, though. I don't want to worry them any more than they already are."

"What about a video chat?"

Angie smiled and settled, as best she could, against Sean's shoulder.

"Good idea. Without the gauze on my head. It's not a good look."

"I can do your hair for you."

"No thanks. I'll ask Mom or Zahra for help."

"Your loss. Don't sleep on my beautician skills. I'm all the rage among bed-ridden mommas."

"You're ridiculous and not funny."

"I'm the funniest husband you've ever had."

Warm, full lips pressed against her forehead, and an arm snaked across her stomach.

"You have no shame taking advantage of my situation."

"None whatsoever. I'm going to kiss and touch you as much as possible. Nothing inappropriate that'll get me slapped, but I'm going to feel you up in the most respectful way."

"Those two things don't go together. You're not supposed to feel up your injured wife, no matter how respectful you claim it to be."

Sean's soft as cotton lips kissed Angie on her scraped cheek.

"Right now I'm selfish and needy and don't care. I thought I would lose you and that scared the shit out of me. Even now, with you awake and talking, I still feel the constriction in my chest. I'm afraid to look away in case it turns out to be a dream. I know nothing has changed between us, but can we table all of that, at least until you get out of the hospital? Will you trust and rely on me during your time of need? Will you look at me as your loving and devoted husband, even if only for a little while? I'm not asking only for myself, Angie, but also for you. You don't need the additional stress. Healing will take up most of your time and energy. Let me do the rest."

It wasn't a plea for forgiveness but for a temporary truce. Sean desired the former but would accept the latter. At least for now. In truth, Angie had no interest in maintaining the distance she'd put between them. Not while she healed. It was all she could do most days to stay awake long enough to speak with her stream of visitors and not to reveal the depth of her concern about potential long-term effects of her injuries.

"Thank you."

"Does that mean you accept?"

She could hear the controlled happiness in his voice and feel him move closer to her.

"You're going to crush me, and I do accept."

"I'm going to take good care of you."

Sean always took excellent care of Angie. She may not trust him in certain areas now, but she did in this one.

"I know. Not to seem ungrateful but get out of my bed."

The odd angle and dip weren't doing her neck and shoulder any favors. She'd also see about taking off the neck brace before she spoke with the girls.

"I am kind of uncomfortable."

"Only kind of?"

"The idea was better in my head. All romantic, you know?"

"I can't see how being perched on a bed made for one, when you're over six-feet tall, could have seemed romantic."

"It's not, when you put it like that." Sean slid from the bed, and then straightened Angie's white covers over her. "Do you want me to read to you before I have to leave? We finished *Bound Souls*, but I brought another one of your books with me."

"The paranormal romance one with witches and were-cats?"

All summer, she'd meant to read the new books. As far as guilt gifts went, Sean's novel selections were good ones. It shouldn't have taken a near-fatal car crash for her to take the time to read them. Technically, she wasn't reading the novels at all. Sean, if he ever gave up law, could have a career as a voice actor, so convincingly did he take on the persona of each character, even the females.

"I remembered that was the one you wanted me to read next, so that's the book I have with me today. From the look of you, though, I think I'll only get through the prologue and first chapter before you fall asleep."

"Probably."

While Angie liked the stories, she enjoyed the sound of Sean's voice more. Smooth and relaxing, like rhythm and blues slow jams.

He dug into his black messenger bag and pulled out the paperback.

Angie closed her eyes. She thought Sean would begin to read. When he didn't, she opened them. He watched her, not with a fun-loving smile, but with an all-too serious expression he'd frequently worn since her crash.

"I love you." Leaning on the bed with an elbow, he repeated, "I love you. It's important to me you know how much I do."

Angie knew. Not just knew but felt his love for her. Perhaps Sean had been the one to forget how much he cared for Angie. Maybe it was he who needed the reminding.

"I know you do."

There went his beatific smile. "Good. I wanted to get that straight before you conked out on me. I'll tell you again tomorrow."

"I have a concussion, not memory loss."

"Doesn't matter, I'm telling you anyway. Right after I kiss your forehead and suck your fingers."

"You're not sucking my fingers."

"What part of you can I suck, then?" Light-brown eyes lowered to her chest. "I'm open to suggestions." Sean raised his index and middle fingers. "Two suggestions, really."

Angie almost said something about Sean milking this situation but stopped short when he kept staring at her breasts, a long tongue coming out and licking lips she remembered all too well on her body.

"Just read."

"Party pooper." Sean rested back in the chair and began to read.

Her husband was dangerous when he was being charming. But Sean's allure was most lethal when he looked at her with earnestness, openness, and love.

It had been a week since Sean mailed off the paternity test kit. He'd told her three to five days after arriving in the company's lab, the results would be known. Had the company contacted him? Did he know whether he was the father of Trinity's baby? If he did know, when would he tell her?

Angie closed her mind to that hurtful train of thought and focused on the story and the pact she'd made with Sean. Soon enough, she'd know the truth. But for now, Angie wanted to bask in the sound of her husband's voice.

With a scowl Sean didn't even try to conceal, he watched Dr. Derrick Murphy, the provost's smile too wide, his proximity to Angie too close, and his presence too much for him to handle.

"You look great."

"I've never known you to be a liar, Derrick."

Dr. Murphy smiled down at Angie, his hand still holding hers long after the greeting handshake.

"I would never lie to you, Angela." He raised one hand to his chest and over his heart. "I swear, I've never seen a lovelier patient."

"Spent a lot of time at the hospital, have you?"

"I will if you have to stay here much longer. The first time I was here you were unconscious. The second time I came you were asleep. I guess the third time is the charm. All things considered, you do look great. How are you feeling?"

Sean listened as Angie gave Dr. Murphy an abridged version of her medical condition. She deleted much and didn't share information about her temporary paralysis. At least Sean hoped her paralysis proved to be short-lived.

Edward tugged Sean's arm. "I'm hungry. Let's go to the hospital cafeteria."

"Go by yourself or take Mom. I'm visiting my wife."

Edward's voice lowered to a whisper. "Unless you're planning on kicking that guy's ass for flirting with Angie right in front of you, I suggest you take a deep breath and a walk."

"I'm not leaving."

Brenda stepped into Sean's line of sight, impairing his vision of Angie and Dr. Murphy. Her hand went to his chest and her eyes to his. "Take you father's suggestion. I'll stay here with Angie and her colleague."

"But—"

"He's being overly friendly, and she's being courteous. But you're working yourself into a firestorm of jealousy borne of guilt. Angie doesn't need that, so leave, and don't return until you're either calm or Dr. Murphy is gone."

"Everyone misses you at EU. Jeanette tells me your mailbox keeps filling with emails of concern and well-wishes. That executive assistant of yours is managing everyone and everything, including your exec team while you're in here. So, don't worry about EU. We got you covered."

"I didn't doubt it for a minute. EU isn't one person. It's all of us, from the president's executive team to the faculty to the custodians. I do thank you, though. It means a lot to know my absence hasn't interrupted the operation of the university."

"It's an old, huge school. It'd take bulldozers to shake something up at EU. But that doesn't mean your absence isn't keenly felt. If nothing else, you've given me an excuse to buy you flowers. I hope you like these better than the ones I bought you for your birthday."

Sean glared at the bouquet of red roses Dr. Murphy had placed on the windowsill next to Sean's own vase of red roses. Sean didn't like Dr. Murphy bringing his wife flowers, especially since his arrangement was larger than Sean's.

"Did I get it right this time?"

"The flowers you gave me for my birthday were lovely."

"Which is your kind way of saying you liked the lilies, but you prefer red roses. An observant man can learn, Angela."

"And so you have. Thank you. They're beautiful, but please don't make a habit of bringing me flowers. It isn't necessary."

"They're not just from me, but the entire team. They figured it would be best if one of us visited instead of everyone. Jeanette's still coming, though, if she hasn't already been here."

"Yesterday, before visiting hours ended."

"I should've known. But the flowers are from all of us. I'm pretty sure we can write that off as a business expense."

"You've just gone cheap on me."

Dr. Murphy laughed, and Sean had had enough. He stormed from the room, Edward behind him.

"One of these days that guy is going to make me hurt him."

Sean stalked away from his wife's room and down to the cafeteria, grabbing sandwiches, chips, and bottled water for his parents and himself. Brenda hadn't come down with them, but she'd been at the hospital all morning too, and hadn't eaten lunch.

Sean and Edward sat at a table near a window-wall. On the other side of the glass was a patio garden. Its babbling brook and daffodils reminded Sean too much of Dr. Murphy's damn roses for him to relax and appreciate the tranquil garden.

"The chicken's already dead. You don't have to bite into your sandwich like you're trying to kill the poor bird for a second time."

He swallowed, not even tasting the sandwich, having demolished half of it in less than a minute.

"Every time I see that guy, he's in Angie's face and space. He's a little weasel."

"He's not your basic weasel, and that's a problem."

"What do you mean?"

"Real talk here, Sean. Can we have a real conversation without you turning it around on me and biting my head off?"

"Not if it's about you cheating on Mom."

"Then I can't help you."

"I didn't ask for your help."

"I know you didn't, but you need it." Screwing off the plastic top, Edward sipped from his chilled water. "Brenda and I have been here a week. Do you know what we've seen in those days besides your house and this hospital?"

"I have no idea."

"Styles upon Styles. They're here all the time. If not Angie's father's people then her mother's. I tell you, I don't know how they expect her to rest if they're always here and sucking up the air in her room."

"That's just how they are. They're a close-knit family."

"Maybe a little too close."

"Maybe our family is too distant."

"We are, but you're missing my point."

"I don't think you have a point. Eat your sandwich, Dad. All of it. You need to gain weight."

"I'm not going to wolf my sandwich down. I like to chew my food and not choke on it. And I do have a point. My point is that people who live the straight and narrow can miss the crooked and broad."

"I have no idea what you're talking about."

"It means you married into a goodie two-shoes family. Don't get me wrong, I love Angie and like her family. You married the proverbial nice girl next door, if next door was Buffalo. And I know why. So do you."

Sean did know. Angie and her family were nothing like his. The package appealed, and he'd wanted that kind of life. Now he had it. But everywhere he looked, something or someone threatened to take it away from him.

"That's why you need my help. I, unlike your in-laws, understand weasels. Listen to me for a minute. Dr. Murphy is playing the long game, which doesn't make him the normal kind of weasel. That was me. Some men are all about the quick win and the quicker getaway."

"You mean no-strings sex."

"You got it. As a married man who wanted his cake and ice cream, playing the weasel worked for me. I only messed around with women who wanted the same thing from me that I wanted from them."

"I told you I didn't want to hear anything about you cheating on Mom."

"You did, but you're also listening because you're beginning to see this weasel has a bit of insight. Your wife isn't naïve or blind. She knows Dr. Murphy's concern is more than collegial."

Sean paused, thought, and then asked, "You think he lied about the flowers being from the group?"

Scooting his chair closer to the table, Edward leaned forward, shoulders hunched to his ears and eyes serious pools of knowledge. "No, and you're still missing the bigger point. He's too smart to lie about something so easily verified with one phone call to Angie's secretary."

"Jeanette. That's the name of Angie's executive assistant."

"Whatever." Sean nodded to Edward's sandwich and his father took an obliging bite before continuing. "Dr. Murphy isn't interested in an affair with Angie, not even a quickie in one of their offices or a hotel room after hours."

"You could've fooled me. I think that's exactly what he wants."

If his father leaned forward anymore, he'd be on Sean's side of the table. "If that's all he wanted, he wouldn't have set his sights so high. He's a single, good-looking man on a college campus. Dr. Murphy has plenty of options. But came here to personally deliver flowers to his boss when he could've hired a service to do it for him. Why do you think that is?"

"I have no idea." Sean sighed, already tired of this conversation.

"That's because you're thinking like a man who cheated with a woman you didn't want in the long-run. Dr. Murphy is thinking like a man who wants a woman. Not simply sex with a female he's attracted to, but the whole woman and everything that comes with her. That man I saw upstairs genuinely cares for Angie. I wouldn't go so far as saying he's in love with her, but there's no doubt, if given the chance, he'd swoop in and fill whatever space you left. He's the guy that, in subtle ways, let's a woman know if she wants to make a change in her life, he's there to help her, and she won't have to be alone."

Edward's shoulders finally relaxed, and so did the rest of him, his back going to the chair and his lips to the bottle of water.

"You're saying I need to worry about Murphy trying to take my place?"

"No. I'm saying he's letting Angie know she has options, and he's one of them. He's smart, stable, handsome and probably a boatload of other shit women find attractive. Angie works with him, which means they know a lot about each other. From their interaction, it's easy to see they get along well and have developed a friendship. If you and Angie divorced, in time she could easily come to see him as more than a colleague and work friend. The transition from that to lovers and more wouldn't be difficult. Angie may not see that now. But she will if your marriage dissolves. That's Dr. Murphy's long game. He won't put his life on hold for Angie or even directly proposition her. But he'll do just enough to remind her he's a good choice for a family-and-work-oriented woman."

Sean crunched on his barbeque potato chips, grinding them into tiny bits before swallowing them along with his father's tarnished perspective.

They ate in silence, Edward slowly making his way through half of his chicken salad sandwich and Sean digging into the bag long after the chips were gone. He stared out the window-wall, the babbling brook wasted on him.

"Is this karma for me cheating on Angie?"

"I don't believe in karma. Life is what it is. Good things happen to bad people. And bad things happen to good people. It's just the way it goes. Angie doesn't want him, by the way."

"How do you know?"

"The same way I knew something was wrong in your marriage. Her eyes. With him, they're kind and polite. But in the way of a woman who's trying to keep things level and calm. Angie can manage her co-worker. Trust me, she's been handling him long before you realized his interest in your wife."

"You know all of this because of your years of cheating, huh?"

"I do know a lot about different kinds of men and woman. But mainly just from living. I may not be able to offer you much, but I know people. The good, the bad, and the ugly. To varying degrees, people are all three. Even with your short-lived affair, you're firmly in the good column. Angie may still be hurt and angry, but she knows this fundamental truth about you. And that's why Dr. Murphy could never have a real chance with her as long as the two of you are together."

"I don't plan on us not staying together."

Edward's smirk wasn't patronizing but it did convey something akin to calling Sean naïve. "When a man is in the doghouse with the missuses, little is up to him. Lucky for you, you don't have a wife who will make you jump through a bunch of hoops."

"Hoops would be better than having no idea where I stand."

"That's your problem. You've always seen the glass as half empty instead of half full. Despite yourself, your glass is half full. If you cheat again, it'll be completely empty, and you might as well step aside for Dr. Murphy."

"I'm not going to cheat again."

"Don't tell me, tell your wife."

Edward drank the rest of his water but left the chips untouched and rewrapped his half-eaten sandwich. Sean would make sure Edward finished his lunch. His father did need to gain weight.

"What do you think I should do about Dr. Murphy?"

"Not a damn thing."

Sean didn't expect that answer but was curious about his father's reasoning.

They took their time transitioning from the cafeteria up to Angie's room, with the men taking a detour to the patio garden before going back upstairs. It was almost the time Malcolm was slated to visit, bringing SJ with him.

Sean stopped Edward halfway down the hall to Angie's room. "Why shouldn't I do anything?"

"Unless you think she's done something with him and, from my experience, he wouldn't be sniffing behind her if they had, it's best to keep your mouth shut because your jealousy in light of your affair will only anger her." They stopped in front of Angie's door. "Besides, she'll eventually put him in his place. You'll probably never know when it happens, but she'll do it and he'll get the message loud and clear and will respect her even more afterward. That's a professional woman's superpower."

"What if she doesn't and the weasel gets a foothold?"

Slim shoulders shrugged. "Then maybe karma is real. You did cheat on her, and payback is said to be a bitch."

"Why do I bother talking to you?"

Sean pushed into his wife's room and hoped Dr. Murphy had had the good sense to have left while he'd been gone. He smiled. Karma hadn't caught up to him yet. The weasel was gone and sitting in the chair beside Angie's bed was a person he now thought of as a family friend.

Malcolm had struck gold when Sky had agreed to date him.

Sean handed his mother her lunch, and then greeted the new visitor. "Hello, Sky. It's nice to see Malcolm hasn't run you off yet."

"No, not yet."

He kissed his wife's cheek, enjoying the truce which meant she didn't recoil from his touch or skewer him with her eyes.

SJ came barreling into the room, fast and careless, and knocked into the end of Angie's bed.

"Watch what you're doing. This isn't a football field." Sean turned to Angie, worried. "Did he hurt your legs? Are you all right?"

"Sorry, Mom."

For seconds, Angie didn't respond, her focus on the foot SJ had hit with his arm.

"Angie, honey, are you—"

"It's fine. SJ, touch my foot again."

"But …"

"You didn't hurt me, but I need you to bump my foot again." He did. "One more time, please." When SJ ran his hand over Angie's foot for a third time, tears fell, and she smiled. "I felt that. I felt every glorious touch."

CHAPTER TWENTY-TWO

"You go in first." Holding Angie, Sean backed away from the front door of their house and made room for Malcolm and her wheelchair." When her brother didn't move, an agitated Sean asked, "Why are you just standing there? Go inside the house."

"No, you take my sister inside first."

"That doesn't make sense. If the wheelchair is already in there, I can put her in it when I bring her in."

"She doesn't need to be put in the wheelchair when she first gets inside."

Angie's brother and husband continued to argue, as they had since the doctor had cleared her to leave the hospital. Her only saving grace, with two men fighting over who would take care of her, was the absence of her fath—

The front door swung open. "I can hear you two idiots inside the house. Sean," Charles said, "bring my daughter inside, and take her into the living room. There're people in there waiting to see her. She can sit on the sofa instead of in that damn wheelchair. Malcolm, you pull up the rear." Big hands came together in a loud clap that got the frowning men moving.

Angie smiled at Charles and held on to Sean as he made his way into their house. It felt like months since she'd last been there instead of only weeks. The place smelled of a mix of cleansers and home cooking.

Sean's arms tightened around Angie, and she tried not to look at him. With two broken legs, Angie couldn't manage on her own. While she disliked having to rely on Sean to carry her into the house and everywhere she needed to go the wheelchair couldn't, her husband reveled in her temporary dependence. Reveled might be too extreme of a word to describe Sean's feelings, but it couldn't be far from the truth. He hadn't stopped smiling since he'd helped the nurse get her into the wheelchair. His smile grew larger when he'd lifted her from the wheelchair and loaded her into his truck with a, "You're going to be great for my biceps and triceps. I'm hitting the gym and weights more often, so I can take care of you while you're in those casts."

"Mommy, Mommy." Zuri ran straight for her. "You're home. Yay!"

"Hi, baby. I am home, thanks to Daddy and Uncle Malcolm."

It didn't take Kayla and SJ long to join them in the hallway. Kayla nearly knocked Zuri over to get to Angie.

"Daddy was gone forever." Kayla buried her face against Angie's shoulder, one arm going around her neck and holding tightly. Her daughter wept softly. Of the three children, Kayla was the one who'd kept her emotions most under control while Angie was away. Now, however, Kayla let loose and her sadness and relief to have Angie safe and at home was painful to witness.

All the children crowded around her, awkward in their efforts to hug her while not banging into her legs.

"Guys, guys, come on. Let me take your mother into the living room."

"Not the living room," Angie said tiredly.

Sean stopped a few feet from his destination. "What do you mean? I can hear people talking in there."

So could she. Too many people, all of whom she'd probably seen the three weeks she'd been in the hospital and who could wait a little longer.

Her mother and aunts had obviously cooked, which was all her family needed to entertain themselves.

"I'm tired."

"Too tired to say hello to your family?"

"No," she acquiesced reluctantly. "We should go in and thank them for coming, but I don't want to stay. If you wouldn't mind, I'd like to be taken to my bedroom." She wanted, no needed, time alone with her children. From the look of them, especially Kayla and Zuri, they needed it too. "Once I'm settled," she told the children, "get a plate of food, if you haven't already eaten, and join me in bed. How does a talk and a movie sound?"

"Really good." SJ kissed her cheek. "We've eaten, but I'll fix you a plate and bring up popcorn and juice for us."

"I want nachos and cheese." Zuri whined and pouted in an un-Zuri-like way, brown eyes wet and little hand on Angie's arm. "I want nachos and cheese, Mommy."

"That's fine. You can help your brother fix them. Be sure to thank him."

"I will."

None of the children moved, not even when Malcom passed them with Angie's wheelchair and Charles came out of the living room and gruffly asked, "What's taking you so long, Sean? Angie weighs a buck twenty, even with the casts." Charles pulled a black marker from his pants pocket and waved it at her. "I'm going to be the first to sign your casts."

"She's not twelve," Kim yelled from the living room. "You don't get to sign your daughter's casts."

"This is an A and B conversation, Kim. C you're way out of it."

"If granddad's signing, I want to sign too." SJ's eyes brightened, and Angie could see an idea forming. "Granddad, do you have more markers? Colors other than black?"

"Sure do. I bought a whole pack. You want to see?"

"I want to sign Mommy's casts." Zuri didn't leave Angie's side, but her attention had shifted to Charles. "I want a red marker."

Kayla pushed her sister's shoulder, gentle and playful. "You write everything in red."

"It's my favorite color."

"Purple is mine. Do you have a purple one, Granddad?"

"Not purple. What about green or blue?"

Sean whispered in her ear. "You know there's no way you're going to be able to get out of this situation, right?"

"You're only saying that because you've thought of something you want to write on one of my casts."

"You make it sound as if I want to write something nasty."

"You don't?"

"Of course, I do. You know me. But I won't because everyone will see. I'll write something appropriate and save my nasty thought for another time."

Sean eventually managed to end the conversation in the hall and take her into the living room. As she'd suspected, some members of her family were there, as were Zahra and her sisters, and Sky.

Malcolm sat next to Sky on the loveseat, his lips to her ear. Whatever her brother said to his girlfriend had the woman lowering her eyes and shaking her head. A small smile played around her mouth, however, telling a different tale.

They were a sweet couple. Malcolm had dated his share of women, but none of them had brought out this anxious-happy side of him the way Sky did. When Malcolm and Angie had spoken in May near Peace Bridge, the same day she'd met Sky, he'd told her he wasn't yet in love. From the way Malcolm snuggled with Sky on the loveseat and the fact he'd invited her to Angie's homecoming, his feelings for his girlfriend went much deeper than a shallow office romance.

Angie may not know whether Sky returned Malcolm's love, but she had two functioning eyes. What they saw pointed to reciprocated, although restrained, affection from Sky.

"Thank you all for coming and for taking such good care of Sean and the children. Your love and support mean so much."

Angie stayed in the living room longer than she'd intended. Sean had placed her on the sofa, giving her time to speak with her visitors before hoisting her back into his arms and carrying her upstairs. Everyone had signed one of her casts, Charles first followed by Zuri who drew a red heart with her name inside. Sean and Sky were the only ones who hadn't taken a turn.

Sky's action hadn't surprised Angie. For as many times as they'd talked, Sky rarely discussed her family, leaving her with the impression that she was an only child who'd had limited contact with children her age beyond school. To some, the younger woman may appear aloof, perhaps even snooty. To Angie, Sky Ellis was an introvert who filtered her surroundings through her highly analytical brain before deciding on a course of action and her next words. While Sky may not have felt comfortable signing one of Angie's casts along with excited members of her family, she had visited her at the hospital, several times, without Malcolm. She counted Sky as a friend and hoped to get to know her better.

What had surprised Angie, after their conversation in the hall, was Sean's attitude shift from playful and flirty to thoughtful and quiet. He'd remained silent through the excited proceedings, her family and friends swapping markers and one-upmanship with their drawings. Leave it to her family to go beyond a simple signature to full-blown caricatures. All through the silliness and fun, Sean had sat in a chair in the alcove of the living room, looking out the window until she had asked him to take her upstairs.

"Thank you." Using her arms, Angie readjusted herself on her bed until she was propped comfortably against the headboard. "I arranged for an in-home aide. She'll begin tomorrow."

The smile that had formed with her small words of gratitude fell. "Why did you do that?"

"Because you've not gone in to work for three weeks, and I don't expect you to put your job on hold and stay with me until I'm out of these casts."

Sean pointed a thumb at himself, his frown firmly fixed. "That's for me to decide."

"You can't—"

"I've been working from home. I don't have to go in to the office every day. That's a benefit of being the boss."

"It's going to be several weeks before the doctor will remove the casts. I don't expect you to cater to me."

"Thirty minutes back at home and you're already trying to get rid of me. Is our truce over, now that you're out of the hospital?"

"The car crash didn't change our problems. I don't know why you act as if it did."

"You almost died," he said, his voice lingering on the last word with an angry emphasis.

"I know. I don't need you to remind me. The mirror and my broken legs are enough to remind me."

The bed smelled of Sean's shaving cream and favorite cologne. She'd also noticed items on her nightstand and dresser were in different places from the last time she'd been in her room. Brenda and Edward, after driving Kayla home, had spent a week and a half in Buffalo. Although they'd stayed in the house, for some reason, it hadn't occurred to Angie that Sean would've moved back into the bedroom so his parents could use the guest room.

From the spotless room, he'd cleared out his things before bringing her home. Maybe he did realize her hospital stay hadn't altered the state of their marriage to the point of her being fine with them sharing a room and bed again.

It hadn't, and she wasn't.

"I know we still have a lot to work out." Sean found a spot on the edge of the bed beside Angie and sat facing her. "You're still entitled to your anger and distrust. Listen, there's something I've wanted to tell you but didn't feel I should until you were released from the hospital and at home."

"About the baby?"

"Yeah."

Her pulse quickened. She'd refrained from asking but hadn't been able to stop thinking about the paternity test result, no matter how hard she tried. She'd waited months to learn the truth. Angie hadn't been able to consider moving on with Sean and their marriage until the paternity of Trinity's baby was known. She'd told herself her marriage would be over if Sean's affair had resulted in a child. There were times when Angie tried to envision a life with Sean--when his child by another woman wouldn't bother her. She'd tried and failed each time.

Angie would like to think herself bigger than resenting an innocent child who had no control over the circumstances of its conception. How would their marriage change with the inclusion of Sean's fourth child and the relationship he would have to have with Trinity as they raised their kid? When Sean had informed her he'd intended to go to Trinity's home to have the paternity test done, guilt and secrets in his voice and eyes, she'd known he'd been to her home before, and not for professional reasons.

Yes, the anger and distrust remained, a pitiless weight her spirit and mind were exhausted from carrying. No, Angie couldn't continue their marriage if her worst nightmare was to come true.

Taking a slow, deep breath, Angie nodded for Sean to continue. Her legs were broken and her body covered with healing cuts. What would one more wound matter? She'd survived what could've been a fatal crash. Angie would survive this too.

"I got a call from Genetic Industries Northeast three days after you came out of your coma." Sean scooted closer, and Angie wished she could run away from the truth and her future pain. His hand reached tentatively for hers but fell inches short. "The baby's not mine."

Angie's head fell against the headboard and the fists she hadn't known were clenched relaxed. Then the tears came.

"Honey, I—"

"Are you sure?"

"Positive."

Hands covered eyes, and Angie shook Sean off when he made to comfort her. Beyond relieved, she didn't know how she felt about the news and what it could mean for their marriage. One thing she did know, and that was she couldn't deal with Sean right now.

"Would you let the children know they can come up now."

"Are you sure? I thought we could talk, now that you know."

"I need time to think and process everything. Once I have, we'll talk. But I'd really like to spend time with the children. Kayla and Zuri are more upset than I knew. I wish you would've told me. How many nightmares has Zuri had since I've been in the hospital?"

"Too many. She wakes up screaming for you. I do my best to soothe her, but she cries for you until she falls back asleep."

Sean hadn't said a word. He'd stayed at her side every day, keeping silent about his and their children's stress. As she observed her husband, ready to shoulder the entire responsibility for her homecare, she knew she'd made the right decision when she'd arranged for help. Sean needed to rest and to start taking care of himself. He wouldn't do that if he was worried about her and their children.

She may not be able to walk, but she wasn't useless. Angie snatched the phone from the cradle and dialed her son's cell.

"Hello."

"SJ, are you and the girls ready for our movie night?"

"Yup. We have the snacks and your plate of food."

"That's good. Ask Grandma to make a plate for your father and bring it up when you come."

"You got it. Comedy or action?"

"PG anything until Zuri falls asleep, then action."

"Yes. I know exactly what we can watch. Be up soon, Mom. Bye."

Angie ended the call and tossed the phone onto the bed beside her.

"I'm not hungry."

"Eat anyway then take a shower and go to sleep."

"I'm not tired either."

Could Sean sound more petulant?

"I can't make you. But please do as I ask. You've been burning the candle at both ends since my hospitalization. You can't possibly have gotten enough sleep these past weeks, no matter what you claim. The dark circles under your eyes are still there. You need to sleep."

"What if you need something while I'm sleeping?"

"The house is full of people. I'll ask my brother to bring the wheelchair into the bedroom and have him place it beside the bed. I know how to get from bed into the chair. I also know how to maneuver from the chair to the toilet. You added the toilet rails, right?"

"I did but—"

"Then I'll be fine while you get some much-needed rest. Eat, shower, sleep. If you won't do it for yourself then do it for me."

Her girls came rushing into her room. Zuri and Kayla made a beeline for Angie's bed, jumping on with bouncing gusto and wide grins. SJ and Malcolm followed, each carrying a tray laden with a plate of food.

Sean leaned in and kissed her cheek, lingering before pulling away and taking the tray from Malcolm and sitting at her desk.

By the time Malcolm brought up her chair, Sean had eaten half of his baked chicken, mashed potatoes and gravy, green beans and moist corn bread.

SJ and Sean talked while Angie ate. The simple action took on a decidedly difficult bend because Kayla and Zuri were glued to her sides.

"Kayla, tell me about your last week of dance camp."

"I don't want to."

"Why not?"

"You and Dad missed the final performance." As they had downstairs, Kayla's eyes filled with tears. "Dad called and told me you were in an accident, and the two of you wouldn't be able to make it. Granddad and Grandma were there, but it wasn't the same. I shouldn't be upset. It isn't your fault. I don't know why I'm even crying."

"Because we weren't there to support you. I'm sorry we weren't."

"It's not your fault," she sniffled.

"Feelings don't always work that way, sweetie."

SJ removed the tray from her lap and, with help from Sean, she slid down the bed until she reclined flat on her back.

"Help me with Zuri, please."

Sean helped Zuri to cuddle comfortably against Angie's chest.

"Come here, Kayla."

Angie's sensitive ten-year-old came, snuggling next to her and resting her head on her shoulder.

She held both her daughters, rubbing their backs and fingering their braids.

"I'm sorry I haven't been here for you kids. But I'm here now, and I'm not going anywhere."

"Promise?" Kayla sniffled again.

"I promise. You kids are my heart and soul. I love you."

"We love you too, Mom." SJ's smiling face loomed above Angie. "My sisters are greedy Mom hogs. I don't like it."

"You're too big, SJ." Zuri lifted an arm and shoved her brother's leg. "You saw Mommy in the hospital. That wasn't fair."

"That's a perk of being fifteen, squirt."

Zuri began to poke her tongue out at SJ but looked to Angie who shook her head at her youngest child. She settled her head back on Angie's chest and closed her eyes.

From this angle, she couldn't see her husband, but she didn't think he'd left the bedroom.

SJ made himself comfortable on the bed and turned on the television, the volume low. Crunching on popcorn, he watched a movie. Angie caught him stealing glances at her every so often.

"I'm fine. I really am," she assured him quietly.

"You look better but still not quite yourself."

"I know. Now that I'm home, I'll get even better. I'm glad you came to visit." Seeing her son had done wonders for her spirit and will.

"Dad is sleeping. Should I wake him?"

"Does he look uncomfortable?"

"He looks like he's going to fall out the chair. I should probably get Dad up and help him to his room." SJ's gaze returned to Angie. "Is Dad still staying in the guest room? He slept in here while you were in the hospital."

There was a larger question behind the one SJ posed. A discussion she wasn't yet prepared to have with her husband, much less her son.

"I'll be in here and Dad will be in the guest room."

"Oh."

How could so much disappointment live in a two-letter word? Angie reached across Kayla to SJ.

"I'm fine. I get it," SJ said with feigned nonchalance.

How could he understand when she had no answers herself?

"I'll get Dad out of the chair and into his bedroom."

"No need. I'm up."

Without another word, Sean left her bedroom. They'd have to talk soon, but not tonight.

SJ watched television until he grew tired.

"Mom, I'm going to go. Do you want me to wake Kayla and Zuri so they can go to their rooms?"

"No. Let them stay the night. You can stay too. You're already here and under the covers."

"I haven't slept in your bed since I was a kid."

"I know. You don't have to stay if you don't want to."

"No, I want to." SJ slid down the bed and pulled the comforter up to his shoulders.

"Are you comfy?"

"I feel like a baby, but yeah, this is nice."

It was nice to be home and have her children close. In time, the security her car accident had stolen from the kids would rebuild as their fear for her health diminished. Tonight's need for physical closeness was but one step on the road to her children recovering from almost losing her.

"I'm home, SJ."

He sniffed. "Yeah, I know." Another sniffle and then another.

One step at a time.

Angie fell asleep, warmed by her children's love and nearness.

CHAPTER TWENTY-THREE

Sean closed the front door, turned, and almost ran into his daughter. Hands on her nonexistent hips, Kayla frowned up at him.

"What's with the look?"

"Mommy's going to be mad."

"No, she won't."

"Ms. Pedri is nice and so was Ms. Halco. Mommy's going to be mad."

"I can take better care of your mother than they can."

His ten-year-old's head shake and knowing eyes made her seem older than her years. The girl wasn't wrong and knew it.

"You aren't better than aides, Daddy."

"Says who?" he asked, playing with his too-serious daughter. "I'm better than every in-house aide."

"They have special skills and training."

"So do I." Sean plucked Kayla's hands off her imagination, as his mother used to call his sisters' preteen hips. "I have many skills."

"As a lawyer, not as a person who takes care of people in their home. That's why Mommy's going to be mad."

"You worry too much. I'm the best at taking care of Mommy."

Kayla's long braids, white and blue beads on the ends, shifted when the girl shook her head again. Then, in a matter of seconds, Kayla's face morphed from disapproval and judgment to cunning and optimism. "Hey, what about a bet?"

He didn't like the sound of that. "What kind of bet?"

"If Mommy doesn't get mad you fired another aide, I'll do something for you. If she does get mad, you do something for me."

"Let's negotiate the terms of this bet."

They walked to the kitchen and sat on either side of the island, facing each other. Sean couldn't help smiling as his daughter with her hands folded in front of her, as grown-up as she wanted to be.

"What are you putting on the table if I win?"

Kayla pretended to mull his question over, eyes twinkling when she replied. "I'll vacuum your truck once a week for a month and take your turn reading to Zuri at night."

"For how long?"

"A month."

"Wow, a month for both. That's one heck of a deal. What do you want from me if you win?"

Again, Kayla pondered his question. This time, however, her act wasn't as well played. The scheming rascal had a plan and didn't want him to know she'd already thought this all out. Sean's firing of Ms. Pedri only served to give Kayla the opening she'd needed.

"I was thinking, for my birthday this year, I could participate in the family celebration."

The Styles had a cool tradition in which they celebrated birthdays as a group. They honored each person born during their birthday month with dance and song. Spouses celebrated spouses, parents celebrated their young children, and adults celebrated their parents.

"What exactly do you mean? I always sing for you, while your granddad likes to use the evening to dance with Grandma."

Malcolm also performed for his mother and niece, although he shared his October birthday month with both females and should be on the receiving end. When Malcolm married, he'd have a wife who would honor him in whatever loving way she chose during the Styles October celebration.

"I know it's my birthday, but I want to perform a dance with you for Mommy."

Ah, Sean understood. "The final dance from the AileyCamp?"

"We were allowed to choreograph a small part of the final show. I thought you could sing and I'd dance."

Kayla was so much like Angie, a tender heart encased in a lioness's body. She wanted to perform for her mother and thought no one would let her because children didn't participate in the celebration beyond being the recipients.

"Tell you what, we can choreograph a song/dance routine together."

"Really?" she asked, her smile reaching joyful, wide eyes that shimmered with excitement.

"Yes, really. We can buy matching outfits and everything. It's October, so a Halloween theme, obviously."

"You're going to buy me a new dress?" Her squeal was ear-piercing but also heartwarming. Sean loved making his girls happy.

"I have no idea what to get you, but I have a credit card, a truck and I know how to get to the mall."

"Yes, yes, yes." Kayla jumped from the stool. "I know everything I'll need."

He assumed as much. Thank goodness, because he had no clue. When it came to purchasing the girls' clothing, Sean left that task to their mother. Jeans, sneakers, boxers and sweats--SJ was easy, pretty much because the teen wore the same types of clothes as he did. Dress clothes, however, were Angie's domain.

A fist pump and a toothy grin preceded Kayla's, "This is going to be epic."

Sean didn't know about all of that, but Kayla's enthusiasm was infectious.

Kayla hugged him before running from the kitchen. A minute later, she returned. "Um, Daddy … ? You should call and make up with Ms. Pedri. Mommy really is going to be mad when she finds out what you did."

"I'm not afraid of your mother," he joked.

His daughter sighed, gave him a pitying look, then ran down the hallway and up the stairs.

Maybe Sean should take Kayla's advice and call Ms. Pedri. A little groveling might be in order after he'd fired her without cause or warning. If he did that, though, he'd have no reason to stay home with Angie. In the three weeks since learning he hadn't fathered Trinity's baby, his wife had retreated into her shell. He'd thought their relationship would improve, but it hadn't.

True, Angie had softened somewhat toward him, but the chill of distance remained. If he didn't stay close, helping Angie with her basic needs, she'd continue to shut him out until she was ready to give him an answer about their marriage.

"We can talk when I return from the salon with Sky and Zahra," she'd told him this morning. "I'm sorry it took me so long. I wasn't trying to string it out or to hurt you with my indecision. I needed time and didn't realize how much of it I would require."

"When you get back?" he'd repeated, confirming her statement as a promise.

"Yes."

Sean picked up the kitchen phone and dialed. Before speaking with his wife, he needed to ask his mother a couple of tough questions. Until Trinity, he would've never considered posing such personal questions to Brenda. Not that he hadn't thought them, over the years. When Sean lived at home, he couldn't help but ask himself those questions, but he'd been too angry and embarrassed to speak with his mother about his father.

Sean had, however, answered those unasked questions for himself and hadn't liked the answers. Would he like the actual answers any better than his conjured ones? Probably not.

"Hello."

"Hey, Mom. Do you have a few minutes to talk?"

"Are you sure?" Enia rolled Angie in front of the full-length mirror then pulled her hair back and off her shoulders. "This should give you an idea how your hair will look if I cut it. You've never had me cut your hair so short before."

"I know. But it's time for a change."

"Girl, you had to be wheeled into my shop. I think that's enough change for you this year. Tell her, Zah. Once I cut her hair, that's it. It'll take a long time to grow back."

Zahra bent beside Angie and looked at her in the mirror, Enia still holding her hair back. "You have the prettiest eyes and facial features. I think short hair will look good on you. What do you think, Sky?"

Sky didn't answer, and the three women shifted to look at her. She sat on the sofa against the far right wall, cell phone in hand and typing away.

"She's in a Malcolm zone," Zahra whispered. "The girl can't stay off her phone. What do you think your brother texted her this time?"

"No clue."

"Something sappy, I bet."

"Always."

Enia tapped Angie on the shoulder and winked. "Malcolm's a real cutie. You should've had him bring you to the shop today. I haven't seen that sexy brother of yours in months."

Enia was a thirty-three-year-old stylist from Philly who Malcolm described as "pretty but cultish." A fondness for piercings and black clothing, even graphic tees with images of pentagrams, devils and skulls, did not make Enia part of a cult. She just had a fondness for occult clothing and pushing people's buttons.

"I think I'm too much for him, though. Too many men are intimidated by a strong, independent woman."

Sky kept typing, her eyes lowered to her phone.

Zahra shoved Enia's leg and mouthed, "You're so bad."

True, but Zahra didn't know Sky as well as Angie did, and Enia didn't know Sky at all. Today's outing to Enia's salon was the first time she'd met Sky, and all she knew about the quiet woman was that she was dating Malcolm.

"A man like Malcolm Styles can be broken and made to see the light. That stallion can be tamed, if ridden right and prodded with sharp enough spurs."

Too far, but she'd soon learn.

Enia's cell phone dinged, and she retrieved it from the pocket of her black smock. "Someone sent me a text, but I don't recognize the number."

"You use your cell phone number for your business, I doubt you recognize the number of half the people who call you."

"Good point."

Angie glanced around Enia at Sky, who hadn't raised her head from her cell, and then back to the stylist.

"Some asshole sent me this."

She turned her cell phone to Angie and Zahra.

Zahra burst out laughing. "Oh, shit, that's good. An emoji with piercings everywhere and a don't symbol across its' face."

"Who in the hell would send me—" Enia swung toward Sky. "You undercover ninja bitch." She hooted. "You're good. I like you. Come back anytime." Shifting from playful to professional, Enia examined Sky more closely. "Your hair is natural. It doesn't know if it wants to be curly or wavy, does it?"

"The biggest battle of my childhood." Sky finally looked up from her phone but not at Enia. "Zahra's right. Between your striking eyes and high cheekbones, a short style would enhance your natural beauty. I am partial to your longer hair, though. Why do you want to cut it?"

Good question. She liked the length of her hair. It lent itself to more versatile hairstyles than shorter hair would. But every time Angie looked in the mirror she saw a car crash victim.

"No one was with me when the nurse unwrapped my head for the first time. I'd asked Sean to leave. I didn't know why at the time but was glad I had after I saw myself in the mirror. I think one of the nurses may have tried to wash the blood out of my hair, when I was in a coma, but some of it was still there. I could see it. Feel it. Dried and crusty. I could also see where Dr. Bandari had parted my hair to stitch my scalp. I guess I should feel lucky he didn't shave my head to get to the wounds. When I viewed myself in the mirror, my hair was just there, limp and lifeless. I hated the way it looked. But I hated the way it made me feel even more."

Angie had cried, even after the nurse had gone in search of Kim and her mother had washed the blood from her hair.

"I told Kayla that feelings don't always make sense." Angie spread her hair over her shoulders and examined her image in the mirror. "I have two broken legs I can't do anything about. I have aches and pains I need painkillers to dull and scars where unblemished skin used to be. I feel unbelievably vain for noticing and for caring. I'm alive and I'm grateful, but I can't help but be sad and angry over the changes forced on me. But this" her fingers combed through her hair, "I have power over. It's a change I can make."

Zahra bent over and hugged Angie. "You should've told me. I would've brought my husband's clippers over and hooked you up with an old school high top fade."

Angie laughed and swallowed her tears.

"I've got it." Enia beamed at Angie, her smile classic bad girl mischievous. "What about a short part style with line?"

Angie's reaction was an eye roll, followed by a playful arch of her eyebrow. "Don't you dare. I don't want a haircut so badly I'd let you do that to me."

"Be that way. I'll find someone who will appreciate my skills. Oh, Sky, you should let me cut your hair. All those wavy-curls would look great in a frohawk."

"You're not touching my hair."

"Why? Because Malcolm likes your hair that mix of tamed and wild?"

"He likes a lot of things, none of which you'll ever find out."

"Yup, a straight up ninja bitch." Enia clicked her tongue, showing Sky her tongue ring. "Anyway, I have several hairstyle books you can view before you make your final decision, Angie. It's no rush. My next client won't be here for another hour, and she never knows what she wants."

For fifteen minutes, Angie thumbed through Enia's hairstyle books. Zahra had pulled up a chair to sit beside her, commenting on the styles she liked and disliked. Sky, on the other hand, had relocated to the back of the salon to take a private call.

"Are you sure Sky and Malcolm are back together?" Zahra asked.

"Positive. I think their relationship was moving too fast for her, and she got cold feet and needed time to think."

"So, not really a break up but a breather to clear her head and get some perspective."

"That's a good way of putting it. I never asked her."

"Why not?"

Angie pointed to Sky, who stood as rigid as any pole, an arm crossed over her chest and cell phone up to her ear, nodding but not speaking.

"She's private."

"Obviously. Who do you think she's talking to on the phone?"

"I don't know." But based on how tight-lipped Sky was about her father, she could hazard a guess.

Private people were that way for a reason. In Sky's case, Angie sensed her private nature not only stemmed from her introversion but from family pain. Closing oneself off emotionally was one method of dealing with hurtful events. Angie could relate.

She closed the hairstyle book and lifted her skirt to show Zahra the words Sky had written on the cast of her left leg.

"May I sign your cast now?" Sky had asked.

They'd been sitting in Angie's living room, waiting for Sean to store her wheelchair in the trunk of Sky's car so Sky could drive them to a little grab-and-go café they liked before meeting Zahra at the hair salon. Since the house didn't have a wheelchair ramp, Sean had little recourse but to make two trips to the car.

"Sure, but I don't have a—"

Sky had pulled a marker from her purse and had written five words.

Now Zahra read them aloud, "Turn your wounds into wisdom." She looked up at Angie. "I think I've heard it before. Or maybe I read it somewhere. I'm not sure."

It had sounded familiar to Angie too, but she hadn't been able to place it. While Sky had driven them to the salon Angie had looked up the quote on her cell phone.

"It's a quote by Oprah Winfrey," Angie informed her.

"Makes sense. Oprah's life has included many wounds, but she didn't permit any of them to suffocate her dreams or impede her forward movement. Wounds into wisdom. I'll have to remember that."

So would Angie.

Sky had told Angie, recapping her marker and smiling up at Angie from where she'd knelt on the floor in front of her, "It's one of my favorite quotes. It's hard to remember there can be something good on the other side of pain, heartache and fear. Wisdom is deep and personal and must be earned. It can't be stolen or even given."

Sky's smile had then dimmed some, and it wasn't hard to see she'd recalled a specific moment or series of moments in her life where she'd been wounded. Had she gained wisdom from her wounds? Had her wounds been the impetus for the distance she'd put between herself and Malcolm?

Angie read it to herself now, over and again, shutting out the conversation between Zahra and Enia. It wasn't until later when Angie was sitting in her wheelchair in her bedroom, Sean in a chair in front of her and the new painting on the wall behind him, that it all clicked into place.

Sean hadn't signed her cast, hadn't drawn a picture, and hadn't written a thoughtful quote. What he had done, the day after she'd returned from the hospital, was purchased a painting and hung it on her bedroom wall above her bed.

Angie's eyes shifted from the painting to her waiting husband then back to the painting. An African American woman, dressed in white and blindfolded, stands at a cliff's edge, feet bare, one foot in the air and stepping forward. Raging ocean water smacks against the overhang. Head held high and shoulders straight, she walks forward, unseeing yet confident and trusting. She should plummet to her death, but she doesn't. For under her outstretched foot, the step of faith she willingly takes, is a large, translucent hand that extends from the sky, ready to catch her, to support her, and to keep her from harm.

"What's your decision, honey? Do you want me and our marriage? Are you willing to give me a second chance?"

Angie's gaze lifted to the painting again and the woman in the blindfold. Without that hand, she'd surely fall to her death. Yet the hand was exactly where she needed it to be, even though she couldn't see it.

Turn your wounds into wisdom, her mind repeated. *Turn your wounds into wisdom.*

Sean held out his hand to Angie, face grim and eyes beseeching her to take it. Not just his hand but the same leap of faith the woman was taking in the painting. A gift from her husband. His final plea for Angie to step into the unknown with him, trusting he wouldn't let her fall.

Fear kept her hand in her lap, but an image of a teary-eyed Sean, when she'd awoken from her coma, had her taking the biggest leap of her life.

Angie took Sean's hand. Not translucent or huge, as the hand of God in the painting, but solid and so very real.

"I love you. You won't regret giving me, giving us, a second chance."

CHAPTER TWENTY-FOUR

Angie looked up from her laptop to see a frowning Sean leading a smiling Derrick through the back door onto the patio where she was enjoying an unseasonably warm September evening. Ten minutes earlier, with Kayla holding the back door open for Angie, she'd retreated to the solitude found on the patio, leaving her children to their homework and her husband to his exercises.

She hadn't asked SJ or Sean to help her move from her wheelchair onto the sturdy outdoor furniture. A month of using a wheelchair had taught Angie a lot about her capabilities, as well as the resilience required of permanent wheelchair users.

"You didn't have to bring the papers to me."

Derrick joined her on the wicker sofa, and Sean slammed the door when he returned to the house.

Her colleague raised his face to the sky, eyes closed and the sun shining down on his smiling, upturned face. Derrick breathed deeply. "It's a nice day to be outside." Angie recognized in his expression the same appreciation of peace and quiet she experienced when sitting there. "The leaves are turning colors and the smell of autumn is in the air." Derrick nodded to the folder of documents on his lap. "I know I didn't have to deliver the papers but coming here was a great excuse to leave work early. Everyone's back on campus."

She'd wanted to at least attend the first day of freshman orientation, delivering her customary welcome speech. But she didn't have a medical clearance to return to work. EU's Board of Trustees may have called and emailed her their "get better soon" wishes but legalities trumped their impatience to have their CEO back on-duty.

"Jeanette attached yellow arrow stickies in all the places you need to sign. Here." Derrick handed Angie the folder and a black pen. Opening the folder, she dutifully went through the small stack of papers, reading and then signing where needed. "Don't forget this one," he noted, pointing to a signature line she'd missed. Derrick sighed and leaned his back against the plush red cushions. "You have a nice home, and this is a great backyard. Do you guys barbeque out here a lot?"

"Not as much as the kids would like."

Rarely this past summer, with Kayla gone and Angie disinclined to spend time with Sean in what would normally be their "quality" family time in the evening.

Angie re-clipped the papers and returned them to the folder. "All done. Thanks, again, for bringing them by."

"Are you kicking me out?"

Angie did hope he'd leave soon. She had no interest in entertaining Derrick or ignoring his tedious flirting. The time had come for her to have a serious conversation with him. Angie had miscalculated. She'd thought, with time, his interest in her would fade, especially when she gave no response he could interpret as reciprocated feelings. But her lack of a rejection seemed to either fuel his interest or his resolve.

"I assumed you had someplace better to be, on a Thursday night, than at my house on a work errand."

"No place, really. I have time, if you want an update."

Jeanette was great, and she'd kept Angie abreast of everything intended for the president's office. But, tucked away in the admin building, and only venturing past its halls coming to and leaving from work, didn't make her executive assistant a reliable source on the types of informal information she required. Derrick, however, walked the campus and spoke with a wide range of EU constituents, the way she used to. Her provost knew the pulse of the campus, information she found invaluable as a leader.

"An update would be great."

Angie handed Derrick the folder, and he began to speak. Unsurprisingly, he had much to share. The more he talked, the more she realized how much she missed her job, and the wonderful feeling of purpose that infused her at the beginning of each school year. But there was nothing like being home when her mother dropped the children off from school, excited chatter and laughter heralding their arrival.

When Derrick wasn't flirting with her, she enjoyed his company. Angie respected Derrick as a professional and liked him as a person. If she was the matchmaking type, she'd introduce Derrick to Zahra's sister, Ella.

The backdoor banged open and out came Sean, dressed in a sleeveless tank, spandex shorts and tennis shoes with anklets. In each hand, he carried a heavy-looking, adjustable dumbbell. His neck sported a black jump rope with a skull on each handle. Sean dumped the jump rope and cast-iron hand weights on the grass several feet in front of the patio, before going back into the house and returning with Angie's purple yoga mat.

In a matter of minutes, Sean had the mat unrolled with the dumbbells next to it and was lying on the non-slip surface, doing a series of stomach crunches. His back was to Angie and Derrick and his earbuds were in, but he was most likely eavesdropping on their conversation instead of listening to music.

"As I was saying, Angela ..."

She tried to focus on the conversation and her guest and not on her silent but imposing husband. He'd pulled his exercise equipment from the basement and dumped it in their backyard, becoming a deliberate distraction.

"What do you think?"

She thought her husband should've left his T-shirt on and stayed in the house. Sweat clung to Sean, rolling down his glistening back and over well-defined muscles. He stretched, bending forward, his spandex shorts form-fitting and leaving little to the imagination. When Sean had let Derrick in, he'd been wearing a pair of baggy sweats and an old T-shirt, his normal gear for working out.

Angie shook her head and forced her attention away from Sean's testosterone display. She didn't know whether her husband sought to remind her of the physical pleasure his ripped body could give her or to let Derrick know, physically, that he couldn't compete. Perhaps the second message was meant for Angie, too.

Regardless of his motivation, she couldn't deny the validity of both unvoiced claims. Her husband was an impressive physical specimen and knew it. However, arrogance combined with jealousy wasn't a good look for him.

"I think it's a good idea."

"You do?" Derrick laughed and patted Angie's shoulder. "I don't think you've heard a third of what I've said, for the last fifteen minutes."

"I was listening."

"Your ears were listening, but your mind and eyes were on your husband. I get it. He's a big guy with muscles. Each of those dumbbells are at least fifty pounds."

Derrick could boast his own fit physique. But few men compared to a six-three, former college football player, with an active gym membership he used at least three times a week.

Unlike Angie, whose attention had strayed, Derrick's focus, during their conversation, had stayed on her. It still did, despite the topic change.

"Short hair looks good on you. I meant to tell you that, when I arrived. So beautiful," he said, low but not whispered.

Derrick seemed not to have realized he'd said the last sentence aloud, or how long he looked at her before pushing to his feet and grabbing the folder of signed documents. But she'd noticed and, apparently, so had Sean.

All at once, Sean's back was no longer to Angie and Derrick. Her husband faced them, earbuds out, face drenched with sweat and brown eyes slitted in warning.

Yes, Derrick and she would have to have a frank conversation. So would Angie and Sean. But Sean kept doing things, like today's foolish stud display and the firing of her in-home aides, that had most of their conversations turning into arguments.

"The next time you'll see Dr. Styles-Franklin, she'll be back at work."

"Everyone will be happy to have Ange—"

"Dr. Styles-Franklin," Sean repeated, with a ground-out emphasis. He didn't move, not even a single step toward Derrick. But his nearness wasn't necessary to push home his point, and neither were the words that followed. "She's your boss. If she were a man, would you call your boss by his first name?"

Sean's attitude had nothing to do with sexism and double standards.

"Umm, ah …" Derrick scratched his head and Angie felt like smacking Sean upside his. "We're friends, as well as colleagues. She calls me Derrick and I call her Angela. Not all the time, of course. I know when formality is required and when it isn't."

"No one calls my wife Angela, and formality, with your boss, is always required."

"Sean." She didn't yell his name to get his attention. They had a guest and while Sean was being incredibly rude and Derrick smugly provoking, she wasn't a rope to be tugged between the two men. "Sean," she repeated, tone calm and voice even.

His heated gaze swung to her, and she didn't feel a need to say more. Despite Sean's anger, his temporary silence told her he'd heard and received her warning for him not to continue his train of thought.

"Okay, well, I should be leaving."

"You can leave that way." Sean pointed to the gate that led from the backyard. "Walk around the house to the front. It's a shortcut."

It wasn't a shortcut.

Tight lines at the edges of Derrick's mouth gave away what the rest of his body did not. Ignoring Sean, he spoke to Angie. "When will the doctor remove your casts?"

"In a few more weeks."

"Perfect. You'll be back on your feet in no time," he said with forced joviality. Securing the folder under an arm, Derrick walked to the gate and opened it. He smiled back at Angie, and then to Sean. In the seconds before he spoke, she glimpsed the open challenge in his eyes. "See you in October ... Angela."

The gate creaked behind him, his retreating words a, "kiss my ass" to Sean.

"The first and last time. If he comes here again," Sean balled his fist and punched the air, "he'll get a hard taste of Jersey. It's bad enough to have him flirt with you in the hospital and in front of me, but it's even worse for that asshole to do it in our home. You better set him straight, Angie, before I do it for you."

"You have no moral standing to say anything to me." Angie didn't care Sean had a point about Derrick's behavior and her failure to address, months ago, Derrick's unspoken but obvious romantic feelings. "When you came out here, you were already upset. Derrick calling me beautiful was a slip. He's never done it before."

"But he's thought it."

"So what. I can't control what he says let alone what he thinks, any more than I can control what you do, so stop firing my damn in-house aides."

Their building argument wasn't about him firing her aides or even about Derrick, but what they both symbolized. Anger and frustration for her. Guilt and fear for him.

"He wants to fu—"

"Don't say it."

Sean stomped across the grass onto the patio, stopping directly in front of Angie. "Me not saying it doesn't make what that asshole wants from you any less true." He dropped to the cushion where Derrick had been, hands balled into fists but eyes soft. "I know I have no moral standing to judge you, but we're still married."

"Which means what?"

"It means Derrick Murphy should have more respect for you being a married woman. He doesn't. He's a little weasel waiting for you to throw a bone his way. By bone, I mean—"

"I know what you mean. How is Derrick any different from Trinity? What did she throw your way before you took a nibble and then a whole damn bite? Don't start this shit with me, Sean. I'll speak with Derrick, not because you don't like his flirting, but because it's a conversation I've avoided having for too long. But this jealous husband routine is beyond tired and absurd."

"Tired and absurd? You act as if I don't have a right to be upset or to even worry about you and your provost."

"Everything is an argument with you."

"With me?" Sean pointed a thumb at his chest, then dropped his hand to his knee. "Come on, let's be real. We can hardly talk, anymore, without it blowing up into an argument."

"Whose fault is that?" Angie asked, the question coming out like lightning striking a rooted tree, a direct hit with heavy damage.

"Mine. Every damn thing is my fault. Cheating, my fault. Lying, my fault. Paternity scare, my fault." Fists pounded against knees. "What in the hell are we doing?"

"Fighting. Again." Angie rolled tense shoulders and slumped against the cushion behind her.

It's all they'd done since Angie had agreed to give Sean a second chance. Almost every conversation devolved into an argument. Angie was unable to get past Sean's affair. She had no idea where to begin, which left her floundering and with a sense of inadequacy.

"Go back to work. You being here all day doesn't help."

"Why, so it'll make ignoring me and our problems easier for you?"

Angie rolled her shoulders again, the action doing nothing to relieve her stress, so she snorted and glared at her husband. "The fact you believe any part of this is easy shows how little you understand me. I'll hire another aide and you can return to work."

"None of those aides can lift you. Every morning, I bring you downstairs. There you would stay until I returned home from work to carry you upstairs in the evening. Our house isn't equipped to handle your temporary condition, which means you're limited to whatever floor I carry you to. And don't pretend you wouldn't be bothered by that kind of restriction."

She would be, but while she appreciated his care and help, the intimacy of his assistance left her feeling vulnerable. Little of her daily routine occurred without his help. In Sean's mind, she was his wife, and no barriers to her body existed. For Angie, she grappled with disentangling images of him touching her with the hands he'd used to caress and hold Trinity.

Then there were the scars from the crash Sean never mentioned but his eyes invariably traveled to when he helped her wash and dress. Pride kept Angie silent about both, the two different but equally incapacitating forms of insecurity. She would hire another aide and send Sean's ass back to work before he forced her to kill him.

Refusing his help, Angie held on to the arms of the wheelchair and hoisted herself into the seat. The switch from sofa to wheelchair wasn't graceful or quick, but she would take fumbling independence over pitying assistance any day.

"This isn't working."

"What do you mean?" he asked, voice cracking in a way that told her he knew precisely what she meant.

Angie pointed between them. "Us. This. Our marriage. It isn't working."

Leaning forward, elbows on knees and the anger from earlier washed away with the harsh tide of reality, Sean watched her for several seconds before speaking. When he did, it was with frustration but also with determination. "That's because we don't know what in the hell we're doing.

We need professional help. I researched a few marriage therapists. If you want, I can email you the information."

"I'll think about it."

"Don't sound so enthused."

Her tempered flared, intermittent sparks she tried to control. "Because spilling my guts to a stranger is something I should look forward to?"

"I'll have to spill mine too."

"That's not a selling point that'll have me jumping on the counseling bandwagon. Knowing is painful."

"So is telling and being judged. Do you want to go in? It's beginning to get a little chilly."

"No, but I'd like some privacy."

"Always trying to get rid of me." He sighed. "Fine, I'll clean up my stuff and take everything inside." He kissed her cheek. "We'll get through this."

"So you keep saying, but we haven't yet." Maybe they never would, and they were deluding themselves into thinking they could mend the rift between them. "Send me what you have on the therapists, and I'll review the information."

Angie wouldn't promise him more than that, but she wouldn't continue to turn her back on one of the few options that could help them salvage their marriage.

CHAPTER TWENTY-FIVE

Sean stood outside Angie's bedroom, the door partially closed. He could hear her inside humming to Zuri, who'd awakened from a nightmare. Since Angie's return from the hospital, Zuri's nightmares had decreased. He hoped, once her casts, the last visual reminders of Angie's accident, were removed, Zuri's anxiety would ebb to nothing, taking her bad dreams with it.

Like Malcolm, Angie didn't have the greatest singing voice, but she hummed beautifully, and the melodious sound had the rewarding result of soothing their youngest daughter.

He leaned against the wall, his mind full of a conversation he'd just had with Malcolm before he'd headed home. The younger man had arrived on their doorstep, as he'd done six months ago, wanting his sister's help with Sky. Malcolm, the rare unmarried Styles at age thirty-six, had finally found a woman he wanted to marry. The problem for his brother-in-law was the woman of his heart wasn't as keen on marriage as he was. More likely, Sky needed more time to get to where Malcolm already was in their relationship.

Sean couldn't fault Malcolm for his impatience. Every time he became frustrated and angry with Angie over her snail's pace in forgiving him and moving on with their marriage, he would upbraid himself for his lack of patience and sensitivity. Sean could no more speed up Angie's recovery from his affair than Malcolm could will Sky to take him as her husband before she was ready. They'd have to wait, but that didn't equate to inaction on their parts. Malcolm would continue to romance his Sky while Sean intended to push the issue of marriage counseling with his Angie. He'd emailed her the information Thursday night. Two days later, she still hadn't given him a definitive response, the way she'd promised.

His head fell against the wall and he remembered part of his conversation with Malcolm.

"You're saying Angie's not ready to truly deal with our marriage, although she was the one to make the decision to stay together. That sounds about right. She won't be in those casts forever. In another month or so, she'll be back at work and my time with her limited."

"Back at work with Dr. Murphy, you mean?"

"That guy has a thing for my wife."

"It doesn't matter. Who else looks or is interested never matters. It only matters when we allow it to."

"Is that your way of asking me why I cheated on my wife?"

"No. That's my way of saying you should've ignored your legal assistant's interest in you. I'm saying if you were attracted to the young woman you should've fired her ass instead of fucking her. I'm saying I don't think my sister is heartbroken or vengeful enough to screw around with Murphy or any other man to get back at you. And, let's be real here, Sean, if Angie had fucked around after she'd learned about your affair, your ass would never know. Men get caught. Women rarely do, unless they just don't give a damn."

"That's kind of harsh coming from you."

"Maybe, but I'm right. Do you really think Angie had no idea you were messing around before you confessed?"

"Is that what she told you?"

"No. We're close, but Angie doesn't tell me everything. But I know her, and I know women. I'm sure she at least suspected."

"If she suspected I was creeping around on her, why didn't she say anything? I damn sure would've."

"Because to admit, even to yourself, that your spouse is cheating, means you must decide to do something, even if that something is to ignore all the awful signs of infidelity. Men, on the other hand, we want to break shit and beat the hell out of the guy fucking our woman because we're possessive and revert to our primal state when it comes to the woman who owns our heart."

Until his conversation with Malcolm, it hadn't occurred to him his wife may have suspected him of having an affair. Last December, the day Angie and he had gone Christmas shopping then spent the evening in bed making love while the children were at Malcolm's house, Trinity had called a couple of times. He hadn't answered her calls or the subsequent text messages until much later.

He'd waited for Angie to leave the bedroom and go to the kitchen before he'd checked his messages. That's when he'd found out about the pregnancy. Angie had caught him staring at his cell phone, mind whirling at the prospect of what Trinity's news could mean for his life and family. Angie had asked him about the text messages, most of which had been from Darryl. But not all, and not the most important of the bunch. But Angie had said something else to him, after he'd explained why Darryl had called and left so many messages. Within the truth he'd told Angie was also a significant lie of omission. Sean now recalled Angie's words to him.

"If you have something you'd like to tell me, I wish you would."

He'd had too much to tell her and not enough guts to do it then. Perhaps Malcolm was right. What would it mean if he were? Sean didn't know, but he intended to find out.

Sean no longer heard Angie's humming, which meant one thing. He entered the bedroom, quiet as he pushed the door fully open. As he suspected, Zuri was asleep, her head on a pillow in Angie's lap.

"I've got her." He went to scoop up their daughter, hoping Angie wouldn't ask him to allow Zuri to stay the night. They needed to talk, which wouldn't happen if Zuri bunked with Angie. With Kayla and SJ at the movies with a couple of their young adult cousins, Angie and he had the house to themselves.

When Angie didn't stop him, he took care to lift Zuri without waking her. He made short work of getting Zuri back into her own bed and tucked in. In the few minutes it had taken him to take care of his little girl, Angie had removed her dress and was struggling into a nightgown she'd taken to storing under her pillow for ease of access.

"Let me help you."

Angie waved him away. "I got it."

She didn't. The cotton material was bunched up at her waist.

"I got it," she assured him again, as he continued toward the bed.

He watched Angie wiggle until she had the nightgown pulled under her bottom and over her thighs, a Herculean task considering she had two leg cylinder casts.

When friends asked after Angie's health, Sean told them she had two broken legs but was fine. It wasn't a lie, but his response also wasn't the full truth. Most people, when they thought of a broken leg, envisioned a short leg cast that stopped below the knee, not a long cast that went from ankle up to below the buttocks. A leg cylinder cast, which both of Angie's legs were placed in, were for lower leg fractions and knee dislocations. She'd require physical therapy, once the casts were removed.

"Please stop looking at me like that. It makes me self-conscious. You, Zuri, and Kayla wear the same look. I'm not going to die."

"I know."

"Your eyes say differently."

He wanted to kiss her lips. Sometimes, when they argued, Angie's sexy lips would pull him in, despite the harsh words rolling off them. She had to know how much he wanted her. Sean never hid his feelings. Even if she could have pain-free sex, she gave no signal she wanted to reestablish their sexual relationship. As it was, she tolerated his chaste kisses and touches. Although, sometimes, like two days ago in the backyard and when he carried her upstairs tonight, he swore she desired him in return.

Moving her wheelchair from beside her bed, Sean slid the chair from under her desk and placed it in the cleared spot.

"We need to talk."

"I assumed as much, since you planted yourself where my wheelchair should be."

"I have two questions and I'd like for you to answer them honestly and for us to, for once, not argue."

"It's not my honesty that causes our arguments but your inability to handle what I have to say. You can't ask to have a heart-to-heart and then turn around and get mad and hurt when I say something you don't like. It's all or nothing with me. I can hold it in and say nothing or I can let it all out. I try not to let it all out. Trust me, I do. I also try not to be mean or bitchy, but I'm capable of both. I don't like acting out, so I'd rather stay silent."

"That's not healthy."

"My anger or my silence?"

"Both."

She exhaled a soft, warm breath of air. "I know that about myself. I won't resolve that personality flaw tonight, so go ahead and ask your first question."

For a second, Sean considered letting it go. But when he took in his wife, her willingness to dive into the deep end of the pool with him because he'd asked for her honesty, he realized she was right. He couldn't always handle her truth, regardless of its delivery.

"Did you know I was having an affair before I told you?"

He'd asked for his wife's honesty, which she could've taken as an insult, considering his own lies. To his knowledge, she'd never looked him in the face and lied. That streak continued today.

"I suspected, but I didn't know for certain until you told me. I didn't want to know the truth, so I buried my suspicions. I shouldn't have, but I did."

It was as Malcolm had thought. Did that also mean Malcolm was right about Angie's ability to have revenge sex and not tell him? The thought angered him as much as it hurt.

"I wish you would've said something."

"Why? Would you have owned up to it? Stopped? Even if I did confront you and you stopped sleeping with Trinity, so what? How long would that have lasted?"

The first thought that came to mind was a defensive statement of, "Of course I would've stopped." But he took a breath and really thought about his wife's reply. Not just her words but the unsaid implication.

He'd ended his affair because of internal motivations rather than from external demands. Sean had also confessed his sins to Angie without an uncomfortable accusation, and there seemed to be value in that for Angie.

The revelation, while wonderful, wasn't enough to relieve his tension. He still hadn't asked his second question.

"I understand your point. I hate so much about what I did during that time. Now, to know you suspected, and how that must've made you feel …" His wife kept far too much inside. More than Sean had known. More than he deserved. "I'm sorry." How many times could one man say those words? Each time was like ripping a bandage from a wound. It hurt but he felt compelled to do it over and again. "I really am sorry."

Angie looked down at her hands, and silence descended between them. Again, Sean wanted to kiss his wife, to use pleasure to take away the pain he'd put inside her heart. But it was too soon, and he hadn't earned that kind of gift from her.

Raising her eyes, she met his gaze with a blank stare. "What's your second question?"

"When we were talking to Malcolm earlier, you said something about turnabout being fair play. I know you meant that in terms of Malcolm's situation."

"I knew you were going to bring that back up. Is that your question? You want to know if I've ever cheated on you?"

Sean wanted to know if she'd cheated on him as a reaction to his affair. But Angie had framed the question to include their entire relationship.

"Yeah, that's what I want to know."

Angie paused, and in those heart-thudding seconds he understood why she had buried her head in the sand. What would he do if she had cheated? Would he have a right to be upset? Could he forgive her? Did he even deserve her fidelity?

"I haven't had intercourse with anyone else, since we became intimate."

His racing heart slowed but only a little. He'd cleared the biggest hurdle, but she hadn't fully answered his question. A lot of cheating could take place outside the realm of intercourse.

Sean remained silent, their eyes locked and him trusting his wife to uphold her promise of complete honesty.

"When you and the children were in Newark, visiting your parents after Edward's stroke, I agreed to meet Jason for dinner."

His heartbeat sped up. "Who in the hell is Jason?"

"The bartender I danced with at Zahra's bachelorette party. You said you smelled cologne on me that night. It was from Jason."

His wife had danced with another man so closely he'd left the scent of his cologne on her dress. He'd known it had to be something like that and, dammit, he'd done the same as Angie. Sean had known she had gotten close to a guy that night but hadn't pushed for details because he hadn't wanted to know. He'd also believed Zahra when she'd told him Angie hadn't done anything sexual with any man at the club.

Had Zahra lied to him? He hadn't thought so.

"You hooked up with Jason, when the kids and I were out of town?"

"It depends what you mean by 'hooked up.' We talked for a little while on the phone, the night you left. The next night, I met him at a bar."

As easy as that. He'd done something similar when Angie would work late. Hours were simple to fill with an illicit liaison when a spouse was preoccupied.

Sean didn't want to hear any more. Didn't think he could take it if he did. Yet, the hurt and guilty part of him needed to know every goddamn detail.

He gritted out, "Why did you meet him?"

"Seeing you upset and trying to suppress it should taste like sweet tea on my tongue. It doesn't, though. The flavor is bitter, and I get no pleasure from your pain. I didn't have sex with Jason, so you can cease that train of thought. But I did allow him to kiss me, and I returned the kiss. I crossed the line, and I thought about it before doing it--not premediated but intentional."

She'd kissed another man but hadn't gone further. Why?

"I knew I shouldn't have gone to the bar, or even answered my phone when he called." She shifted, readjusting the pillow behind her back. "But I wanted to know."

"Know what?"

"How you could do it." Her eyes fell to her lap again, but they were soon back on his. Hurt and anger radiated in their depths. "I wanted to know, to understand, so I met Jason and permitted a kiss I knew was wrong. He sat across from me, clear in his willingness to take the meeting wherever I wanted it to go, including back to his place or to a hotel."

All the blood in his body must've settled in the heart racing too fast and in the fists ready to find Jason and beat the shit out of him for kissing and propositioning his wife. Only his guilt kept him from flying off the handle and driving to the nightclub where Angie had met the bartender and putting his fist through the man's face.

His jaw ticked, and his leg muscles jumped, but he remained seated.

"I didn't want to go that route, not even to spite you. I'd never use my body for revenge, and I simply had no interest in having sex with a man I didn't know. And, before you ask, not even with a man I do know, like Derrick. I don't want Derrick, even though it would be easy to have him."

Easy to have him? Sean didn't like the sound of that, Angie's complete awareness of Derrick's attraction and the power she wielded to turn a professional relationship personal and sexual.

"I didn't have sex with Jason because that's not who I am or the kind of person I'd like to become."

There was the judgment. It lurked behind most of their conversations.

"When we kissed, I felt awful, and it had nothing to do with the quality of the kiss. Jason's a good kisser," she added, as if it was any other detail.

"I don't want to know what kind of kisser that punk is."

"You're right. I'm sorry. My point is that I didn't take any pleasure from the kiss, not even a guilty pleasure, the way I thought I would. It just felt wrong--so, so wrong. Then I thought of you and your two months of cheating. You did much more than kiss Trinity. I thought how callous you must've been to have sex with her and not feel enough guilt not to do it again or to stop before kisses and touches escalated to sex. Then I thought maybe you were so attracted to Trinity you didn't care you were breaking our vows because having her was more important than being faithful to me."

He opened his mouth for a rebuttal but shut it. Sean had asked for honesty, and Angie had given it to him in ugly detail. When she'd picked up the children from Newark, he'd known something had happened over the weekend. As usual, Angie had kept it to herself. But she couldn't hide her anger at Sean, even when she'd given him a birthday card. Now he understood why.

"I thought if I could understand how you were able to cheat then I could stop being so damn mad and hurt. But I don't understand beyond concluding you must've really wanted to be unfaithful, and you pushed past your morals and reservations and once you did, it became easier to do it again and again."

Edward had made a similar comment about the first affair being the hardest and each subsequent affair less so. In a way, it had been the same for Sean. The last time he'd had sex with Trinity was damn sure easier than the first time. Angie would've learned the same terrible lesson if she'd pursued the relationships both Jason and Derrick offered. It wasn't so much that Angie was incapable of finding Jason's kiss pleasurable but the fact that she hadn't granted herself permission to relax and open up to the feel of a man other than him.

"I don't think I can ever understand that mindset, and I don't want to."

There went the judgment again. Sean took it on the chin, because he deserved it and his wife could've sought solace and revenge in Jason's bed but had chosen not to.

"Kissing Jason could still be considered cheating. It was wrong, and I'm sorry for doing it and for not being brave enough to tell you before now."

Angie sounded as contrite as he had when he'd confessed, despite what had to have been a short kiss she didn't repeat or follow-up with something more carnal.

It still hurt, though. Not only the fact she'd kissed another man but the reason she'd met Jason in the first place. It all hurt because Angie's actions stemmed from Sean's affair and her pain.

She fiddled with the hem of her light-blue, cotton nightgown, the design simple, the cut loose but the lowcut V-neck and spaghetti straps were tempting. "Our marriage is so broken. At times, I feel we are too."

Scooting forward in his chair, long legs hit the side of the bed. "We aren't broken and neither is our marriage."

"Maybe not broken but definitely strained. It can't get tauter before popping."

True, but Sean wasn't a quitter, and neither was Angie.

He rose from the chair, rolled it from the bed and back to the desk where he unplugged Angie's laptop. Without asking permission, Sean joined Angie in bed and against the headboard.

He opened the laptop and a new tab and typed in his search.

"What are you doing?"

"There's a questionnaire we need to complete."

"I know the one you're talking about. You included the link in the information you sent me Thursday."

Meaning she'd taken the time not only to read the documents but to also check out the links in the main email.

"Marriage counseling, Angie. We need it."

The site he wanted appeared first in the long list and Sean clicked the hyperlink. Two more clicks had him on the intake questionnaire page for Dr. Alexis Naylor of Two Hearts Marriage Center, a licensed marriage and family therapist.

Sean scrolled slowly down the page while Angie and he read each question, then he returned to the top of the page.

Angie tilted the laptop screen forward, so she could better see while she read. "Twenty-five extremely personal questions. You'd think, if Dr. Naylor wants business, she'd ask fewer and less intrusive questions."

"She's a marriage counselor. She's supposed to ask intrusive questions. We better get used to it now." Sean eyed his wife. His heart hadn't stopped its erratic beat since they began this courageous conversation. If Angie agreed to the counseling, they'd have many more. "Tell me what you want to do. You know how I feel. I'll fight for you and for us, with everything I have. But it can't be all on me. You'll have to want it too. Do you?"

Angie looked away from Sean and to her laptop. "What problem(s) in your relationship have caused you to seek couples therapy?" Angie read. "Dr. Naylor gets straight to the point with the first question. This should be fun. I can't wait."

Sean grinned. He'd take sarcasm as long as Angie agreed to counseling. Which, thank God, she just had.

He kissed her on her lips and not at all chastely. He'd be damned if the last good kiss she'd received was from a man other than himself.

CHAPTER TWENTY-SIX

Angie never thought she'd find herself sitting on a couch in an upscale Buffalo office across from a woman who specialized in adultery counseling or, as Dr. Naylor's brochure read, "couples therapy for extramarital affairs." Yet, there she was on a Tuesday evening in her first therapy session.

"Do you understand why I asked to speak with you and your husband separately?"

Dr. Alexis Naylor, a fifty-something African American woman with light-brown eyes that watched Angie too closely, crossed her legs and leaned forward in her chair, a pen and legal pad held firmly in her hand.

"You'll use the solo sessions to determine our readiness for marriage counseling. I also assume the strategy is intended to garner answers not influenced by the presence of our spouse."

"Yes, that's correct. The questions I'll ask you and your husband will help me assess whether my services are a good fit for your needs. It's also my hope, through our discussion, you'll get a clearer picture of your counseling goals. Everyone isn't ready for counseling, even when they believe they are. Or they have misconceptions about counseling, which may serve as a barrier to reaping the potential benefits of therapy. At any point you want to stop and take a break, let me know. The same is true if you have a question."

Take a break as opposed to leave. Angie could leave whenever she wished and no one, not the professionally-dressed and articulate Dr. Naylor or a nervous Sean sitting in the waiting area, would stop her.

"Are you comfortable? Is there anything I can get you?"

Until she saw the therapist's eyes fall to Angie's legs, she thought her questions were about her comfort level with this initial session. Nothing about this situation put Angie at ease. She felt defensive, annoyed, and uneasy with the prospect of divulging her innermost feelings to a stranger, even to a woman with "training and experience in treating infidelity," something else she had read in the good doctor's brochure while they'd waited to be called into her office.

"I'm fine. Thank you."

That came out curt, but Dr. Naylor only smiled and nodded. Angie's reaction couldn't be new for her, especially at a first meeting and under tense and emotional circumstances. She'd read Angie and Sean's answers to her questionnaire and knew they were there because of Sean's affair. What kind of patient could enter Dr. Naylor's office free of anxiety? No one sane, Angie reasoned.

The therapist smiled at Angie and sat back in her chair, legal pad in her lap. Dr. Naylor hadn't written a single word yet. No doubt that would change.

"I have only a few questions. I'll pose similar queries to your husband. After Sean's session, we'll reconvene together and talk about next steps."

Angie wondered if Dr. Naylor sat in front of a mirror and practiced the art of body language, as well as speaking to herself and rehearsing what she thought to be a confident and reassuring voice. Were verbal and non-verbal communication skills a class she'd had to take for her license, or had she learned, over her twenty-plus years of practice, what worked best for her patients to yield her desired effect?

"What are you thinking right now?"

"Inconsequential and distracting things. Pointless, really. Are you going to write that on your pad?"

Laughter. Unrehearsed. "No. But I can use an electronic device instead. For some patients, they relax more when they don't see the pad. An electronic device makes it easier for them to forget the session is being recorded and they feel as if they have my full attention."

"I don't doubt I'll have your complete attention, even if you're scribbling notes on your pad. No, I don't have an issue with this form of notetaking. What's your first question, Dr. Naylor?"

There went her smile again. Calculated. Yes, the woman understood the importance of gestures, expressions, and postures. Likely, she knew body language specialists. EU employed a couple of them in the Department of Communication.

Angie rolled her shoulders and halted her wayward thoughts.

"According to the pre-session questionnaire, your husband had an affair with his employee."

Angie didn't respond to Dr. Naylor's statement. The woman knew what Angie and Sean had typed on the questionnaire, including details of Trinity's pregnancy and the result of the paternity test.

"You've known about Sean's affair for seven months but haven't sought to end your marriage. Why?"

"We have three children."

She'd spoken matter-of-factly, as if placing a period at the end of a sentence that needed no further explanation. But the four words and incomplete response required so much more than Angie wanted to supply. She would have to, though, which grated. So, she was unsurprised by the therapist's follow-up question and probing eyes.

"And that means what to you, Angie?"

"It means I have to consider their feelings and future as well as my own."

"Are you saying you decided not to file for divorce because of your children?"

"It's not that simple. My children's happiness factors into every decision I make about my life. Even still, they aren't the foundational reason why I've stayed with Sean or why I'm here."

"What do you view as the foundational reason?"

"You mentioned seven months as if that's how long I've been considering what to do about Sean and his affair. That's not true. I knew, from the beginning, if Sean was the father of his former lover's baby, I wouldn't be able to stay with him. I couldn't see myself being able to get past him fathering a child with another woman and their constant presence in our lives. What I didn't know, what I didn't allow myself to think about, until recently, was what I would do if Sean wasn't the baby's father. You have a perfectly neutral expression on your face, Dr. Naylor."

"I can smile and nod more if that will make you more comfortable."

"It wouldn't. I know when someone wants to mine for more than what I've given them. That's how I interpreted your expressionless stare. You heard what I said, but you also know there're chunks of thoughts and feelings I've left unsaid, either because I'm not self-aware enough to know them, or because I'm deliberately keeping them from you."

"Which one is it?"

"Likely, a little of both, but mainly it's my reluctance to dredge up those painful memories and feelings. I know I'll have to if I'm committed to counseling and repairing my marriage."

At that, Dr. Naylor smiled and wrote several lines of notes on her legal pad. Angie was never one to fill the air with unnecessary chatter, so Angie remained silent until the therapist finished writing whatever she thought Angie had said that had warranted recording for later reference.

"So, you are committed to repairing your marriage?"

"I'm committed to not giving up on twenty years of my life without first working to salvage it."

"Do you believe your marriage is worth salvaging?"

"If I didn't, I wouldn't be here. I thought Sean and I had a solid marriage, a great marriage. I don't know when that changed for him. Obviously, it did, though, and I missed the signs."

"Do you blame yourself for his affair?"

Dr. Naylor wrote during and after Angie's answers but never when she posed a question. Each question was delivered with her inquiring eyes and unblinking stare.

"Sometimes." She shrugged, but not for lack of anything else to say. If Dr. Naylor wanted a deeper answer, she wouldn't get it tonight.

She wrote another sentence on her pad, and Angie regretted having turned down her offer to use an electronic device for notetaking. It wasn't so much the sight of the legal pad that made her uncomfortable but the therapist's cherry picking of her responses. Each time she wrote on her pad, Angie felt judged. Common sense told her that wasn't the case. Dr. Naylor was only doing her job as a neutral third party. Still, if Angie returned, she would request the use of the therapist's cell phone or whatever she used to electronically record her sessions.

"All right. We'll return to that topic another time. I only have two more questions for you, Angie, before you can return to the waiting area and I speak with your husband."

Wonderful. Diplomacy prevented Angie from speaking the word aloud and with a heavy dose of sarcasm. Diplomacy and the fact that Dr. Naylor didn't deserve her bad attitude. Angie had agreed to the counseling, with no coercion from Sean. She did want to be there, but she also didn't, if that made the slightest bit of sense.

"You're an internal processor."

"In the extreme, I've been accused."

"By your husband?"

"Yes, but also by my parents and brother. They're all over sharers and often say the first thing that pops into their mind or that's on their heart."

"But not you. Why?"

Angie shrugged again, and Dr. Naylor's face revealed none of her thoughts. She didn't even add another line of notes to her pad.

"You still have two questions left, and I know the ones you just posed weren't the questions you were referring to earlier. They were short detours you hoped would provide you with better insight into a patient with partially open doors."

"True. Let me be plain. If you want to reap the best possible benefits from therapy, you're going to have to open all your doors--not only to me but to your husband. And he'll have to do the same for you. Secrets and evasions are counterproductive. Are you willing to change, in some areas, if it means healing yourself and working to heal your marriage?"

Angie pondered Dr. Naylor's question, reading between the lines and then acknowledging what she'd concluded months ago. Sean's cheating was a symptom of an existing issue in their marriage. While Angie wasn't to blame for Sean's affair, she was responsible for the role she'd played in the weakening of their marital bond. That train of thought had never set well with her.

In all that Dr. Naylor had said, Angie had latched on to a single word. Heal. Yes, Angie needed healing.

"You're saying therapy is as much about Sean and me as individuals as it is about us as a couple."

Dr. Naylor leaned forward again. "Couples enter therapy for a myriad of reasons. Even when both are committed to the marriage surviving, it doesn't always work out that way. In those cases, gaining closure becomes the goal of the counseling. Closure strengthens the couple as individuals. They are more confident as they move forward into a future not as a married couple."

At the thought of a future without Sean, Angie glanced to the closed door, knowing he sat on the other side, as nervous as a student outside the principal's office, unsure of his fate but determined not to run away from the consequences of his actions.

"I'm open to change."

"That's good. Final question. Do you believe cheaters can change?"

"You should've led with that question. It would've made the other ones pointless."

"Not pointless, Angie. Every question served a purpose and they are interrelated. However, if I began with the question I just posed, your partially open door would've slammed in my face."

Angie couldn't help but smirk. The good doctor had spent the last twenty minutes softening her up for the million-dollar question. Of course, she'd asked herself the same question after Sean had told her he wasn't the father of Trinity's baby and had asked her to consider giving him a second chance. Her struggle with the answer was the reason it had taken her weeks to arrive at a decision about the potential future of her marriage.

Fear had made her indecisive. Even after she'd agreed to work on their marriage, fear still haunted her. As Angie contemplated her response, fear of being wrong bubbled, like acid, in her stomach.

"I guess it depends on whether the cheater is truly guilty and feels remorse."

"Does Sean feel guilty? Is he remorseful?"

"I'm sure you'll ask him the same question."

"I will. But I'm also asking you. Do you feel your husband regrets his affair?"

For the first time, since this conversation began, Dr. Naylor had asked Angie an easy question and one she didn't want to avoid with a shrug.

"Yes."

"I can wait, if you want to accompany your wife to the bathroom."

For a second, Sean considered taking Dr. Naylor up on her offer and darting after Angie. But only for a second. Sean didn't have a death wish. Turning away from the closed office door, he smiled at the therapist and hoped she didn't think him an overprotective husband.

"The restroom for the suite is around the corner from the waiting area and down a short hall. It's ADA compliant, so Angie should be fine. If you think otherwise and don't wish to go into the women's bathroom, I could have my receptionist check on Angie for you."

"No, she would hate that. Angie knows what she's doing."

"I'm sure she does. After what happened to her, it's only natural for you to worry about your wife's wellbeing."

Sean hated thinking about Angie's car crash. Images of her wrecked car and post-surgery body invaded his dreams, most nights. Like Zuri, after a nightmare, he awoke breathless, frightened and in need of comfort. Unlike Zuri, he couldn't crawl into Angie's bed and snuggle against her, reassuring himself of her safety.

Some nights, though, when the nightmare was especially bad, Sean would peek in on a sleeping Angie. He wouldn't stay long, despite his yearning for closeness.

"You saw a news report about Angie's car crash?" Most people he knew had.

"I did." Dr. Naylor, round faced with a pug nose and a large mole above her right eyebrow that should probably be surgically removed, placed a pen and yellow pad she held on the side table next to her. "Would you like to talk about the impact of Angie's car accident on you?"

"On me?" No one except his and Angie's parents had ever asked about him. The children, of course, but never how he was coping.

"Yes. You and your children may not have been in the car with Angie but she's not the only person affected."

"I appreciate your understanding. I almost lost my wife and the mother of my children. It hurt like nothing I want to experience again. First, we thought she wouldn't survive the surgery. Then we thought she wouldn't emerge from her coma." Unconsciously, Sean's hands rubbed from thighs to knees. "For days, she had no feeling below the waist, and we feared the crash had taken away her ability to walk. As you saw, Angie's in leg cylinder casts. Her doctor assured us once they're removed she'll be able to walk."

"Sounds promising."

"She's scared as hell the doctor is wrong, and so am I."

"Does Angie know how frightened you are and how much you worry about her?"

"She knows. Angie says I look at her as if she's going to die."

"How has the car crash impacted your relationship with your wife?" Dr. Naylor picked up her pad and pen from the side table and set them on her crossed leg. "I mean in terms of your affair."

Tense and unsure what to do with his hands, he shoved them into his pants pocket only to pull them right back out and place them on his knees again. "We're pretty much where we were before the crash. Well, not exactly where we were. We talk more now, which isn't saying much considering Angie barely spoke to me before her accident. More talking also means we now argue a lot."

"You didn't argue about your affair before the accident?"

"Not really. I would want to talk things out, but Angie wanted me as far away from her as our three-level house would allow. She shut down on me and built a wall around herself to keep me out. I don't blame Angie. My affair hurt her."

"Do you feel guilty about your affair?"

"Of course, I feel guilty," Sean snapped. "What kind of question is that? You've met my wife. She bends but doesn't break. She survived all that crap I just told you about her car crash, yet she gets up every morning and doesn't complain because she's more worried about me and the children than her post-traumatic stress. I'm going to take Angie car shopping after her casts are removed. But she holds her shaking hands when she rides in a vehicle."

"After what Angie went through, PTSD is normal."

He knew that. But what in the hell was Angie going to do when she returned to work if being a passenger in a car frightened her?

"You're missing my point. Until my confession, I'd seen my wife cry twice, both times at the funeral of a grandparent. Do you have any idea how it feels to hurt your spouse so badly she breaks down in a bathroom, sick to her stomach because of something you did? I hope you don't because it rips you in two. So, yeah, I feel guilty about my affair. It's like a layer of dirty skin I want to scrub away, but I know I earned the dirt because I put it there myself."

"Forgiveness is critical to healing, Sean."

"I'm sure it is, but Angie hasn't forgiven me yet."

"I meant you being able to forgive yourself for betraying and hurting your wife. However, despite how awful you feel, a cheater's guilt is also important to the healing process. Without it, re-earning Angie's trust will be difficult. But guilt alone isn't enough."

"What do you mean?"

"Are you remorseful for your affair."

"Are you asking me if I regret having an affair?"

"I am."

Perhaps they had selected the wrong counselor for the job. What kind of patients was she used to dealing with that she needed to ask that kind of question?

Sean scooted to the edge of the sofa, elbows on his knees and irritation in his voice. "I regret everything about the time I spent with Trinity."

"Because your affair hurt your wife?"

"Of course, but not only that. My affair was wrong on so many levels. I know I'm not a perfect man, and I don't try to be. The temporary sexual pleasure was just that, fleeting and not worth the repercussions to my life and soul. Sex with Trinity was the worst decision of my life, but I can't take it back. I can only move forward and hope Angie will want to move forward with me. Regret and guilt are paltry words for what I feel."

Dr. Naylor's nod annoyed Sean, as did her notetaking right after he'd bled on her plush sofa cushion. The woman could at least let him know if he'd passed her silent test.

"One more question. Do you believe cheaters can change?"

Sean thought back to Edward's years of infidelity and his recent claim of monogamy. After having spent time with his parents this past summer, he believed his father no longer cheated on his mother. He didn't know what had changed within Edward or whether he'd just grown too old to run around anymore. Sean would have to tell Angie and the therapist about his parents, but not today.

After only a few questions, Sean was spent. No wonder Angie had looked as if she was ready to go home when she'd exited Dr. Naylor's office. Therapy was emotionally exhausting, and they hadn't even discussed the why of his affair yet.

"Cheating isn't like an incurable disease. Cheating involves choices. I had control over my choices, and I chose to cheat. I don't have a porn addiction. I don't sext or participate in online sex chat rooms. I don't have an emotional attachment to Trinity, and I have no interest in maintaining any connection to her. I broke off the affair because it was wrong, and the guilt was killing me. That's also why I told Angie, even though I was scared to death she would leave me. A part of me is still afraid she will. I have to believe cheaters can change. That *I* can change. I want my wife and marriage back. And I want Sean Franklin back."

He thought Dr. Naylor would add more notes to her legal pad, but she didn't. Instead, she reached over to the phone on the side table and picked up the receiver.

"Clarice, send Dr. Styles-Franklin in, please. Thank you."

Sean jumped from the sofa and rushed to the office door, opening it for Angie. She appeared as she had before--annoyed but willing to follow through with her promise.

He walked behind Angie as she rolled herself to the sofa. Sean sat on the sofa cushion closest to his wife, smiling at her instead of listening to whatever Dr. Naylor was saying to his left.

"Sean." Angie nodded in the therapist's direction. "Our hour is nearly up, and Dr. Naylor is trying to tell us something."

"Right, right." Sean's attention shifted to Dr. Naylor, but he reached out and held Angie's hand. If he couldn't look at his wife's beautiful face, he would soothe his anxiety with the touch of her soft skin.

"Based on my discussion with each of you, I recommend co-and-solo therapy sessions. Both would occur once a week for the next two months. After eight weeks, we would reassess. I don't expect an answer now.

You'll need time to process today's session and to discuss my recommendation with each other. Marriage counseling is a big emotional and financial commitment."

Neither Sean's nor Angie's medical insurance covered this type of therapy. Not that it mattered. When Sean had recommended counseling, he'd done so with the intention of incurring all financial costs.

"If you do decide to return, we'll begin with the development of a therapy plan. This is what you must understand: you cannot reclaim your former marriage. It no longer exists. What you must ask yourself is whether you are prepared to create a second marriage together."

CHAPTER TWENTY-SEVEN

The only benefit of Angie's refusal to speak with Sean about his affair, these past months, was the free pass she'd given him to keep the what and why of his affair to himself. Angie never asked questions or probed for details, not even when they'd argued. For that, Sean had been grateful. Then he'd gone and pushed for marriage counseling. A smart yet stupid move for the civil rights lawyer. Why? Because of this moment.

"Last week," Dr. Naylor began, "I had an opportunity to meet with you both about today's co-session. I must admit, I was surprised the two of you hadn't had this discussion before. Most couples who come to me already have, and that topic is normally the first one they'd like to discuss."

Sean's eyes wandered to Dr. Naylor's large eyebrow mole. It wasn't an unattractive feature of the therapist's face, just a conveniently distracting one. Sean would rather look anywhere than at his wife. This way, with his gaze locked on Dr. Naylor's mole, he gave the appearance of attentiveness.

Their first joint session had occurred two Mondays ago. At that initial session, Angie and Sean had done exactly what Dr. Naylor had said they'd do if they decided to employ her as their marriage counselor.

They'd created a therapy plan, much of which included activities to help build a healthy relationship and to reestablish trust. Thursdays and Fridays were their solo session days. Today was their third co-session, and Sean wanted to chew off his tongue.

"Remember I talked about the importance of being an active listener." Dr. Naylor's eyes moved from one to the other, making sure to include them both in everything she said. "For the two of you, active listening should not only involve listening to learn and to receive information but listening with an open mind and an open heart."

They'd also talked about not using accusatory language. Instead, they were supposed to express themselves by explaining how their spouse's actions and decisions made them feel.

"Angie, Sean has something he'd like to share with you. He's agreed to be open and honest. He also agreed to answer any follow-up questions you may have. His goal, for this session, is full-disclosure." Her attention shifted from Angie to him. "Sean, Angie has agreed to listen and not to interrupt. She also agreed not to punish you with silence and to also be open and honest. Is there an agreement either of you would like to add before we begin?"

Sean sucked in a deep breath and lowered his gaze to Dr. Naylor's eyes. "No. I think you covered everything."

Angie's response of, "I have nothing else I'd like to add," didn't surprise him. If her solo session was anything like his had been, she and Dr. Naylor had discussed today's session. The therapist would've sought to prepare Angie, as best she could, just as she'd done for him. Angie wasn't the type of person to make last-minute changes to an agreed-upon plan if it wasn't necessary.

When they'd arrived, one of two table chairs had been placed against a wall, leaving room for Angie's wheelchair. Unlike Sean, who'd chosen to begin the session in his normal spot on Dr. Naylor's sofa, Angie had parked her wheelchair at the wooden table. Sean now stood from the tan, rolled arm sofa and moved to sit across from his wife at the circular table.

"As I explained in last week's solo sessions, think of me as a silent observer. I'm not a referee. I'll never take sides, and you shouldn't direct your comments to me but to your spouse. Of course, if you have a question or concern during the process, feel free to pause your discussion, and I'll be here to support you. As always, if you need a break, you may take one. If I feel the discussion has veered off course and into unhealthy territory, I'll interject. The purpose of these discussions is to learn, to understand, and to grow."

For a therapist, she had plenty of disclaimers. Sean was already nervous. The more Dr. Naylor prefaced the impending conversation, the greater his tension headache. No offense, but he wished she would shut up and let him get this confession over with. At last Thursday's solo session, he'd had an epiphany about his affair. The conscious acknowledgement of a deep-seated desire had embarrassed Sean, leaving him feeling like a pathetic loser.

Angie hadn't spoken a word the entire drive to the therapist's office. She appeared to be as nervous as he felt--back straight, hands in her lap and eyes on the shiny wooden table. Soon enough, Angie's cool orbs would be on Sean, and he'd have no choice but to explain why he chose to betray her and himself by having an affair with Trinity Richardson.

When Dr. Naylor finally stopped speaking, she nodded to Sean, legal pad and pen poised to record his shame. For this session, Angie and Sean, both of whom disliked Dr. Naylor's preferred method of notetaking, thought it a better option than having a recorder on the table between them, thus ruining the illusion of a private conversation between spouses.

Angie raised her eyes, and Sean could see the pain already there, as well as the anger. He couldn't change either, so he dove into the icy ocean, no life preserver but hoping his swimming skills would be enough to keep him from drowning.

"You never asked me why I cheated. Not even the night of my confession. I don't know if I would've been able to tell you back then. I'm not even sure I knew the real reason. I mean, I gave myself excuses. And maybe those excuses were part of my motivation to cheat. I'm unsure."

He was rambling, but the way Angie watched him, cold but not un-feeling, it made opening up to her difficult. Sean didn't know how else she should look at him. With a big stupid grin on her face, as if she was thrilled to learn why her husband had screwed another woman? No, An-gie was doing what she'd agreed to do—listen without interrupting. She hadn't agreed to mask her feelings for Sean's comfort.

His hands came to the table then he dropped them back into his lap. "It began with little compliments. You know, the kind of stuff some em-ployees tell their supervisor to stroke their ego. Harmless, when only a little brown-nosing. Trinity asked a lot of questions and was eager to learn, so she started joining me in my office for lunch. I didn't invite her, at least not at first. But lunch proved the perfect time for me to answer her questions and to discuss the cases she was working on with me. I began to look forward to our lunch discussions and her questions. I en-joyed the interest she showed in the cases and in what I did for a living. I liked having someone to listen to me and who made time for me. Things escalated from there into a physical relationship. I don't want to tell you the actual details of the affair, not only because I'm ashamed of my ac-tions, but because the details will only hurt you more. I don't want to do that, but I agreed to answer any questions you may have. I'll honor that agreement."

There was more to tell, although she could surmise most of it from what he'd already shared. Much of his reasoning had to do with Trinity filling a void. The next part wouldn't be new to Angie. Sean had men-tioned the issue to her before. The problem, he now understood, wasn't the validity of his discontent but his failure to let his wife know how big the issue had gotten for him. Instead of explaining the seriousness of his concern, the way he had last December, too late and months after his af-fair, he'd remained silent and let his unhappiness with the situation fester.

Unhappy. The word felt like a peptic ulcer, an open sore he'd left un-treated for too long.

"I enjoy spending time with you, Angie. I love your smile, so I try to make you laugh. You're intelligent and passionate, and I've always felt lucky to have you in my life. When I see you with our children, my heart squeezes. You spoil them, but you also hold them to high standards, never giving false praise but always words of empowerment."

Sean couldn't understand how a man could stay with a woman, even his wife, who didn't love, cherish, and protect their children. As dysfunctional as his parents' marriage had been, Edward loved his children and Brenda had never used them to hurt him.

"Ever since you became EU's president, we don't spend much time together. You work long, late hours. Many weekends, you're at a function, which cuts into our family time. Before that eyebrow of yours raises any higher, I know you spend time with the kids. I see the effort you put in to get home before they go to bed, to help them with their school projects, to make sure there's healthy food in the house and they have home-cooked meals. You squeeze in all of that, and more, after work, between meetings, and on Sundays, the one day you never work. I know you have an important job that demands more than forty hours a week. You told me, before you accepted the position, the hours you'd have to spend at EU."

Angie had done more than that. She'd come to Sean when she'd first considered applying for the job. They'd discussed the pros and cons, as well as the probability of Angie being selected for the post. Considering the president of EU's board of trustees had suggested she apply for the position, months before the former president had retired, the chance of her earning the spot had been high, although not guaranteed.

"That's your dream job and you worked hard to get where you are. And you're damn good at it. I couldn't be prouder."

Sean had encouraged her to apply and to push past her uncertainties. He'd believed in her. The same way Angie had believed in and supported his dream of opening a law firm. He'd reassured and encouraged and thought he was prepared to absorb the personal sacrifices for her career, the way she'd done for his. He'd had no idea how difficult it would be to share his wife with so many people and how hurtful it was to end up on the bottom of his wife's list of priorities.

"I didn't have a clue how much of your time EU would take up. I didn't know how it would make me feel to no longer have your ear and time the way I used to or how much I would miss our quality time together. I discovered I'm needier than I thought and more jealous too. I'm envious of the time you spend at work, with your family and even with our kids. I know, when it comes to the children and your parents, I'm normally part of whatever is going on. But that's not what I mean. I'm talking about Sean and Angie time. That's what I've missed. That's what I wanted, and I was angry because it seemed as if you didn't miss us at all. I felt as if you made time for everything and everyone except for me. I felt like an afterthought or another box to check-off on your to-do list."

Where was a glass of water when a man needed one? Better, a hole in the floor he could jump into, hiding from the tears filling his wife's eyes caused by the truth of his emotional needs. Sean felt no embarrassment for wanting unrushed and non-children-related conversations with Angie. For expecting her to show more than a compulsory interest in his cases. For wanting to laze in bed on a Saturday morning, making love and talking, and for desiring nothing more than to go on dates with his wife. None of Sean's needs embarrassed him. His response to them not being met did.

"I should've talked to you about my emotions instead of feeling guilty about them and instead of being angry with you for failing to see we were beginning to grow apart. Sometimes, I thought you did see but didn't care because you had the job you always wanted, and being a college president trumped being my wife. I'm not saying that's how you actually felt, only that, some days, it felt that way to me."

Sean swallowed saliva and willed his shaking legs to still. He needed to share his epiphany but felt too dehydrated to continue. A bathroom break was tempting. A splash of water to his face would be nice, a stiff drink he could wash down his humiliation with would be even better.

Men were eighty percent more likely than women to have an affair. Affairs occurred fifty percent more often in big cities compared to other regions. Men were less likely than women to forgive an affair. Women were more likely to forgive a cheating partner when the affair wasn't emotional. He'd read each fact, and more, on the half dozen marriage counseling sites he'd visited before choosing Dr. Alexis Naylor. He'd also read that lack of relationship satisfaction was a common reason given for cheating, according to major studies on extramarital affairs.

Sean hadn't been unhappy in his marriage, per se, but he also hadn't been satisfied, which, shit, had made him unhappy.

He swallowed again and kept going, wanting this over and refusing to think about his fall from marital grace.

"Trinity reinforced my ego. She told me what I wanted to hear. I liked her attention. The respect, the awe in her eyes when I won a case. I didn't have to have sex with her. I shouldn't have had sex with her. I didn't want to lose you. And I thought, until last week, I didn't want you to learn about my affair, especially when it was going on. I know you remember that night I asked you if you'd known about my affair. You said you'd suspected but didn't know for sure and chose not to confront me. That had been a huge blow and I didn't understand why it hit me so hard. At first, I thought it was because you'd suspected, and the knowledge of my infidelity had hurt you for much longer than I'd known."

He hadn't given his feelings about her answer to his question much thought. She'd not only made her own confession about Jason but had also agreed to counseling. That night, he'd gone to bed with more hope than he'd had in months. Excavation of his feelings about Angie's suspicions of his affair had come later and on Dr. Naylor's comfortable sofa.

"I now know I began my affair because I wanted to get a rise out of you. I wanted you to see me, to listen to me, to remember I'm more than the father of your children and the man who shared your bed. I didn't want to get caught, but I also did. I had no idea what else to do to make myself noticed except to do something you couldn't ignore. And yet, even when you saw, when you suspected, you chose to remain ignorant, rejecting me yet again."

That last part of his sentence fell within the range of accusatory language, Sean drawing a conclusion based on Angie's actions. Dr. Naylor didn't interject, so he continued.

"I acted out in the worst way. Like a damn child deliberately breaking rules to get his parents' attention, even if it's negative attention. It's a sobering and painful realization."

"That you had an affair to garner my attention or that you selected the most devastating behavior you could think of to hurt me for me hurting you?"

"That wasn't—"

"What you were trying to do? Sure it was. According to you, I ignored you after earning my promotion. You felt as if I shoved you to the margins of my life and heart. I didn't listen when you asked me to reduce my workload and for us to spend more time together. I didn't listen, which meant I must not have cared about you. My behavior didn't change, therefore, my feelings for you must've. You built it all up in your head until you convinced yourself I had betrayed and victimized you." Long, painted nails tapped the wooden table, an angry beat betraying Angie's fraying self-control. "Contempt, neglect, indifference, violence." Angie pushed from the table. "There are a multitude of ways to betray your spouse. For you, it was fucking Trinity. Apparently, for me, it was neglect and indifference."

"Angie." Dr. Naylor got to her feet.

"Active listening, I know. Silence, I know. No accusatory language, I remember that too. I'm done."

"What do you mean?" Sean moved to Angie, who'd turned in the direction of the office door. "You agreed to have an open mind and not to run away."

"I didn't promise not to run away. And I'm not." Shaking her head then rolling her shoulders, she glanced from the door to Sean. "I need a break, and I'm taking one. Unless you want me to respond now." A loathing gaze raked over Sean, cutting him to his bleeding ulcer. "I suggest you don't take that option."

"Sean, open the door for your wife. If you want her to respect your voice and feelings, you must respect her need for space and private contemplation."

Against his better judgment, Sean let Angie go.

"That went well." Dr. Naylor reclaimed her chair, sinking onto soft-looking upholstery.

"You can't be serious." Sean followed her lead and sat.

"Quite serious. You expressed what you've been holding in for a very long time. She listened and, I believe, truly heard you."

"I hurt and upset her. Again."

"That's unavoidable, as we already discussed. It's all painful, Sean. As you know from personal experience, remaining silent doesn't reduce your pain."

"It makes it worse, I know."

"It can. When she returns, it'll be your turn to listen. You told me you aren't good with handling Angie's truth, which she knows."

"Are you saying part of the reason Angie doesn't talk to me, even though I'm always the one asking, is because I become defensive?"

"Guilt can make many people defensive. What you and Angie must discover, together, is the legacy your affair will have on you as individuals and as a couple."

Sean thought about the word legacy. Edward's serial cheating had been profoundly impactful on Sean--much greater than he'd ever wanted to admit.

"Angie hired another in-house aide."

"You're upset. Why?"

Again, he felt like a petulant child. When in the hell had Sean become so needy and covetous of his wife?

"She hired a linebacker this time. All her other aides were women and too small to assist her up and down the steps."

"I understand. Are you upset because she removed your only valid argument for staying home to take care of her or because you think you'll lose whatever traction you've made if you return to work?"

"Both, but mainly the latter."

For fifteen minutes, Sean and Dr. Naylor waited for Angie to return. When she did, her cell phone was on her lap, and her purse was hooked on a push handle. Whoever she'd called, likely Malcolm, but maybe Zahra, had given her whatever she needed to return to the session and to sit across from him, her composure reestablished.

Damn, he loved his wife. She'd taken everything he'd said, the ugly and the shameful, and matched it with grit and dignity. He owed her no less.

"I can't believe you're telling me this now," Angie had said to her mother.

After retreating from yet another one of Sean's damn confessions, Angie had ridden the elevator to the lobby. She'd found a secluded area in a corner and called Kim after failing to reach Malcolm on his cell and landline.

"I know I should've told you and your brother years ago, but I couldn't bring myself to do it."

"And you think now, and over the phone, is the best time to tell me about an old affair of yours?"

"You're so much like your father when you're angry."

"I didn't call for this."

"I know you didn't. You wanted advice and to talk. Do you still want either? From me, I mean? Charles is downstairs, if you'd rather speak with him."

Kim had blown her away, and she hadn't been in the right frame of mind to deal with her mother's confession and guilt on top of Sean's.

"I'll get your father."

"No, that's okay. I've been away from the session too long. I need to get back before Sean thinks I've abandoned him."

"Were you considering that option?"

"Leaving my only source of transportation home wouldn't be a good decision. Besides, if I call for an Uber or taxi, Sean would likely find me before the driver got here."

Not that Angie had had any intention of leaving today's session unfinished, no matter how painful listening to Sean's rationale for his affair had been.

"Your father can pick you up," Kim had suggested after a long pause between them. "But I don't recommend leaving your counseling session. You and Sean can rebuild your marriage."

"The way you and Dad did, you mean?"

"It took a long time, sweetie. ... You're mad at me. I can hear it in your voice."

Angie had felt deceived by her parents. By her mother. Did she know Kimberly Styles at all? How could the mother she thought she knew also be the same woman who'd carried on an affair and for much longer than Sean's two months? Malcolm and Angie weren't privy to every aspect of their parents' lives any more than their parents were entitled to unfettered access to theirs. Intellectually, she knew this to be true, but she'd still felt betrayed.

"I have to go, Mom," she'd told Kim.

"Okay. I know. Whenever you're ready, we can talk."

"Think about also telling Malcolm. I don't like him being the only one of us who doesn't know. I also don't want to be part of a big lie of omission we're keeping from my brother. He would hate that as much as I would."

Kim's lengthy pause had told Angie all she'd needed to know about her mother's opinion of her suggestion. Malcolm wouldn't want to know any more than Angie had. But she did know. Apparently, so did Sean. Kim had shared that unasked-for confession too.

Now, she sat, yet again, across from her husband. Angie loved and respected her mother. Kim's adultery hadn't altered her feelings toward her mother. If Charles hadn't forgiven Kim, Malcolm wouldn't exist and who knew how Angie's life would've turned out if her parents had divorced.

She looked at her husband. Really looked at him. He'd driven directly home from work, gathering up Angie so they'd be on time for this meeting. He'd spent the better part of the day in court. Yet his black suit and white shirt were no worse for wear. The same couldn't be said about his fatigued eyes and uneasy expression.

Angie placed her hands, palms-down, on the table, keeping her tapping in check. "Together, we weighed the advantages and disadvantages of me becoming EU's president."

"I know."

"We both knew the time commitment, especially for the first two years when I would be under the microscope the most. I'm so tempted to call bullshit on most everything you said in this session. And, trust me, I listened carefully."

Not responding hadn't been difficult. Being a college president meant people often sought her time and ear. Angie knew how to listen before speaking, when to challenge a speaker and when to walk away, whether mentally or physically. On more than one occasion, she'd caught herself treating Sean as she would an EU constituent vying for her precious and limited time. She would smile, not feigning interest but portraying a deeper focus than was true.

"I know you have a point about us not spending as much time together as we used to. You're not the only one who noticed. Just because I don't express myself the way you do or the way you think I should, it doesn't mean I don't care. And yes, I know I'm not always there for you. Of all the balls I have in the air, I lost track of yours. I let it fall and didn't know I had. I must own that and how my lack of awareness and sensitivity made you feel. You fell off my radar, despite you being right beside me all the time. I trusted you, relied on you and, ultimately, took you for granted. For that, I'm sincerely sorry. You aren't expendable, and I should've listened more."

Angie paused and relaxed the fingers that wanted to ball into fists and pound on the table. She could no longer throw herself at her heavy bag the way she once did to relieve stress, but she'd managed to still control and release her anger that way. Learning to workout in a wheelchair had been an adjustment she'd viewed as a trial to win rather than a contest to lose.

"None of that, however, excuses what you did. Every lunch date and conversation you had with Trinity, you could've used that time to call or text me. We've been married twenty years. I'm not going to stroke your ego, nor do I expect you to stroke mine. You may have initially slept with Trinity because you were lonely and enjoyed the fawning of a young woman, but that's not the reason you had sex with her for two months. You enjoyed the sex, the novelty of being with a different woman and the thrill of having sex with her under the noses of your colleagues."

Despite her best effort, her fingers began to thud against the table. Not as hard as she wanted to strike it but rough enough to draw Sean's attention away from her face to her hands and then back to her eyes.

"Maybe you did do it as an extreme wake-up call to me and in response to our lack of emotional intimacy. Answer me this, Sean. What are you going to do when I return to work? Even if I work fewer hours and make a concerted effort to spend more time with you, I can't change the nature of my job. Being a college president will always keep me busy, and we'll never have the time together we used to. Are you going to assume I don't care about you, that I don't miss spending time with you? Will you keep the depth of your unhappiness inside? Will you find another woman to make you feel needed and special?"

Unexpectedly, she stopped tapping. Angie wouldn't ask him questions about his time with Trinity. She had no interest in pouring salt on an open wound. She wouldn't torture herself with questions that forced him to compare her to Trinity or to even tempt him into lying to her by asking a stupid question about whether he'd enjoyed the sex. Two months of Sean going back for more answered that question. Her husband, like most men, enjoyed sex. Why would she think he wouldn't with a full-figured and pretty young woman? Angie didn't need the additional blow to her self-esteem by asking pointless questions she knew would hurt.

Sean's elbows came to the table, his hand holding his forehead. He watched her, mouth closed and eyes the same shade of worried brown he wore during every conversation they'd had about his affair. She'd grown to dislike the shade and all it represented--Sean's sadness, guilt, and at times, his hopelessness. Angie didn't see hopelessness today, though.

"We have a mountain to climb." He got to his feet, walked around the table, and knelt beside her. Sean brought Angie's hand to his chest and placed it over his heart. "I know I've given you no reason to believe me or to even trust me again, but I won't cheat on you. I'd sooner cut my heart out than put us through this again. Hyperbole, but it's how I feel."

No, not hopelessness. Purpose.

"You're asking for my trust and forgiveness?"

"No, I'm asking you not to erect barriers to the possibility of me re-earning both."

"Your infidelity makes me question everything, including my judgment. I trusted you and you took advantage of that trust. I worked and came home to you and our children every day, and you used my job as an excuse to betray me. I don't want to wonder, when I have to work late or on a weekend, if you're going to interpret those acts as a lack of commitment to our marriage. I can't be responsible for your insecurities, any more than you can be responsible for mine."

"I know." He held her hand even tighter to his chest.

"I'm still so angry with you," she admitted.

"I know that too. We're here to work on ourselves, which will make us better partners to each other. I'm going to put in the work, honey. I hope you see I've already begun. Slow and steady wins the race, right?"

She had no idea, but she nodded because he had been putting in the work. It was time for Angie to make her own overture. A healthy marriage can't exist with one person doing all the work.

"The mayor sent me two tickets for this weekend's 4U concert. They're playing at the University at Buffalo. The concert is supposed to be 'a symphonic celebration of Prince'."

They hadn't attended a concert in years. Angie normally refrained from taking personal gifts from politicians, particularly those who donated to EU. But she'd received many gifts after her car crash. With so many acts of kindness, she'd questioned the prudence of returning the gifts, considering the circumstances under which they were given.

"Are you asking me on a date, Dr. Styles-Franklin?"

"Not if you're going to grin at me like that during the concert."

Sean kept grinning, although he said, "I promise to keep my smiling to a minimum, if you promise to let me hold your hand and to feel you up when we get home."

Sean kissed said hand, his grin even brighter.

"We have an audience, if you've forgotten."

"I haven't and Dr. Naylor is used to my humor. She knows I'm joking."

"About taking advantage of me after the concert?"

"Hell no, about keeping my smiles to a minimum. I'm totally feeling you up after the concert and," he kissed her hand again, "holding your hand while listening to Prince's greatest hits. Do you think 4U will play *The Most Beautiful Girl in the World*?"

"I have no idea."

"If they don't, I'll sing it to you when we get home. You know, when I'm feeling you up."

Angie looked over Sean's shoulder for help from Dr. Naylor. The woman who vacillated between blank expressions and calculated smiles and nods was laughing.

What in the hell happened to neutrality?

CHAPTER TWENTY-EIGHT

Swollen, discolored, and bruised, those were the words that had come to mind when Sean had seen Angie's legs after her casts had been removed. His wife had always had sexy legs, smooth and firm and delectably cute. Now, they were unrecognizable, hairy and with a layer of dry, flaky skin from thigh to ankle.

"You're going to fall, if you get in like that." Holding Angie around her waist, while allowing her to grip his right hand, he helped her into the tub of warm water. "Take it slow. The last thing we need is for you to slip and fall."

Since Angie's release from the hospital, Sean's anger at the at-fault driver had ebbed. He'd been so happy to have her safe and at home, he'd stopped wishing for the man's untimely and very painful death. But a rush of fury had surged through him as Angie's casts were cut away, revealing scabs from her surgery and legs that looked too weak to hold her small frame.

"Thank you. I'm fine now."

Ignoring Angie's indirect suggestion for him to go away, he opened a bar of the mildest soap he could find at the grocery store and grabbed a washcloth from under the cabinet sink. Angie needed his help, not just with the first bath she'd taken in weeks, but even with climbing the stairs. Sean's eyes traveled to the cane propped against the closed bathroom door and he felt like breaking the damn thing in two, right after he snapped the driver's neck who'd done this to the woman he loved.

"I know you want to help, but I need a few minutes to myself." Her voice trembled and then cracked, and his blood boiled. "Please, Sean."

Dr. Naylor's voice echoed in his head about space and private contemplation, which Angie hadn't had since returning from the doctor's office. By the time they'd arrived home after stopping at the grocery store for a few supplies for Angie's legs, his in-laws were there. Between their excitement to have her out of her casts and nearly knocking her over with their hugs, she hadn't had time to process the sight and condition of half her body.

Sean should leave Angie to her solitude and wait for her in the bedroom until she finished her bath. It's what Dr. Naylor would recommend, and Sean was paying the woman a small fortune for her expertise.

Off came his shoes and socks, followed by shirt and pants. For the sake of a modesty he didn't feel, he kept his boxers on. Angie may have had no choice but to undress in front of him, but they still weren't sharing a bed, let alone having sex. If he was going to disregard her request for privacy, he could at least demonstrate enough respect for her boundaries to keep his dick from winking at her.

"Sean, that isn't necessary."

Climbing in behind Angie and all but forcing her to scoot forward to accommodate him, he sat with his long legs on either side of her, knees bent.

"Sean, I—"

He pulled her against him, her skin warm and soft and the best thing he'd touched in months. This closeness wasn't about sex but emotional support, so Sean made sure to keep his hands around Angie's waist and away from places she would construe as sexual. No matter how many times Sean had told Angie he'd feel her up, his wife had taken the statement as he'd intended it. As a joke.

"I got you. Just relax. The warm water will help some of the excess skin fall off. I'll use the gentle soap and washcloth to get off even more. But I can't scrub it off, and you aren't allowed to scratch."

"I know." Angie groaned, and relaxed fully against him. "My legs look awful and they feel even worse."

Sean had purchased a bottle of water and had filled her prescription-strength Ibuprofen at the grocery store. He'd handed Angie the bottle of water and pill bottle as soon as he'd returned to the truck. She'd wasted no time downing two pills, half the 3200 milligrams recommended daily dosage. He hoped the pills would help alleviate her pain. Sean doubted they would do much for her swelling but had confidence the circulation exercises and leg elevation, at regular intervals, would do the trick.

"Dr. Mucci said your legs are in good condition, considering the trauma they experienced. With rehabilitation, you'll be as good as new before you know it."

"When did you become an optimist?"

"The day you agreed to give me a second chance."

"My legs—"

"Will heal. I know, when you look at them, it's hard to believe you'll get back to normal, but you will."

Angie shifted until the side of her face pressed against the length of his right arm. When Sean felt liquid on his biceps he kissed the top of her head, staying silent while she wept.

This had been the reason she'd wanted him to leave her alone in the bathroom. Angie's body had endured much but so had her self-image. To him, she was as beautiful as ever, although he doubted she viewed herself in the same flattering light.

"I don't expect anything," Sean told her. He again lowered his mouth to the top of her head for a kiss.

Sean had been shocked when Angie had returned home from the hair salon sporting a short, sexy do. He hadn't known if he should comment, so he hadn't. Then he'd overheard Dr. Murphy compliment Angie's new hairstyle, and he'd wanted to smack his forehead for waiting so long. After Murphy's compliment, Sean couldn't very well follow behind the provost with his own.

"Expect what?"

"I don't expect you to suddenly forgive or trust me because I'm helping take care of you. I also don't expect you to be any less furious with me because you're taking comfort in my arms. I know it probably goes without saying, but I wanted to be clear. Hurt, angry or overflowing with joy for each other, this is us. This is what we do for each other, who we are to each other. My love for you is the one part of our marriage I don't mind you taking for granted. I give it to you without reservation."

"Thank you."

Angie squeezed his arm, the sensation gentle for the silent gratitude the touch expressed and the trust and faith she still had in him, not the trust and faith he'd shattered with his affair but the rest of him his wife knew she could rely on through sickness and in health.

"You're welcome. Are you ready for me to wash your legs?"

"Yes. Afterward, would you help me while I shower? I don't want to stay in this water with my dead skin any longer than I must. It's disgusting … and depressing."

"No problem. Dr. Mucci gave me three printout pages of your at-home exercise program. There're four ankle exercises you're supposed to do twice a day to begin. There're also two knee exercises. You should also do those twice a day until you can walk without assistance. Then you'll do those exercises once a day."

"That's six. I thought there were more."

"There are, but I can't remember the rest. Do you?"

"Not really. After the first five minutes of Dr. Mucci explaining the program, I tuned her out."

"Because you knew I was listening, or because you could refer to the printout later?"

"Both. Does our talk and shared bath count as a healthy relationship building activity? Don't laugh, Sean. I'm serious."

"I know, that's why it's so funny. Here we are, you naked and me damn near, and you're trying to wiggle your way out of our daily relationship building activity."

"We're sitting in nasty dead skin water and your semi-erect penis is pressed against my behind. Really, Sean?"

He hugged Angie and kissed her bare shoulder. "I'm sorry. I was thinking only non-sexual thoughts. I promise. But, you know, you do have a nice ass, and I've missed being this close to you. That's beside the point, though, and you're trying to distract me."

"It's exactly the point, which is sticking me in my backside. I thought you were going to wash my legs."

"I'm going to wash you all over, and this bath and conversation don't count as a healthy relationship building activity."

"One, we're communicating instead of arguing."

"We're literally in the middle of a disagreement."

"It's still not an argument, so I'm counting it as one of the criteria. Two, bathing is something we can do together. Three, we can do it regularly."

"You didn't even want me to join you. Are you now saying you want us to regularly take baths together?" He slid forward, emphasizing his point. "I'm all for it, if you are. Fourth criteria, the activity must be enjoyable for both of us." Sean poked her with the tip of his penis again, torturing himself with how good she felt and the dead-end street his flirtatious teasing would take him down. "This is pleasant for me. What about you?"

"Weekly CEO meeting?" Angie suggested, ignoring his question.

"We did that four days ago and it has the word *weekly* in the title for a reason. What about cuddle time or soul gazing?"

"This bath is nothing but one soggy cuddle time. Sean, come on. I'm peeling and want to get out of this nasty bath water. It's gross."

"You're such a girl."

"Yes, hence, your semi. And you're the one who picked the sappiest activities on Dr. Naylor's list of suggestions."

"I accept your bi-weekly CEO meeting but add cuddle time. It's called being romantic, not sappy. In fact, I want us to have cuddle time every day. I made a playlist for us."

"Of course, you did. We can cuddle before bedtime."

"Fine, but I don't want you falling asleep again."

"I won't."

She would, which suited him just fine. When Angie fell asleep, he got to hold his wife much longer than she would agree to if she were awake. As much as Sean enjoyed their banter, he disliked how they negotiated activities to build a strong relationship and to ward off the chance of divorce. They weren't limited to Dr. Naylor's suggestions and, in the weeks since they'd begun counseling, they'd devised their own, making certain they adhered to the four criteria their therapist had outlined.

Angie was right. Sean preferred activities that put him in physical contact with her. While Angie was partial to relationship builders that had them talking and opening themselves up to each other on a level beyond the physical both types of activities demanded something different from the couple. What they had in common were the requirements of openness and honesty, a prescription for a healthy relationship, according to Dr. Naylor.

Sean had no secrets from his wife, except for one. But it was a good kind of secret. Sean wouldn't ruin Kayla's surprise by revealing what his daughter and he had worked on for the last month. Everything was set for the Styles family Halloween and October birthday month celebration.

Using an arm, Sean encircled Angie's midsection, giving her a tender, loving squeeze. "All right, my lady, let's get you deskinned."

"You're not funny."

"I can feel you laughing. I like it. Your breasts graze my forearm when you do. Laugh again."

"You're shameless."

"Guilty as charged. Come on, time to get you squeaky clean."

"How many of these knee exercises am I supposed to do?" Angie used her hands to pull her right knee, now 'squeaky clean', toward her chest. Pain radiated from her hip and down to her knee. Not a sharp pain, thank goodness, but the dull ache was fierce and unforgiving. "How long should I hold this position again?"

"Hold for ten seconds, and you need to do fifteen of them on each side."

Reclining on her bed, she grimaced, not at Sean, who knelt beside her, but at the pain that refused to go away.

"How many have I done?"

"Four."

"That's it," she huffed out. Angie repeated the exercise, switching legs and conscious of her husband's matching frown. "Talk to me."

"About what?"

"Anything. Tell me how the case against the other driver's insurance company is going."

"Our lawyer is handling it. You're going to have a very good settlement by the time Desiree is finished. You don't care about the case, though."

She didn't, but Sean did. He had needed an outlet for his frustration. Since murdering the man who'd caused her injuries wasn't an option for him, taking the driver's insurance company for as much money as his lawyer friend could get, mollified her husband. Somewhat.

"I need a distraction from the pain, so tell me something you want to share."

Being told Dr. Banduri had had to operate on her two broken knees was one kind of knowledge. Seeing those same knees swollen and with an incision line from the top to the bottom was a deeper, more painful knowledge level. Her knees weren't the only parts of her legs that had been broken, though.

Angie closed her eyes and repeated the exercise, alternating legs. Angie understood Sean's anger, as well as his frustration. She shared both emotions. Some days, like today, she wanted to cry--and had. No matter how many pep talks her brother and husband gave her, or how many daily affirmations she read, she had to accept reality.

Angie would never be as she'd been prior to the car crash, neither her body nor her mind. She had a drawer with three tubes of "safe, clinically proven and doctor recommended" scar removal cream, care of Zahra. Aunt Charlene and Aunt Debbie had called to let Angie know they intended to stop by tomorrow with a light paste made from baking soda. According to her aunts, the paste was a natural exfoliator and would aid in the removal of scar tissue. Angie had no idea which home remedy she'd have to submit to first because her mother had also called and said something about roasted turmeric powder and desi ghee. She loved Kim and appreciated her need to mother her forty-six-year-old daughter, but she could do without having clarified butter spread on her legs.

"That's fifteen on both sides. Are you ready for the next exercise?"

"Not really." She opened her eyes and saw that Sean had moved to recline beside her, his eyes no less worried for his more relaxed posture. "Will you place a pillow under my left knee?"

"You can take a break, if you need one."

"I want a break too badly to take one now. If I do, I won't want to restart."

She waited for him to shake his head and call her stubborn. Sean didn't. He simply nodded and adjusted a pillow under her left knee for the next exercise.

"Flex your foot, toes pulled up, then lift your heel off the bed and straighten your leg. Yeah, like that. Try to keep your leg straight and hold that position for five seconds. Good, now nine more times before you switch sides. Do you still want to have another CEO meeting? I know you only brought up the lawsuit because of me and the funk I get in when I'm reminded how much that asshole hurt you. But we're supposed to select a topic we both are interested in talking about."

She wished Sean would go to his room and get some much-needed rest. He may have returned to work, but he made sure she was dressed, downstairs, and fed before her aide arrived and he drove the kids to school. By six, Sean was home, unless he had to stay late at the office. With Wesley's help, she managed to cook dinner and complete light housework. Even though she'd hired Wesley to spite Sean, she never asked him to carry her up and down the stairs, which meant she couldn't do laundry during the day. She did, however, have Wesley drive her to the grocery store. Angie was also capable of helping the children with their homework.

For all she could do and did do, most of the household responsibilities still fell to Sean.

"Tell me three things that made you happy this week."

"Oh, I'm the CEO today." Sean moved the pillow to her other leg, his hand skimming her thigh with more than clinical concern. She pretended not to notice. "I like it when I'm the CEO."

"That's because you like talking about yourself."

"Is that your way of calling me self-centered?"

"You wouldn't consider it an insult, if I did. I'm supposed to add a weight around my lower leg. One to five pounds."

"I have ankle weights in the basement. SJ also has a set in his closet. I could get them for you, but I think you should hold off on adding weight until the swelling has reduced and your pain has lessened. You're sweating."

"I'm not."

Leaning closely over her, he swiped the pad of his thumb over the top of her lip, producing a ripple of unwanted awareness. "Yes, you are. Right here." Two fingers from the same hand cleared away a path of sweat from her throat and halfway to her cleavage, setting off sparks she'd been trying to suppress since the moment he'd undressed and joined her in the bathtub. "And a little here. I could go—"

"No." A whispered command, but Sean's fingers stilled. "I don't want to add that weight to an already heavy day."

"I'm sorry. I didn't mean anything by it."

Angie sucked in a breath and pushed it slowly from her mouth. "All your touches have meaning."

"You're right, they do. I shouldn't have touched you like that. We haven't even talked about sex in our joint sessions."

They would soon, though. The sex conversation, Sean's testing the waters touches, and Angie's push-pull desires were all inevitable.

"So, what are three things that made you happy this week?"

It wasn't time to cuddle, yet Sean slung his arm across her stomach and spooned against her side the second she'd finished her tenth and final leg lift.

"This makes me happy."

"Sean."

"I'm serious. Being in our bed and holding you makes me happy. I know you won't tolerate this as much as I'd like, but the progress is significant to me."

This physical closeness was progress. She'd permitted short kisses to the lips and pecks to her cheeks, but those were chaste, except for the night she'd told Sean about Jason. That night, Sean had kissed her with a possessiveness unlike him. Angie hadn't returned the kiss, which hadn't diminished the fervor with which he'd claimed her lips.

"What else?"

"Darryl's oldest son's wife gave birth to his second grandchild. A big, eight-pound baby boy. He brought pics into the office yesterday. Old school, actual four-by-six glossy prints. You should have seen him, Angie. He couldn't stop smiling or talking about the baby."

"How's the mother?"

"Lena is great. He had pictures of her too. Exhausted from the delivery but looking good. They named the baby after both grandfathers. Darryl Michael O'Neal."

When SJ was born, Angie had made the same suggestion, but Sean had balked at naming his son after Edward. As with many unyielding behaviors and perspectives Sean had taken with his Newark family, Angie hadn't pushed for an explanation and he'd never offered details. Since last summer, the relationship between Sean and his parents had improved but it was still strained. Perhaps the next time they played the truth game, she would ask about his parents.

"You still have four ankle exercises to do then I'm taking you downstairs. If I keep you up here much longer, the children will break down the door and tar and feather me for keeping you to myself for so long."

"You're exaggerating."

"Barely. Do you want to know the third thing that made me happy this week?"

"You sound like a big kid wanting to tell me what you got for Christmas."

"It is a gift, but not mine. SJ has a girlfriend."

"A what?" Her head swung to Sean and her heart stopped beating.

"Damn, Angie, you can't be that kind of mother."

"What kind?"

"The kind that cuts with her eyes every girl her son dares to bring home to meet her. You're going to scare them away."

"No, I won't. It doesn't matter, anyway, because he's too young to have a girlfriend."

"Fifteen isn't too young, and girlfriend may be too big a word for it. He has a girl who likes him. Kim saw them together when she picked SJ up from school last Friday."

"Mom didn't tell me." Angie sat up and glared down at Sean. "Why are you the only one Mom told?"

"Because, when it comes to this and SJ, I'm the sane parent."

Flopping onto her back, she snorted. "Sane, huh? Wait until Kayla has her first boyfriend then we'll see who's the crazy parent."

"I have a gun and a chastity belt and I'm not afraid to use them. Now stop getting yourself worked up. I have a few more minutes of cuddle time, so stay still and let me hold you. Anyway, like I said, I don't think she's actually his girlfriend."

Angie wasn't worked up. Okay, she was, and she'd been fourteen when she'd had her first boyfriend. Charles had had a similar reaction to Angie's when her boyfriend had called the house, except he'd snarled and hung up on poor Reggie and had threatened to ground her if "that boy called again." Thankfully, Kim had intervened. But the damage had been done. The next day at school, Reggie had avoided Angie, and their short-lived, youthful relationship had suffered a quiet, uninspired death.

"Our boy is growing up. It's nice to see. He also has a crush on Sky."

"I noticed, and so has she. Sky's sweet and polite and would never hurt his feelings. As far as crushes and older women go, SJ made a good choice."

"Crushes are better when they can actually go somewhere."

Angie opened her mouth to ask if that's what had happened between him and Trinity. She caught herself before the painful question slipped free. But Sean hadn't missed her hesitation and the subtle shift in her mood.

"Your face shutters whenever you think about Trinity and me and you don't want to give voice to whatever is on your mind. Go ahead, ask your question."

"Every question doesn't need to be asked, and I don't need to know every answer, even if I think I want to. I didn't mean to ruin the moment."

"It's fine." Sean sat up and grabbed the exercise printout from the nightstand that used to be his. "You need to finish your exercises."

"Sean, I—"

"I'm good. Let's get back to work."

She'd hurt him, even though she'd stayed silent to keep from achieving that useless end. Her husband had yet to learn the difference between silence for the sake of distance and avoidance and silence in the name of caution and sensitivity.

In silence, Angie began her next exercise.

They still had so far to go.

CHAPTER TWENTY-NINE

"What are you doing in here?" Sean caught Zuri by the waist and lifted her into the air, swinging her around. "I left you in the living room with Sky and your mother. What are you doing in the kitchen?"

Sean kept swinging his daughter, incautious of the crowd of people in his kitchen and Zuri's little feet threatening heads and plates of food.

Her giggles were among Sean's favorite sounds and, thankfully, she laughed a lot, her life full of security and joy.

"I'm getting water for Mommy."

He could take care of that for his wife, as well as a little favor for his brother-in-law.

Sean placed Zuri back on the floor before grabbing a bottle of water from the fridge and handing it to her.

Music pulsed through the house, classic rhythm and blues with soul-stirring vocals and finger-snapping melodies. Sean had looked forward to tonight's celebration for weeks. Wherever the Styles gathered, good cheer followed. Angie was in one of her cool but light-hearted moods. Some frost still clung to the perimeter of their relationship, but they argued less, and Angie smiled more.

Reaching inside a cabinet, Sean pulled out a bag of Halloween candy and opened it. He knelt to Zuri's level, her eyes automatically falling to the bag he held.

"You like Dr. Sky, right?" A short nod and no eye contact from his sweet-toothed little girl. "Good. I need you to do me a favor. Zuri, look at me. Thank you. When you return to the living room, I need you to call Dr. Sky Aunt Sky."

"Aunt Sky?"

"Yes. When she marries Uncle Malcolm, she'll become your aunt. But you can start calling her Aunt Sky tonight."

Zuri's eyes lowered to the candy bag again as her lips lifted into a huge grin. When he'd described Zuri as a pixie-cherub to Malcolm and Angie last month, he'd meant it. His daughter possessed the face of an angel but the stature and mischievousness of a pixie. Zuri may be too young to comprehend the rationale behind his request, but she knew a bribe when she heard one.

A chubby hand dug into the bag of Halloween candy, drawing out a fistful of chocolate eyeballs.

"Aunt Sky," she repeated.

Since he'd turned Zuri into an accomplice and had already gone against Angie's wishes not to use their daughter to soften Sky up to the idea of marrying Malcolm, he added one more request.

"Mommy's legs still hurt a little. But you can ask if you can sit on Aunt Sky's lap. I'm sure she won't mind holding you."

No one could resist a smiling and soft-spoken Zuri. The girl oozed charm and innocence, and she resembled Malcolm enough that Sky would find it difficult to look at her and not see a child she and Malcolm could create.

"Okay, Daddy. I have Mommy's water and my candy." She'd already shoved half of her bribe into her mouth. "Aunt Sky and lap. Got it."

He kissed her baby soft cheek. "That's my girl." He needn't waste his time telling her to keep their conversation a secret. Sean had no idea what

Zuri's career path would be, but she had the early markings of an excellent spy. "Thank you, baby."

Off she went, darting around legs, squeezing past relatives, and then disappearing into the sea of bodies.

Satisfied, Sean went upstairs, stopping at Kayla's room before going to his own.

"You're not dressed yet?"

A rhetorical question. Sean's jeans and sweatshirt were answer enough. Hands on Kayla's imaginary hips and the roll of her eyes, neither action she'd take with Angie, revealed the depth of her eleven-year-old impatience and small bout of pre-performance nerves.

Sean entered his daughter's room, the orange ball gown he'd bought her on the bed instead of on her body.

"You aren't dressed either. Do you need help?"

"Mommy usually helps me, but I think I can manage by myself."

"It has a zipper on the back. Put the dress on while I'm here and I'll zip you up. Then I'll go to my room, get dressed, and then check on your grandfather, brother, and uncle."

"They're in Mommy's room."

"I know, now put on your dress."

Underneath her robe, Sean was pretty sure Kayla wore stockings and all the tween underthings she'd had him purchase when he'd taken her shopping. The items would've covered her from chest to ankles, but he still turned his back.

It didn't take Kayla long to put on her dress. Before Sean knew it, he stood opposite a vision in orange. The mannequin hadn't done the dress justice, or maybe his daughter was just so damn gorgeous he couldn't help but think her lovely in her birthday dress. Sweetheart neckline, beaded bodice with tulle accents and an A-line tulle skirt, that's how the saleswoman had described the dress to Sean, who'd looked at her with what had to have been a confused expression. He hadn't commented beyond handing her his credit card, a beaming Kayla beside him.

"If this is what eleven looks like, sixteen is going to kill me." Angie was right, when Kayla began dating he would be the insane parent.

"I can't wait until I'm sixteen, but I haven't even turned twelve yet. Mommy did my hair." Kayla turned in a full circle, making sure he saw every side of her head. "Do you like it?"

He had no idea how Angie managed both their girls' hair. The braided patterns were creative and age-appropriate. Kayla's ballerina-inspired design was braided going back and pulled up in a classy bun.

"You're gorgeous. Tonight is your special night."

She'd turned eleven a week ago, and they'd celebrated her birthday with cake and ice cream. Malcolm and the grandparents had visited, and gifts were given. But tonight's celebration would kick off the Styles holiday season of festivities and fun.

"Thank you." Kayla pushed Sean toward her bedroom door. "It's your turn. Go get dressed."

"I'm going." He laughed. Then, because a vision of Sean escorting his daughter down a church aisle popped into his head, he hugged her to him and uttered what every father should tell their daughter. "Know your value and hold on to it with both hands, especially when you're tempted to lower it or when others seek to diminish you."

At eleven, Kayla may not comprehend the depth and importance of the single sentence. But Sean would repeat it to her time and again as she grew into womanhood and any time after that she needed a reminder.

After leaving Kayla's room, Sean took a quick shower and shaved. He'd done both this morning but wanted to look and feel his best. He wouldn't disappoint his daughter. Like Kayla, he also wanted to impress Angie with their routine.

Twenty-five minutes later, he entered Angie's room to find Charles, SJ, and Malcolm putting the final touches on their matching outfits. He tossed his fedora onto the dresser, to join the others. Sean may not like wearing suits, but he looked damn good in them. "Don't think you're going to upstage me this year," he said to his brother-in-law.

Standing in front of the mirror as if he owned it, Malcolm adjusted his orange bowtie. "I'm better than you. After all this time, you need to face facts."

"You're delusional. Your sister takes pity on you every year and throws you a sympathy vote. It's pathetic."

Malcolm glanced over at SJ, whose focus was on the new cufflinks Sean had bought him and not on his joking father and uncle, and then he flipped Sean the bird.

"Neither of you have a chance of outperforming me."

In unison, Sean and Malcolm turned to face Charles. The older man wore his black suit well. The undone tie in his hand, not so much.

"You can't even tie your bowtie, and you think you're going to beat us." With care typical of Malcolm, he removed the silk tie from his father's hand. "Arthritis acting up again?"

"A little. I could've managed, but thanks for the help. You need me to sit on the bed?"

"In what universe is five-ten short? You're only six feet, Dad, I got this."

"Five-ten is average for a man, Uncle Malcolm."

"Thank you, buddy."

"What are you thanking him for?" Sean asked. "He called you average. You'll never convince Sky to marry you if you're just average."

"Oh, good, a sex conversation." No longer preoccupied with his cufflinks, SJ moved to stand beside Sean.

"What makes you think we're talking about sex?"

"Please, Dad, give me some credit. I turned fifteen over the summer."

"So, what do you think you know about sex?"

"We've had the talk. I know about sex. I'm just saying. You made an average joke, and you're talking about Dr. Sky. That was a joke about Uncle Malcolm having an average-size dick, right?"

"Don't say dick. For god's sake, Sean, is this how you're raising my grandson?"

"You've got to be kidding me. I've heard you say far worse than that around SJ."

"Come on. I'm not a kid. It's just us men in here. We can say stuff like—"

"We're men." Sean pointed to himself then to Malcolm and Charles. Finally, he pointed to SJ. "You're fifteen, like you said, and in your mother's bedroom. Have more respect, even when she's not around. Angie wouldn't want you talking like that."

His son's face hardened, and sudden anger radiated from him. "Respect? You haven't slept in here in almost a year. You think I don't hear the two of you? You think I'm too young or stupid to know what you did? Is that what respect looks like?"

Yeah, Sean had been waiting for this, although he didn't think it would happen today. Angie's car crash, hospital stay and return home had compelled everyone in the household to step up and work together. For SJ, that must've meant putting aside his anger at him. He'd always blamed Sean for the discord between his parents. Until this moment, Sean had no idea SJ had known the reason Angie and he no longer shared the master bedroom. The hurt he saw in SJ's eyes, as well as the disillusionment, brought back painful memories of his own childhood. Sean had looked at Edward in the same way the first time he'd learned his father had had sex with women other than his mother.

He'd vowed to never give his children cause to see him as a cheater and liar. Self-reproach had Sean remaining silent when he should've spoken up, but Charles stepped into the breach, a life-preserver when a man needed one.

"Come here, SJ."

As only a moody teenager could, SJ took his own sweet time moving over to Charles, glancing first to Malcolm. Like everyone else in the room, Malcolm's smile had disappeared, his expression serious.

"At your age, we all thought we knew everything. It's not until you get older and look back on your teenage years that you realize you didn't know shit. You're full of piss and vinegar, right now. I get it. But what happens between your parents is grown folk business you couldn't possibly understand. This is what you do understand, though-- your father hasn't gone anywhere. He's here. Not perfect. Not faultless. But still here because that's what responsible men do. When you've made a few fuckups of your own, you'll find out what it means to be a man and whether you are one."

"Are you saying I don't have a right to be upset?"

"You have every right. What you don't have a right to do is to allow your attitude to spoil everyone's good time. Tonight isn't about you or your dad but about your Uncle Malcolm. It's also about your sister and your grandmother. Tomorrow will come, and you'll still be mad at your dad, which is your right. Did you hear me when I said he's still here?"

"Yes."

"Good. Do you know what that means?"

"That Dad and Mom aren't getting a divorce?"

When Sean was a kid, his parents getting a divorce had been his biggest fear, too. By sixteen, he'd changed his tune, wishing his mother would grow a spine and get rid of Edward's serial cheating ass.

"It means as long as your dad's around you can mend the rift between you. It means you get to see the worth of a man, not through his accomplishments, but in how he handles his mistakes. Do you understand me?"

"Yes, sir."

With a beefy hand, Charles slapped SJ on the shoulder and then hugged his grandson. "For the record, Styles men don't have average-size dicks, no matter how short your uncle is. When we sit on the toilet, our dicks get a drink of water. That's how well-hung we are."

SJ's laugher was pure teen male who relished "manly" conversations with the older men in his life.

"Dad, come on with that."

"What? This is real talk. The boy needs to know what he can look forward to. By the way, when are you going to pop the question and get started on your own family? You'll be thirty-seven in almost two weeks.

It's time for you to release those little swimmers and add to the Styles clan."

"We aren't there yet. Stop pushing. We're taking things slow. I'll propose when the time is right and not a day before. I don't want to screw this up. Sky means too much to me to rush into anything and not get it right."

"I didn't see you as the slow starter type. By now, I thought you would've been married for a decade. You got the house, what's taking you so long to fill it with a wife and kids?"

Malcolm appeared no more pleased to be the center of his father's attention than Sean had felt having his son voice his pent-up anger and fear of the disintegration of his family.

Malcolm grabbed the fedoras and distributed them, taking care to look at the size inside each before handing them out. "I'm not a slow starter. Just because you and Mom had your first kid at twenty-three, doesn't mean I had to. I do things at my own pace."

"A snail's pace. Okay, I get why you didn't marry one of your other girlfriends. They weren't right for you. But Sky is."

"She's hot," SJ said with too much enthusiasm.

"Watch your mouth," the three men said in unison.

"Sorry. Too soon for me to add to the conversation again?"

"If there's a fifteen-year-old girl at school you want to talk about," Sean said, "share away. Sky's going to be your aunt. You can't find your aunt hot."

"Even if she is?"

"Especially if she is." Forget what he'd said to Angie about SJ's crush on Sky. Hearing it come from his mouth sounded more like teen lust and less like little boy cute. "You can't crush on your uncle's girlfriend. She's Aunt Sky. That's what I told Zuri to call her."

"You what?" Damn, Malcolm had said that as if Sean had told him he'd set Sky up on a blind date. There was far too much male emotion in this room. "Why in the hell would you do that?"

"I thought you wanted the pixie-cherub's help. I saw Zuri in the kitchen getting Angie a bottle of water, so I slipped her a couple of chocolate eyeballs in exchange for her calling Sky 'Aunt.' "

More than a couple of chocolates, but why add fuel to Malcolm's fire.

"You bribed your kindergartner with Halloween candy. Angie's going to kill you, if she finds out."

"Snitches get stiches, Uncle Malcolm."

"I'm going to kick your wannabe thug ass."

"What? I can't say that either?" SJ whined, dropping onto the bed before jumping up almost instantly. "Hey, why didn't you ask me? I like chocolate eyeballs."

Just when he thought he understood teenagers, SJ did something to prove him wrong. The boy's emotions were all over the place, and Sean couldn't keep up. Charles, on the other hand, had no problem responding in an age-old way of older black man to young black male.

He smacked SJ upside his head. "Because your father has a brain. If you called her Aunt Sky, it would've come off as a teen boy's wet dream. All creepy and with a pubescent hard-on to boot. Zuri has that angelic darling thing going for her. I bet she gobbled up her bribe before going back to Angie, all sweet as pie innocent. That girl has everyone fooled."

"All right, all right, that's enough." Malcolm's voice silenced Charles. A miracle and it wasn't even Christmas. "One last wardrobe check then we get Cinderella."

Considering how late they were retrieving Kayla, she'd probably greet them with an imperial frown and hands on her hips.

They did look good, though. Three generations of men.

Sean and SJ would have to talk. He had no idea what he'd say to SJ, especially about Trinity and Trayvon. He'd also have to tell Angie SJ knew about his affair, which wouldn't make her happy. But those were troubles for another day.

Angie didn't know if she should cry or fan herself. Probably both. With their not-so-clandestine meetings in the basement, she'd known Sean and Kayla were up to something, but she would've never guessed this. Kayla looked stunning in an orange gown she had never seen before but one she would've selected for her daughter because the color and design fit her dark, sienna skin tone and lithe form so well.

The dress moved with Kayla as she used the living room as her personal stage, the gathered Styles enraptured by her ballet routine. Her daughter danced with confidence and a ballerina's grace. More, her smile radiated passion for the art form, while her body reflected years of training and hard work. Kayla's talent was on full display.

"Isn't she lovely," Sean serenaded, singing the song Stevie Wonder had written for his daughter Aisha. Angie's husband, brother, son, and father wore matching three-piece, black suits with orange bowties, handkerchiefs and black fedoras. They'd wowed the crowd the moment they'd entered the living room. But it hadn't been their admirable lip-syncing of Gladys Knight's *Love Overboard*, the men as The Pips and Kayla as Knight, that had Angie's heart thudding with love for her daughter and desire for her husband.

Those reactions were due to the singing/dancing duet of father and daughter and the utter pride and pleasure on Kayla's face. Sean had a wonderful baritone voice, which, surprisingly, considering how much he enjoyed showing off, he didn't publicize often. These family birthday events were the rare times Sean displayed his singing talent, normally to compete against Malcolm who was a better dancer than he was.

This year, however, there was no competition, at least not for Angie, who usually liked to pop Sean's bubble by voting for Malcolm instead of for her husband. The group voting was inconsequential and done in good fun, but Malcolm, Charles, and Sean had turned it into a true competition, making voting against Sean even more amusing.

Sean tracked Kayla with his eyes and voice, following her lead as she played up the crowd. When she needed, he gave her a hand, supporting her when she twirled around him, the best partner a girl could ever have.

With over two dozen people crammed into Angie's living room and spilling out into the hallway, her attention was all for her husband and child. She saw the love they shared--a father's devotion and a daughter's trust. Sean and Kayla were in-sync in a way Angie and Sean hadn't been in months. Hell, for longer than that, if she was being honest. Sean had been right. The two of them had begun to drift apart and she'd been so consumed with proving an African American woman could successfully lead an Ivy League university she hadn't noticed the strain she was putting on her family and marriage.

Kayla's straddle split leap ended her fabulous routine and the crowd went wild. They vaulted to their feet with applause and shouts, drowning out Sean as he concluded Wonder's song. Kayla hopped into his arms and he swung her around the way he had when she was small. He kissed her cheeks and whispered words into her ear, causing her to beam even brighter.

Angie couldn't have chosen a better man to be the father of her children. Her heart reached for him, as did her body. Her mind, however, wasn't so easily won over. It warned Angie to proceed with caution.

SJ retrieved Zuri from Sky's lap where she sat beside Angie on the sofa. Sky had been as taken by Malcolm's performance as Angie had been by Sean's. Her son danced with his sisters, singing along to Sister Sledge's *We Are Family*. At that, tears did fall. But she didn't have time to dwell too long on her happy, spirited children before Malcolm drew her onto the dance floor.

"Come on, I can't let my nephew outdo me in the brother department."

"Oh, that's the only reason I'm your dance partner?"

"You're the best dance partner."

"What about Sky?"

Most of the people in the living room were dancing, including a shy Sky who Sean had invited to dance. While Angie still had trust issues with Sean, she didn't view every female as a threat to her marriage or to Sean's renewed monogamy.

"She's great, too, but I loved you first. Now, stop stepping on my toes. You're terrible at this."

"Be quiet, I'm a good dancer."

"I hate to break it to you, but you've never been a good dancer."

Angie snorted a laugh. "I thought you said I was your best dance partner."

"You are, which doesn't mean you're actually good."

"You're the worst brother ever, and I'm returning the birthday gift I bought you."

"You better not." He dipped Angie, as careful as ever, and she laughed.

Her laughter ended abruptly, after she'd been returned to her seat, when an exuberant Zuri jumped onto her thighs, landing with hard, pointy knees. Angie didn't scream, but she sure wanted to. Sharp pain exploded at the point of contact and radiated down to her knees. Closing her eyes, she sucked in a breath and rode the wave of discomfort.

"Where does it hurt?" Sean asked, and she didn't have to see him to know her husband was worried.

"Give me a minute, and I'll be fine. Zuri took me by surprise is all."

"You don't look fine. Let me take you upstairs and to bed. Everyone will understand."

Angie forced her eyes open and to her husband, who sat beside her looking concerned. Music played and her children, along with Sky and Malcolm, gazed on with the same alarm as Sean.

"I'm fine. Don't look at me like that."

"You're one stubborn woman."

"I know. I don't want to upset Zuri. Sky's holding her?"

"Yes."

Sean must've handed Zuri over to Sky after he'd pulled her off Angie. He'd been gentle with their daughter, but he'd wasted no time removing Zuri's weight from her legs.

"That's good. She likes Sky, which means she'll be asleep in less than five minutes, even with the music and laughter." Looking up at her brother, she asked, "When Zuri falls asleep, will you and Sky take her upstairs and put her to bed?"

"Of course."

"Make sure to turn on the camera and bring down the baby video monitor."

"I can take both of you upstairs," Sean offered in that gentle but pushy way of his.

"I won't lie, my legs do hurt, but not as much as you seem to believe. As I said, I'll be fine. But I won't stay down here much longer if that'll put your mind at ease. I want to watch my parents dance and see Malcolm's tribute to Mom. After those two things, I'll submit to you babying me."

"Submit?" Sean cupped her cheek and stroked with his thumb, suffusing her with sensual warmth and desire. "You don't know the meaning of that word, but I'll accept the compromise."

"Thank you."

"You'll have to come up with a better payment than your thanks. I have a few ideas, if you're interested."

"I'm not."

"I think you are, but don't want to admit to that either."

Angie was interested and, no, she wouldn't admit it.

It was another twenty minutes before Angie and Sean made their way upstairs, leaving the party early and their guests to fend for themselves.

"I could've walked," she said, from the cradle of Sean's arms, still awed, after all this time, by how easily he lifted and carried her.

Sean pushed her bedroom door closed with his hip. "You could've, but we would still be at the bottom of the stairs. You watched your parents dance, you saw old family pictures Malcolm had turned into a vid for Kim, and you saw Charles put Sky on the spot in front of everyone. I can't believe he did that. She's not a member of the family yet, no matter how much we'd all like her to be."

Sean lowered Angie's feet to the floor beside the bed, and she held on to him until she felt steady.

Angie scanned her room. "Why does my room smell like cologne and why is the comforter ruffled?"

"We used it as our dressing room."

"Dressing room?"

"Malcolm and Charles did. SJ and I got dressed in our own rooms. Do you need help getting those pants off?"

"No, I got them."

Sean watched her for all of ten seconds before shooing her hands away from her belt.

"I said I don't need your help."

"You said the same thing downstairs. I'm going to take your pants off, so I can look at your legs. Do they still hurt?"

"A little."

"A little? Why don't I believe that?"

Because it wasn't true. Angie had left her studio pouch with her pain medicine in the living room. Fortunately, she had another bottle in her nightstand drawer.

Large hands slid over her backside, Sean's gentle touch deliberate as he pushed Angie's dress slacks over her bottom and down her legs.

Holding on to his shoulder for balance, she toed out of her shoes.

"Step out of your pants." She did. "Good, now sit down and I'll examine your legs." She did that, too.

He removed her trouser socks, which left her in a flowy, burgundy, tassel-tie blouse and black panties. Although Sean had seen her in far less, since they'd stopped sharing a room and bed, she felt self-conscious and exposed. The way his big, familiar hands glided over her skin created heat everywhere he touched.

Ankles. Calves. Thighs.

"Do you feel anything?"

Yes, too much. The pain was still there, but now it existed as background impressions. The pads of Sean's probing fingers, his back and forth motion and tender kneading heightened her awareness to a simmering flame of womanly heat. His deep tissue massage, great for chronic aches and pains, had Angie reclining on her bed, eyes closed and mouth open.

Her husband was a man of many talents, and she didn't mind when he chuckled at her sigh, or maybe it was a moan of pleasure.

"Good?"

"You know it is."

"I like verbal confirmation of my quality work."

"Then consider it confirmed. Where did you learn how to do this?"

"YouTube."

Angie laughed and then, *mmm*, this time the sound she made had been a moan, an uninhibited response to the firm press of his fingers into her muscles.

"This is a bad position for you. You're not supposed to let your legs hang like this. You pull them onto the bed while I take off my suit jacket and tie."

He'd left his fedora downstairs.

Eyes still closed, Angie resituated herself more comfortably onto the bed and waited for Sean to do whatever he needed to make himself just as relaxed. When his hands found her legs again, she smiled.

They'd been so busy prepping for tonight's get-together, they hadn't engaged in today's relationship building activity. Now was the perfect time. Angie wanted to offer Sean something, wanted to let him know how much his and Kayla's performance had meant to her.

"You're an amazing father, Sean." She'd opened her eyes when she made the declaration and saw his hands still and eyes raise to hers. "I've told you before but not as often I should. You're wonderful with our children. I was reminded how much tonight. You and Kayla were beautiful together. I loved every minute of your duet. You made our daughter very happy."

He smiled, then shook his head. "She worked the hell out of me."

"What?"

"You heard me. The girl's a damn taskmaster. She's bossy as hell and will probably grow up to run the Alvin Ailey American Dance Theater, if not form her own dance company."

They laughed, and Angie forgot about the pain in her legs.

"Thank you for saying that. It means a lot. I try my best. Honestly, half the time I don't know what in the hell I'm doing. I think about their feelings first and then what they need to be successful in life and take it from there."

For Angie, she began with examples her parents had set for her, the behaviors they'd modeled, and the lessons learned they'd passed down to her. From there, she added what she wished Charles and Kim could've done with her. She omitted parts of their teachings she disagreed with, choosing to, in certain areas, parent her children differently than how she and Malcolm had been raised. She got the feeling much of Sean's parenting was him doing the opposite of how Brenda and Edward had raised him. Her husband was in too good of a mood for her to bring up the sensitive topic of his childhood and parents.

"Tell me something weird about yourself."

Sean resumed his massage. "We're playing the truth game. Nice. But you know all the weird stuff about me."

"I doubt it."

"After twenty years of marriage, you know most everything that makes me weird. But I guess there are a few things I do in the bathroom you'd probably consider strange."

"Like what?"

"Odd bathroom behaviors. Some of the weirdness revolves around the trajectory of my pee and pee bubbles. There's also the poop thing. Ever since SJ sent me that damn smiling poop emoji last year, I can't help but look at my poop before flushing. I don't know if I'm expecting it to smile back or what, but I do it every single time now. Oh, I also blow my nose in the shower."

"That one's not so weird."

"I mean without a tissue."

"That's nasty."

"I make sure it goes down the drain, and you've never noticed."

"It's still nasty."

"It's only nasty if you've stepped in my snot. Do you want me to use lotion?"

"No, it's fine." Lotion would feel better, but Angie didn't want to lose contact with Sean's hands, even if only for a minute. "Your turn. What question do you have for me?"

Sean pretended to think but asked her a question so quickly it was clear he'd been waiting for the right time to pose it.

"When I touch you like this, do you feel sexual desire for me?"

"That's unfair."

"The only rule in this game is honesty, Angie."

"But I asked you a silly question."

"You did, and I'm asking you a serious one."

"It still isn't fair."

"I'm trying to win you again. Fairness is irrelevant. But fine, I'll ask another question." Straddling her waist, Sean leaned down, his chest to hers and his mouth sinfully close. "Have you thought about kissing me tonight?"

Angie had ... and more. She didn't want to make that confession, but she couldn't wimp out of this question, too. The purpose of this activity, like the others, was to strengthen their connection. Strictly speaking, Sean wasn't wrong to pose his first question. The truth activity could range from lighthearted and playful like Angie's question, to heavy and revealing like Sean's.

"I have."

His body lowered to hers, heavy and warm and hard everywhere. Then he kissed her. Soft, full lips moved over hers, sucking then teasing with his tongue. Lips parted, and he entered her, licking her tongue and the inside of her mouth.

She moaned, and he kissed her deeper.

Her head swam with yearning and trepidation. She wanted him. It had been nine months since they'd last made love but only one month since she'd felt the slightest stirrings of desire for him. Yet, every time she envisioned them making love, she saw images of Sean with Trinity.

Even now, as Sean moved against her--his arousal a delicious weight she ached to touch and to have inside her--Trinity's words kept replaying in her head. *I recall Sean liked my hair, pulling on it when he had me sprawled over his desk and fucked me from behind.*

Angie pushed against Sean's shoulders. He didn't stop kissing her. If anything, he kissed her harder and used his big body to cage her in, keeping her firmly under him.

Yanking her mouth from his, she gulped in a lungful of air, her heart racing and Sean's eyes two glassy pools of lust. They stared down at her, a mixture of confusion, want, and disappointment.

Sean rolled off Angie but stayed close. "Your face is shuttered again."

"I know. I'm sorry."

"Why are you apologizing? I'm the one who cheated. You're having flashbacks because of me. I can't be mad about that."

Not mad, but hurt.

Dr. Naylor had explained flashbacks, how they could be something that triggers thoughts of the affair in the mind of the cheated-on spouse. Movies with infidelity could be a trigger, as could sad love songs. For Angie, it was the recurring image of a smug Trinity Richardson and her graphic description of having sex with Sean. Angie's mind filled in the rest with images she found difficult to ignore, especially when Sean tried to close the physical divide between them.

"Do you want me to leave?"

Angie reached for Sean, her hand finding his and lacing their fingers.

Bringing her hand to his lips, he kissed the palm and held her hand. "When I was a college freshman, I used to buy all kinds of crap I didn't need from the store, so the cashier wouldn't think I only went in there to buy condoms."

She smiled, grateful for Sean's patience and resolve.

"I thought of something else I do that could be considered weird. I applaud every time a plane I'm on lands safely."

Sean laughed. "You do. Thanks to you, the kids do it too. I don't know if we come across as a bunch of overly thankful passengers or extremely paranoid ones. Probably both." Leaning over, he kissed her cheek, her hand still in his. "I have to recite the entire alphabet to remember the order of the letters."

"When I was ten …"

CHAPTER THIRTY

"Hey, SJ." Sean peeked his head into his son's room. "Grab your shoes and coat and come take a ride with me."

The fifteen-year-old sat on his bed, laptop beside him and face buried in a school text. "But I'm doing—"

"Homework, I know. We won't be long. Thirty minutes. Maybe an hour. Get a move on. The sooner we leave, the quicker I can get you back home and to what looks like a great book."

"Real funny, Dad. Geometry is boring."

"You're great at math. Even better, you actually like it."

"That doesn't mean it's not boring."

Sean remembered finding a few high school classes boring, too. Those were usually the ones taught by uninspired teachers or classes that didn't challenge him. More than halfway through October, it was still early in the school year. Sean would have to find out what was going on in SJ's math class before his son used boredom as an excuse to play around in class. Better yet, he would inform Angie. This was her field of expertise, although, with her being an educator, she could be more critical of ineffective teachers than the average parent.

"Have you talked to your mother about geometry?"

"Yeah." SJ slipped into a pair of black hiking boots and grabbed a red-and-blue Buffalo Bills hoodie off the back of his desk chair and pulled it on. "I think she scheduled a phone conference with Mr. Reyes."

He should've known Angie was on top of it and that SJ would've gone to her for anything school related.

The minute they stepped out of the house SJ asked Sean, "When is Mom going to drive her new car?"

Sean's truck and Angie's new sedan were parked in the driveway. He'd talked her into purchasing a white car instead of another red one. According to a few online articles Sean had read, white cars were the "safest" color for cars.

"I mean, I know she's driven it, but not that much."

Anxiety assaulted Angie every time she got behind the wheel of her new car. Less and less each time, fortunately, but still enough unease that Angie kept her drives short and solo. She'd refused to drive the children until she'd conquered her anxiety, so afraid she'd cause an accident. Sean had a similar fear. He didn't doubt her driving ability, but the thought of her driving away and never returning home because some asshole rammed into her car, this time killing her, was a fear he hadn't been able to escape.

"The accident shook her up. Mom's taking it slow, but she'll get back in the swing of things. Did you ask her if she wanted something while we're out?"

Sean waited for SJ to buckle up before pulling out of the driveway. He and Angie always made sure the kids wore seatbelts, but the routine now had an unspoken weight they all felt.

"Mom doesn't want anything, but I have a list from Kayla and Zuri."

"A list?"

"You know how they are."

Sean did, and SJ was no better than his sisters. He bet he also had a list and a store where he wanted him to stop before returning home. Too bad, this wasn't that kind of outing. If the kids really needed something purchased for them, they would've mentioned it earlier.

For ten minutes, Sean drove. He had no destination in mind but stayed within a few miles of the house in case Angie or the girls needed him. The radio played low and Sean and SJ sat in awkward silence. He'd spent three days plotting the best approach to take with a conversation he dreaded having with his son. Nothing he thought of seemed adequate for the questions SJ would likely pose.

How did a father explain cheating on a boy's mother? Sean had no idea, especially since his own father hadn't attempted to explain himself to any of the Franklin children. When he'd had that thought, this evening, he'd known what to do. Sean didn't need a plan, he only required the courage to open a door and permit his son inside.

Sean turned in to a shopping center. He drove until he found an area with few cars and parked his truck, leaving the vehicle on but turning the radio off.

Undoing his seatbelt, he shifted to face SJ, who copied his actions. "You said some things the other day we need to talk about."

"I thought you loved Mom."

It may have taken Sean three days to work up the nerve to have this conversation with SJ, but it took his son less than twenty seconds to verbally punch him in the gut. Damn, kids had an amazing knack for going straight to the core of an issue while also missing the complex nature of relationships.

"I do."

"Then how could you do that?" SJ played with his fingers, looked out the window then finally back at Sean. "I think I knew something was going on between the two of you all those months ago, when you went away on business. You didn't really leave Buffalo, did you?"

"No."

"Mom made you leave the house?"

"She did."

"Because she found out you cheated on her, right?"

Sean nodded, but the non-verbal response wasn't enough. He needed to speak the words, to take responsibility in every way. "She did. I confessed."

SJ's eyes lowered, and head nodded.

Sean kept his mouth shut while SJ processed the confirmation of his suspicions. He'd told Angie what had happened in her room with SJ, their son's indirect accusation and open hostility. Her pissed-off reaction hadn't surprised him. For them, progress was two steps forward and one step back. Their son's knowledge of Sean's affair had refreshed his infidelity in Angie's mind.

Forty-eight percent of couples who went through counseling for extramarital affairs reached a state of relationship satisfaction. To Sean's dismay, it took those couples five years to achieve that level of success. The flip side was the thirty-eight percent of couples whose relationship deteriorated during the same five-year period. The other fourteen percent of couples had no noticeable change in their relationship. Like the divorce rate, marriage counseling success and failure rates were nearly the same percentage. Sean liked to think his and Angie's odds for full recovery were above the norm. But the way she'd walked away from him mumbling curses, when he'd told her their son knew about his affair, made him rethink that optimistic view.

"Why would you do something like that, if you love Mom? I don't get it."

His son sounded both puzzled and angry. But it was SJ's eyes that exposed his hurt, not simply on Angie's behalf but on his own.

"I remember those two weeks when we were told you were out of town. Mom was in an awful mood back then, quiet, sad, and angry. I kept thinking she would feel better if you were there. Then I wondered if you'd done something to make her that way. I know people cheat. I just never thought my dad would be one of them. I overheard you guys arguing. I know I should've gone back upstairs, when I heard you fussing in the living room, but I didn't."

SJ's focus turned away from Sean again and out the window. At a little after six on a Tuesday, but parked in front of a bank that closed at four, there wasn't much by way of scenery or people for SJ to take in. The teenager was thinking again, his age and inexperience making it difficult for him to untangle the hero image he'd had of Sean from the reality that his father was as flawed as everyone else. More, SJ had to separate the parents who loved him from the man and woman married to each other and the myth that his parents' marriage must be perfect because they'd created a safe and supportive environment for him.

Reaching out, Sean laid a hand on SJ's shoulder. The boy didn't jerk away, but he also didn't turn back to face him.

"This is what you need to know, SJ, and it's a painful but important truth you'll understand better when you're older. People are capable of both loving someone and of engaging in actions that will hurt that same person. People do all kinds of stuff that's not good for them, and they do it knowing the repercussions could hurt them or someone else."

SJ's nod had him returning his attention to Sean, who removed his hand from his son's shoulder and placed it on his own knee.

"You mean like stealing or doing drugs. I know kids at school who do both. Some of them steal from their parents to buy weed … or worse. They actually brag about it in class as if it's something to be proud of."

"Behaviors that hurt you or people you love and who love you are nothing to brag about. There are many reasons why people boast about poor choices, but rarely are those reasons based on true pride. I'm certainly not proud of what I did. I also have no intention of repeating my mistake."

"It doesn't mean you won't, though, does it?"

Angie had made a similar comment during a counseling session, but also during a couple of their heated arguments. He hoped SJ hadn't overheard those too.

"When everything is stripped away, all a man has are his actions. Values and beliefs only have meaning through our behaviors."

"Granddad calls that walking the walk. He told me I can't go around telling people what a great basketball player I am if I don't have the skills to back up my big talk. He said it's better to let my game on the court do the talking for me."

"That was some impressive paraphrasing." Sean smiled at SJ, but his son didn't return the gesture. "How many curse words did Charles's pearls of wisdom include?"

"A lot." At that, SJ did smile but less in camaraderie with his father and more with fondness for his grandfather. "I know what you're saying, Dad. I really do. It's just … well, it's hard knowing you did something so terrible to Mom and not to be mad at you. I am mad. But I hate feeling that way. I know it doesn't make any sense but …"

"No, it makes perfect sense. You're entitled to your anger, even to your disappointment. I'm disappointed in myself. But I can't let that mistake be unforgivable. I've chosen to forgive myself because I needed to, and I hate the way shame makes me feel. I know I'm not a bad person, even if I feel that way sometimes."

"I wasn't implying you're a bad person, Dad. I know you aren't."

"I know you don't think that about me. But when you commit an act that hurts someone you love, you feel like the worst kind of person. Well, you do if you have a heart and a moral compass. I'm sorry for what I did and the impact it has had on Angie and our family. We're in counseling and doing our best to work things out."

"If you can't, then what?'

Sean didn't like thinking about that possible outcome, but he had. Dr. Naylor hadn't included marriage counseling stats on her brochures and webpage for nothing. The good doctor wanted to ensure her patients knew the cold, hard facts from the outset. The thing about statistics, however, was behind each data point were real-life people with stories. For Sean, counseling wasn't a cure-all. People got out of it what they put into it. A therapist, no matter how skilled and smart, couldn't work miracles on people for whom divorce was the best option. Some individuals didn't need to be married to each other, while others shouldn't marry anyone.

When SJ's gaze skidded away and his fingers began playing with the hem of his hoodie, Sean, slow on the uptake, realized what kind of dream his son had had about Malcolm's girlfriend. More, it dawned on him that SJ neither knew who he'd slept with nor about Trinity's claim that he was Trayvon's father. Thank god.

"It was *that* kind of dream."

"Yeah, and now I feel awful. You were right, I can't have a crush on my uncle's girlfriend. He wants to marry her, you know."

Everyone knew. What the family didn't know was whether Sky Ellis would accept Malcolm's proposal, whenever the younger man got around to asking her.

"Buckle up. We can talk about it on the drive home."

"I was hoping we could stop at a store for chips, a candy bar, and soda."

"Did you wake up with a hard-on after dreaming about Sky?"

"Yeah."

"Then no junk food for you."

"That's not fair," SJ whined. "It's not my fault she's—"

Sean turned on the radio.

"That's so extra, Dad. You could've just told me to be quiet."

SJ's comment didn't require a response, so Sean strapped in, backed out of the parking space, and then lowered the volume on the radio. "Tell me about the girl Kim saw hanging all over you."

"I think you're talking about Teona."

"How many girls hang on you that you have to guess which one I'm referring to?"

Looking both ways, Sean made a left out of the shopping center and headed toward home.

"I don't ship Teona, she just wants me to." SJ sighed and slumped in the seat, melodramatic and funny as hell. "She is pretty, though."

"Then go for it."

"I don't know if I'm ready. I'm still raw from losing my Dr. Sky."

Sean snapped his fingers in front of SJ's face, hoping to snap him out of his teen delusion. "Newsflash, Sky was only yours in your wet dream."

"Savage, Dad." He clutched at his hoodie around the area of his heart. "So cruel."

"I got your savage and cruel right here." Sean punched his son in the shoulder, a manly love-tap.

"Ow," SJ deadpanned, rubbing his arm as if Sean had hit him full force. "If you ever want to, you know, take Mom out or something, I can babysit Kayla and Zuri. You don't have to call in the grands or Uncle Malcolm."

"Thanks. I think I'll take you up on that offer."

"Great." SJ perked up, sitting up straight and smiling. "That'll be twenty bucks an hour."

"Or chips, a candy bar, and a soda?"

SJ shrugged, a con artist in the making. "If you insist on paying me with junk food, fine. I'm a flexible guy."

Sean laughed, punched SJ in the shoulder again, then drove toward the closest convenience store. He'd been suckered by a fifteen-year-old. But dating his wife, especially after the good time they'd had at the Prince tribute concert, was a great relationship building activity they needed to do more often.

Sean would do his part to make sure they did.

CHAPTER THIRTY-ONE

"If I don't see you again before Thanksgiving break, enjoy your time with family and friends."

Variations of the same well-wish were returned to Angie by members of her executive leadership team but with an additional, "Be safe" and "Take care of yourself."

With smiles, they filed out of her office. They were a great team and had filled in during her absence with skill and effectiveness, despite strong personalities and different styles of leadership. Still, Angie detected friction between two members of her team, more than had existed before her medical leave of absence. She would address the issue after break, instead of allowing it to grow the way she had the matter she would deal with right now.

"Dr. Murphy, if you have a few minutes, please."

He stopped at her office door, then moved to the right so Dr. Mateosky could pass. The tall blonde waved at Angie again, her smile as sweet as the woman herself.

"Did you have a question about my report?"

"No. Close the door, please, and join me."

Angie leaned against the conference table, having stood when her team began their exodus. Now, she slipped back into her chair, her cane beside her desk on the other side of the room. Thanks to her physiotherapist, her legs were stronger and her walking more sure-footed. She didn't rely on her cane as often as she once had, and, with Sky's help these past few weeks, her upper body was getting as much of a workout as her lower half.

At the Halloween/October celebration, Sky had offered to workout with Angie, going so far as to drive to her home, pick her up and take her to Sky's apartment building. At first, Angie had been intimidated. Sky ran like a woman possessed and was in excellent shape. But, when she'd taken Angie to the fitness center in her apartment building that first time, and had talked her through a series of manageable core and arm exercises, her tension had eased. Now, she looked forward to their Saturday morning exercise routines.

She wasn't, however, looking forward to this conversation. While Angie valued honesty and straightforwardness, they were like one of those rubber door wedges elementary school teachers used to hold the classroom door open. Once the door was propped open, anyone could see inside the classroom and choose to enter. With counseling, Angie's life had turned into an open-door classroom, compelling Angie toward honesty and straightforwardness when she'd rather slam the door shut and ignore what happened on the other side.

Derrick pulled out the chair beside Angie and sat. Today he wore a charcoal suit and a smile he used with Angie when they were alone. She'd dismissed this smile countless times, as well as the meaning behind it. She wouldn't any longer, not because she feared Derrick would do or say something that would give Sean the excuse he wanted to act the role of possessive husband, but because Derrick had crossed the professional line in a dozen little ways. And she had allowed it to happen. Ignoring his interest had seemed the wisest course of action.

She'd been wrong.

Angie didn't fear confrontation. What she'd wanted to avoid was an uncomfortable work environment.

"We need to talk."

"Sure. About what?"

Their knees touched because, when Derrick had sat next to her, he'd positioned himself so they would. A seemingly innocuous action and easy to dismiss, but it was one of many ways he deliberately crossed the line without being overt.

"Move your chair back."

"Excuse me?"

"I said for you to move your chair back." Eyes glued to Derrick's, Angie lowered her chin in the direction of their knees. "Today will be the last time you do something like that."

He scooted his chair to the spot where he'd pulled it from. "You asked to speak with me, so I sat. A little too close, I guess, but I've sat beside you like this before."

"You have, and you've grazed my leg in the same way before too. Just as you've brought me flowers before, although I've told you not to. Just as you've asked me to lunch and dinner, when it would've been only the two of us."

"We're friends. That's what friends do."

"You're right. Going out for meals and giving gifts are what friends do. However, we are colleagues who have a good working relationship, which I'd like to maintain. We are not friends. At least not in the way you'd like to define that word."

"If this is about what happened between Mr. Franklin and me, he got it wrong. I like and respect you, Angela. That's all he saw that day. I was also worried about you. Everyone at EU was."

"Not all of EU visited me at my home. And Sean didn't get it wrong. He's smart and perceptive. He saw what I have been aware of for months and should have put a stop to sooner. I hoped I was reading you incorrectly. But I wasn't. Let's stop dancing around this."

"I don't—"

"Stop," she said firmly, raising a hand, palm out. "I'm not asking you to confess to anything. I'm also uninterested in having a discussion about what we both know to be true. I see you. You've made sure of it. I see you and know what it is you're offering. I know I will never accept. You need to know this too. This isn't a discussion. This is me telling you, in no uncertain terms and as nicely as I can be on the subject, to cease and desist."

"Angela, I'm just——"

"EU's provost and a valued member of my executive leadership team. That's it, Dr. Murphy. Take my statement as a verbal warning."

"A verbal warning?" he questioned, surprise in his voice and distress in his eyes. "I haven't done anything that could be construed as sexual harassment. I would never do that to you or to anyone else."

Angie hadn't viewed Derrick's actions as sexual harassment and, legally, she doubted they rose to the policy's standards. She wasn't going to permit him, however, to drag her into a policy debate that would serve no purpose but as a distraction he could hide behind.

"You're a bright man. You know what I'm talking about, so please don't insult either of us by pretending otherwise." Angie rolled tense shoulders. "If I must be plainer, … well, neither of us will enjoy it if I'm forced to deal with you in a way I'm trying very hard not to. Besides, it's the middle of the day, and I'm ready for lunch. So, I'll say it one more time. We're colleagues and nothing more."

Using the armrests of the chair, Angie pushed up, walked to the door and opened it. "Thank you for your time, Dr. Murphy. Have a wonderful Thanksgiving."

Derrick didn't immediately move or respond to Angie's polite dismissal. His face had fallen, and his shoulders had slumped. When he did come back to himself, it was with a blink of the eyes and a shake of the head.

"I apologize," he said from his spot at the table before he rose to leave. "I apologize," he repeated when he stood in front of her, hands in his pockets and voice contrite. "I … I … you and your family have a wonderful Thanksgiving, too, Dr. Styles-Franklin. I'll see you after break."

Angie smiled and extended her hand to her provost, who accepted the handshake. " 'Every moment is a fresh beginning,' Dr. Murphy."

"T.S. Eliot." Derrick didn't prolong the touch, which meant more to Angie than his return smile.

"It's my husband's quote of the day."

"I saw the single red rose in the vase on your desk. I assume it is from Mr. Franklin as well?"

"Yes. He gives me a rose and a quote on a message card three days a week."

"Why three? Favorite number?"

"Something like that."

Nothing like that. Sean gifted her with a single red rose and a New Beginning quote on the days of the week they had counseling. Three mornings a week she found the items on the passenger seat of her car. They began arriving the day after Dr. Naylor had recommended using a journal to record their feelings about themselves, their spouse, and their marriage. She taped each message card inside her journal and pressed a flower petal next to it. It filled the journal, but probably not in the way Dr. Naylor had intended. Next to each quote, Angie answered two questions: How are you feeling about Sean and your relationship today? and What is one thing you love about your husband?

No matter how busy or stressful her day, she answered those two questions, even if the response was scribbled in her journal before she turned in for the night or written in bullet points. On the days they argued, answering the second question forced Angie to remember what she most loved about her husband. Invariably, the question reminded Angie why she'd chosen to stay with Sean after his affair and why he was worthy of a second chance.

"I have an appointment at one."

Derrick's expression reflected his chagrin. "See you next week."

Derrick left, and Angie closed the door behind him, relieved. That had gone better than she'd anticipated, which made her feel awful about not having nipped it in the bud months ago. It was the same lesson Sean and she were working on owning. They needed to keep the lines of communication open and to stop making decisions based on assumptions.

The second Angie grabbed her lunch from the microwave and sat at her desk, her cell phone rang. One o'clock on the dot. She answered, accepting the request for a video call.

"Hey, beautiful."

Angie didn't recognize the room behind her husband. Most of their lunch dates occurred in their offices. Occasionally, Sean would be away from the firm and they'd have a quick chat and chew while he sat in his car. Today, however, there was nothing but a plain white wall behind him.

"Where are you?"

"I've been tossing around an idea and it led me here."

"You didn't answer my question," she said between a forkful of spaghetti and a bite of garlic bread. "I thought you had a deposition today."

"I did, but that was this morning. I keep telling you we need to sync our calendars."

"Why? You already have access to my personal Outlook calendar, which is synched to my work calendar. You've literally inserted yourself into my work day."

His flirtatious wink was as clear as the picture of him on her cell phone screen. "Like a virus, you mean?"

"Yes, like a virulent plague. And I know who you are. I don't need you to write: Sean Franklin, Esquire, Your Loving and Devoted Husband on my calendar every time we have something planned together. By the way, I'm capable of adding our dates to my calendar. You don't have to do it for me."

"I like being able to *do it for you*. I also like *inserting myself* into something of yours." Sean winked again then took a big bite of a cheeseburger.

Unable to stop herself, Angie rolled her eyes at his shameless flirting. They hadn't attempted sex again since that night in October when she'd had her flashback. It hadn't been the first or last flashback, unfortunately, but her rejection hadn't cooled his attempts at intimacy. Sean would kiss her, as often as she'd let him, which wasn't as frequently as he'd liked. What she permitted was as much physical intimacy as she could handle.

At least for now.

"Getting back to the original topic. Where are you?"

"You'll find out Sunday."

"What's going on Sunday?"

"SJ's going to watch the girls while we go out for a couple of hours. I'll bring you here and explain my idea. I want your opinion. Is that spaghetti you're eating? I thought it was gone, that's why I bought this greasy burger for lunch."

"You love greasy burgers and fries, and I packed the last of the spaghetti last night and hid it behind a big bag of kale. It's the one place you and your greedy son wouldn't think to look in your endless pursuit to devour everything in the kitchen. I cook large portions for a reason, Sean, and it's not to give you and SJ more food to gorge yourselves on, but so we don't have to cook every day."

Another two large bites had Sean polishing off his burger, then cramming ketchup-smothered fries into his mouth. Angie, on the other hand, still had half a bowl of spaghetti left and most of her garlic bread.

"You act as if my son and I don't leave any food in the house for you and your daughters."

"That's because you damn near don't. I'm pretty sure it's you who's been eating Zuri's applesauce cups."

"Come on, cinnamon applesauce is the best and Zuri is the biggest food waster in the family. So you see, I'm actually helping you save money."

She snorted. "By taking food out of the mouths of our children?"

"No, by teaching them the importance of being first."

"You're awful," she laughed. "Stop eating my baby's applesauce."

"What about the carrots and peanut butter combo pack you get her? Oh, and the veggie chips and the honey turkey lunch meat?"

She laughed again and again, Sean never one to leave the stage when he had a captive audience.

For a month, they'd scheduled virtual lunch dates. Unless something important arose, they didn't cancel. Some days, like today, they had thirty minutes to talk. Other days, five minutes was all they could squeeze in. They didn't measure the quality of their lunch dates by the minutes but by the concerted effort they made to keep and stay connected.

When she'd told Sean, in Dr. Naylor's office, he could've called and talked to her during his lunch hour rather than assuming she'd be too busy to make time for him and, instead, choosing to spend that time with Trinity, he'd heard her. More, he'd acted, and she had found herself looking forward to their dates, including the ones they now took on weekends, when time allowed.

With flexibility and consistency, they'd discovered opportunities to fit each other into their lives in a way they hadn't in a very long time.

"Are you going to the gym after work?"

"After what I just scarfed down, I better. Are you going to be busy, when I get home?"

"A little. I'm still playing catch-up. If you also have work, we can share the same space."

"Your bedroom?"

Sean sounded hopeful, but Angie knew what would happen if he spent too much time on her bed. She didn't want to feel pressured into renewing their sex life before she was ready. Their lack of physical intimacy was the topic of several of her solo sessions with Dr. Naylor. No doubt Sean wrote about it in his journal, her husband more diligent than she when it came to that therapy strategy.

"No, the basement or living room."

"That's fine. I'll just sit obscenely close and kiss your cheek, maybe your neck, if you're in a good mood. How about you lower your cell, unbutton your shirt, and give me a little peep show."

"I'm at work."

"And behind a closed door, I bet. Just a quick peek."

Her eyes shifted to her office door, then back to Sean. "You want to see my bra?"

"I want to see your beautiful bare breasts and suckable nipples, but I'll settle for admiring whatever lacy bra you're wearing and imagining the rest."

Angie wasn't an adventurous woman. Sean'd known that about her when they'd married. She lived her life by the rules and seldom ventured beyond them. When they'd dated and a few times since they'd married, he'd talked her into doing something she wouldn't ordinarily do, such as having sex in a public park, swimming with dolphins, and riding the tallest roller coaster at Cedar Point.

She unbuttoned her shirt, tilted her phone downward and bit her bottom lip, as she let Sean take his visual fill of her. Angie felt exposed, literally and figuratively.

Redoing her shirt and propping the phone back on the desk, she ignored Sean's grin. It wasn't a smug smile, though, which she'd expected. What Angie hadn't anticipated was Sean's, "Thank you, honey. I know each act of trust is like taking a leap of faith over and again."

It was, and she appreciated his awareness of how challenging the process of forgiveness and trust rebuilding was for her.

"Before we end our lunch date, I want to ask you a question. You don't have to answer it now. In fact, I'd prefer if you wait until tonight because I want you to give my question serious thought."

"Okay. Don't make it sound so ominous."

"I did, didn't I. It's not bad, but your answer matters to me. So, how can I make you feel more loved? Think about the question in terms of the next few days, but also the next few months. The timeframe could be from tomorrow to your Valentine's Day birthday. How can I make you feel more loved, Angie? I want to know."

"You mean you want me to create a list?"

"A list would be good. You look confused. Did my question throw you?"

"Yes. But it also seems one-sided."

"It isn't. Do you know why?"

Angie had no idea, so she shook her head.

"You flashed me in your office. You've altered your work schedule to spend more time with me and the kids. You attend every therapy session, without complaint, and you approach every relationship building activity with openness and respect. I don't remember the last time you told me you loved me, but you make me feel loved every single day. Even when we argue, I know it comes from a heart that I hurt but that I'm grateful still loves me despite my faults. I love you. Enjoy the rest of your day, Angie."

With a kiss to his phone's screen, Sean ended the call.

He had thrown her in more ways than one. How could he make her feel more loved? The question pleased her but not as much as the fact that her husband hadn't mimicked one of Dr. Naylor's relationship building questions but had created a question of his own.

Feeling loved wasn't about the knowledge of being loved but deliberate acts of care and affection. Sean had demonstrated his love for Angie time and again, especially since his affair and her car crash. He didn't lack creative, even practical, ways to show his love. What Sean was really asking for was a formula to Angie's forgiveness and trust. If a formula existed, it would include time, honesty and patience.

She would answer her husband's question. Angie would even text it to him, although one line did not constitute a list. But her answer would be her truth. His response, however, if he followed her suggestion, would make his future actions toward her more meaningful and more deeply felt.

"I'll give the two of you time to talk." The realtor, Ms. Garza, pulled out her cell phone and was checking her emails before she'd finished her sentence. Walking toward the front door, she waved over her shoulder. "I'll be in my car. When you're done, I'll lock up." Then she was gone.

Sean didn't know how the woman sold homes with her nonchalant attitude and cell phone addiction. For all the help she'd been, Ms. Garza could've unlocked the house then returned to her car because she spent most of her time either texting or responding to emails. Good thing Sean had explored the house earlier in the week, the realtor no more helpful then than she'd been today.

Angie had all but ignored Ms. Garza, following Sean on what amounted to a self-guided tour of the house. Now, it was Sean who followed behind Angie like a puppy waiting for her to hand him a treat and scratch behind his ears. It wasn't the perfect analogy, but it was marginally better than viewing himself as a horny dog wanting to hump any part of her she'd allow. To date, his wife hadn't allowed much. He couldn't blame her, though.

If the tables were reversed, Sean couldn't see himself having gotten this far in the reconciliation process if Angie had been the one to cheat. Thinking of his wife in the arms of another man would've driven him crazy, if not to murder. He wasn't proud of the double standard. If Sean ever had to find out if he could weather that storm, it would mean the steps they were taking now had failed. He would do all in his power to ensure that didn't happen.

"What do you think?"

"It's a beautiful Victorian house and in a great community. It's also not far from EU's main campus." Angie walked to the room's front window and peered outside. "There's a For Sale or Lease sign on the front lawn. I noticed it when we arrived." She turned back to him. "You want to move?"

"Yes, but not in the way you mean."

Angie returned to his side, face upturned with questions but also with patience. He took her hand and pulled her down to the shiny wooden floor, their backs going against a white wall and his hand holding hers. Thanksgiving had been fun, despite an argument they'd had before leaving to spend the day with the Styles at Malcolm's home. As the day had drawn on, they'd settled into the spirit of the family gathering. By the time they'd returned home that night, they were smiling, and she'd agreed to cuddle time. They hadn't made love that night, unfortunately, but that would come in time.

"My lease on the executive suite I use for the firm ends in January. I've had the renewal contract for weeks but couldn't bring myself to sign."

"Why not? You've been there for years. The suite was a nice upgrade from the shared office space you had when you first started out."

"I know. But it's time for a change. Business is great, and I'm ready to expand."

"You mean you want to bring on another lawyer or two?"

"One definitely. You looked at the space. What do you think?"

"There are four rooms upstairs that would make for good offices. The space we're in now, the dining room, I assume, is spacious and the closest room to the front door. It has that big front window over there, which lets in a lot of light. This would make a nice reception area. I'd have to examine the house again, through a different lens, now that I know you're considering the building as a business. Buy or lease?"

He should've better prepped her for today's visit. But if he'd told her sooner, he'd feared she wouldn't have come.

"I thought we could decide that together." He raised their linked hands and kissed the back of hers. "Like you said, the location isn't far from EU. We could meet up, some days. Maybe even drive in together, sometimes. You could drop me off here and then drive to campus or I could take you to work before coming here. If there's an emergency, we can reach each other a lot easier than we can now."

"You left me a rose and message card in my car today, although it isn't one of our therapy days. Why?"

" 'Every new beginning comes from some other beginning's end.' When I saw that quote by Lucius Annaeus Seneca online, it resonated with me." He kept her hand in his, needing the comfort of her warmth. They rarely spoke directly about Trinity but the shadow she and their affair cast over their relationship was long and dark. "All beginnings aren't good ones. I leave you those messages because we've embarked on a new beginning. But starting anew doesn't erase old beginnings and fresh hurt. You haven't visited me at work since I told you about Trinity. We haven't talked about it but it's there between us."

"Sean, I—"

"I know. Trust me, I do. The law firm is tainted territory for you, and an epicenter for flashbacks. What you may not know is that it is for me, too. Just to be clear, I don't sit in my office reminiscing about the times I spent in there with Trinity."

"I don't want to hear about that." She snatched her hand from his. "I can't."

"And that's the primary reason I want to move to a new location. It doesn't have to be this house or this neighborhood. I hate that you are so repulsed by my place of business you don't want to visit me there because all you can think about is me with another woman. If it's an unwelcome reminder for me then I know it's even worse for you."

Sean reclaimed her hand, and for several minutes they sat in silence. As much as they communicated and shared nowadays, it was still hard discussing Trinity and his betrayal. It was for Sean, too, but his discomfiture and guilt didn't rival Angie's pain of the reminder. In this light, five years to full recovery made sense. Nothing about the reconciliation and healing process was quick or painless.

"Letting the lease lapse, relocating, and upgrading the law firm would be good professional decisions, but an even better personal choice. In therapy we learned about the importance of holding on to the healthy and the happy and letting go of everything else." He claimed her hand again, kissing it. The warmth that had reassured him minutes ago had leached away. "Talk to me."

"Let go of my hand."

With reluctance, he did. Angie, dressed in tight jeans, a form-fitting red turtleneck, and leather ankle boots with low heels, bolted to her feet and left the dining room. Sean stayed where he was on the floor. Angie hadn't exited the house. He could hear her walking around downstairs, the clack of her boots making it easy for him to track her movements, including her ascent to the upper level.

Now that Angie had, for the most part, stopped hiding her feelings from him, he was able to witness the full scope of her efforts to deal with his affair and her decision to work toward growth and relationship satisfaction. Seeing Angie grapple with her emotions and his choices of a year ago was painful. He'd done this to her, and he needed to see the effects of his actions on the woman he'd pledged his heart and fidelity to.

Sean stared up at Angie when she reentered the room. Her face bore no sign of tears, which he had come to learn wasn't a reliable barometer of her emotional state. He also knew better than to touch her, even a heartfelt hug, when she was feeling exposed and angry, so he stayed seated and waited for her to decide how this outing would end. The way Angie looked at him, though, cold wrapped in frost, she challenged the heat coursing through the house for dominance.

The only silver lining in the dark cloud that had descended over his wife and inside the house was his certainty he'd made the right decision for them both. Sean had considered Angie's feelings, including her unvoiced ones about his office. No way would she forget what had occurred between Trinity and Sean there. That knowledge would always exist, but his office didn't have to serve as a physical reminder. It was one thing for Angie to accept him after his affair, but she shouldn't also have to come face-to-face with or avoid the location of his adultery. Angie may not be able to see it now, but the move would be a much-needed, new beginning.

She entered the room and went straight to the front window, her back to him. "I like the house and your plan. I understand the personal reasons behind your motivation to move out of the executive suite." Facing him, her arms crossed over her chest, she blew out a long breath. "You're right. I can't see myself ever going back to your current law offices."

She turned away from him again, severing their weak connection. He wanted to touch her, physically and emotionally, so he withdrew his cell phone from his sweatshirt pocket and located one of a half dozen cuddle time playlists he'd made for them.

While he sat, and she stood staring out the window, music played. Not romantic ballads of love and desire but the theme songs to Angie's favorite childhood television shows. Sean had compiled the list after one of their lighthearted relationship building conversations. He'd included several of his favorite songs as well, such as the theme song from the *The A-Team*.

By the fifth song, her shoulders shook, and her right hand covered her mouth.

Laughter.

"*Knight Rider*." She swirled to face him, icicles melted and a rainbow in her eyes. "Of course, you would like that show."

Sean jumped to his feet. "A tricked-out talking car. What's not to like?"

The next song played, and Angie's grin widened. "*Miami Vice*. God, Sean, you're a walking male trope."

He looked at her pointedly, with raised eyebrows and ticket off on his fingers, "*Fame, Charlie's Angels, The Jeffersons,* and *The Brady Bunch. The Brady Bunch*, Angie? You've got to be kidding me with that one."

Angie looked only slightly embarrassed, protesting, "Be quiet. Is that the theme song to *Smurfs* I hear? It must be one of your favorites because it's not one of mine."

"It's a classic cartoon."

"They were all related, had one female in the group and one older male. Deconstruct that dynamic and see what you come up with."

"That is so wrong. How dare you malign a perfectly good kid show of the '80s."

Angie's smile brightened the room and warmed his spirit. Sean couldn't help it. He leaned forward and kissed her.

And, hell yes, she kissed him back.

CHAPTER THIRTY-TWO

"You're distracted today. Care to share?"

"Did you mean to make that rhyme?"

"No. Between the two of us, you're the jokester." Dr. Naylor smiled at Sean, a notepad in her hand. "Tell me what's on your mind."

Reclined on Dr. Naylor's sofa, but still tense, Sean's long legs stretched in front of him, and the therapist waited for his response, as patient as ever. "My brother-in-law's girlfriend invited my family to Maryland for Christmas. The in-laws too. It's supposed to be a surprise for Malcolm since he's willing to give up spending Christmas with his family to accompany Sky to Annapolis so she could spend the holiday with hers."

"Malcolm. Your brother-in-law, right?"

"I told you about him. We're still on the outs but we're doing better. His anger towards me has lessened. I think it helps that his sister and I are in counseling and he's in love. The kids are excited for Christmas and the trip."

"Sounds like fun and an opportunity for you and Malcolm to spend quality time together. Maybe talk and work on mending your friendship?"

"I'd love that. All signs point to him using Christmas as an excuse to pop the question to his girlfriend."

"Christmas and an engagement, two happy occasions in one. Tell me why you've delivered what should be happy news as if you've foreseen storm clouds in your future."

"Despite my current mood, I am looking forward to getting away with the family. Annapolis won't be as cold as Buffalo, which should be nice. Malcolm deserves the love of a good woman, and he's found that love with Sky. They're a great match and will have a wonderful marriage."

"How does their happiness make you feel?"

"I'm not jealous, if that's what you're getting at. I'm happy for them and wish Sky and Malcolm the best." Sean sat up straight. "In almost three weeks, it'll be a year since my confession."

"Ah, I understand now."

"I'm glad you do because I feel like I'm going to lose everything."

"Has Angie mentioned separation or divorce?"

"No, but she's retreated. She seems to be mad at me again, although I don't think she ever stopped being angry with me."

Dr. Naylor crossed her legs, her knee-high stretch boots a pretty shade of burgundy and a contrast to her normal pointed toe black pumps. "Retreated how?" she asked.

"We still have our daily relationship building activities, but she no longer wants to do cuddle time or any other activity that involves physical contact. We talk and that's still good. But there are times she's distant. The closer we get to the anniversary of my confession the more distant Angie becomes. It feels like I'm losing her all over again."

Angie would say Sean was being dramatic. Edward would concur, arguing Sean was seeing the glass as half empty instead of half full. Dr. Naylor may agree, but the therapist was subtler in her analysis than either Angie or Edward would've been.

"You're not losing Angie, and what you both are feeling is normal. As I've told you before, every day won't be a step forward. Some days will feel like you've fallen down the same flight of stairs you just walked up. For you, you can look back on that day as the moment you came clean and cleared your conscience. You may even feel proud of yourself for telling Angie the truth, which is understandable. Your confession gave you peace of mind but took away hers. With every succeeding year, the anniversary of your confession will hurt her less."

"I don't regret telling Angie the truth. She deserved to know, and it was the right decision to make. Sometimes, though, I also feel it was a selfish choice. You're right, I did want to clear my conscience. I couldn't stand the guilt and I was scared as hell Trinity would decide to punish me for breaking things off with her by telling my wife about us. Angie and I have been through a lot, and I hate, as Christmas approaches, her mind is filled with awful memories and the pain I caused her."

Despite the legal pad she held in her hand, Dr. Naylor, per Sean and Angie's request, used a recorder for their sessions. He wondered if the therapist realized her unconscious attachment to her legal pads and how their constant presence revealed them as her preferred form of notetaking.

"Looking back is unavoidable, Sean. We like to remember the good times, but we also recall the bad ones. Let's go back to what you said. It's almost a year since your confession and a little longer than that since you ended your affair."

"I know."

"This time, a year ago, did you think you'd be in marriage counseling and preparing to take a holiday vacation with your wife and children?"

"Of course not. I couldn't fully enjoy Christmas last year because of my lies and affair. I was so certain Angie would leave me, I kept putting off telling her the truth. I began the new year with old fears and tired lies."

"Christmas is in a few days. How are you feeling about it this year?"

"Much better. I hear you, doc. I'm not where I was a year ago, which I'm grateful for, trust me. Angie's also not where she was a year ago. I just want all of my wife back."

"Every session I remind you to practice patience, and I'm reminding you again. Her healing isn't the same as yours. It's uniquely hers, and you must accept that, no matter how much you hate seeing her regress and sometimes pull away. You also tend to view her distance as negative. That's not always the case. Distance, in the short-term, can help one gain perspective."

"I can see your point and admit that's how Angie sometimes uses it. But not always."

"Very true. Tell me the other way Angie uses distance."

He knew this strategy. Dr. Naylor used the method often. Sean and Angie also used the strategy with their children, asking them to explain why a poor decision wasn't the wisest course of action. They believed, as did Dr. Naylor, that the power of knowing was strongest when voiced by self and not by an external party. The therapist knew the answer but had shifted the responsibility of verbalization to him.

"Angie doesn't like hurting my feelings, which she knows she's capable of doing when upset. In her mind, she's sparing me by putting distance between us. She thinks that's a kinder method of dealing with her anger than unleashing it on me."

"Is it kinder?"

"Her distance feels like rejection, which hurts. But, yes, it is kinder than having her rip my throat out. My wife is the woman you want at your back when all hell breaks loose. It's great when her ire isn't directed at you, but when it is, she's fierce, and everything she says is brutally honest. That's what it is. Her honesty feels like a quick, unexpected jab to the chin that knocks you on your ass."

Sean touched his chin, recalling when Angie had struck him there. During a co-session, she'd apologized for taking her anger to a physical level. "I had no right to hit you, no matter how upset I was at the time. No one would excuse you, if you did the same to me in a fit of anger." She'd reached for him and caressed his chin. "I shouldn't get a pass because I'm a woman and you're a man. Hitting is unacceptable inside a marriage, regardless of who throws the punch. I'm sorry. It won't happen again."

Until she'd sat across from Sean, in Dr. Naylor's office, offering him an apology, he hadn't thought he needed or deserved one. He was wrong on both accounts. He'd wanted to embrace her, but she was wrapped in shame and anger, an insulated down jacket that left no room for him. So, he settled for stopping by her favorite Mediterranean restaurant where they gorged themselves on charcoal rotisserie chicken, falafel salad, rice pudding and baklava.

"Are you still with me, Sean?"

He hadn't been for a moment, but he was now. "Yeah."

"Good." Dr. Naylor placed the legal pad on the table next to her. "If you accept the kind and sensitive parts of Angie, you must also accept the quiet, brooding and sometimes brutally honest parts of her, too."

"I know, and I do. I just ... she took away the one thing I had going for me this Christmas. And I was stupid enough to include her birthday in the deal."

"I don't understand."

"I asked Angie to tell me what I could do, over the next few months, to make her feel more loved. She asked if I meant a list, and I thought a list sounded like a great idea."

"I take it you disagreed with what she included on the list."

"She wrote one line, doc, and it wasn't a suggestion of what to do, so much as it was a recommendation as to what I should stop doing."

"I'm lost again."

Sean retrieved his cell phone from his back pocket, found Angie's text message, and handed the phone to Dr. Naylor.

After reading the text, she nodded.

"You agree with her?"

"It's not for me to agree or disagree. But I can see, from your perspective, how her suggestion could make Christmas and her birthday a challenge for you. At the same time, Sean, you did ask."

"How in the hell can I show my wife how much I love her if she doesn't want me to spend any money on her? She sent me this in late November. I'd already purchased her Christmas gifts. If I do as she requested, I can't give any of them to her. Last year's birthday was a total bust. We've never had such an awful Valentine's Day before either."

"What did you buy Angie for her birthday last year?"

"A necklace."

"Expensive?"

"Of course. It was her birthday and Valentine's Day."

"Did your expensive birthday and Valentine's Day gift make her feel loved?"

Sean's gaze shifted from the therapist to the recorder and legal pad, and then back to her. "I wasn't trying to buy my way back into Angie's heart."

"Are you sure?"

"I like buying my wife gifts. I always have. Angie knows that about me."

Dr. Naylor handed Sean his cell phone. "Yet she asked you to show your love in ways that will cost you nothing financially. She didn't even tell you how. Angie left the specifics up to you. Why are you so displeased with this development?"

"I'm upset because ... because ...." Sean slammed his hand down on his thigh. "Dammit, I don't know why."

"I think you do," Dr. Naylor said, her voice a composed contrast to his own. "Have you told Angie about your parents?"

Sean shook his head. He had written about Brenda and Edward in his reflection journal, but he hadn't found the right time to broach the subject of his serial cheating father with Angie.

"I know I need to." He dropped the cell to the cushion beside him and leaned back. "I visited my parents, a few months ago. While there, my father sent me upstairs for his medication. I looked in the drawer where I thought he told me he put the bottle. It was in the next drawer over. But the first one I looked in had a cotton sheet on the bottom and on top of the sheet were all kinds of jewelry. Bracelets, rings, watches, all piled on one side of the drawer."

"A lot of men like jewelry."

"They weren't my father's. The jewelry belonged to my mother, but I couldn't recall her ever wearing any of them. But I did remember Dad bringing her gift-wrapped boxes when I was a kid. Not all of them could've been jewelry because some of the boxes were too big. But I remember, and the gift boxes always came after a fight and Mom's discovery of another affair. I'd forgotten until I saw the pile of gold and silver guilt gifts." He slapped his thigh again, harder than the first time, causing it to sting. "Dammit, every time I think I'm not like him, I do something that reminds me that I am Edward Franklin's son."

Dr. Naylor paused and watched Sean, her eyes lowering to the thigh where his large hand still rested. When he didn't speak or further hurt himself, she nodded.

"You aren't your father. But I do recommend exploring your relationship with your parents in more depth. I think you're beginning to see the extent to which your parents' marriage has influenced your thinking about self and consequently, how you view Angie and your marriage." Dr. Naylor's timer went off and she silenced the subtle phone alarm with a swipe to the right. "That's our hour, Sean. Think about having that conversation with Angie. Trust your wife not to judge you based on your father's actions. Trust is a two-way street. You can't expect Angie to give you hers if you aren't willing to give her yours. Enjoy Christmas in Maryland, and I'll see you and Angie next year."

Sean did intend to enjoy the holiday season. For that to happen, he had to shake off his moody blues and create his own festive spirit. Thanksgiving may have passed, but Sean had much to be thankful for, mainly a healthy wife and happy children.

A day later, Sean seated himself beside Angie in a ridiculously large truck Charles had rented for the trip south over the objections of his wife and daughter, who were displeased with Charles's choice of driving over flying. Sean had kissed Angie's cheek, slung his arm around her shoulder, and talked her ear off the entire drive to Annapolis. By the time they'd arrived, tired and in need of a good stretch, he had decided on the perfect Christmas gift for his wife. A gift that could cost him more than anything he'd purchased for Angie in year's past.

Angie couldn't peel her eyes off the four-poster bed. The king size would accommodate Sean's tall frame and swallow up Angie's petite one. Why had Sky put them in the same guest room? That's right, the younger woman didn't know Angie and Sean hadn't shared a bedroom in nearly a year, despite her knowledge of the couple's marital troubles.

The thought of sharing a bed with Sean scared the hell out of her, for the emotional dangers and physical temptation the proximity would offer.

"SJ was right, Malcolm, Sky's home is amazing. Professionally decorated, I bet."

Sean went on about Sky's million-dollar home. Angie couldn't blame him. The woman had given no indication of her wealthy background. From the little Angie knew about Sky's life in Maryland, she was raised by her mother and this was her childhood home. The Styles had met Sky's father and her sisters when they'd arrived. Angie had known Sky was of biracial parentage, so seeing Sky's white father and sisters hadn't surprised Angie. While Sky looked nothing like her father, Robert, she had inherited his olive hazel eyes, as had her sisters, Carrie and Olivia.

This Christmas had the ingredients for a complete fiasco or a sentimental Hallmark holiday movie, from Sky's estrangement from her Ellis family to Malcolm's engagement dreams to Angie and Sean's sleeping arrangement.

"I'm going to take a shower," she announced to her brother and husband, hoping they'd take their conversation out of the bedroom. When they kept talking about Malcolm's plans to add more decorations to Sky's home--as if what Malcolm and Sky's cousins, Brandon and Jeremiah, had already put up wasn't enough to sate any lover of the yuletide holiday--Angie located her toiletry bag and pulled out a robe and an outfit for later.

She'd shower then take a nap. Sky had jogged past them on their drive up to her house, waving but not stopping. Some people ate or drank too much when upset. Sky ran. In a way, so too did Angie. Not physically, which at least had great physical benefits for people who chose that form of evasion, but emotionally, an unhealthy approach to stress.

Angie entered the bathroom and closed the door. Like the main room, the bathroom exuded elegance. The room was all soft beiges on the walls, natural wood on the floor, shelves, and mirror frame, with a white tub behind a glass shower door. Brightly patterned rugs and wall art added color to the room, reminding Angie of Sky, who normally dressed in monochromatic colors but added a dash of red, purple, orange, or pink to brighten up her ensemble.

Turning on the brush chrome faucet, a modern touch in the nature-inspired bathroom, Angie drowned out her husband's and brother's voices as she brushed her teeth and washed her face. She removed her shoes, socks, sweater, and pants, folding the clothes and placing them on a wooden shelf catty-cornered to the double sink vanity.

The bedroom door closed and seconds later the bathroom door opened. A smiling and half naked Sean stood in the threshold, eyes blatant in their perusal of her body. Her scars had healed, and most were no longer as obvious as they'd once been. Someone looking at her wouldn't know the trauma her body had endured. Her legs were still a source of mild, daily discomfort, and although Angie no longer walked with a cane, she'd been known to limp at the end of a tiring day.

None of those details seemed to matter to Sean, his scrutiny carnal and his muscular chest and arms spectacular.

She turned away from him, busying herself by unpacking her toiletry bag and storing the items in a top drawer of the wooden vanity.

"We should shower together, or that tub looks big enough for the both of us, if you prefer a bath."

Like the bed, the size of the tub hadn't escaped her notice. Angie closed the drawer and turned to face her husband, who'd entered the bathroom, his frame imposing and smile full of heat.

Angie shut her eyes and leaned against the vanity, the granite countertop cool under her palms. She'd avoided this very situation for weeks. It had been a long time since they'd had sex. Angie wouldn't lie to herself and pretend she didn't want her husband. With each passing day, she desired Sean even more. It was hard not to, especially when he strutted around the house in tank tops that showed off his broad chest and large, long arms that had gotten even harder and stronger with the increased frequency of his weight training.

This trip was a much-needed respite from Buffalo and work. They'd gained much from marriage counseling and were more communicative. They were closer too, despite her tendency to hide behind her protective wall. She'd tried not to shut him out and to remember her discussions with Dr. Naylor.

Angie had been doing well, too, until Sean had mentioned going Christmas shopping. The simple reminder of their annual trip to the mall for Christmas presents had brought back memories of the year before. Sean had been upset Angie had gone in to work on a Saturday and had forgotten about their plan to use the day for last-minute shopping. There was so much she hadn't known back then, but the signs of Sean's guilt and his displeasure at her long work hours were there. Angie hadn't seen them. Her blinders had been convenient and firmly in place.

Less than a month later, it all fell apart. The illusion of domestic harmony had crumbled to ash, blown away in the barber wind of Sean's confession, the damp snow and spray of it freezing Angie on contact.

Lips pressed to her neck, and she didn't open her eyes. Angie couldn't. When closed, she could imagine, pretend, and forget. She'd dreamed of giving herself to Sean again, the way she had since falling in love with him. He was still so much of the man who'd stolen her heart with his smile and humor. But also not. He'd matured in a way she found pleasing and attractive, taking on the roles of parent and spouse with a smooth transition most people, including herself, stumbled through before finding their rhythm.

Sean's hot mouth traveled from her neck to her shoulder, his hand pushing down the bra strap so his mouth could claim the skin underneath. "You taste so good. I want my tongue all over you."

"I love the sounds you make when you come. You sound even better when you're pulsing around my dick." Sean kissed her again, his fingers still inside and staking his claim even though they no longer moved in and out of her.

Angie wanted his mouth on her, his tongue replacing his fingers. Sean would do it, too, if she asked. But Angie wouldn't ask. She couldn't take more pleasure from her husband without returning it. Angie didn't think she could, neither oral sex nor intercourse.

She scooted away and further onto the countertop, Sean's fingers slipping out of her. For her sake and his, she shouldn't have allowed him to go so far. She tingled for more of him, ached to have her husband fill her, his gorgeous body all hers.

But he hadn't been all hers, dammit, and she found it difficult to let that shit go. Angie needed to, though, because holding on to it wasn't doing either of them any good.

Sean dropped his pants and boxers. His erection bobbed out, long, dark, and thick, and Angie couldn't look away. He took himself in hand and began to pump. Sean's other hand came to Angie's thigh, squeezing and caressing.

Their gazes locked, but she couldn't hold it. Drawn back to the hand stroking his length with a firm grip she knew he liked, she watched him masturbate. Enthralled.

Her sex ached anew, and her breathing quickened along with his.

"This is what I do, when I think about you. I imagine you fisting my dick, like this, your thumb over the head, spreading my pre-cum between your soft, warm fingers and drawing it down me before going back up for more. Up and down. Up and down, you'd go, with a little twist of the wrist at the top."

He did exactly that, jerking his hand up and down. Over and again he pleasured himself, hand moving faster and faster.

She gulped, mouth dry and panties soaked. Frozen, Angie could do nothing but watch Sean jerk himself off, his grunts deep when he came in a rush of breaths and sperm. Seeing him like that, hand around his engorged dick and chest heaving, was erotic as hell, and she'd enjoyed the sight far more than she'd thought possible.

She barely noticed when he wiped his soiled hand on the same wash-cloth she'd used to wash her face. But she didn't miss when he wrapped his big hands around her waist, slid her to the edge of the countertop again, and lowered his head.

"Sean, wait, wait…" Hot breath then warm mouth found her center. "Shit, Sean… please."

Flat tongue licked up and over drenched panties, and Angie lost her ability to protest.

"I had to bust-a-nut before I did this. You were killing me, all supple and doe-eyed. We gotta work this out."

"I know." She did but … Sean's mouth went to work, unbothered by her panties or their position. "Sean. Sean." Hell, what was she trying to say? With his mouth on her, she couldn't think clearly. He'd wanted her to feel more and think less. Dammit, she couldn't help but do both. But when Sean moved her panties out of his way and licked her sensitive flesh, her scream shut off all upper brain functions.

Angie was feeling now. Sean's stubble. His hands, mouth and tongue. She felt it all and tried to control the flood of emotions threatening her heart and overpowering her mind. Eyes closed, she allowed him to pull her from the countertop and onto a colorful rug.

Off came Angie's panties and in between her legs he went again. Sucking, slurping, licking, Sean exemplified the term eating pussy. He had her wide open. Her back was arched, and hips lifted off the floor, offering herself up to him. In that vulnerable moment, Sean could've entered her with more than his first two fingers. Angie wouldn't have resisted if he'd penetrated her with his penis, but he didn't, for which she was grateful.

This tryst in the bathroom was a huge step into the unknown, and Angie feared the repercussions on her heart. What would Sean think it meant? What did Angie want it to mean? Would she be able to go further than this in the near future? Was Angie enough for Sean? Could she trust him?

A powerful orgasm ripped through Angie. She was unable to stay still, her hips twisting. Sean kept licking her, his middle finger driving into her while he sucked and licked her clit.

"Oh, god," she screamed. "Oh, god, oh, god."

He licked and licked, his tongue slick and firm, his finger swift and accurate. She came again, her mind a whirlpool of emotions, her body an erupting volcano.

A tender tongue licked her down from her high, keeping her aroused but not trying to tip her over the edge again. Sean's mouth stayed on her, kissing her thighs and stomach before moving back to her center. Angie's hand rested on the crown of his head, eyes lifted to the ceiling and legs on either side of his shoulders. It felt good and right but also frightening.

Angie's eyes slipped closed, and she moaned, Sean's tongue dipping inside her once more.

CHAPTER THIRTY-THREE

"They're not coming." Charles walked from the opening of the living room, where he'd stood waiting for Malcolm and Sky, to the sofa nearest the seven-foot Christmas tree. He plopped onto the sofa next to Kim. "We should start without them."

Sean brushed his shoulder against Angie's and whispered in her ear. "Trust me, Sky and Malcolm are definitely *coming*. Just not down here with us as spectators to their personal Christmas celebration." Angie didn't smile, but he could tell she wanted to. "They've already started opening Christmas gifts. If they open any more presents, Sky's floor will collapse, and her bed will fall on our heads. Wouldn't that be a merry Christmas, your brother's bare ass greeting us."

"Be quiet," she shushed him.

"I mean, come on, we're down here and they're still upstairs. The walls may be solid and the beds sturdy, but the rooms aren't soundproof. I swear, when we passed Sky's bedroom I heard Christmas bells ringing, reindeer clapping, and Saint Nick singing."

"Stop it." Angie buried her face in her hands.

the sofa and squeezed between him and the cushion he reclined against. Reaching out her small hand, Zuri pulled down the collar of Charles's robe.

"Hey, what are you doing back there, squirt?"

"No price tag, SJ." Zuri sniffed her grandfather's robe. "It smells really good and feels soft."

"I knew it," SJ laughed, hyper and loud.

"Sean, is this how you're raising my grandchildren? To disrespect their elders?"

"Why am I always the one who gets blamed when the children do or says something rude? I mean, look at your daughter."

"I am looking at her." The moment Zuri had yanked on Charles's robe and declared his clothing fresh, Angie had fallen onto the floor, laughing her ass off. "Angie gets a pass."

"Why, because she's your daughter?" Sean stood from the sofa, pointing at his laughing wife with as much indignation as he could muster while howling on the inside.

"Yes, because she's my daughter. I don't need a better reason than that."

"You do, if you're going to accuse me of raising disrespectful children."

"Your daughter implied I smell and don't wear decent clothes."

"That's not what she meant, is it, Zuri?"

She nodded, and they broke into another round of laughter. The older man pointed at Sean, and not with his index finger.

"Out of the mouths of babes," Kim said. "I told you that new cologne you bought was pungent. The smell stays on your skin and gets in all your clothes. Even Zuri doesn't like it." Kim grabbed Zuri and set her on her feet and between her legs, holding the little girl around the waist. "You're right, Kayla, I did take your granddad shopping for a new robe, slippers, and pajamas."

"Dad doesn't wear pajamas. Not once, when growing up, did I see him in slippers, much less real pajamas."

"A man doesn't need slippers or pajamas in his own home. It's a waste of money."

"You need a robe, though," Sean added, all attempts at feigned seriousness gone. "I didn't need to see you walking around your house in underwear and nothing else. I've never wanted to wash my eyeballs more than the first time you flashed me."

"I didn't flash you, and you were in my house. I'll wear what I want in my own home."

"Or nothing at all," Angie said. "Thanks, Mom."

"What are you thanking her for?"

"For having the sense to keep you covered while in Sky's home. Dad, Malcolm wants her to become a member of our family, not have his father scare her away with stretched-out tighty-whities."

"I see what's happening here." Charles began to flip Sean off again, but Kim caught his hand and pushed it down. "You've turned my baby girl against me."

"How did what Angie said swing back to me? I object."

Kayla popped up. "You're not in court, Dad, you can't object."

"I am in court. My reputation as a father is at stake. I object," he repeated, pointing an index finger at Charles. "This is the case of Sean Franklin versus Charles Styles. I'm suing for slander and emotional distress."

"For how much?" SJ got to his feet and stood next to Sean. "A mill?"

"Traitor, SJ." Charles booed his grandson. "Give me my Christmas gift back."

"Not a chance. Cold, hard cash, Granddad, love it. From your wallet to my hands. Money beats a gift card any day." SJ ran to Charles, hugged and thanked him for his Christmas present, then darted back to Sean's side. "I represent Mr. Franklin."

Zuri, mimicking her brother said, "I represent Grandad Styles."

"Thank you, baby."

"Then I'm the judge." Kayla stood, cute in her pink-and-white Ballet Is My Life T-shirt.

The unopened gifts were forgotten, the family engrossed in the hilarity of a mock civil trial.

"I award a million dollars to Mr. Sean Franklin. Cash, credit, or debit?" Kayla asked Charles, one hand on her hip, the other palm up, waiting for Charles to cough over the settlement.

Cash, credit, or debit -- his daughter spent too much time shopping with her mother.

"The entire case is bogus," Charles complained. "My lawyer is short and more interested in stuffing her mouth with Christmas candy than my case, and the judge has a conflict of interest. I'm not paying Mr. Franklin a million dollars. The most he'll get from me is a two-cent piece."

"Dad, that's no longer in circulation."

"A three-dollar bill then"

"Also out of circulation."

"Angie, stop correcting me and ruining my comeback."

"I guess she's not your baby girl now, is she? Consider my payment a belated dowry for taking Angie off your hands. With twenty years of inflation, a cool mill may just cover it."

Angie snorted. "Off his hands, huh?"

"Most definitely. You're kind of high maintenance. The price of step stools alone has been exorbitant." Sean smiled down at Angie when she strolled up to him, hands on her hips and eyes amused pools of dark-brown. Damn, she was hot as hell, sassy yet playful. Except for sexy Angie, spirited Angie was his favorite version of his wife.

"I'm high maintenance?"

"Since the day I met you." Angie was the least high maintenance person Sean knew. If anything, she didn't rely on him as much as he'd like. "Charles's dowry is way overdue. Twenty years and three kids overdue, to be precise. You look upset, Mrs. Franklin. I don't know why, I just said you were worth as much as a Jaguar C-X75 Supercar."

"Mrs. Franklin?"

"You heard me." Mirroring her, he placed his hands on his hips and lowered his face to hers. "You're my wife, which means you take my name and like it."

A wildfire had less sizzling heat coming from it than what he saw in Angie's eyes.

Charles laughed. "That hole you're digging is pretty deep. She's going to kick you're a— Okay, Kim, stop with the elbow already. I get it. No cussing. Damn, woman."

Angie stepped even closer, their foreheads mere inches apart. "Are you finished?"

"I haven't received my settlement yet. If I don't, I may have to return you to your father."

"Good burn, Dad." SJ moved away from Sean and closer to his grandparents. From the corner of Sean's eye, he saw Kayla do the same. "It's been nice knowing you. I'll say good things about you at your funeral."

"Give me a break. I'm not afraid of a little woman with cute manicured nails and fingers made for scratching my back and cooking my dinner."

The thing about being a jokester, over six feet tall, and a button pusher, Sean overestimated his ability to handle the response to his provocations. To prove he wasn't afraid of his wife, he made to deliver a gentle shove to her shoulder. Wrong move.

She intercepted his hand, grabbed his wrist and twisted. Sean didn't know what in the hell she did, but the maneuver had his entire right arm up and taut. Angie added pressure and increased the rotation of the twist and her body. Down Sean went to his knees, right arm extended upward and his hand and wrist in Angie's control. A woman her size shouldn't be able to bring a six-foot-three man to his knees, but she had and with embarrassing ease.

"How does that wristlock feel?" Charles's bark of mocking laughter barely penetrated the fog of Sean's quick defeat and the pain in his wrist-joint. "Fifteen years of jujitsu classes. Besides Angie's college tuition, it was the best investment I made in my daughter. A star pupil, if you couldn't figure it out."

SJ knelt in front of a wincing Sean. "This isn't a good look. I'm tempted to take a pic and post to Snapchat, but I don't want my friends thinking my mom beats up my dad."

"You're not helping."

SJ shrugged. "What am I supposed to do? She's Mom."

"I'll remember this, when you want me to pay for driving lessons."

"Shady, Dad."

Angie pressed on his wrist and he fell completely to the floor. The joint lock hurt, but not nearly as much as it would've if Angie was doing more than making a point. He'd make her pay for this in the bedroom, not that he could offer up that threat in front of his children and in-laws.

Angie narrowed her gaze at him, but there was an impish twinkle in her eyes. "Say it."

"Say what?"

"An apology. Say it and I'll let you go."

"Fine. You're a bully. A tiny Christmas bully who revels in emasculating her husband in front of his children."

"Emasculating? You asked my father to pay you for taking me 'off his hands.' What kind of sexist thing is that to say about your wife and the mother of your children?"

"You Styles don't know how to take a joke."

"I thought I was a Franklin."

"Nope. I take that back. You're all Styles. You don't deserve my last name."

"Good, I didn't want it anyway."

Small but strong fingers released him, and Sean attacked. He wouldn't give Angie another opportunity to use more martial arts moves on him.

Grabbing Angie by her waist, he yanked her onto the floor beside him. She yelped her surprise, and Sean covered her body with his, holding her down with one hand while tickling her with the other.

Angie bucked and fought, yelling but also laughing at the power reversal.

"No, you don't, Mrs. Franklin. I got you now."

"Styles-Franklin. My name first then yours." She tried to bite the arm closest to her. "Get off me and stop t-tick-tickling me."

Sean didn't stop. His fingers moved to every spot he knew would make her squirm and holler. A weight hit his back, and then thin arms came around his neck and legs around his waist. Zuri. Sean tumbled to the side, careful not to squish his daughter. They fell in a heap, Zuri laughing and digging her fingers into his side the way he'd done Angie.

"You're a big bully, Daddy."

"I got your bully." Sean hoisted Zuri from beside him and next to Angie, pinning them both and alternating attacking one then the other. Between raspberries and deft fingers, he had them both laughing and fighting to get away from him.

Another body landed on Sean. Unfair, three Franklin females against one Franklin male.

Sean tussled with his wife and daughters, losing the battle but doing his best to stay in the fight.

He could hear Kim and Charles in the background, clapping and laughing but doing nothing to help their only son-in-law.

"I got your back, Dad." SJ jumped into the fray, tackling Kayla. The girl screamed and giggled. Then it was on between sister and brother, two athletes going at it—SJ strong and fast, Kayla limber and sneaky.

His family rolled around on Sky's floor, coming close to toppling her birthday Christmas tree, destroying presents, and smashing gift boxes. They were acting like five, drunken idiots, and he couldn't have been happier, even when Angie caught him in another joint lock and made him tap her leg in defeat.

His family was wrapped up in each other, all arms and legs, loud laughter and sweaty bodies.

A throat cleared.

They stopped, and Sean looked over his wife and children and toward the opening to the living room.

"Are we interrupting?"

Sky's maternal uncle, Kenneth, and his wife, Yvette, stood at the threshold of the living room. Their faces registered shock, and for a second, Sean felt guilty at having brought his family's brand of silliness and fun into Sky's home. They were guests, after all, and Sky wasn't there to excuse or justify their raucous behavior.

Then Kenneth, a bear of a man, grinned, and Yvette, a tall woman dressed in black pants and a red blouse, lifted a professional-looking camera to her eye and snapped off several shots.

They'd met the couple yesterday, along with their grown sons, Brandon and Jeremiah. Sky may not have been raised by her father and accepted fully into his family, but her maternal family couldn't have been more kind and welcoming.

Kenneth laughed again, his large belly shaking. "Where is my niece? We'd like to wish her a happy birthday."

Charles made his way across the living room to greet Kenneth and Yvette, shaking Sky's uncle's hand. "She and Malcolm are still upstairs."

"But it's after ten."

"I know," Charles agreed, seeming happy someone finally agreed with him. "We've been waiting for them to come downst—"

Sean and Angie fell into each other, laughing with abandon. Sean's Christmas couldn't get much better than this. He understood Angie's request now and why she'd asked him not to spend money on her. He still didn't like it, but no price could be placed on the last thirty minutes he'd shared with his family. Sean felt loved and, from the way Angie hung over him, eyes filled with laugh tears and a big grin on her face, so did she.

The day drew on and Sky's Ellis family converged on her home. Malcolm and Sky had finally joined everyone, embarrassed to find more than two dozen people waiting for them and the knowledge that every adult in the house knew what had taken them so long to make it downstairs.

Gifts were opened after dinner, Sky the center of attention since it was her birthday. Being an introvert, she couldn't have enjoyed the spotlight, but she accepted the love of family and friends with smiles and grace.

From across the room, where Sean sat on an ottoman next to his wife's chair, he caught Malcolm rise from where he was sitting beside Sky and move to the entrance to the living room. For several minutes, Malcolm watched Sky open presents, his brother-in-law not as jovial as he'd been earlier in the day.

"Something is bothering Malcolm," Angie said to him.

"I noticed. I'm going to check on him."

"Thank you."

He kissed Angie's cheek. "Keep my spot warm. I'll be back in a few."

Twenty minutes later and seated at Sky's kitchen table, Sean knew what had put Malcolm in a worrisome mood. Sean didn't doubt Sky would accept Malcolm's proposal, but most men, prior to popping the big question, feared being rejected by the woman they loved. Hell, twenty years into Sean's marriage, he still feared being rejected by the woman he loved.

After their talk, Malcolm, more confident than he'd been when Sean had followed him out of the living room and into the kitchen, strolled away with a pep in his step and a proposal plan to execute.

Sean had remained seated, mind replaying a portion of his conversation with Malcolm.

"You're my brother, and I love you. Sky is amazing, and you're perfect for each other. The two of you are every corny love song."

"*Baby Love*, The Supremes," Malcolm had thrown out, quick to catch on and feed Sean's love for music and romance.

"*Endless Love*, Diana Ross and Lionel Richie."

"I'll raise you a duet with a quartet. Boyz II Men's *I'll Make Love to You*."

Sean liked the clean-cut group, but he could do better. "Bet. Rihanna featuring Calvin Harris. *We Found Love*. The song was on Billboard's hot one hundred chart for ten weeks. Don't ask me why I know that bit of worthless information."

Tempted by the container of delicious-looking brownies on the table in front of him, Sean had helped himself to two.

"Was the song before or after the Chris Brown incident?"

"I have no idea, but Brown's image hasn't been the same since he was arrested for abusing Rihanna. Are you folding?"

"No, but I have a song for you. Al Green's *Let's Stay Together*."

"Just because we're alone in the kitchen, it doesn't mean I won't tell your sister you hit on me."

They'd slapped hands and laughed like old friends. Not since Angie's car crash and their bedside vigil had Sean felt so connected to Malcolm. This weekend, Malcolm on the cusp of becoming a fiancée, he'd sensed their friendship reforming.

"What I've learned from counseling," he'd told Malcolm, "is that staying together is only one step. An important step, don't get me wrong, but still only one. For months, I thought if I could just convince my wife to stay, then everything would be fine. But it wasn't. Staying is just that. I stayed. She stayed. But we were stuck. Staying together isn't enough."

"So write the rest of the lyrics to Green's song."

Malcolm had offered up the suggestion, not as if mending the rift Sean had created in his marriage was as simple as snapping his fingers, but as a challenge for him to keep moving forward and not to give up.

"That's what I'm trying to do."

"Don't try. Do."

Yes, definitely a challenge.

Reflecting on all the songs Malcolm and he had swapped, as well as Angie's desire for him to spend no money on her, an idea began to form. He had less than two months before Angie's birthday and Valentine's Day. That should be enough time to organize everything.

Sean grinned, pleased with his budding plan, and then got to his feet. He needed to clear the house of guests and straighten the living room before Malcolm returned with Sky from his pre-proposal outing. The man would need privacy and a romantic atmosphere when he popped the question. Sean would make sure he had both.

Pulling his cell phone from his pants pocket, he added a new notes page: Angie's Valentine's Day Surprise.

"Why are you looking at me like that?" Sean sat up in bed, naked except for boxers. "Why are you up and all the way over there?" Glancing at the clock on the nightstand, he added, "At one o'clock in the morning. Come back to bed."

She'd missed sharing a bed with him. Not the sex, per se, although she missed that as well. What she missed was the intimacy of the act and the security his arms offered when he coiled his big body around hers.

"You have no idea how I'm looking at you. Most of the moonlight falls on your side of the room."

The lamp on the nightstand flicked on. "Were you plotting my murder?"

"I've done that once this month. I hate to be redundant, so you get to live another night."

"Very funny." He patted the vacant spot beside him. "Come back to bed, or you'll force me to come to you."

She didn't move.

A put-upon sigh and long strides had Sean in front of her a few seconds later. He loomed over Angie, his frame large and cut to mouthwatering perfection. His eyes slid from her face to the hand holding the rings he'd given her.

"Intending on returning those? I thought we'd gotten past that hurdle."

"We have." She scooted over when it became clear he intended to plop his big body on the settee whether she moved or not. "There isn't enough room for the both of us."

"Yet here we are, fitting on this sofa together." His arm rose to the back of the settee and around her shoulders before his face lowered to her hair. "You always smell good."

"We showered with the same soap."

"It smells different on you." He sniffed. "Better." Another sniff. "Sexier."

"Cut it out. You're acting like a Bassett Hound on the hunt."

"Is that your subtle way of calling me a dog?"

"I don't like when you joke like that."

"Too soon? Sorry." Sean kissed her cheek, the way he often did when he needed physical reassurance but didn't know whether if he asked for it she would reject him. "I can replace those rings. I don't know why you won't let me."

Because Sean was still her husband and his rock-hard body felt amazing, she slouched against him, her head going to his chest, the symbols of their marriage in the palm of her right hand.

"I didn't have much money when I bought you those rings. I can afford so much more now. I can get you rings on par with what Malcolm purchased for Sky."

She'd seen the engagement ring. He'd taken a picture and had sent her a text, asking her opinion. Angie had given it. The ring was elegant, expensive, and perfect for Sky.

"I don't want different rings. I loved them twenty years ago when you were a struggling lawyer just starting out, and nothing has changed." The last part of her sentence wasn't strictly true in the broader sense. So much had changed in the intervening years, some unavoidable, others undeniable.

Sean removed the rings from her hand. "I saved for a year to buy you these."

"I know."

"Why did you take the rings off, if you love them?" With the same reverence with which he'd placed them on her fingers the first time around, he returned the rings to where they belonged. Once on, Sean raised her hand to his mouth and kissed. "I'm glad you still want them. And I regret ever giving you reason to want to give them back."

They sat in silence, Angie choosing not to answer Sean's question. He held her to him, her head pillowed against his chest and over his heart. Today had been one of those days where she found herself wanting to bask in the light of Sean's magnificent rays, but apprehension had kept her from losing herself in his warm allure.

"If you want to get rid of me, you're going to have to be the one to leave because I'm not walking away from you."

So he'd said a dozen times, and he still didn't get it. When Sean had slept with Trinity, he'd been the one to leave Angie.

She pushed from him and grabbed his journal. "Here, take it back."

"No, it was a gift."

"I don't want it. Please, take it back."

"I won't. I have a closet full of Christmas gifts I can't give you because you asked me to show you my love without spending any money. You know how hard that is for me, but I'm trying to respect your wishes. I didn't make the decision to give you my journal lightly. I wanted you to know how much I trust you with my heart. I thought we were beginning to get back what we once had, even if only a little."

"We are. I'm just not ready to read what you've written in your journal. If it's full of details about your affair with Trinity, I'd rather not know." She shoved the journal against his chest, but he still didn't take the book from her. "I'm trying. I really am. But it still hurts. Every time we have a good day, like today, and we feel like old times, I remember I felt the same way right before you told me about your affair. I can't trust this yet. God, Sean, I want to. My life would be simpler, if I could."

Angie desired simple and safe. Yet the heart and life promised neither.

"I wouldn't ask you to read my journal if I thought it would cause you more pain. I didn't waste a single page on Trinity, at least not directly. But the journal does include my invisible blood and tears. The act of writing out my thoughts and reflecting on them were more therapeutic and painful than I thought possible. I came to several realizations. I could tell them to you, but I'd rather you read them first. Afterward, we can talk about anything in the journal you'd like to discuss. But that's not the bigger issue of why you're up tonight and left the bed. You're retreating again, afraid, like you said, of letting me fully in and making yourself vulnerable. You feel that way because you still don't trust me not to hurt you again."

She hated this. Hated how her valid emotions hurt him. Hated how her heart and body betrayed her mind. Hated how his love for her shone in the eyes that held hers, but the impact of his love was dulled by the truth of his words. No, she hadn't reached the point of being able to trust that he wouldn't cheat on her again. Her mind told her he regretted his affair and wouldn't stray again. Her heart, however, wasn't yet convinced, although it pulsed and begged for reassurance.

She told herself tonight what she had before. If Sean cheated again, their marriage would be over. No more therapy. No more apologies. No more chances. Just over. Dr. Naylor and she had discussed her decision. The future offered no guarantees, and neither could Sean, even if he meant his promises. All Angie had control over was how she would respond if the unfortunate happened and Sean broke his vow of fidelity again. Viewed in that light, trust had more to do with Angie trusting herself to follow through with her plan and less about her trusting Sean to keep his word.

What she trusted was his desire to maintain their marriage. She trusted his love for her and their children. She trusted his good intentions and heart. Angie didn't lack trust in Sean, but rather faith, a higher and deeper standard that rested solely with her. Trust could be earned, but faith had to be given. The two were connected but not interchangeable.

Angie placed the journal on the floor and resettled against her husband. "Let's talk about something else. Do you think Sky accepted Malcolm's proposal?"

He held her and didn't force the issue. Today had been a good Christmas. Angie hadn't wanted to ruin it, so she'd given herself permission to do as Sean had asked—to feel and not to think. When she'd allowed herself to enjoy the holiday and not give in to negative and distracting thoughts, she had relaxed and opened herself to love and laughter.

At the beginning of the year, when Sean had confessed, Angie wouldn't have predicted the two of them would still be together by year's end. That thought helped put tonight's feelings into perspective. Neither knew what the future held. This time next year, they could be in a better place than they were today.

"Of course Sky accepted Malcolm's proposal. I can go check on them, if you want."

"It's after one. You just want an excuse to harass my brother. Leave Malcolm alone and let him enjoy the first night of his engagement. You have the rest of our vacation to pick a fight. I'm glad the two of you are getting along better." She leaned up, facing him. "Thank you for helping Malcolm tonight. I don't know what was bothering him, but it seemed, after his talk with you, he got over it."

"A little case of cold feet. Nothing serious. Malcolm only needed someone to remind him of what he already knew."

"That Sky loves him and wouldn't be so foolish as to turn him down if he proposed?"

"Ding, ding. The prize goes to the beautiful college president. How late do you think they'll come downstairs tomorrow? Well, later today."

"That will depend on how long Malcolm can go without food."

Sean chuckled. "Good point. Come here." He hauled her on top of him, forcing her to straddle his hips. "That's better." Sean didn't try anything. His hands stayed on her waist, his eyes at face level. "I'm a patient man."

She snorted. "No, you aren't."

"You're right, I'm not. But when it comes to you and us, I damn sure am. I'll never grovel or beg. That's not who I am or even the kind of man you want me to be. I made an awful mistake. I can't change what I've done, but I can assure you it'll never happen again."

Nothing she hadn't heard from him before. Still, Angie couldn't deny she needed to hear it over and again. No guarantees, she knew, but it felt good to have him say it. It felt even better that Sean knew it needed saying and didn't hesitate to voice Angie's fear and to claim responsibility for his future actions.

"You don't believe me. I don't know what to do about your lack of faith in me. I can tell you a hundred times a day, but words won't stop you from questioning who I'm with and what I'm doing when I work late. Words and promises won't restore the security my lies ripped away. I have no proof I haven't cheated on you before or since my affair. I have nothing to give you but my word. It must still be worth something because you haven't thrown in the towel, but it isn't worth enough to put your mind at ease. I don't know what else to do."

"Neither do I. That's why we're in counseling. I wish we were a better example for Malcolm and Sky."

"We're a real example for them. Marriage is work and not always the good kind that takes place in bed. They'll have their own struggles because they're flawed people, just like everyone else. Neither are looking for or expecting perfection. They're realists, even Malcolm. They'll have an imperfect but wonderful life together. They are each other's gift of Christmas present."

"You're right. I only want the best for them."

"So do I." Fingers glided from waist to arms and up to shoulders, kneading. "I want the best for us, too." Hand around nape, Sean pulled Angie's face to his. "Sometimes, when you're right beside me, you're a million miles away. I know it's selfish to want all of you when, for a time, I shared with someone else what belonged to you. Yet I want everything you have to give. Your trust and faith. Your smile and warmth. Your witticism and sarcasm." His lips pressed to hers. "Your love and body."

Angie's eyes slipped closed. Heart raced. Desire and caution waged a war inside her body, as they'd done for weeks. Caution had proven the consistent and undisputed winner. Tonight, however ...

"Give me a real second chance, Angie. Let me make love to you."

Opening her eyes, she straightened, putting a little distance between them for the conversation Sean seemed to want to have. "I have given you a real second chance."

"Have you forgiven me?"

In the months since they'd started therapy, he'd never asked her that question. It was reasonable, if not overdue, but him putting it out there had still taken her by surprise.

"I've been afraid to ask. You have no idea how many times I've wanted to but backed away from the question at the last moment."

"Why are you asking now?"

"You gave me a vintage pocket watch with the names and birth dates of our children engraved on the back. As much as I love that Christmas gift and all that the watch symbolizes, it's not the present I most wanted this Christmas. I didn't think I wanted anything special for the holiday until we played and laughed this morning. The way you looked at me, even when you had me in a joint-lock, was all I'd been missing and everything I almost threw away."

"How did I look at you?"

"As a man you loved. A man you were devoted to. A man who hadn't hurt you. Those are the ways you used to look at me before my confession. I hadn't realized it until it was gone. For a while today the look returned, and it was like the dawning of a new day." A hand rose to her face and cupped her cheek. "The look vanished when I gave you my journal, and it's still gone. You're guarded again, although not as much as you once were. I'm feeling brave, so I asked you two questions I'd like you to answer."

"Have I forgiven you, and will I allow us to make love?"

"Yes. I'd like to know."

Fair questions and ones she'd pondered. They were also difficult questions for the emotions linked to them, as well as the possible implications for their marriage.

Sean said he wanted to know, but he appeared scared to death of her answers.

Angie turned into the hand caressing her cheek and kissed the palm, giving herself a few seconds to gather her nerve and to shed her cloak of protection. In posing the two questions, Sean had made himself vulnerable to Angie. She could and would do the same for him.

"I used to think forgiveness was for the recipient. It is, but forgiveness is also for yourself. I didn't know if I was capable of forgiving you, even when we began therapy. Sometimes, I questioned whether you were worthy of my forgiveness. But I had to self-correct that kind of thinking. If I didn't think you were worthy of my forgiveness or myself capable of forgiving you, for my sake and for yours, why should I continue our marriage, much less be in couple's therapy? A part of me had to believe both. Otherwise, what in the hell was I doing?"

"What are you saying?"

Closing her eyes and breathing deeply, she centered herself before looking at Sean again and responding. "It means I needed to forgive you for my own sanity and peace of mind. Anger isn't my friend, but we were swinging partners for months. It hurt to be so mad at you, as much as it hurt to have a reason for so much anger. It wasn't healthy, and I had to let it go."

"By forgiving me?"

"Yes, by forgiving you."

Sean's hand dropped from Angie's face and to his side, eyes solemn. "You forgave me because it's what you needed to do to help yourself heal and to move on?"

"Yes. It's the same reason you forgave yourself, right?"

He nodded. "I guess I was hoping your forgiveness would have something to do with me."

"It does, but it has more to do with me. I know what you're thinking and why you're more upset than relieved."

"I am relieved. Honey, I'm so happy you've forgiven me. The thought of not having your forgiveness hurt like hell. But forgiveness isn't a guarantee you'll stay."

"No more than guilt and shame can guarantee you'll be faithful."

Blunt, maybe harsh, but also true. Honesty didn't come with blinders or training wheels.

"What about the second question? The other day in the bathroom was great. You responded to me in a way you haven't in a long time. But not fully. Do you want me?"

"That's not what you really want to know. I watched you masturbate and let you give me oral sex and multiple orgasms, so me wanting you is obvious. Speak your heart, Sean, and I'll speak mine."

"I want you to want me, not because we haven't had sex in almost a year and you're horny and needy, but because you want *me*. The person.

Your husband. The man you love." Sean glanced away from Angie, a too familiar sign of his shame, and then back to her. "I want you to not see me as a cheating asshole. I want you to just see me when we make love."

He was referring to her flashbacks. They'd lessened but not disappeared. Angie didn't know when or if they would. "You were a cheating asshole, but that's not who I see when I look at you. I do see Sean the person. I also see my husband and the father of my children. We're friends, too. I see that person when I look at you as well."

A triumphant grin brightened Sean's face and had him rubbing Angie's thighs. "What else?"

"Don't get cocky."

He winked. "I'm hoping you'll want me to get cocky. You called me an asshole."

"I've called you worse in my head."

"That's cold. Tell me you love me."

"No."

"Why not?"

"I thought you wanted to make love."

"I do, almost as much as I want to hear you confess your love for me."

"You're assuming I still love you."

Full, warm lips nuzzled her neck. "It's a safe assumption, but only because you haven't murdered me in my sleep. I want to be inside you." A bite to her earlobe and then a nip to her shoulder. "As deep as I can go. I've dreamed about it." Fingers slid the straps of her black, silk nightgown down her arms. "Jerked-off to thoughts of making love to you. I fucked you with my mouth in the bathroom. That's not what I want to do now. It wasn't even my intention when I joined you in there. But I was desperate and greedy and would have you anyway you allowed."

He plied her neck and shoulders with worshipful kisses, his lips soft and tender and the hands roaming her body the same. Angie had also thought of Sean, her vibrator no match for a full-bodied hard male. His mouth and hands felt so damn good. Sean never disappointed, when it came to giving her sexual pleasure.

A thought that would've had Angie stopping Sean was shoved away as quickly as it had arrived. She wouldn't allow a flashback to ruin this moment between spouses. Sean was right. Angie was horny and needy. But only for him. She had to clear this hurdle. Angie was tired of denying her urges and giving in to her fears. It wasn't romantic to think of what would happen between them tonight in those terms, but it was her truth.

She couldn't continue to withhold sex, punishing him and denying herself. Sex wasn't a reward for good behavior to be revoked and held over another person's head when they did something that displeased their partner. Sex could destroy a bond as much as it could affirm one.

Placing her hand at the nape of Sean's neck, she pulled him to her and captured his lips in a slow, burning kiss. For lengthy minutes, they luxuriated in the kiss, unrushed and thorough. They hadn't kissed like this in years, taking their time and enjoying the act, not as a prelude to sex but as a gratifying interlude in and of itself.

He nipped, and she sucked. He licked, and she moaned. The kiss went on and on, Angie's body heating, Sean's hands wandering. Her hair. Her shoulders. Her breasts. Yes, her breasts. Heavy and aching for his touch, for—"Mmm, yes, there"—Sean's mouth on her nipples.

He'd yanked her nightgown to her waist, far less gentle than his kisses had been. Sean's tongue rimmed her nipple, circling the areola over and again before taking it into his mouth and sucking. His left hand fondled the other breast, squeezing and running a thumb over the pert nipple.

Angie's moan, throaty and heartfelt, seemed to encourage Sean. He opened his mouth wider and engulfed as much of her breast as he could, sucking hard and greedily. There was nothing gentle or slow about Sean now, which suited Angie just fine.

Horny didn't begin to describe her level of need or the groundswell of lust his mouth and hands had unleashed. Hips moved of their own volition, rocking back and forth over Sean's growing erection.

Back and forth.

Back and forth.

"Shit, that feels good. I thought I could do better than I did in the bathroom, but it's been too long. I don't want this to be a quick session, Angie."

She pushed off him and got to her feet, legs weak and panties drenched with evidence of her desire. Angie removed them, along with her nightgown.

Sean had followed her up, his boxers quickly discarded. Grabbing her around the waist, he lifted and pressed her to the closest wall.

"Right here," he rasped, voice thick with arousal, but not as thick as the erection pressing against her stomach. "I'm going to hold you up and you're going to ride me."

"You want me to—"

He readjusted his arms and her legs, supporting her under her knees and holding her legs open. With a quick upward motion, Sean was inside her.

Angie gasped at the sharp, hard entry and Sean stilled. "Did I hurt you?"

A little, but she wouldn't tell him that. Sean was big, and it had been a while since they'd done this. Not just sex but what was about to be athletic sex.

"I'm fine."

"Are you sure?" He kissed her, pressing into her with his soft tongue and rigid dick.

Yes, she was sure, as long as he kept up the double penetration.

"Wrap your arms around my neck. Yeah, just like that." Sean moved away from the wall, taking the entirety of her weight. Weightlifting had done his body good. "Now ride me."

One arm around Sean's neck and the other pressed to his chest, Angie moved up and down his length, aided by his supportive hands on her ass.

In the middle of Sky's guest room they made love, the lamp and moonlight illuminating their physical reconciliation. No sounds could be heard in the hallway or next door. The only noises came from Sean and Angie, heavy breaths and pleasured grunts.

Up and down.

Up and down.

Damn, he couldn't be any deeper or she more open. Breasts and nipples slid against sweaty pecs, gliding over a dusting of curly hair. The sensation of chest against chest electrified her skin and sent quivers of delight straight to her groin.

Mouths collided and the exploring kisses they'd started on the settee continued. This time, they were hard and deep and punctuated with pulls, bites, and panting.

Sharp nails raked down the center of Sean's chest, not breaking skin or drawing blood but hard enough to get the kind of reaction from him they enjoyed.

Sean slammed Angie down onto his dick, wrenching control from her. She scratched him again, harder and adding a bite to his collarbone.

"Hell, yes. Keeping doing that."

Angie obliged, and Sean responded in kind. Up against the wall she went again, her lower half held up and pressed against him. Hands gripping her bottom, Sean's thighs were miraculous, their strength admirable.

They kissed through it all.

Angie had no idea how long Sean held her against the wall, kissing her and proclaiming his love, hips in constant, driving motion. What she did know was, as he settled her on the bed, putting his face between legs hoisted over his shoulders, she couldn't go back to celibacy. He'd obliterated any part of Angie that may have thought she could have sex with Sean and not lose herself in the love she felt for him.

It wasn't the sex that made Angie feel this way. But the sex, and it was damn good sex, had her emotionally open and receptive to her husband, as well as hopeful for a happily-ever-after and not just a happy-for-now. This was cuddle time to the nth-degree.

Sean's hips, thighs, and penis had done most of the work, so it didn't take but a few swipes of his tongue to send her into another dimension. Back bowed, hands fisted sheets, and mouth opened on a decadent scream of release.

Crawling up Angie's body, Sean kissed her again, and then pushed into her, not giving her time to catch her breath or to float down from the cloud he'd catapulted her onto.

"So good," he moaned into her ear. "So damn good. I could stay inside you all night."

She laughed, bit his neck and then soothed it with butterfly kisses.

"Do that again."

After the orgasm he'd just given her, Sean could ask her for damn near anything and she'd gift it to him.

Angie bit and kissed his neck again, and all through their lovemaking, enjoying each groan and grunt she pulled from him.

Sweaty and slick, he moved inside her, her legs around his waist and holding him close.

"I'm going to come."

She knew. Sean's pace had increased, and his controlled breathing had begun to falter. Reaching between them, Angie found her clit and rubbed, stroking his surging penis in the process.

"Shit. Damn, that's … that's …"

She clenched around him, the beginning of her orgasm triggering his. Sean powered into Angie, his body hard, strong, and carnal from the forehead pressed against hers and all the way to the toes digging into the mattress.

Scrumptious came to mind, and then *mine*.

"So good," Sean breathed. "You wrecked me."

"You're the one who did the wrecking. I may need my cane to help me walk tomorrow."

"Flatterer."

Angie wasn't trying to be. She could already feel where she'd ache in a few hours.

"Do you want to take a shower or bath?" She may have posed the question, but she didn't so much as move an inch.

"I do need to get up and brush my teeth, but I don't think I can stand. You wore me out." Sean pulled Angie to him, settling her in front of him, his too-warm body spooning around hers.

She would overheat, if they slept like this. Yet, Angie had no desire to fall asleep any other way. The notion didn't frighten her as much as she thought it would.

"Angie, I love you. You won't regret trusting me with your body again." He leaned up and turned off the nightstand lamp. "I promise. Have faith in me."

Faith. A weighty word to be only five-letters long.

"Go to sleep, honey. I need you to get a good night's rest because, come morning, I'm going to pin you to the bed and fu…"

Angie reached behind her and found Sean's flaccid penis and stroked it to fullness. He shut up, and she slid down the bed, unwilling to wait until morning to have her husband again.

By the time she finished with him, they would both need to brush their teeth.

CHAPTER THIRTY-FIVE

"I can carry her."

"You have our luggage. I can manage Zuri. Thank you, though."

Sean watched Angie make her way up the stairs, Zuri's legs and arms wrapped around her mother. The little girl had fallen asleep the last three hours of the drive from Annapolis to Buffalo. When Charles had dropped them off, Angie lifted Zuri from her car seat before Sean could, leaving SJ, Kayla, and him to haul their bags from the truck into the house.

"She's faking," SJ said, standing beside Sean at the foot of the stairs. "She's a big, tiny faker and Mom falls for it every time."

Kayla bumped SJ's shoulder with hers. "We used to do the same thing."

"Yup. Mom fell for it then too."

"Nope, you're wrong." Kayla bumped SJ again. "Mommy doesn't fall for baby tricks like that. She played along because it made us happy to think we tricked her. She knew how much we liked her spoiling us."

"You're the one who's wrong. Tell her, Dad."

Four years may have separated brother and sister but, in certain respects, Kayla outpaced SJ. His son still interpreted life too literally, missing the spectrum of colors that made up the world. His oldest daughter, however, had grasped the concept of sarcasm by the age of seven.

"Kayla's right."

"Told you," Kayla sing-songed. She poked her tongue at her brother at the same moment Angie reappeared at the top of the stairs.

"Young lady."

"Sorry, Mommy."

"It's late. The two of you need to bring up your luggage and bags of presents. You don't have to unpack tonight, though."

"Do we have to go to bed now?" SJ asked.

"No, you have one more day of your winter break left. But I have to go in to work tomorrow."

"Got it. You want us quiet. No problem, Mom."

"I'm going to see if Zuri is finished brushing her teeth, then I'll turn in for the night. But I'll come to your rooms and wish you both a good-night first."

Angie disappeared, and the children wasted no time following her orders. They should've driven home two days earlier, giving Angie time to settle from her trip and to prepare for her return to work. But she'd insisted on spending as much downtime with the family as possible. Her spring semester would be busy, so he understood her motivation.

She'd explained, no matter how she readjusted her schedule to spend more time with him and the children, she couldn't meet the demands of her job by working less than fifty hours a week. Sean truly got it now. They had to make a consistent effort to spend quality time with each other and not to allow outside obligations to dominate their relationship. Relationship building activities were key to them staying connected and continuing to grow and bond as a couple.

This was easier to achieve, obviously, when Angie was on medical leave and they were on vacation. Even when she'd first returned to work, it was on a part-time basis. Now, with the beginning of a new semester, Angie would be back at work full-time, and so would Sean. He had to move his firm out of one building and into another. January and February would be busy for them both.

After depositing Angie's rolling suitcase in her empty bedroom and noting his wife was in with Zuri, reading her a bedtime story, he'd dragged himself to his room. Once inside his dark, lonely bedroom, he dropped his luggage, yanked off shoes and clothes, and headed straight to the bathroom for a shave and shower. Despite them having shared Sky's guest room and renewing their sexual relationship, they hadn't talked about post-vacation sleeping arrangements.

Sean hadn't wanted to risk the rapport they'd achieved by bringing up a topic that could lead to an argument. The night they'd made love, Sean couldn't have been happier, except when he'd awakened to find Angie curled against him. They'd made love that morning and as many times as he could drag her back to the bedroom without being too obvious and embarrassing his wife. There was no getting anything past Malcolm and Kim, however. Luckily, his mother-in-law had only smiled at them, and his brother-in-law had had no interest in talking about his sister's sex life.

"Are you stalking Mom?"

Sean swung around from where he stood in front of Angie's partially closed door, pondering his next course of action--return to his room and go to bed alone or start a conversation with his wife that could go south.

SJ stood in his doorway, grinning at Sean. "She's got you shook."

"What do you know about being shook?"

"I know what it looks like." A finger rose and pointed at him. "It looks like you. Things are better between you and Mom, right? I mean, you guys were cool towards each other when we were visiting Dr. Sky. I haven't seen Mom laugh so much in a long time." SJ pointed his index finger at Sean again. "You either. You're kind of obvious, Dad."

"Obvious?"

"Happy, I mean. It was nice seeing you and Mom happy ... and together. Are you moving back into your bedroom?"

He heard the water from Angie's shower shut off and had to refrain from imagining his son's mother deliciously wet and totally sexable. It wouldn't do for Sean to get a hard-on in front of SJ while daydreaming about having sex with Angie.

"I don't know. I hope so, but it's up to your mother."

"Like you always tell me, if you don't ask, the answer will always be no. If you do ask, the answer could possibly be yes. But you'll never know if you're too afraid to go for it."

"You're telling me to man up and to go for it?"

"Yeah." SJ grinned. "Go for it. But, umm, close the door and maybe turn on the television."

Before Sean could digest that SJ had just given him sex advice, his son had slipped back into his room and closed the door, leaving him alone in the hallway, stunned and amused. He'd joked with Angie when he'd told her Sky's bedrooms weren't soundproof, implying he'd heard Sky and Malcolm going at it Christmas morning. Perhaps he should've remembered his own words when she and he had spent the last five days having sex behind a locked door, no television or music to muffle the noises they'd made.

Sean knocked on Angie's bedroom door, too smart to barge in on his private wife.

"Give me a minute," she yelled from what sounded like the bathroom.

He waited, impatient and nervous.

"Come in, Sean."

He entered what he hoped would be his bedroom once more and closed the door after him, taking SJ's recommendation. "How did you know it was me?"

Angie sat on the bed, a towel wrapped around her and a nightgown and pair of panties laid out beside her. His question and why he was in her room drained away when she removed her towel and began applying lotion to her feet and legs.

"The kids don't knock as hard as you do, not even SJ." She looked up at him through long, dark lashes, lips curling into a knowing grin. "It's impolite to stare."

422 · N.D. JONES

"You're naked. What did you think I would do, when you took off your towel?" He moved to the bed, invading Angie's space when he knelt in front of her. A memory from two decades ago popped into his mind, a younger version of them in Angie's apartment, Sean on both knees and a monographed, wooden box in his pocket. "Will you marry me?"

Right hand halfway to her face and smelling of peach-scented lotion, she stopped, blinked, and then laughed. "We're already married. Stop being silly."

"I'm serious. I'm asking you to marry me. Again," he clarified.

If Sean had planned this, Angie wouldn't be naked and shocked and he wouldn't be in boxers and his Keep Calm and Call Your Lawyer T-shirt. He should've taken a play out of Malcolm's gamebook and gone for romantic and sweet. But he was down on both knees, and the woman he loved was in front of him, eyes wide and mouth open but silent.

"Dr. Naylor said our old marriage was over. I don't like that idea, as if everything that came before my affair is null and void. But I get her point. We've had to, in many respects, start over. If that's the case," — Sean took hold of Angie's hand, heedless of the squirt of lotion in the center— "will you consider remarrying me? Not on my birthday, like the first time, but on yours, the way we should've done it twenty-one years ago."

"You want to … what? I'm confused. When you knocked, I assumed you wanted to talk about moving back in to the bedroom."

"I did. I mean, I do. But, well, I don't know where the proposal came from. I saw you sitting there, so beautiful and comfortable in your own skin… and with me. When I went down on my knees, the proposal kind of popped out."

Not romantic or sweet. He'd been nervous as hell the first time around, but he'd managed to bumble through his marriage proposal without coming off as a green teenager. Not so this time.

Sean rubbed the back of a lotion-soft hand with his thumb. "Forget I said anything."

"I don't think I can. You really want to renew our vows?"

"I do." Sean scooted back, allowing Angie to finish putting on lotion and to dress. Afterward, he claimed the spot next to her on the bed and held her hand. "I would like for us to renew our vows. As soon as I asked, it felt right. Perfect. A second chance, not just for me but for us. For months, even tonight before I knocked on your door, I kept thinking about you giving me a second chance. My second chance is also *our* second chance. The gift you gave me was also a gift you gave *us*. Whether it's this Valentine's Day or three from now, I'd like to repledge myself to you."

"I don't know what to say."

His marriage proposal had been too spontaneous for him to build a campfire of hope, but that didn't prevent his heart from slowing to a disappointed crawl at her response. She still held his hand, though, and hadn't asked him to leave her bedroom, which had to count for something, so Sean claimed it as a small win.

"I'm scheduled to attend this year's Presidents Institute. I told you, remember?"

"I do. Scottsdale, Arizona for three days."

The conference fell during the anniversary week of his confession. The timing was coincidental, but Angie's decision to attend was her way of putting distance between them without coming straight out and telling him she didn't want to be around him during that time. He wished she felt differently but didn't begrudge her need to deal with memories of that wretched day alone and on her terms.

"May I move back in here?"

"You made that question sound like a consolation prize instead of the huge step forward it would be for us." She raised her head and stared at him before releasing his hand and repositioning herself against the headboard. Angie then reached into the nightstand drawer, pulling out Sean's reflection journal. "I planned on reading your journal before falling asleep. I didn't think you'd want to be in here while I read it, so I decided to wait until tomorrow to broach the topic of you moving back into the bedroom."

He sat on the side of the bed, left foot on the floor and his bent right leg on the bed. "You've thought about me moving back in here?"

"It would've been hard not to after this past week. If you must know, I've missed you."

Sean didn't care if his smile made him look like a lovestruck idiot. His grin was wide and toothy. "I like the sound of that."

He liked, even more, that she had finally decided to accept his Christmas gift. Also, Angie hadn't said she was opposed to them renewing their vows, nor had she rejected the idea of him moving back in to their bedroom. She also hadn't dropped the conference on him at the last minute, any more than she'd denied her need to spend the anniversary of his confession away from him.

Angie had told Sean his affair still hurt her. He couldn't expect her to heal from the wound he'd inflicted quickly or even completely. Hell, he still hadn't gotten over growing up in a house with a cheating father and a weeping mother.

Angie was right, Sean didn't want to watch her read his journal. He had no interest in witnessing the play of emotions cross her face as she soaked in the pages of his childhood trauma and buried pain. At the same time, he didn't want to return to the guest room and fall asleep without his wife beside him.

"Just to be clear, you're letting me move back in here?"

"If you want to."

He reached out and ran a finger down her smooth cheek to her round chin and then across her heart-shaped lips. "You know I want to, but I want to make sure it's also what you want. Just because we shared the same room in Maryland and are having sex again, that doesn't make you obligated to take this step if you aren't ready. As much as I want to be in here, I want you to be sure, to not have any regrets when you open your eyes tomorrow and see me beside you."

"You're sweet."

Sean shook his head and let his hand fall away from Angie's face and onto his lap.

"I wasn't going for sweet. I keep telling you, I want *you* to want *me*. I know, for months, you didn't, and I can't blame you for feeling the way you did. I know it may sound like a switch, the cheater being worried about being wanted by the cheated-on spouse. But it's how I feel, especially since I never stopped wanting you. Some days, I think I want you too much."

Angie didn't comment. She did, however, turn down the covers beside her. It was a silent invitation he wasted no time accepting.

Sean vaulted across his wife, literally jumping over her body to get to the opposite side. Angie laughed, and he moved in for a kiss. But two resolute fingers pressed against his lips, denying him. "What's wrong?"

"Sex or reading? I don't have time for both. You choose."

Sean frowned. "You've got to be kidding me."

"You should know I'm not. It's eleven o'clock and I must be up by five-thirty. If we have sex, it won't be quick because neither of us will want it to be. If I begin reading your journal, I may not want to stop until I'm finished."

"I want to have sex, but I also want you to read my journal. There are things in it we need to discuss."

"I know, and I've put it off for days. I shouldn't have. That's why I decided to read it tonight."

When Sean remained silent with indecision, Angie said, "If you're torn between the two, you must really want me to read what you've written."

"I must be getting old." Sean sighed. "I can't believe I chose you reading a book over us having sex. The either/or option wasn't fair. There should've been a third selection. A little reading then a lot of sex. A little sex then a lot of reading."

"That would've been four choices, and any option that had sex first and reading second would've had the night ending without me reading a word of your journal."

"True." Sean got back out of bed, flicked off the ceiling light and then turned on the lamp on Angie's nightstand. "You read, and I'll dream about having sex with you."

Sean climbed in next to Angie again, less excitedly his time, but no less happy to be back in his room, on his side of the bed, and sharing it with his wife. He was tempted to kiss her goodnight. Instead, he pulled the covers to his waist and stared up at her, his reflection journal in her hands and open to the first page. Her gaze wasn't on the book but on him, so he asked her, "What are you thinking?"

"About your marriage proposal."

His heart leapt but he remained calm. "What about it?"

"It's a considerate, even romantic gesture, like moving your law firm to a new building. Neither should be necessary, but both are like healing crystals, treating our insides by drawing out the negative energy and replacing it with positive, life-affirming energy."

Sean liked that analogy, and it gave him an idea, which he added to the one he'd crafted after his conversation with Malcolm in Sky's kitchen. His brother-in-law had told Sean to write more of Al Green's *Let's Stay Together* song. With Angie's unwitting help, he now had what he hoped would be the perfect Valentine's Day and birthday gift for her.

"If you read quickly, I can give you all the positive, life-affirming energy you want."

Angie laughed and mushed his smiling face. "You chose reading, remember?"

"Not reading. Openness. Honesty. No walls, Angie, not anymore."

"No walls," she agreed, her voice devoid of humor and her eyes full of understanding.

I wish I could forget all the times I heard Mom cry. She yelled a lot too, but she cried even more. The sound used to rip through me. My sisters

and I were unwilling bystanders to her pain and humiliation. To this day, I hate to see a woman cry. I promised myself the only tears my wife would shed because of me would be happy ones. I broke that promise.

A crying woman takes me back to when I was thirteen, listening as Mom cursed and cried, and then finally dropped to her knees, head hung low and a heartbreaking prayer on her lips. This isn't the first memory I have of Mom breaking down over one of Dad's affairs, but it's the first time I remember blaming her for her weakness.

Angie looked from Sean's journal to the man himself. She'd suspected he'd had a troubled childhood. She'd also assumed Edward had cheated on Brenda at some point in their marriage. Not because Angie believed all men were cheaters but based on a few comments Brenda had made about Edward, over the years, and about Angie being "lucky" because Sean was "loyal." Years ago, Edward had even flirted with Kim. Inappropriate was too mild a descriptor for his actions. A man who had no compunction flirting with his son's mother-in-law was the kind of person who wouldn't stop at flirting if the woman returned his attention and attraction.

No, reading of Edward's infidelity hadn't shocked Angie. What had her mouth hanging open, page after page, was the depth and breadth of his adultery. At least two decades, according to Sean, although he suspected much longer.

I never wanted anyone to feel sorry for me. It's not as if I was beaten when I was a kid. I was embarrassed, sure. What kid wouldn't be with a father like mine? That's what I used to tell myself growing up. Dad and Mom didn't beat us, abuse alcohol or do drugs. His cheating and her crying and yelling became the Franklin family normal.

Angie shifted to her side and slid down the bed. Propping on her right elbow, the journal on the mattress in front of her, she continued to read. More than halfway through, she didn't know what to think of Sean's entries and his long-held secrets. Everything she'd read revealed a detail about her husband she hadn't known. They'd been married almost twenty-one years, for god's sake, and Sean hadn't mentioned any of this.

Angie should be mad at him, but she couldn't find it in her to muster the emotion.

He'd said his journal included his invisible blood and tears. The longer she read, the more she agreed. He hadn't wanted her sympathy, so he'd walled off that part of himself. But Sean hadn't let his childhood pain go, even in his silence. His fractured relationship with his parents and emotional need for affirmation and security had influenced every part of their marriage, including his affair. Tonight, he'd said he sometimes wanted Angie too much. Was that how he'd interpreted his mother's rationale for staying with her serial cheating husband? Was his affair an unconscious attempt to refute what he'd viewed as his emotional dependence on her? An acting out, of sorts, that had the dual effect of getting Angie's attention while also affirming his "manhood" and lack of "victim" status?

Angie didn't know, so she continued to read.

I knew it. I didn't want to be right. I called Mom tonight and she admitted what I'd suspected for years. I wanted to know why in the hell she'd stayed with Dad instead of leaving him. Mom's answer was the same excuse I gave for all the fucked-up shit that happened in our house. Dad didn't hit or beat us. He didn't get drunk or high. Dad worked and put food on the table. He made sure we had everything we needed, and he came home to us every night.

Mom stayed. I hated that she did. Worse, I grew to view my own mother as a spineless woman. Even now, I see her as weak to Dad's pathetic. How could any self-respecting woman stay with a man like Edward Franklin? My sisters have thought that way for years. Until recently, I didn't think I shared their harsh opinion of our mother.

Angie turned the page. Some of Sean's reflections were a couple of paragraphs. Most, however, were two to three pages in length. Thus far, this entry was the longest of the bunch, and it was very hard to read and digest. Not due to its length or Sean's doctor-like penmanship, but for the heartache she detected between the lines.

There are many ways to abuse women and children that don't reek of alcohol or come with a fist to the face. I never wanted to view my father as an abuser, but I don't know any other way to think of what he did to us. To her. What hurts the most is that I blame Mom for staying with her abuser. More, I resent her for not getting us out of that house and away from Dad. She loved him more than she loved us, or even herself, at least that's how her decision to stay made me feel. When I graduated high school, all I wanted was to get the hell away from Newark. I thought it was because of Dad. I was partially right. It was also because of her.

Angie felt tears on her cheeks, unaware she'd shed them. She wiped them away. No wonder Sean had selected this indirect method of unburdening his heart and sharing his pain. If Angie had to look into his eyes as he told her this story, she wouldn't have been able to stop the tears from falling. He would've interpreted them as pity instead of compassion.

I didn't want a doormat for my wife, so I didn't marry one. I also didn't want a wife who couldn't stand on her own two feet. That's not Angie. I didn't want a woman who would cry and scream and call me on my bullshit only to diminish herself by accepting and excusing my bad choices. Angie is nothing like Mom. Except, in some ways, she is. Angie can be hurt like Mom. She feels deeply like Mom. She loves her children and wants to keep her family intact, like Mom did. She loves her cheating husband, the way Mom does.

I didn't marry a woman like my mother. I married a woman who can be hurt and who expresses her love in the ways most women do. I'm not my father, despite the one awful act we have in common. I must remind myself of that truth, more often than I like. I am not Edward Franklin. This summer, I've come to realize Dad is more than a selfish whore, as I've thought of him for decades. I want my wife to forgive me, but I've never thought of forgiving my parents. The double standard stings. I have a lot of shit to work on. Too bad I didn't begin to deal with the baggage I brought to my marriage until after I betrayed Angie and threatened the stability of my family.

"It's not an excuse."

Angie slapped a hand over her mouth, quieting her scream. "Dammit, Sean. I didn't know you were awake." She turned onto her left side, head on her pillow, facing her husband. "What's not an excuse?"

"Growing up the way I did. Having a father who cheated on my mother. It's not an excuse for me cheating on you. That's not why I wrote that stuff in my journal or why I gave it to you to read. I should've told you years ago, but I was afraid you'd think I would become like him. I was also ashamed of Dad's behavior. Until I began therapy, I never really wondered what would make Dad do what he did. It was easy to think of him as just a bad guy. A villain, you know?"

Angie nodded. She was empathetic, although she couldn't relate to his experience.

"Four sisters and only one of them is in a stable and long-term relationship. I can't say for certain it's because of Dad and our upbringing. But I can imagine it's difficult for them to trust men, even though they know, intellectually, that not every man is like Dad. I don't want that for my girls. I don't want Kayla and Zuri to settle for *any* man just to have one in their life. I also don't want either of them to be afraid to trust a man with their heart because I've set a bad example of manhood for them."

"You haven't. You're a great father. If you weren't, we wouldn't be together."

"Why couldn't Mom have had that same attitude?" Sean snuggled closer to Angie, a hand going around her waist and rubbing her lower back. "I know that's an unfair question, but I can't help thinking it. You now know all there is to know about me and why I've kept us as far away from Newark and my parents as possible."

"You ran away."

"Running resolved nothing, but it gave me room to breathe and time to learn how to be a man outside of my father's adulterous shadow. It's difficult for me to see the good in him because memories of his affairs and Mom's pain taint my vision."

Sean's hand on her back dipped to her hip and stroked the silk material of her nightgown in a rhythm that felt less sensual for her and more self-comforting for him.

Angie shifted forward and kissed his forehead. "A man can be a good father but a terrible husband. If your parents separated or divorced, you and your sisters would likely feel differently about Edward. His affairs affected you so much because you witnessed the firsthand impact on your mom, so your thoughts and feelings about your father are mixed in with his ill-treatment of your mother. It makes sense. It would be difficult for anyone, especially a son, not to judge his father based on how he treated his mother. The same way it's unlikely you could avoid forming certain opinions about women due to your interpretation of your mother's personality and actions. I won't lie, when Mom first told me about her affair, I thought less of her, which made me feel like the worst kind of daughter. But, for a short, painful time, I did. I got over that initial reaction quickly because I have a lifetime of examples of my mother's wonderful character and the love, trust, and respect between my parents."

"You were right. It all hurts. I'm sorry I hurt you."

"I know you are. Thank you for confiding in me." With a playful slap, she hit his arm. "Better late than never, I guess."

"I love you." Soft, tempting lips kissed hers. "We're going to make it, aren't we?"

"I hope so." Her hand rose from Sean's arm to his face where she caressed his rugged jaw. The lamp behind Angie granted her a view of his handsome yet sad visage. "We're still here, Sean. We're committed to making our marriage work."

"I'm committed to you and our children." The hand on her hip, which had stilled, began moving again, pushing up her nightgown. "I'm also committed to loving you—heart, body, and soul."

They kissed, Sean's hand pulling on her panties and hers tugging down his boxers. When he nestled between her thighs, with them still on their sides and him inside her, she forgot about her five-thirty wake-up call and his journal.

"I know you have to get up early. I promise to make this good but quick." Sean rolled Angie onto her back, his shaft sliding over her clit.

She moaned, and he set a fast, hard pace that had her coming within minutes.

"I'm not ready for this to end," she panted against his lips. "Don't stop."

"You sure?"

She slapped his delectable ass and kissed him hard.

CHAPTER THIRTY-SIX

For a woman who, seven months ago, had two broken legs, it was incredible how Angie skated around the rink at Ice at Canalside--like an honorary member of the Buffalo Sabres. This was supposed to be a fun and lighthearted outing for Angie's birthday, yet she skated with an exuberant aggressiveness that, if she mowed a skater down, might get them kicked out of the place.

Sean shook his head at his wife and told her again to, "Slow down. There isn't a goal on the other side of the rink."

Angie turned until she'd formed a figure eight in front of him. Then, because she was a demon from hell and his ice skating skills a step above needing a training walker, she twirled around him, smacking his ass after every pass.

"You're an ice skating hellspawn."

Zuri and Kayla skated past them, Zuri pushing a Penguin Skate Aid and her sister skating backward with far more skill than Sean could skate forward.

"Show-offs," he yelled after his girls, who snickered and kept going.

"Get a move on, Dad. You look like a big moose caught on the ice." SJ whizzed by, giving him a playful shove to the shoulder that threatened his tenuous balance. "Get in the kiddie lane, if you can't keep up."

Everywhere Sean looked, people of all ages were skating. The sun had set a little before six, and, with it, the temperature had dipped to the low thirties. Ice at Canalside rink was lit with an enticing red and pink glow, the Valentine's Day colors casting the ice in a romantic sheen.

Sean did feel like a big moose, clumsy and awkward, which didn't mean he wasn't having a good time.

Angie's glove-covered hand slipped into his, and he smiled down at her.

"Come on, hold on to me, and I'll guide you around the rink."

She was the reason why he was having so much fun. Until meeting Angie, the only type of sport footgear Sean had worn were cleats. Ice skating had been new to him. After all these years, he still wasn't a good skater, although Angie was a patient teacher. The quality of her tutelage showed with the kids. Not so with him, especially since he usually copped-out and spent his time on an ice bike. Yet, most of their outings there ended with her coaxing him into a pair of ice skates, taking his hand, and leading him around the rink. They would talk and laugh and he would stumble because his wife's smile and voice were more captivating to him than learning how to ice skate.

Angie would speak to him sweetly, softly, providing directions and praise. Then she would be off, leaving him watching after her as she used the rink as her personal playground. Whatever stress Angie may have brought with her onto the ice was burned away in every graceful line and gliding movement. Like SJ on the football field and basketball court, Angie left everything on the ice. She threw her entire five-three frame into skating, filling her lungs with cold air and using it to propel her from one end of the rink to the other.

Now, however, she doted on him, although this was her birthday. Like the kids, he loved being spoiled by her.

They stopped in front of the pavilion, Sean resting against the railing, holding Angie around her waist with his chest to her back.

In silence, they watched their children, as well as Angie's best friend, parents, brother, and soon-to-be sister-in-law, all of whom had met them at the rink to celebrate Angie's birthday. It was a school and work night, so no one could stay out late. Family birthday fun was all well and good, but Sean had something more romantic and sensual in mind for Valentine's Day. That's where Malcolm and Sky came in.

Sean bent and kissed Angie's cold cheek. "Two skate admission tickets and rental passes." Another kiss. "Two vouchers for hot chocolate or cupid cocktails. Considering how cold we are, we should use the vouchers to warm up with the hot chocolate." A third kiss, better since Angie had turned in his arms, her face lifted to his. "Two bags of Sponge Candy and a Fat Bob's Smokehouse coupon."

Going on tiptoe, Angie kissed him, using the scarf around Sean's neck to pull him down to her level. "Canalside's Sweetheart Skate Package. I love it. Thank you."

"All of that for only twenty bucks," he said, half boast and half complaint.

She laughed and kissed him again--just a peck, the way his kisses had been. It may be Valentine's Day and couples were skating while holding hands, like Malcolm and Sky had been, but this wasn't the place for more than a tame kiss to the lips and cheek.

"How much is it killing you not to have gone all out this year? No jewelry and flowers. No fancy restaurant."

"It goes against everything I believe in as a man and as a husband. But it's what you wanted. A no-frills birthday. You don't get more no-frills than a twenty-dollar date. I'm telling you right now, Angie, I want the works for my birthday."

For a second, her eyes lowered.

Last year, they'd neither celebrated his birthday nor their wedding anniversary. Even if Sean hadn't been in Newark and Angie in Buffalo, the two of them were miles apart back then. He'd inadvertently reminded her of that, but it was unavoidable. They didn't pretend anymore, and she had stopped swallowing her truth to spare his feelings. They knew where they'd been and how much further they had to travel to reach full recovery.

She snuggled close, her arms going around his waist and her face to his chest. Sean kissed the top of her head, although he doubted she could feel the light touch through her black turban beanie.

"I can't believe you wouldn't let me buy you a dozen roses, but you accept a hat made from baby alpaca fibers from Sky that had to cost her a hundred bucks."

"One hundred thirty."

"Who in the hell spends that kind of money on a cutesy winter hat?"

"It's a birthday present, and Sky has expensive taste."

"So, do you. Don't act as if you two aren't shopping buddies. I bet you were with her when she bought it."

"You have no evidence to support your contention," Angie said, a smile in her voice and her words mocking the defense attorney from Sean's favorite legal drama television show. Small, exploring hands settled on his ass. "When are we leaving?"

"What do you mean?"

Angie leaned back from Sean just enough to meet his eyes. She didn't have to say, "Cut the bullshit," because her face said it for her.

"How in the hell do you do that? How could you possibly know I have something planned for just the two of us?"

"Because you've been uncharacteristically good for almost four months. You haven't given me a single present you bought for Christmas, although it must be driving you crazy to know they're in the guest room closet, unopened. New Year came and went and still no presents. My birthday is almost over, and you haven't spent more than sixty-dollars here, and that's including paying for the children to skate and eat."

"That doesn't mean anything."

A guy riding an ice bike rode past Angie, too close to her legs for Sean's comfort, but he let it go when she lifted onto her toes again and kissed his jaw.

"Tell me."

"I've kept my promise."

"I know you have, and I appreciate your effort."

"But I draw the line at Valentine's Day. I gave you a cheap birthday present, and it's the last time I will, so don't expect it next year." Since Angie still had her hands on his ass, he didn't feel guilty about lowering his mouth to hers and kissing her with a little tongue and a lot of restraint. "Malcolm and Sky agreed to stay at the house tonight with the children. They'll sleep in the guest room and drive the kids to school tomorrow."

He'd originally asked Charles and Kim, but the scheming older couple had convinced him to ask Malcolm and Sky because, as Kim had said, and Charles had agreed with a vigorous nod, "Babysitting will be a great parenting experience for Sky." The poor woman hadn't married into the Styles clan yet, but her future in-laws were already mentally adding to their grandchildren count.

"Our guest room will not be the place of conception for my first niece or nephew."

Angie's grin contradicted her severe tone.

Sean laughed, then nuzzled Angie's neck. He wanted to do much more, which meant it was time to get the hell out of there. He'd packed them an overnight and a garment bag, storing both in his truck after Angie had fallen asleep last night. All he needed was time alone with his Valentine's Day sweetheart, and their evening of love, romance, and sex could begin.

"I booked us into a hotel a few miles from EU. That way, tomorrow's commute will be short."

They also wouldn't have to get up super early, leaving them time for unrushed morning lovemaking.

Since Sean had finished moving his law firm into the new building, most days he and Angie drove to work together. The extra minutes alone in his truck or in her car, after dropping the children off at school, were filled with good conversation. Per their agreement, they didn't talk about work or the children. Instead, they used the commute for discussion and relationship building activities, like the CEO interview. To his continued satisfaction, he learned a fun new fact about his wife at the end of every interview, as she did about him.

"Do you want to skate more or leave now?"

Angie grasped his hand, and he followed her. "Let's have hot chocolate with the family first, then I'll let you whisk me away."

He loved the way she said that, with a smile in her voice that let him know she didn't object to his plan.

Anxious to be on their way, Sean downed his hot chocolate, burning his tongue and throat in the process and giving everyone, especially Malcolm, Charles, and SJ, a big laugh. But Sean and Angie had had their drink with the family, his wife's single requirement before she would allow him to spoil her the way he'd been wanting to do for months.

A twenty-three-minute drive and a quick elevator ride to the tenth floor was all the time it had taken to begin their romantic evening for two.

Before Sean used the keycard to unlock the hotel room door, he placed their overnight bag on the floor, hoisted the garment bag over his shoulder, and pulled out his cell phone. He wanted to capture everything, so he began video recording the second the lock on the door clicked.

Stepping in before Angie and turning on the light, he held the door open while he trained his cell phone's camera on her.

Three steps into the room and her mouth fell open. Two more steps had her eyes widening, and several more had her kneeling on the bench in front of the rose petal covered bed, a hand over her mouth.

"How?" she choked out. Slim fingers coasted over the white duvet, tracing the outline of rose petals set in a heart shape. "How many rose petals did you buy to do all of this?"

Sean had tried not to purchase Angie red roses today. Tried and failed miserably. And he wasn't the least bit sorry for his weakness.

"How long did this take? Did you even go in to work today?" Angie stood, her eyes still on the decorated bed and his personal message. "I love you," she read, a whisper from her lips to his ears.

Yes, Sean loved Angie, which he'd spelled out with rose petals. He felt the three words to his core. Sean would always love his wife, and he wanted her to know, especially on this special day, how much he did.

He kept recording, feeling no need to answer any of her questions yet. Sean wanted to watch his wife soak in the room decorated with her in mind and guided by the heart she'd owned for half of his life.

Reaching out, Angie grabbed the string from one of two dozen, red and white, heart balloons floating on the ceiling and over the bed. One-by-one, she examined the photo attached to each string, smiling the entire time.

"SJ's first birthday. God, I forgot how small he used to be. Oh, look at this--a picture of you in front of our then new house. We'd signed a thirty-year mortgage and couldn't have been happier to be in debt." She fingered another picture. "Me pregnant with Zuri. She was the smallest of our children, but I gained the most weight with her. I was hungry all the time."

Keeping quiet, Sean shifted positions, making sure to record Angie from every angle.

"This is my favorite picture from this past Christmas. Sky's aunt is an excellent photographer, and it was kind of her to send Sky this picture to give to us."

Yvette Page had captured the wonder and beauty of the Franklins' Christmas morning. They had been all over each other, laughing as they roughhoused in the middle of Sky's living room. Yvette had sent Sky several pics of the Franklins to give Sean and Angie. Sean had had them framed, displaying one on his new desk at work. The other three were divided between the living room and their bedroom.

Angie turned so Sean could record the picture she held in her hand. "I love this one, too. A thirty-seven-year-old you sleeping with a two-month-old Kayla on your chest. I remember taking this picture. You used to tell me she was lonely in her crib, which was why she cried, and why you brought her into bed with us. I knew it was more about your separation anxiety than Kayla's. It didn't matter, though, because I'd never seen any man more beautiful and loving than you with our children."

Angie hadn't explored the suite beyond the bed. Sean had spent a lot of time preparing the room for his wife, including everything they'd need for an aromatic bath with pink champagne and strawberry bath salts in a bathroom aglow from strawberry-scented candles he'd light before climbing into the tub beside her.

"This is the best Valentine's Day gift you've ever given me. You're sappier than Malcolm, and I have no complaints about that today."

Sean narrowed his gaze at his wife. "You're awful. I know that look. You're planning on comparing whatever sugary-sweet Valentine's Day gift Malcolm gave to Sky to what I did for you." At her hearty nod, Sean found himself returning her smile. "Hell, yes. This beats anything Malcolm could've come up with for Sky. Wait." Sean stopped recording and texted Malcolm several pics of the suite and his Valentine's Day handiwork. Malcolm had done the same to Sean when Sky had treated him to a birthday getaway weekend last October. He laughed at his brother-in-law's response. "He sent me a brown-skinned middle finger emoji."

I love you, too, bro. Sean replied. *Thanks for watching the kids. We appreciate it. Now, if you'll excuse me, I'm going to have sex with your sister. All. Night. Long. :)*

A green nauseated face emoji appeared on his screen, and he was tempted to send Malcolm another reply. But he refrained, refocusing his attention on his wife, who'd used the time to retrieve their overnight bag from the hallway.

As soon as Angie dropped the overnight bag onto the white upholstered storage bench at the foot of the bed, Sean scooped her into his arms and swung her around.

"Champagne, chocolate, and you. That's all I'm consuming tonight."

"Hmm, am I the main course or dessert?"

"Both."

Sean kissed her, his arms holding her as tightly as she held on to him. Off came coats and shoes, and they tumbled onto the bed of roses. Then they were kissing again, exploring and tasting. Hands stroked and fondled.

Sean broke the kiss, his lips traveling to the supple column of Angie's neck and licking. "I have a present for you."

"I know. I can feel it through your jeans."

Sean chuckled, then moaned at Angie's touch. She'd undone his buckle, button, and zipper and had her hand down the front of his pants. Shit, her hand was so soft, but she stroked him with a balls-tightening firmness that had him biting on her neck and thrusting into her hold.

She could and had brought him this way, and it always felt amazing when she did. But the staid pace of her handjob was mere teasing foreplay that would lead him to the edge but not hurl him over.

When she removed his jeans, boxers, and socks, he yanked off his hoodie and undershirt, leaving him naked but his wife fully clothed. He fell onto his back, bringing Angie with him.

Rose petals clung to him, as did Angie's eyes, watching him with undisguised appreciation.

"You're so handsome and sexy." She fingered the tip of his dick, her thumb gentle and arousing. He twitched, and she licked her lips. "Do you want me to taste you?"

"Hell, yes," he croaked, his dick twitching even more.

"Good, because I want you in my mouth." Angie removed her red cardigan and long-sleeved, black shirt. "Thick and long and touching my tonsils." She slipped out of her camisole, abs tight and succulent breasts covered with a hot pink, mesh lace bra.

Sean reached for her, and she allowed him to touch her through the material of her bra and draw her down into a wet, needy kiss.

Last month, when Angie had traveled to Arizona for the Presidents Institute's annual conference, he'd not only missed her, but had worried about her every day she was away from home. The last time Angie had traveled by herself, he'd almost lost her forever. Sean was sure he hadn't breathed easy the entire three days she was gone.

But she'd returned, safe and sound, and the anniversary of Sean's confession had passed without either of them feeling a need to mention it outside of therapy. So the uneventful day came and went, and Angie didn't call him that day but she did the other two. They'd weathered an entire year, and they were still together. It had been a year of lies, truths and pain, but also a year of forgiveness, healing, and strength.

Warm, wet mouth engulfed him, and his mind went blank. All he could do was feel. His body relaxed and melted into the duvet and rose petals. Sean loved when Angie did this, all her attention focused on giving him pleasure which, in turn, aroused her too.

Never did he feel more submissive, yet powerful, than when Angie went down on him. She responded to his every moan and movement, listening to his body's cues for what she should continue, stop, or do next. Yet he was also at her loving mercy, her hands and mouth capable of bringing him to blubbering tears of joy and release.

She palmed and played with his balls, her touches tender and caring and just a little bit domineering. Angie licked, sucked, and nibbled. Saliva overflowed her mouth and slid down his length to soak into pubic hair he left thick and wild because he wasn't a porn star, and Angie loved the feel of it rubbing against her when they had sex.

Angie made love to him with her mouth, slowing them down from what would've been a quick, frenetic coupling. The reins were firmly in her hands, and Sean went with it.

Slow and gentle, he thrust into her mouth, one hand on her shoulder, the other on her head, touching but not pushing downward. Sean's eyes closed, and he accepted everything his wife gave him.

In his mind, he began to sing one of his favorite Leela James songs. Sean ached to sing the ballad to Angie now, as he'd planned. But the moment didn't feel quite right. Tonight was special, but not special enough for what he'd originally planned. So, Sean sang the song to himself, allowing the warmth of the lyrics and Angie's mouth to wash over him. It was all that kept Sean from falling off the cliff into the orgasmic sea below.

After long, delightful minutes, he eased Angie's mouth off him. "I don't want to come that way."

He helped her remove her bra, slacks, and stockings. Sean paused at the hot pink lace panties that matched her bra, deciding he could work around the sexy lingerie, if it meant he could see her in it while they made love.

"Come here." Sean knelt, sitting on the backs of his feet, and watched as Angie straddled his hips and lowered herself onto his thighs. Readjusting her panties, she moved them to the side so Sean could slip inside her.

They moaned and, for several seconds, neither of them moved. They did gaze into each other's eyes, a deeper and stronger connection than the one below their waists.

Slowly, they closed the distance between their faces, meeting in the middle and drawing each other into a kiss that lingered. They made love, their mouths and sexes fused in an erotic language created by and for themselves. He held her close, Angie's chest against his, her hands on his shoulders, and her sex clenching around him.

He slammed her down onto him, over and again.

"*Yes.* Shit, Sean, *yes, yes.*"

Angie rode him, hard and harder. She could come this way, him deep inside of her and her clit rubbing against his stomach. She could come, and she did, with loud curses that had Sean holding off on his own orgasm and prolonging his efforts to give her even more pleasure.

After Angie's second orgasm, Sean lay her on the bed and claimed her with his mouth. He never got tired of tasting her in this way, especially since she enjoyed it so much.

"I told you you'd be my main course and dessert." He held her legs wide open for his head and shoulders. "So good, and all mine."

Angie had always been his, even when he'd been too blind and arrogant to appreciate her devotion.

She whimpered, squirmed, and sought traction to draw her body closer to his.

Sean didn't believe in keeping a lady waiting, so he dove back in. Where Sean was a hairy beast below the waist, Angie was Brazilian smooth with a sexy triangle leading him to her scrumptious center.

"You're so greedy," Angie moaned, legs quivering and voice cracking. "An absolute glutton, and I love it."

He sucked on her bud, and she screamed and came.

Because Sean was the greedy pig Angie had accused him of being and not yet done with his meal, after she'd regained her breath, he flipped her onto her stomach. Kneeling again, Sean pulled Angie until her thighs were on his and her ass pressed against his stomach.

He pushed into her. The rear-entry position was piquant. The back of her entire body was open to his exploration, and he gloried in being able to run his hands over her ass, down her thighs, and up her back and arms.

As much as Sean reveled in this position, he couldn't hold out much longer.

Angie, as attuned to his body as he was to hers, glanced over her shoulder at him and nodded.

Sean powered forward, grunting, fingers digging into Angie's hips. On a final grunt, he held her to him, giving her everything he had, as if she didn't already own every bit of him.

They collapsed to the bed, their bodies coated with perspiration. Rose petals stuck to skin and littered their hair. Sean was relaxed, sated, and totally in love with his wife. That Leela James song came to mind again, and Sean almost began singing it to Angie.

Angie licked her lips, her pink flag a temptation and a challenge to his body to recover sooner rather than later. "That was sooo good."

Sean beamed at her. "It was." He plucked a rose petal from her hair. "You're so beautiful, especially after sex." Pulling her to him, he kissed her, wanting another taste of her tongue. "I love you."

Sean opened his mouth to fill the uncomfortable silence that always followed his declaration and her lack of a reciprocal statement. This time, however, Sean didn't have to come up with something to hide his disappointment at Angie's unwillingness to voice the same because she filled the void for him.

"I love you, too."

He could've jumped for joy. But a naked man with a flaccid penis jumping up and down wasn't an image he wanted to give his wife on her birthday, so he settled for hugging her, and then kissing the shit out of her.

"Thank you. I've been waiting for you to say it back."

"If you keep giving me mind-blowing oral sex, like you just did, I'll declare my love for you every day."

Sean didn't believe her for a moment. What he grasped, however, was the huge step toward him Angie had taken with her declaration. It wasn't that Sean didn't know his wife loved him. Although, for months after his confession, he'd questioned if she still did. No, he knew Angie loved him. Otherwise, she wouldn't have gifted him with a second chance.

But she'd left the words unsaid for thirteen long months. Sean may have had her love, but that wasn't the same as Angie feeling safe enough in their relationship to voice it to him. Apparently, she did now, and Sean couldn't be happier or more humbled by the trust she'd placed in him.

Sean rolled out of bed, locating their overnight bag from where it had fallen from the bench and onto the floor. He rummaged inside until he found what he was looking for and pulled it out.

"Happy Valentine's Day," he said the second he rejoined Angie in bed. Sean handed her a red, heart-shaped gift box the size of his palm.

"Should we put clothes on?"

"First, I didn't pack you a nightgown. Second, anything you put on I'm only going to take off you. Third, we're getting into the Jacuzzi tub after you open your gift, so, no clothes required for that. Fourth—"

Angie kissed him. "Shut up. I get it. You want me naked the entire time we're here."

"Among other things I want while we're here." Sean pointed to the box Angie held. "But that can wait until after you open your Valentine's Day present."

"You mean another Valentine's Day present." Angie nodded to the decorated suite. "You spoil me."

"I know, but it comes from a good place. You spoil me and the kids. It's only fair I return the favor."

"That's called enabling an enabler."

"True." Sean kissed Angie's cheek. "Open my gift before I open it for you."

Angie's smile of gratitude made everything he'd done for her worth it. She removed the lid from the box, then the black velvet bag. Digging inside, she pulled out her gift. Her eyes twinkled, traveling from her gift to Sean. "A necklace."

He swallowed, suddenly nervous. "You said my marriage proposal, like relocating my law firm, was equivalent to healing crystals, replacing negative energy with positive energy. That analogy made a lot of sense and resonated with me on a deep level."

Sean removed the necklace from Angie's hand. "I researched healing crystals." He touched one of the pink stones. "I learned rose quartz means unconditional love." Still touching the rose quartz, he used another finger to press against the gemstone beside it. "Clear quartz means growth and awareness, like our time with Dr. Naylor in therapy." He'd thought of adding many different healing crystals, but the three he'd finally settled on summed up his feelings for his wife better than ten disparate crystals could've. Sean ran a third finger over a shiny jade gemstone. "Amazonite, it helps to settle conflicting emotions. I had this healing crystal necklace made specifically for you. I hope you li—"

Angie flung herself at Sean, knocking him onto his back. They fell in a heap, his arms around her and she atop him. He hadn't expected such a strong yet mute reaction from his wife. It both pleased and worried him.

He held her tighter. When she still didn't speak, Sean rolled her onto her back and placed his Valentine's Day gift around her neck. Sean had gifted Angie with an expensive necklace for her birthday last year. To date, she'd worn it once, and that was only because the children and her mother had wanted to see the gift on her, and she'd obliged. Sean had no idea where she kept that necklace, probably stuck in a drawer with his other guilt gifts.

This year's necklace, however, wasn't about Sean's guilt but a celebration of their grit, emotional awareness, and resilience.

Angie gazed up at him, her eyes filled with unshed tears. "I can't go back, Sean. I won't."

His heart constricted at her openness as well as her emotional stability. She'd made a statement, not asked him a question, so he didn't have to respond. But he wanted to, even if only with a nod, which he found himself giving her.

She smiled, and a solitary finger caressed a rose quartz on the necklace that hung between her breasts. "Unconditional love." The same finger moved to an Amazonite, her eyes still locked on his. "It does mean emotional balance, but it's also known as the 'hope' stone."

He thought she would move on to one of the clear quartzes, but she didn't. Angie lifted her hand to his face, touching him with the same reverence as she had the healing crystals.

"Topaz," Angie said, voice low and soft. "You forgot to add topaz to my necklace. I'm sure there's room for at least one of those healing stones. Perhaps in the center?"

Tears threatened, and Sean dipped his head to Angie's neck, breathing in their combined scent and the Valentine's Day gift she'd just given him. She'd told Sean, only once, that she'd forgiven him for his affair and lies. Angie had said she'd forgiven Sean for her own sanity and peace of mind. Now, she'd told him again. This time, however, the forgiveness she'd offered was directed at him. He remembered reading about topazes during his research and the gemstone not only meant empathy, which Angie had shown him, but it also meant forgiveness.

"Thank you."

She kissed his forehead, then threw him a curve ball. "What's your favorite Valentine candy saying?"

He blinked away tears. "What?"

"What's your favorite Valentine sweetheart candy saying? Tell me the ones you wanted to receive or gave out as a kid, and I'll tell you mine."

A Valentine's Day relationship building activity. Hell yes, Sean loved the way his wife's mind worked.

"Be Mine," he blurted.

Angie snorted. "Unoriginal but a classic. Mine is Crazy 4U."

"Okay, that's a good one but not better than True Love."

She snorted again. "You gave a girl a True Love candy heart when you were a kid?"

"Hell, no." Sean kissed Angie. Hard to do when he couldn't keep from grinning. "I didn't find my true love until I met you."

She rolled her eyes. "Flatterer."

"And proud of it."

Sean kissed Angie again, and he didn't stop kissing her until they were breathless, he was hard, and she was proclaiming her love for him again, the healing crystals warm and sure between them.

CHAPTER THIRTY-SEVEN

Four Years Later

"When can I tell them?"

Angie shook her head at her impatient husband and opened her closet door. She'd been out of the shower for twenty minutes and, with Sean in the bedroom with her, she'd only managed to lotion down and pull on a white bra and panties set she bought for his enjoyment for Valentine's Day. Angie was certain Sean hadn't looked twice at the sexy lace. Her husband was too busy frowning and posing variations on the same question.

She ignored him, stepping into her closet, one hand on her hip, the other sliding garments to the left. Angie had purchased a new dress, along with the new lingerie her husband hadn't noticed. She sighed. Sean was such a beautifully visual creature of a man. The fact that he had neither commented on her post-shower, nude body nor her barely-there lingerie told her all she needed to know about his mindset.

Angie found what she was looking for--a long-sleeved, wrap, tulip skirted jersey dress. The dress didn't come in red, but garnet was a pretty alternative and Sean had several ties with the same color in them, so he wouldn't have a problem complementing her outfit--if he ever got around to putting on more than his socks and dress slacks.

Dress in hand, Angie turned and nearly ran into Sean. "Why are you so close?"

"When?"

She pushed past him and moved to the bed.

"It's been four years. Five if you count the first year."

"No one will care but us." Angie unzipped the dress, stepped into it and pulled it up. She shifted so her back was to Sean. "A little help, please."

"Why do you think I drove up to Cambridge to bring SJ home for the weekend?" As gentle as always, Sean took his time and zipped Angie's dress, placing a kiss to her nape when he finished. "This looks great on you. I love the color of the suede dress sandals, too, but don't know what it's called."

"Spanish sand."

"Nice. Four-inch heels?"

"Almost."

Arms went around waist and pulled Angie against a hard body. Sean's warm mouth lowered to her neck again. "You smell good, too. But you look and feel even better. I want to tell everyone, that's why I brought our son home. SJ should be here for the news. Besides, it's your birth-day."

Angie turned in Sean's embrace, her eyes lifting to his. She smiled. Instead of paying for SJ to catch a train or plane from Cambridge, Sean had driven nearly seven hours to retrieve their son from MIT. SJ was in his second-year of college, but Sean hadn't fully adjusted to having him away from home. In truth, neither had Angie. To everyone's surprise, including hers, she'd handled the transition with a stiff upper lip, only a few tears, and no momma drama when she had to leave SJ after helping Sean and Malcolm unload his supplies into his dorm room.

It had been Sean who'd had to be shoved out of SJ's residence hall.

"You know," Sean had said to Angie and Malcolm when they were back in his truck near Maseeh Hall, "SJ could've majored in math at EU. He didn't have to go all the way to cold-ass Massachusetts for college. He could've stayed at home."

Malcolm had laughed. "Getting away from home is a major selling point for a college to eighteen-year-olds."

Sean had grumbled. "It's costing us a fortune to send him here. If he went to EU, he would've qualified for tuition remission."

Angie had leaned over and kissed Sean on his cheek. True, MIT wasn't cheap, but Angie and Sean had a college fund for each of their children and SJ, bless his brilliant mathematical mind, had been awarded a couple of decent math scholarships.

Angie refocused on the present, and Sean hugged her more tightly. "It's been five years," he whispered, as if revealing a secret. "I want them to know. It's important to me."

"I know," she said, although she felt as if the significance of their news was different for him than it was for her. "The sooner we get dressed and meet everyone at the restaurant, the sooner we can make our announcement."

Apparently, Angie had said the right words because ten minutes later Sean was dressed and barking orders at the children to, "Hurry up and get into the truck."

Ironically, SJ, Kayla, and Zuri had already been waiting for them in the living room, laughing at their father when he'd discovered them dressed and ready to go.

As they all piled into his truck and buckled up, Sean continued to grumble. "None of you are funny." Sean slammed the driver's side door. "One of you could've answered me, when you heard me calling for you."

"It was funnier to have you look for us, Daddy." Zuri snickered. "Today is the perfect day for family fun and jokes. It's Mommy's birthday and SJ is home from college."

"Dad talked the entire drive home. I'm surprised I still have ears."

"Again, none of you are funny."

"I haven't made fun of you," Kayla said from the seat behind Angie. "I would never make fun of the best father in the whole world. Did you get my Valentine's Day gift?"

Sean turned in his seat to look at Kayla, his face a mix of humor and offense. "You gave me two stuffed love rats and a heart-shaped gelatin mold. Not a cute heart like the drawings you used to give me when you were in elementary school, but a heart shaped like an actual heart."

"I know. Did you like it?"

Angie didn't have to see her eldest daughter to know she wore a straight face, but she could hear Zuri and SJ laughing.

"You're spending too much time with your aunt."

"Aunt Sky didn't help me pick out your Valentine's Day gifts. I thought you would like them."

Kayla sniffled, sounding heartbroken, which had her siblings laughing harder and Angie trying not to mirror her children.

"It took me days to get the gelatin mold to look like a real heart. I thought it was a perfect way to express my love for the best father in the world." She sighed with high drama. "Alas, you've broken my heart. I'll have to make another mold with a knife wound going through it. You wound me, Father, and I'll never recover from your cruelty."

Angie couldn't hold it in any longer, she burst into laughter, adding hers to the children's, including Kayla's, who'd broken character. Her fourteen-year-old did spend a lot of time with Sky, especially since she'd begun high school and joined her school's drama club. Like Kayla, Sky had been drawn to stage acting in high school, making her a wonderful mentor and coach for Angie's daughter.

For Kayla, acting was a verbal extension of ballet, another way to tell a story, requiring different but also similar skills. Ballet was still her first love but acting had exposed her to a broader social network and experiences.

"I have a horrible family," Sean groused. "Every last one of you are awful. I don't know why I put up with you."

"Because you love us," Zuri said in her sweetest voice.

"Because we get our sick humor from you." SJ slapped Sean on his shoulder.

"What about you?" Sean asked Kayla.

"We're Styles and Franklins, what else would you expect from that genetic combination?"

Angie covered her face with her hands and laughed. At this rate, her make-up would be ruined before they pulled out of the driveway, much less made it to Sean's overpriced restaurant. When Sean had pledged to never give her a "cheap" birthday or Valentine's Day again, he'd meant it.

She fingered her healing crystal necklace, with a golden-brown topaz centerpiece, and smiled at the memory of Sean giving her the precious gift. She wore it most days, not only because it was beautiful, but also because the jewelry reminded her of what mattered most in her life and the gift of their second chance.

Angie opened her mouth to tell the children to quiet down so Sean could share their news, but the ringing of her cell phone interrupted her.

"Hey, Malcolm. We're about to leave for the restaurant. Are you guys already there?"

"No, we're at the hospital."

Her brother sounded rushed and worried.

"Why are you at the hospital?"

At that word, everyone in the truck went silent.

"Sky's not due for three weeks, but her water broke. We're at the hospital."

"Which hospital?"

Malcolm told Angie and she relayed the destination to Sean, who drove out of the driveway a second later.

With Sean taking shortcuts, it didn't take them long to reach the hospital. But they were still the last to arrive. Rushing down the hall, she spotted her parents as soon as they rounded the corner. Kim and Charles stood outside a closed door.

Her parents hugged her. "How are Sky and the baby?"

454 · N.D. JONES

Kim squeezed her hand and kissed her cheek. "Happy birthday, sweetie. We don't know yet. The doctor is in the room."

"Where's Maya?"

Kim nodded behind Angie.

She turned to see Sky's father seated in a chair opposite his daughter's delivery room. In Robert Ellis's arms slept two-year-old Maya Sade Styles. She reminded Angie so much of Zuri at that age in size, skin tone, and temperament. But her niece's olive hazel eyes and riot of curly-wavy hair marked her as Sky's daughter.

"He's good with her," Kim said kindly. "Better than Sky thought Robert could be, but he's proven, while he failed as a father, he's more than capable of making a wonderful grandfather. With Sky going into labor early, it's nice he came for a visit when he did."

Robert had been sick and unable to travel when Sky had delivered Maya. Sky's Aunt Yvette had been there, though, standing in for Sky's deceased mother, Sade Page. Like this baby, Maya had also arrived early. Malcolm had been just as worried then. Luckily, daughter and mother, while both exhausted from the delivery, had been fine.

They all turned when Malcolm exited the delivery room dressed as nicely as everyone else in his suit but sans the jacket. He smiled at them, eyes dark from nerves but also with excitement.

"Thank you for coming. I didn't call anyone else. Sky doesn't like crowds, but she wanted all of you here."

"How's Aunt Sky?" Zuri asked. "Is the baby here yet, Uncle Malcolm?"

"Not yet, squirt. Your aunt is working on it." Malcolm stepped close to Angie. "Sorry about dinner and your birthday celebration."

She slapped her brother's arm affectionately. "Don't be ridiculous. I'm going to have a niece born on my birthday. That's the best birthday gift an aunt could ask for."

"What's ridiculous," Sean said, shoving Malcolm harder but with the same love, "is your entire family is made up of people whose birthdays fall on a holiday. That never happens, except in the Styles family. You,

Halloween. Sky, Christmas. Maya, Independence Day. Now, you're going to claim Valentine's Day, too. I guess a third kid would be born on Thanksgiving, scoring you a strange holiday and kid trifecta."

"You're just jealous."

"You cried, when Maya was born."

Sean's response was a non-sequitur, but Malcolm nodded, unashamed of his reaction to the birth of his daughter. Sean had cried when each of their children was born, which they all knew, so his statement hadn't been meant as a playful jibe but more of an acknowledgement of manhood and fatherhood. As Sean had told SJ over the years, real men weren't afraid to reveal their tender emotions through tears.

Sean handed Malcolm a handkerchief from the chest pocket of his suit jacket, and her brother took the offer. "You're going to need this, bro. Your wife is having another girl. What in the hell are you going to do in a house full of females but go broke from spoiling them?"

"That's the best part." Malcolm waved to SJ. "As long as I have my scholar-athlete nephew, I'm good. How's your Linear Algebra class going?"

"Good. The prof is better than the one I had for Differential Equations. You and Mom were right, being a content expert isn't the same as knowing how to teach."

Malcolm accepted a hug from Charles and then one from Kim.

"What can we do for you and Sky?" Charles asked.

"Besides me, the hospital will only allow two other people in the delivery room. Mom, Sky asked for you."

Kim had witnessed the birth of all her grandchildren except for Maya, who'd been born in a hospital with a strict two visitor rule. Malcolm and Yvette had filled the two slots. Kim had been a little hurt, but she'd also understood Sky's need to have the woman who was her closest female relative with her in the delivery room.

It wasn't because Yvette hadn't made the trek north this time that Sky had invited Kim into the delivery room. Sky loved Kim and had shared her decision with Angie months ago.

"I would love that." Kim hugged Malcolm again and then, with a huge grin, walked around him and into Sky's room.

"You, too, Robert."

Sky's father, as interested in her condition as the rest of them, had stood when Malcom had exited Sky's delivery room. Now, he stared at Malcolm through eyes that looked just like Sky's and Maya's.

"Sky asked for me?"

"Don't sound so shocked. You're her father, and she wants you in there with her. Are you up for that?"

"Of course. I just didn't think…" He shook his head, as pale as Angie had ever seen the former state governor and naval captain. "Sky asked for me," he repeated, but it came out as less of a question and more of a surprised affirmation. "This is Sky's Valentine's Day gift to me."

"That's one way of looking at it, I suppose. You won't pass out on me, will you?"

"Sade asked me the same question, but I managed to keep from embarrassing myself." Robert's smile made the man look years younger. "I don't think I ever told Sky I was there for her birth."

"I think she'd like to know." Malcolm claimed his daughter from Robert, the little girl dead to the world. "I've got this one. Go on in and I'll be right behind you."

As happy as Kim had been, Robert hurried into Sky's room.

Reaching out for Maya, Angie took the two-year-old from Malcolm, who kissed her forehead before releasing her into Angie's care. "Sky has made Mom and Robert very happy."

"I know. She wanted you in there, too."

"We can't all be in there. I'll take care of my niece. You, Robert, and Mom support Sky while she gives birth to my birthday twin."

Sean wasn't wrong. It was odd for them all to have holiday birthdays. But it was also beautiful and made for a great conversation starter.

"Thank you." Malcolm kissed her cheek before turning and rushing back into the delivery room and to his wife.

SJ commandeered a waiting room where they sat, talking and watching television, then playing with Maya when she awoke full of smiles and toddler energy.

A few hours later, Malcolm appeared at the threshold of the waiting room, locs out of their confine, tie gone, and sleeves rolled up to elbows. She'd seen her brother looking so awed and dazed only twice before—when he'd married Sky and after Maya's birth.

The room quieted and they all got to their feet.

"Daddy." Maya ran to Malcolm, who scooped her up. "Daddy. Where Mommy?"

"I'll take you to see Mommy and the new baby."

"Baby."

Malcolm nodded and smiled at his daughter, then raised his eyes to the gathered crowd. "Sky and the baby are healthy. The nurses are cleaning them up now. You'll be able to see them once they're moved to another room and Sky has a chance to breastfeed the baby." Malcolm hugged Maya even more, his daughter squirming in her father's embrace. "Two daughters, I can't believe it. She came so fast."

"Did Robert faint?" Sean asked.

"For a minute there, I thought he would keel over. But Robert is tough. He held on to Sky's hand and told her she was beautiful and reminded him of Sade when she'd given birth to her. He talked her through the last few pushes." Angie thought Malcolm would tear-up, but he kept his composure. "They've come a long way. I'm proud of them both."

Angie hugged Malcolm. "I'm proud of you. What did you and Sky name your new daughter?"

"We'll tell everyone, once my girls are settled in their room." He kissed her cheek. Twice. "Happy birthday. I'll give you my gift a little later."

Before Angie could tell Malcolm he needn't worry about giving her a gift on the night of his daughter's birth, he was walking away from the waiting area, Maya's arms and legs wrapped snuggly around him.

Angie turned to face her family. This evening hadn't gone the way her husband had planned, but no one minded. Now wasn't the ideal time or location for their announcement, but new beginnings weren't just for newborns and young, married couples. They were also for tried and true relationships, and for marriages and hearts that had survived the test of time.

Angie linked her hand with Sean's, who smiled down at her when she touched him.

"Your father and I have decided to get married."

"I don't get it," Kayla said, "you're already married."

"Twenty-five years next month," SJ added.

Of their three children, only Zuri had a reaction other than confusion. She clapped, chewing the rest of the chocolate candy bar she'd purchased from a vending machine. "May I be the flower girl?"

"If you want." Sean ran his thumb over the back of her hand. "So, we're really doing this?" he asked her, as if, in the seconds between her announcement and now, she'd changed her mind. "I mean, I know you accepted but I've asked you the last five years."

"And I accepted this time. Zuri, you would make a lovely flower girl."

"You two are serious." SJ fist bumped Sean. "Yes, that's what's up."

"When?" Kayla asked.

Sean looked to Angie. They hadn't discussed logistics. After her acceptance, they'd occupied themselves with details of a carnal nature.

"Next month, and on your dad's birthday."

"Are you sure? We can do it on any other day. The renewal of our vows is supposed to be a fresh start."

"A new beginning, Sean, I know. But our new marriage doesn't mean we throw out everything that came before. I've told you many times, I love that we were married on your birthday. That hasn't changed."

Sean wrapped Angie in his arms and lifted her off the floor.

Kayla still seemed confused but Zuri was happy at the prospect of being a flower girl. SJ, however, understood the magnitude of the announcement. He hugged Angie first, but he hugged Sean long and hard.

Eventually, they all piled into Sky's room. She looked tired but also good. Sky's hair was longer than when Angie had first met her, and it was everywhere, falling into eyes and over shoulders. But when Malcolm pushed Sky's bangs out of her face and behind her ear, Angie could see the same joy that had taken up residence in Malcolm's eyes mirrored in Sky's.

Charles clapped Malcolm on the back. "Congratulations to you both. She's beautiful. Every Styles female is, so I wouldn't expect anything less from this little darling."

Sky held her newborn to her, swathed in a light-pink blanket, her head covered in an equally pink hat.

"The baby is so tiny," Zuri observed. "How are you feeling, Aunt Sky?"

"Better now that she's here." Sky glanced to her father who held Maya and to Kim standing next to him. She smiled at the duo, and they returned her smile. But then she shifted her olive hazel gaze to Angie. "Happy birthday. Sorry you had to cancel your birthday dinner. You can blame your niece."

"Oh, I do. I'll never let her forget she ruined my celebration. But, if I must share my birthday with anyone, I'm glad it's with my brother's child."

"I'm glad you said that." Malcolm reached for Angie's hand and pulled her next to him. "We have a birthday gift for you."

"But, M and M, it's …"

Sky lifted the sleeping baby to Malcolm who handed her over to Angie, careful to hold the newborn's head in the delicate transfer.

Adorable and precious were the first words that came to Angie's mind. Children were blessings to be cherished and nurtured, and Malcolm and Sky had been granted two of them. There was no better birthday present.

"Everyone," Malcolm said, "Sky and I would like to introduce you to Soleil Angela Styles." Malcolm slung his arm around Angie's shoulders and kissed her temple. "Happy birthday. I hope naming my daughter after you makes up for ruining your birthday plans." The arm around her tightened, and Malcolm kissed her temple again. "I love you."

"I love you, too, M and M. You're such a wonderful sap."

"I am. I hear there's going to be a wedding next month."

"There will be," Sean confirmed. "If you're nice to me, I may ask you to be my best man."

"Nice to you," Malcom scoffed, letting Angie go and moving toward Sean. "You were my best man, it's only fair I get to be yours."

"I was hoping I'd be Dad's best man."

"You? I don't think so, SJ."

"Come on, Uncle Malcolm, why not?"

"Because you don't have the hair to pull something like that off."

"What? That doesn't make any sense."

"I'm the father, so I'm giving the bride away. My role in the wedding is guaranteed."

Her father, brother, son, and husband launched into an asinine argument, with Robert playing referee through bouts of laughter.

Kim took Maya from a laughing Robert and moved to stand next to Angie. "They're going to get us kicked out of here. I bet you're not even planning an elaborate ceremony."

Angie handed Soleil back to Sky. "I was thinking we could have a small service at our house. Zuri wants to be my flower girl, so that's a must. SJ as Sean's best man would be sweet and would make him happy."

Sky discreetly fed Soleil, a strategically placed receiving blanket covering her chest. "That only leaves Kayla. She'll probably want to dance at the reception. Although, she may want to recite a poem or perform a dramatic reading."

If Angie and Sean were to renew their vows in a month, they would have much to do in a short period of time. Including their children in their second wedding was a great idea.

Sean cleared his throat and Malcolm shoved him before returning to Sky's side.

"There's a birthday and Valentine's Day gift I've wanted to give to my wife for five years. The time never felt right, not even after Angie accepted my marriage proposal. But being here with Malcolm, Sky and their family, and surrounded by my own, my wife happy and my life full of joy, this seems like the perfect time."

Sean cleared his throat again, though the room had gone silent, all eyes on him.

Like a magnet pulling on the force of her heart energy, she walked to stand in front of him. His hands found hers and placed her palms on his chest, one over his heart. Then he began to sing, and Angie closed her eyes.

Sean hadn't sung to her in years. Until this moment, she hadn't realized how much she'd missed the melodic treat.

Leela James had a strikingly powerful voice but her song, *All Over Again*, sounded marvelous in Sean's baritone voice.

He sang about looking into her eyes and falling in love with her again, about being unable to deny his love for her and the feeling of starting over and of starting something new. Sean sang, and Angie allowed herself to drift away on the harmonic message of the lyrics. This was more than a simple birthday gift or even a Valentine's Day present. She touched her healing stone necklace and opened her eyes.

He repeated that she was his lover and friend, claiming he couldn't love her more -- someone else's words but Sean's sentiment. Angie believed him, even without the public declaration.

Angie hugged Sean and they swayed through the last lines of the song.

She heard her mother say, "Romantic" and Sky murmur, "Sweet." Charles growled, "Show-off" and SJ mock-whispered, "I'm the only real man in a family of saps." Kayla and Zuri clapped, and Malcolm remained uncharacteristically silent. Knowing her brother, he agreed with Charles and was plotting a sugary-sweet action he could take with Sky to outdo Sean. Considering his wife had just given them another child and her birthday wasn't until December, he would do well to focus on finding time to sleep and breathe with a two-year-old and a newborn in his home.

All of that faded into the background as Angie pressed into Sean and his steady arms wrapped around her. She loved him. When they first made love, Angie loved Sean. When they had their first child, she loved him. When Sean fretted over winning and losing cases, she loved him. When she found a lump in a breast and Sean soothed her fears, she loved him. When he confessed to his affair, she loved him.

They had twenty-five years of love between them.

The second chance Angie had gifted them wasn't simply about love, any more than her forgiveness or Sean's regret could be boiled down to that ethereal emotion. Their second chance was born of everything they'd shared from the moment they'd met—up to and including their pain and heartbreak. It was hope, winter, and sunshine, but also frost, future, and trust. It was a faithful leap and a daring plunge into the unknown. It was bravery and tears, perseverance, and good, old-fashioned, hard work.

It was Charles and Kimberly.

Malcolm and Sky.

Angie and Sean.

A Styles of love trilogy, a perk, a wish, and the best kind of gift.

THE END

If you enjoyed the novel, the author invites you to leave a review.

REFLECTING ON INFIDELITY: SURVEY RESULTS

These are the exact words from survey respondents. They were not edited in any way.

Cheated-on partner: Do/Did you blame yourself for your partner's affair? Briefly explain.

- No, never cheated, but my husband visited a strip club after promising that wasn't his thing but still went with his boss to "prove" whatever. I obviously have trust issues now
- No he blamed me though. Because I wasn't doing something right.
- No. Because no matter the reason if you're not happy being honest and upfront is the only way to go. Letting the other person know that you're not happy and that you're leaving is

the only honest thing a person can do. Before things get said, I'm referring to a normal relationship not an extreme one.

- Yes. Distance (a part of our relationship was long-distance) and thinking also that I didn't fulfil his needs - I should've been "enough", know what I mean? If I hadn't failed somewhere, he wouldn't have gone looking elsewhere, right? Except, no - some people are pathological liars and will always seek more never mind how much you are giving

- Nope. There is a problem tell me. Control yourself.

- Absolutely not. It was his choice to cheat during our relationship. If he was unhappy with me or the relationship, he should have ended it prior to initiating an affair. As the saying goes, "You can't have your cake and eat it too."

- Yes to begin with however then realised he still chose to do it.

- No. I mate had affair and a child was born

- Partally for not being there for them when they needed me but mostly angry at myself for noticing the changes in our relationship.I would be willing to hear where the relationship had the problems so the love that brought us together is the focus. Even if its scheduling our couple time.

- No

- Sometimes I do and have blamed myself for what happened in past relationships where cheating and leaving the relationship has happened. I also think to myself that my partner has a responsibility for their self-care and how they communicate their needs to me.

Cheated-on partner: Are/Were you willing to change, in some areas, if it means healing yourself and working to heal your marriage/relationship? Explain.

- I wouldn't change myself at all. You either love me or you don't

- I know there was something's I needed to change in which I did just not with him.
- I would be willing to try, with the understanding that the first thing my partner would have to do is regain my trust towards him or her. I would have to also deal with the fact that the person decided that cheating was an option instead of talking to me. Healing would depend on both of us changing and making better decisions.
- Yes. Like I mentioned, distance - change as in being more present, more available (esp. for sex). But it is more that you want to take all the blame on you and think if you do the work, all will be well. But it is actually the cheater who has more work to do - because he is the one who cheated in the first place
- If it is worth it. Have to find out why he cheated.
- I am willing to make changes to better myself and future relationships; however, there is no chance of healing the relationship because the trust has been lost. I do not see how I could ever get past that, as I would be constantly wondering and worrying that another affair could happen in the future.
- I would have, but when he told me if I can give 5 reasons why we should stay together I knew it was over.
- Yes if that person is Honest about his relationship
- its up to both of us to heal figure out why it happened and move on slowly evev if its hard.
- My husband ran away with a woman baiter for a religious cult.
- Yes. I am willing to try as long as the other person is willing to work too and they do the work. I have been in situations where they do not do what they say and they don't care. They just want to give up or have their way.i believe

Cheated-on Partner or Cheater: Do you believe cheaters can change? Why? Why not?

- No, they won't change
- Anything is possible. But I'm not waiting for someone to change.
- No. Because the cheater's decision to cheat shows the cheater didn't value me or the relationship. I know people make mistakes but there are somethings that should never be done. Somethings that once they're revealed to a person that shouldn't be ignored. Cheating is saying that what we share and what we've built together has no value to the person that cheated and the cheater doesn't care about it. It shows that it was worth losing by the act of cheating.
- If it was a one-time thing, or even the one affair, then yes - maybe there was an underlying issue that, if resolved, means the cheater doesn't feel the need to cheat or go look elsewhere. But some cheaters are pathological - they love the thrill of the chase, of lying, of passing for more 'important' in the eyes of another person
- Yes. if they want to save the marriage.
- Yes, but it is extremely difficult. Having been in both positions, I think women are more inclined to change because of the hurt that have caused the other person. I know that is the case with me; I could never cause someone that kind of hurt again. Unfortunately, I have yet to meet a man who has only cheated once. There has always been a pattern of repetitive cheating with the men with whom I have been acquainted.
- I think it depends on their personalty, my ex was very arrogant and I never felt he really was sorry for cheating, he was more sorry he got caught.

- I do believe they can change but it takes commitment. You have to be willing to continue to go without whatever it was lacking in your primary relationship.
- No . If you cheat 1 time you going to cheat again. Because if he or she did get caught. Some thank they will never get caught
- Yes when with the right person and open communication and both are willing to work on relationship.
- Not if they drink the Kool-Aid!
- I believe that as someone who has cheated or been used to cheat that, yes I can and have changed. I won't continue to cheat. I have learned things and can communicate. Both partners have to be willing to change.ye

Cheater: Do/Did you feel remorseful about your infidelity? Explain. Please note, remorse is not the same as guilt.

- No the relationship was over
- Yes, I felt extreme remorse. I hurt my partner in ways that I had not anticipated. He was planning to propose because he could not imagine his life without me. He told me that my cheating made him question love in its entirety and he questioned whether he would ever be able to experience love in the same manner again. I had no idea his depth of feeling for me, and I immediately wanted to turn back the hands of time so that I would not cause him so pain.
- Guilt almost destroyed me. My partner eventually stuck with me but there was some punishment to be doled out and that made it tough to forgive myself. Also, if there are children involved in the primary relationship, they are negatively affected no matter how much you try to shield them.
- Yes , because it alway in you mind
- Would want to work on himself to figure out why he cheated.

- He didn't! He instead accused me of cheating to our best friends who knew what a liar he was. I worked all through our marriage to support us while he was unemployed for more than 60% of that time.
- Yes I did. I felt awful about cheating or helping another to cheat. Sometimes I did not know the person pursuing me was in a relationship and using me to cheat. I had remorse and sorrow. I want to forgive and be forgiven. I like to communicate and get things out.

Cheater: Why were you unfaithful?

- There is no excuse for being unfaithful. Bringing in another person on an already damaged relationship, just creates another problem.
- My way out of the relationship
- A former "crush" found his way into my life and expressed interest in me that he had not previously. I suppose I wanted to see if the grass was greener with someone else. While I was happy in my relationship, it was lacking "something" on which I could not put my finger. I suspected that the missing "something" might be found with my former "crush." I learned the hard way that was not the case, and I ended up hurting someone profoundly in the process.
- The brief answer - I was bored and lonely, felt taken for granted, my partner wouldn't hear me or seek help. A flirtation led to an affair with someone I would never have a long term relationship with. I was a serial cheater over a period of years.
- He cheater and want to hurt him back. But only hurt my self
- depressed not working and a women I knew before wanted to be with me again.
- My partner at the time had already told me they were going outside the relationship and I should move on. They then did

not keep the boundaries clear. I thought and felt I was free to see others. I thought my partner was done with me. Then they wanted me back.

Cheater: Were you and your partner able to move past your infidelity? Why? Why not?

- Just left the relationship wasn't worth it.
- Initially yes. We were able to reconcile and continue the relationship but clearly the it was not what it was before. Several months after our reconciliation, my partner cheated on me. "Tit for tat," as they say. Although I know he loved me, I also know that he could not completely forgive me for my indiscretion. When he found himself in a situation similar to mine (a former flame re-entered his life), he took full advantage. Although I am sure he thought I deserved it, he was extremely remorseful because he truly was a good man and, after some time, we again attempted a reconciliation. Unfortunately, too much damage had been done and there was no way around it. Despite our best efforts, we made the difficult decision to part ways shortly after we tried to work things out this second time.
- We just celebrated fifty years of marriage so I guess the answer is yes. We were separated for almost two years and he did a few things in retaliation that still hurt, but we managed to move beyond it.
- No we got a Divorce due to have a child outside our home
- Yes through keeping open communication , love and communication no matter how busy you are.
- No! He took off in the middle of the night while we were on vacation with our best friends 4 states away from home and was never seen again.

- We did for awhile. Then a different incident came up. My partner became unhappy again with themselves and with the relationship. They wanted to be able to go see others again. So we ended it.